DEATH WEARS A RED HAT

"Kienzle's second Father Robert Koesler mystery is an intriguing blend of Catholicism, voodoo, big-time crime and vigilante justice."

Philadelphia Inquirer

"Everytime I open a book, I hope this one is going to be really smashing, exciting, outstanding. This one is. *Death Wears a Red Hat* is the kind of mystery that I read the others to find. It has all the right ingredients."

Houston Chronicle

"Another dandy tale of homicide with an ecclesiastic twist...A fast-moving plot with amusing sidelights."

New York Daily News

"There are few authors whose books a reader anticipates from the moment he finishes the last effort....Add William X. Kienzle to that list."

Dallas Times Herald

DEATH WEARS A RED HAT

A FATHER KOESLER MYSTERY

WILLIAM X. KIENZLE

BALLANTINE BOOKS • NEW YORK

Library of Congress Catalog Card Number: 79-28353

ISBN 0-345-35669-1

This edition published by arrangement with Andrews and McMeel

Manufactured in the United States of America

First Ballantine Books Edition: August 1989

Gratitude for technical advice to: Ramon Betanzos, Professor of Humanities, Wayne State University; Margaret Cronyn, editor, *The Michigan Catholic*; Jim Grace, detective with the Kalamazoo Police Department; Sister Bernadelle Grimm, R.S.M., Pastoral Care Department, St. Joseph's Mercy Hospital, Detroit; Sister Mary Clodovia Lockett, S.S.N.D., Biology Chairman, University of Dallas; William Lowry, Ph.D., Chief, Regulated Substances Laboratory, Institute of Forensic Sciences, Dallas; John Malone, M.D., Mt. Carmel Mercy Hospital, Detroit; Sergeant Donald Nash, Detroit Police Department; Noreen Rooney, TV Department, *Detroit Free Press*; Werner Spitz, M.D., Wayne County Medical Examiner, Detroit; Art Zienert, Auto Engineering Consultant. Any technical error is the author's.

For Fiona, sine qua non iterum

One

BLESSED
SACRAMENT
CATHEDRAL

"Shut up! You're in the cathedral!"

Mrs. Landry swatted her daughter Lucy's arm in a distracted gesture. Lucy, nine years old, had been blissfully humming her way through the terminal stages of liturgically induced boredom. The two were attending an adult confirmation ceremony at Blessed Sacrament. Lucy's father, Mrs. Landry's husband, was being confirmed as a Roman Catholic, having been received only recently into that faith.

In the loft, the members of the choir were killing time between hymns with casual conversation, reading or absently gazing down into the body of the church, where long lines of men and women, with their sponsors, each waited for their thirty-second sacramental encounter with the bishop. The lines were moving, but almost imperceptibly.

Bishop Art Kenny, the confirming prelate, may have held the world's record for prolonged confirmations. There were no stats for this sort of thing. The interminableness of Bishop Kenny's confirmations was due entirely to the fact that he refused to confirm an unsmiling candidate. He made no secret of this. In his introductory remarks before each ceremony, he always explained in great detail that confirmation was a joyous occasion and that he would

1

therefore not confirm anyone who was not smiling.

This approach was offset by the reluctance, particularly on the part of Catholic laity, to smile in church. Thus, with nearly every candidate there was an additional monologue.

"Now, you know," His Excellency would say, giving a good example by smiling himself, "that I am not going to confirm you until you smile. So, relax, and give us a big smile for Jesus."

Generally, that was enough to elicit at least the kind of smile found on drivers' licenses. Which was enough for the bishop. Which was just fine with the attendant priests, who wanted, more than anything, to get this over and relax at the end of a demanding Sunday.

Priestly attendance at cathedral confirmations was not obligatory. But ordinarily, if anyone from any of the other parishes was being confirmed, at least one of that parish's priests would attend. And attendance usually meant participation.

Priestly participation in a confirmation ceremony involved either reading, pushing, or wiping. Readers stood at either side of the bishop, took from between the fingers of the *confirmandi* the card whereon the new name selected for this occasion was typed, and read that name aloud. Which name was then incorporated into the ceremony by the bishop, as, for instance, "John, I sign you with the sign of the cross and confirm you with the chrism of salvation. In the name of the Father and of the Son and of the Holy Spirit."

Pushers stood at the foot of the altar steps on either side of the line of candidates. It was the pusher's job to guide—not push—the candidate up the steps and into a kneeling position within anointing distance of the bishop.

There were normally four wipers, operating in pairs. As each freshly confirmed candidate approached, the wiper located and wiped off the small dab of oil the bishop had traced on that person's forehead. Standing near the wipers were altar boys, each holding two small baskets, one containing clean cotton balls, the other a receptacle for used cotton.

Of all tasks, that of the wipers allowed the most opportunity for conversation. Usually, they engaged in small talk, mainly to stay awake.

Fathers Patrick McNiff and Alfred Dalton had managed to position themselves farther from the altar than the other wipers. Thus, bothered with fewer foreheads, they had more time to talk.

"Did you hear what happened to Archbishop Boyle last week?" McNiff deposited an oily wad of cotton in the used-ball basket.

"Somebody picketing the Palmer Park mansion again?" Dalton balanced a cotton ball on the tip of his index finger.

"No, it was at a confirmation at St. Kevin's. Everything started okay. They had the procession and all. But while the Arch was facing the congregation, praying from the ritual, hands outstretched, this little altar boy gets confused, forgets there are going to be readings, and removes the chair from behind the Arch."

"You don't mean—" Dalton was reluctant to dare hope that the worst had happened.

"Yes." McNiff's eyes betrayed joyful gratitude that this had not happened at St. Mary Magdalen, his benefice. "The Arch sat down—all the way down to the floor."

Dalton strangled a guffaw. "If the people in that parish had been smart, at that moment everybody in the church would've sat down on the floor."

Lucy Landry could scarcely remember ever having been this bored. The choir was nice when it sang, but that was infrequently. Meanwhile, there was just the tedium of shuffling feet and periodic coughs. Lucy had long finished counting the pillars and windows.

She nudged her mother. "What's that?" She pointed to a spot of brilliant red suspended from the high ceiling directly over the main altar.

Mrs. Landry squinted, her eyes trying to focus on the distant object. "Oh, that's the Cardinal's hat."

"What's it doing on the ceiling?"

"All Cardinals used to be given a hat like that when they became Cardinals." Mrs. Landry sighed. "That one was given to Cardinal Mooney when Pope Pius made him a Cardinal."

"When did he wear it?"

"Never. It's too big and heavy to wear. A picture of it goes on the Cardinal's coat of arms. Then, when the Cardinal dies, they hang his hat from the ceiling of the cathedral."

"Why?"

"Read your prayer book." Mrs. Landry concluded the dialogue she considered pointless.

The two priests between Fathers McNiff and Dalton and the altar ran out of cotton. Rather than sending for a new supply, they retired to the large sacristy to rest weary bones and perhaps snatch a smoke.

And so, business had more than doubled for McNiff and Dalton, who, by this time, were so deeply committed to their conversation that their ministrations had become increasingly perfunctory. Wiping foreheads distractedly, they frequently missed the oil spot entirely.

"Actually, that's kind of nice, the way Kenny makes people smile while they're being confirmed." Dalton, tall, balding, older than his classmates due to time spent in the Navy during World War II, was pastor of St. Rita's on Detroit's east side.

"He may resemble a TV game show host at confirmations, but you should've seen him at my place last month. He raised some kind of hell." McNiff, short, paunchy, silver-haired and black-browed, was a pastor in Melvindale, a western suburb of Detroit.

"What happened?"

"You mean you haven't heard?" In his eagerness to tell the story, McNiff missed several oil spots. "Well, first, you may have heard that we got this new $75,000 altar from Italy—"

4

"Yeah, carved out of one solid block of marble, wasn't it?"

"Yup. And that's the point. Or part of it. It's got a huge tabletop, must be four-by-ten feet. Then it slopes down, very graceful-like, to a single, small base."

"Hey, wait a minute. Haven't you got a problem without four posts, one at each corner?"

"That's it!" McNiff almost yelled, warming to his righteous wrath. "The chancery says if it doesn't have four legs, one at each corner, it can't be a permanent altar!"

"Canonically portable!"

"Canonically portable, hell! I'd like to see one of those chancery dudes try to move it. Must weigh five, six tons."

"Whoever tried to move it would become Chinese."

"Chinese?"

"Yeah, One-Hung-Low." Dalton laughed alone.

McNiff overlooked the attempt at humor. "Then you know what they made me do?"

"What?" Dalton shook his head as he pounded a cotton ball against a forehead. It was a clear case of overblot.

"Since it's not a permanent altar, they made me have a piece cut out of the central tabletop for a twelve-inch square altar stone."

"No!"

"Yes! And then the stupid janitor cuts out an exact twelve-inch square, one-inch deep hole. So when his nibs Kenny comes to bless the new altar, he puts some cement in the hole, then puts the altar stone in the hole, and, of course, since the hole was cut for the stone and no allowance was made for the cement, the stone sticks up above the surface about a quarter of an inch. If you set a chalice down and hit the edge of the stone, the chalice'll tip over."

"No!"

"Yes. And when Kenny gets done and starts to leave, I pick up the hammer and go to give it a good whack to try to settle it in. And Kenny turns around and sees me and says, 'Don't touch that!'"

"But if the stone won't fit in the altar because of the

5

cement, what good would it do to whack it?"

"I could do it!"

Suddenly, the monotony was shattered by a series of shrieks that would not stop.

Lucy Landry, her eyes widened in genuine horror, was screaming uncontrollably. Head tilted, she was pointing at the ceiling.

Mrs. Landry, sensing her daughter's terror was unfeigned, clutched the child closely as her eyes followed in the direction of the girl's outstretched finger.

Shortly, many in the cathedral joined in the pointing and the screaming.

Ushers and priests instinctively tried to restore calm and order. But it was clear to anyone with halfway decent eyesight that tucked firmly inside the crown of Cardinal Mooney's big red hat hanging from the lofty cathedral ceiling was a human head.

Two

ST. CECILIA

Lucky Louie Licata stared at the television screen. Monday morning traffic was heavy in the corridors of the Wayne County Morgue on the corner of Brush and Lafayette. Licata, however, was oblivious to everything but the face appearing via closed-circuit transmission from a room on the floor below. And that's all it was, in black-and-white. No color. Just a face. No body. Just a head lying on a stretcher.

"Holy Mother of God," Licata breathed with almost forgotten fervor, "it's Rudy! It's really Rudy!"

"Well, it's all we could find of Rudy for the moment." Dr. Wilhelm Moellmann, Chief Medical Examiner for Wayne County, had been studying Licata while Licata had been mesmerized by the scant remains of Rough Rudy Ruggiero. "But you do positively identify the remains as being one Rudolph Ruggiero?" The doctor, never once glancing at the television screen, continued to look intently at Licata.

"Jesus! Willya look at him!" Licata responded obliquely. "God! His mouth is wide open and his eyes look like they're gonna bug out. We been through a lot together. We been up against death more'n I could count. But I never seen him look so scared!"

"But that is at least the head of one Rudolph Ruggiero? You're certain?" Moellmann persisted.

7

"Yeah," conceded Licata, "that's Rough Rudy. But whereinhell is the rest of him?"

"Your guess is as good as mine. Finding the rest of Rudy is the responsibility of the police. My job is to determine the cause of his death."

"Well," Licata turned toward Moellmann, "what was it?"

"Gott in Himmel, how am I supposed to know!" The sudden vehemence of Moellmann's response startled Licata. "They bring me bits and pieces of bodies and expect me to guess—that's what it comes down to—guess at the cause of death!"

"Hey, Doc, I didn't—" Licata found no dialogue entrance.

"Coroners *guess*! Quincy on TV *guesses*. Movie medics *guess*. A medical examiner, Mr. Licata, is a man of science." The wiry, sandy-haired, bushy-browed doctor, his intense hazel eyes penetrating and his loose-jointed arms flailing, had backed a bewildered Licata to the wall. "A medical examiner, Mr. Licata, doesn't guess. Either he knows or he doesn't know. The human body has many vital organs. If any one of these is attacked, the human can die. How can a man of science determine a cause of death when he is presented with only a toe or an elbow or a head?"

Suddenly, Moellmann leaned close to Licata, his voice reduced to a conspiratorial tone. "Do *you* have any ideas?"

His basic manic personality aside, Wilhelm Moellmann fancied himself an actor. And having seen his share and more of police work in movies and on television, he regularly strove for the Perry Mason effect. Willie, as his associates referred to him, desired not only to determine the cause of death of each cadaver presented him; he also wanted to catch the perpetrator of the crime. He was unusually competent at the former and seldom successful at the latter. But he tried.

Actually, he might have succeeded with Licata, for he had caught Lucky Louie with his guard down. But when

Licata immediately shook his head negatively, he did so with rare sincerity.

"Then," continued the undaunted Moellmann, "you wouldn't happen to know where the rest of Ruggiero is?"

Again Licata shook his head negatively.

"Very well." Moellmann turned from Licata. He seemed to perform an eccentric two-step, as he left Licata standing, hat in hand, in a bemused state. "Before you leave," he called over his shoulder, "fill out the identification form at the main desk in the lobby."

Licata turned back to the television screen. What, he wondered, could possibly have frightened Rough Rudy so horribly? The two men had been through many thoroughly harrowing experiences together. There had been times, he had to admit, when he, Licata, had been unnerved. But never Ruggiero. He had faced violence, even probable death, with a coolness that Licata had never seen ruffled. Whoever or whatever so obviously had robbed Rudy of his self-control must have been incredibly terrifying. And if it were that terrifying; if whatever it was had so reached Rough Rudy, Licata wondered whether Rudy had been literally scared to death.

He turned from the screen with its macabre bodyless head, shuddered, and made his way to the lobby.

"That mother must be three feet wide!" commented Detective Sergeant Daniel Fallon.

"What was that about a mother?" Father Fred Dolson asked.

"Nothing, Father," said Lieutenant Ned Harris, covering Fallon's hyphenation. "Sergeant Fallon was wondering about the size of the hat."

"It's actually twenty-four and one-half inches in diameter," Dolson clarified.

The previous night, after the head of Rough Rudy Ruggiero had been discovered securely fastened within the crown of the enormous red hat, Inspector Walter Koznicki, head of the Detroit Police Department's Homicide Division, had been notified, as he routinely was in any case of suspicious death. He had phoned Lieutenant Ned Harris and told him to initiate the necessary investigation. One of the specialties of Squad Six was execution-style killings. And Ruggiero's death did appear to have been an execution.

Harris and six of his squad—half the roster—had started the investigation immediately, shipping the head off to the medical examiner. Then Harris had called Koznicki with the details.

Now, early Monday morning, ten members of Squad Six were at the cathedral. Six were scattered in various sections of the building and its adjacent rectory, asking questions, making phone calls, or merely getting acquainted with the locale. Later, in their cluttered squad room, they would share whatever information they had found. Meanwhile, Sergeants Dietrich Bernhard and Charlie Papkin, armed with a search warrant, had gone to Ruggiero's residence.

Lieutenant Harris, black, on the tall side of six feet, slim but powerfully built, was immaculately groomed, with close-cropped hair. He and several other members of Squad Six were standing around Cardinal Mooney's red hat, which now lay empty on the floor of Blessed Sacrament Cathedral's sanctuary. Sergeant Dan Fallon wore a slightly stained blue suit that looked slept-in; Sergeant Fred Ross' blue suit looked as if it had just fallen off the retail rack. Sergeant Patricia Karnego, a tall, well-groomed brunette, stood next to Father Fred Dolson, one of the cathedral's assistant pastors.

Father Dolson was wearing, in addition to his black cassock and Roman collar, a long white surplice. This puzzled Fallon and Karnego, both of whom were Catholic and knew that surplices were worn only during the liturgy. However, unknown to them, tucked into Dolson's sash belt was a small-caliber revolver. Ordinarily, it rested in its small holster on Dolson's nightstand near the phone in his bedroom. When there was trouble—and this situation definitely qualified as trouble—Dolson always managed some-how to wear his weapon.

Dolson, if the truth be known, liked guns and felt com-fortable with them. A member of the National Guard, he was probably the only chaplain fully armed during De-troit's '67 riot. On his way to be chauffeured in a Jeep to the riot scene, Dolson, wearing a sidearm and carrying a rifle, brushed by a parishioner. "But Father," the startled parishioner observed, pointing at the armament, "you're a chaplain!"

Pointing to the small cross insignia on his khaki collar, Dolson shot back, "You think the snipers can see these from the tops of buildings?"

Fortunately for Dolson now, none of the police sus-pected he was armed, or he wouldn't have been.

The five had been silently staring at the hat for several minutes.

Dolson broke the silence. "Lieutenant, I'm curious: ex-actly how was that head attached to the hat?"

"Oh," Harris emerged from speculation as to the reason the hat itself had been used, "those braided cords stapled to either side of the crown—they're red, as you can see, but not the brilliant red of the hat—they were tied beneath the chin and neck of the head, thus holding it firmly within the crown."

"By the way, Fred," Harris addressed Ross, "make sure those cords are held as evidence."

"Pity he used a square knot," Ross commented. "It's not going to be much help. Too common."

"Too common?" Dolson asked.

"Yes," said Harris. "Knots can reveal a lot. Whoever tied them might have been a seaman or had other special training that would evidence itself in the loops or inter-twinement. Or perhaps a knot may be tied in a singular or unique way.

"Unfortunately for our purposes, almost everyone ties a square knot just about the same way. However, these cords and the knot may prove valuable if we encounter a similar incident."

"What I'd like to know," said Ross, "is how in the world could anyone wear a thing that big."

"Oh," answered Dolson, "it wasn't meant to be worn. It was just symbolic. Years ago—centuries, I suppose—most clergymen wore the kind of hat that this one became symbolic of. It was a black hat with a small crown and wide brim—nothing like this brim, though—with ribbons you could tie under your chin to keep the hat in place.

"Then, the galero—that's what the hat was called—just grew." Dolson made an expansive gesture. "And as it grew, it became symbolic of the office. In the late Cardinal Mooney's case, for instance, during one of the ceremonies in Rome when he became a Cardinal, this hat was placed on his head for just a second. It was then shipped home and not used again until it was placed on his coffin for his funeral and then suspended from the cathedral ceiling. That's what happened at the death of all Cardinals. Only not anymore. Pope Paul VI discontinued the custom of the ceremonial red hat."

"What about the tassels?" Ross asked.

"Ah, yes, the tassels . . ." Dolson had no special mastery of all this trivia. When the head had been discovered in the red hat the previous evening, Dolson had figured questions would be asked. He then spent hours studying so *he* would be the one providing answers to the police and the news media. "Well," he continued pedantically, "as you can see, there's a cluster of fifteen tassels on each of the two ribbons that hang from the hat's brim. The thirty tassels, as well as the brilliant red color, signify that it is the hat of a Cardinal."

"That's all very interesting," said Harris, who didn't really find it all that interesting. "But how is that hat raised—and lowered?"

"That's the funny thing," said Dolson, quite seriously, "there's a very strong wire located in the rear of the sanctuary, behind that pillar there." He pointed to a huge gray stone pillar that rose to the cathedral ceiling. "The wire ascends the pillar to a pulley and then to the hat. The hat can be raised or lowered by the wire. But that's what I can't figure out . . ."

"What's that, Father?" asked Harris.

"Very, very few people knew about that wire, and it was expertly camouflaged—so no one would fool around with it."

Harris looked significantly at his three partners. "That *does* put a new twist on things."

Detroit's downtown Greyhound terminal was a busy scene, as it usually was during peak hours. Not only was the low rectangular flat-roofed building a bus terminal, it was also a parking garage and boasted a better-than-average cafeteria. A steady flow of buses met and passed by each other, departing and arriving.

Standing near the wall opposite the arrivals section was an extremely tall, pencil-thin black man, garishly dressed and sporting a black Stetson. Roosevelt Harding, whose street name was Stud, was one of Detroit's most affluent, prolific, and well-known pimps. A good argument could be made that he was at the very pinnacle of his profession. And the bus terminal was one of his most fruitful shopping centers.

Bus terminals in major cities throughout the country are notorious as way stations for young women running away from home. Young women who become outstanding prey for pimps. Usually the girls are frightened, unemployed, penniless, and friendless. In such a situation, pimps are usually successful at ensnaring them. Harding was a master at the game.

The midday bus from Chicago had just arrived, and the passengers were coming through the arrival gate. Harding leaned against the wall, his capped teeth turning a round toothpick through compressed lips, while his eyes, behind smoked glasses, carefully scrutinized each of the arriving passengers.

Suddenly, there she was: white, blond, in her late teens. Her nervous eyes darted about, not in expectation of being met, just trying to size up a strange place, looking for an appropriate bearing.

Harding approached from the rear.

"Hi, honey doll. Lost?"

She spun around and found her eyes level with a brown leather midriff. She looked up at the black face smiling down at her.

"I . . . I . . . just got here from Chicago," she stammered.

"Know anybody here, honey doll?"

"No . . . not really."

"Got a job?"

"N . . . no."

"If you come with me, honey doll, I'll make sure you get a job and a nice place to stay. I'll even have you meet some good folks. Come on, honey doll."

Alice Reardon, fresh from the Chicago suburb of Cicero, hesitated. She had had her consciousness raised long ago by her peers at St. Mary's High School. She was sure that a refusal of this offer of help would be a racist reaction. After all, she had no place to stay, no friends, no job. All of these had been offered.

"Well, all right. And thank you."

"All right!" Stud Harding wrapped one huge hand around Alice Reardon's arm and escorted her from the terminal. Together they entered a purple Fleetwood, known by most Detroit police as THE Pimpmobile.

A late afternoon autumn sun shone through the many windows of the city room on the third floor of the *Detroit Free Press*. In the large white rectangular room, reporters were engaged in a variety of activities. Some were making phone calls, some were typing; a few stood in groups of twos and threes holding conversations that would solve most of the world's problems. A couple sat staring at their typewriters waiting for the drops of blood to appear on their fingers.

At one side, near the glass panel separating the working area from the elevators, staff writer Joe Cox visited with City Editor Nelson Kane. The two were discussing The Red Hat Murder—the tag that, coincidentally, both the *Free Press* and the *Detroit News* had given the death that had been discovered in the cathedral.

"One thing I think you have to conclude," said Cox, smoothing his newly grown, sandy-colored beard, "this thing has started at the top."

Two years before, Cox, in the first blush of his journalistic career, had earned a Pulitzer Prize for his work in the *Free Press'* coverage of the series of murders of priests and nuns generally termed The Rosary Murders. Cox's work had contributed a great deal to the solution of that case.

Kane looked up from the expense account vouchers he had been scanning. He studied Cox. "That's true," he said, "I don't think anybody would argue that Ruggiero ranked as Detroit's Public Enemy Number One. But what do you mean by 'started'?"

Kane, a six-footer with thinning hair, constantly fought to keep his weight near 200 pounds. He had been with the *Free Press* nearly a quarter of a century, and should have been in management by this time. He would have been, if not for Karl Lowell, executive manager, corporate hatchet man and—although theoretically working for the same organization—in the opposite philosophical corner from Kane.

"I think you've got to conclude," Cox explained, "that Ruggiero was wasted by a rival gang. This should kick off a veritable orgy of revenge and counter-revenge. Right out of *The Godfather*."

"Yeah, you could be right. This has to be the work of a rival who wants to become number one and is willing to pay the price in an all-out gang war. Either that, or some nut has bit off much more than he'll be able to chew."

"But the hat," Cox mused, "whereinhell does that red hat fit in?"

"No idea," Kane offered. "The only thing that comes to

mind is that Ruggiero was, like most Italians, Catholic, even if in name only. But where a cathedral and a Cardinal's red hat make any sense . . . well, it just beats me."

"Maybe the killer means that's as close as Rough Rudy will get to having a church funeral."

"No." Kane leaned back, his hands clasped behind his head. "I think you'll find Rudy, or what we have of Rudy, buried from Holy Family. Some claim that place is practically the Mafia burying ground."

"Well," said Cox, "the hat means *something*."

"Right!" Kane jerked his chair upright. "And that brings us to the purpose of this conversation: go find out what it means!"

It had been a relatively uneventful day for Squad Six. Their investigation into the death of Rudolph Ruggiero had uncovered very little. There were no latent fingerprints on the hat, no body, plenty of motives for the murder, and hundreds of probable suspects.

Lieutenant Ned Harris had inherited the leadership of Squad Six from one of his closest friends, Inspector Walter Koznicki, who had been promoted to the Homicide Department's top spot. Both Koznicki and Harris had been promoted two years previously when, with some considerable help from Joe Cox and one Father Robert Koesler, they had cracked The Rosary Murders case.

Harris knew his greatest challenge in this case was to get maximum effort from his squad. The murder of any notorious criminal never prompted the police to wear black armbands. However, Harris was aware that his squad was neither judge nor jury. Their job was to investigate homicides, identify the perpetrators, make the arrests, and bring sound cases to the prosecutors. And this, with strong mutual pride, Squad Six did regularly and well.

They were gathered now, at the close of this working day, in their squad room, which was the same size as the other six homicide squad rooms—too small. The rectangular room was decorated in basic clutter. Mismatched desks were surrounded by mismatched chairs. The walls, at least where the plaster was not gouged, were covered with posters, some humorous, some official. When the entire squad was present, as was now the case, all the chairs were occupied, with some of the force standing in the corners, others sitting on desks.

"Colleen," Harris asked, "did you check with the medical examiner?"

"Yeah." Detective Colleen Farrell, delicate, blonde, and very pretty, was also very tough and in the van of the women's movement. "I asked him about the head and he almost took mine off."

"Well," Fred Ross commented, "that's the way Moellmann is."

Patricia Karnego smiled. "I don't suppose you let it go at that?"

"Hell, no!" Farrell snapped. "I told him what he could do with Ruggiero's head. And also what I would do to *his* head if he doesn't stop always trying to brush imaginary crumbs off my chest. The sexist pig!"

Harris grinned. "O.K., Colleen." He knew better than to suggest that he should no longer send her to the medical examiner's office. She could take care of herself. "How about the Ruggiero home?"

"Kids are all away at school," said Dietrich Bernhard, consulting his notes. Bernhard, solidly built, methodical, was the essential Teuton. "Boys at military schools, girls at convent schools, widow distraught." He looked up from his notes. "I don't know why; according to the neighbors, Ruggiero was hardly ever home . . . just her and the servants."

"Anything else?" Harris asked.

"It was like a church," said Charlie Papkin. Charlie, of medium build, with a salt-and-pepper crew cut, was one of the squad's jokesters. "There were plaster of paris saints everywhere, syrupy religious pictures all over the walls, and votive candles in front of every damn statue and picture. Very tacky."

"Boy, if that isn't a stereotype," said Dan Fallon.

"O.K., gang," said Harris, "let's knock it off for today. But bring your walking shoes tomorrow. I've arranged for all available personnel in the other homicide squads to work with us. We're going to start at the top of the list of Detroit's criminal elite, and find out what they can prove they were doing at—what time again did Moellmann set for the death, Colleen?"

"Between one and five P.M. Saturday."

"Those cats had better have been busy and in company Saturday afternoon, or we're going to find out what they know about red hats."

"Ray," said Father Robert Koesler, "you'll be as safe in Irene Casey's hands as you would be in the hands of that insurance company."

"Allstate," completed the Reverend Mister Ramon Toussaint.

"Whatever."

Koesler, pastor of St. Anselm's parish, was the former editor of the *Detroit Catholic*, the archdiocesan newspaper. He was visiting with his friend Toussaint, deacon, who, with his wife Emerenciana, had come to Detroit in 1961 from Haiti. It had never been clear exactly why the Toussaints had chosen Detroit. One likely reason could have been the outstanding vitality of the Catholic Church in Detroit under the leadership of Archbishop Mark Boyle. For the Toussaints were deeply involved in Catholicism. One of the unique results of their involvement provided the subject matter of the present conversation between Toussaint and Koesler.

"Your Ministers of Service make a good story, Ray, and it's about time the *Detroit Catholic* did a feature on them. I guarantee, you can trust Irene to do a good job with the story."

Koesler, tall, blond, slender, fished another round toothpick from his shirt pocket. He had recently given up smoking and now chewed toothpicks as an oral satisfaction substitute.

Emerenciana joined the two men, who were seated at the kitchen table in the Toussaint home. The couple lived on Stoepel Avenue, only a block from St. Cecilia's Church, where Toussaint was the resident permanent deacon. "What are you two going on about?"

"Bob here is trying to convince me I can trust Irene Casey to do a good story on our black deacons."

"Of course you can, silly," said Emerenciana. "It's not like it was under the former editor." She winked broadly at Koesler, who smiled in return. "Irene has made sure, since becoming editor, that no one any longer calls the paper *The Detroit Communist*."

The three laughed.

"But," said Emerenciana, as she got up to go to the sink, "I've never understood why they need deacons or Ministers of Service. Why don't they just use priests as they always did?"

"We're an endangered species, 'Ciane," Koesler replied. "After the second Vatican Council, vocations to the priesthood fell off all over the world. Vatican II hit Detroit hard."

"Yes, 'Ciane," said Toussaint, "it's difficult to remember that in the early '60s, the Archbishop built a new high school at Sacred Heart Seminary and was considering a new gym. Now they've given away the high school and closed most of the rest of the buildings."

"'Ciane," said Koesler, "once upon a time, the liturgy demanded that none but consecrated hands could touch a consecrated host. Now there are lots of communicants and comparatively few consecrated hands. So, as the laity is encouraged to exercise the priesthood of their baptism, we have extraordinary ministers. Just so, the diaconate once was a full-time position in the Church. When clergy candidates began to want the entire enchilada, as it were, the diaconate became merely a step to the priesthood. Now that so few want to be priests, the diaconate has become a permanent position once again."

"And then," said Toussaint, "when the members of an entire ethnic minority refuse to give two years of each of their lives to deacon training, we have Ministers of Service developed in two months."

As Koesler crossed to the sink to deposit an ashtrayful of chewed toothpicks in the trash can, he was again aware that at six-foot-three he was still only two or three inches taller than Emerenciana. "And to top it all off, the creator of the Ministers of Service is ordained a deacon without having to go through the length of the white man's training time."

A smile briefly crossed Toussaint's usually impassive face. "The Archbishop owed me that," he said. "After all, I saved black Catholic Detroit for him."

"What there is of it," commented 'Ciane.

"It is," said Koesler, "perhaps a variation of Parkinson's Law. That, as the number of priests diminishes, hitherto strictly sacerdotal tasks tend to become part of the natural province of the laity."

"Or," added Toussaint, "if you stand in one place long enough, everything will return to what it once was."

Koesler laughed and moved toward the back door. "I must be leaving now."

"Oh," said 'Ciane, "can't you stay for dinner?"

"Sorry; got to get back for a finance committee meeting. Then there's catechism for the high schoolers."

"All right," said 'Ciane, "but as you leave Detroit, know that you are leaving all the action behind you. *We're* the ones who have a gangster's head in the red hat at the cathedral."

"Funny," commented Toussaint, "murder and the Catholic Church somehow connected. Reminds me of those Rosary Murders you were involved in a couple of years ago."

"Well, there's at least one big difference," said Koesler,

as he opened the door to leave. "I can't think that I'll be tripping over any clues this time around."

Alice Reardon had long since ceased screaming and pleading.

She lay nude, curled in the fetal position, her body convulsing with muted sobs. The bed with its filthy mattress, a few straight-back chairs, and an old refrigerator were the room's only furnishings.

Five naked men sat in one corner of the room, drinking beer, conversing softly, and laughing. For the better part of the day they had been sexually assaulting, degrading, and humiliating the girl. They were pausing now only to wait for a recurrence of vigor to continue their attack.

For several minutes, Stud Harding had been standing in the hall gazing into the room through a one-way mirror. His angular body was ramrod straight as he absorbed the spectacle. It was one he had seen and participated in dozens of times. The scenario was always so similar that he had nearly lost interest in it.

Stud had a few high-priced hookers in his stable. But little Alice from Cicero fit into the least common denominator group. A runaway, not particularly beautiful. Youth and a firm body were what he would sell. But first, just as with a wild horse, she must be broken. In the case of a girl, that meant she must be violated, assaulted, abused, degraded, exposed to every imaginable carnal experience. The "cowboys" were easy to find. The exercise was their reward. After one or two more gang rapes, Alice would be sufficiently broken, if not on the verge of a complete emotional or physical breakdown.

At that point, Stud would "rescue" her. He would dismiss the rapists and treat her tenderly. The routine seldom failed. The girl would do whatever he demanded, partly because he was her father-lover substitute and partly because she knew she could be returned to the "cowboys" at a moment's notice.

Stud turned and climbed one flight to his own personal suite on the third floor. He owned the building, which had once been a respectable hotel. But Stud Harding had turned the Selden Avenue structure into a six-story brothel.

As he entered his apartment, he reflected on the affluence of his life-style. When he was growing up in poverty in Detroit's Black Bottom, he had vowed that one day Roosevelt Harding would have nothing but the best. Which is precisely what he now had.

He stripped and stepped into the shower. As he soaped, he frankly admired his body. It was as smooth as black satin. There was little if any fat, just sinewy muscle that was regularly massaged and stimulated.

As he stepped out of the shower, about to towel, he thought he heard a sound in the adjoining room. Dropping the towel on the wash basin's marble counter, he stepped into the bedroom.

The sound was of moaning. The moaning of many women, only at some distance.

The room made a one-quarter revolution and the two doors disappeared. Stud became aware of an unpleasant sulphurous odor. He heard the hum of the television set, which had, seemingly, turned itself on. The picture, as it formed on the screen, was of Alice Reardon. No longer did she cower and sob. The picture was a close-up of her face. She was laughing hysterically, demoniacally. As the picture widened, her attackers appeared, backing away in uncertainty. She lunged at them as they fell back to the wall. Then, moving quickly from one to another, she tore their male organs from their bodies. The picture faded, their screams of agony dying away into silence.

Stud Harding became aware that he was sweating profusely. The sulphurous odor became more pungent.

Something diaphanous was taking shape in the far corner of the room. As it crystallized, it formed into a woman. A naked woman who somehow seemed familiar. It was Estelle, one of his girls. She'd been killed last week by some crazy john whom Harding had been unable to identify.

Now there were bruise marks at her throat and many bloodless wounds on her torso.

Harding was oddly unafraid. But as she approached, zombielike, he wanted none of her. He swung as if to strike her. But his hand passed through her face, touching nothing. He stepped back. As he did, she swung her right arm in an arc. As her finger passed in front of him, he felt a sharp pain. His chest had been cut, as if by a sharp knife, diagonally from his shoulder to his waist. Blood came from the cut, first seeping, then flowing freely. As he looked in horror, her arm arced once more, and his chest again was cut. It was now bleeding profusely in the form of an X.

He looked up from his wound, but Estelle had disappeared. His heart was pounding so wildly he was surprised he could not see it throb out from his chest.

The odor in the room was by now unbearable. A blast of heat swept over him as the far wall began to glow. Slowly, an image formed in the glow. The most disgusting, horrifying sight Stud Harding had ever seen. A huge face, greenish, salivating, grinning, covered with open sores. As its mouth opened, he could see a sea of flaming lava within.

Harding's mind reeled as he staggered backward, trying to escape the face. Somehow, he knew he was about to be swallowed, to disappear in that foul mouth. A dizzying swoon fought for possession of his mind. With rapidly diminishing strength, he fought the unconsciousness. If he were to fall into this coma, he knew it would be an eternal drop.

As he came in contact with the wall, he shuddered. A massive convulsion shook his body. He pitched violently to the floor, his eyes fixed wide in terror, his mouth stretched open seeking another breath of air that would never come.

"Walt, it was, at one and the same time the funniest and weirdest sight I've ever seen."

Lieutenant Ned Harris was beginning his third scotch-on-the-rocks at Code 30, a favorite restaurant-bar located in a near eastside building owned by the Detroit Police

Department. Among Harris' virtues was his ability to remain largely unaffected while and after consuming considerably large amounts of alcohol. He never drank on duty. He was now unwinding in the company of his close friend and superior officer, Inspector Walter Koznicki.

"Yeah, I saw the photos. I can just imagine what the real article looked like." Everything about Koznicki was large. Six-feet-four-and-a-half, approximately 250 pounds, yet he was not fat. If he were ordered to pare off, say twenty pounds, the weight would have to be surgically removed.

He sat with Harris on the upper level of the dining area near the bar, sipping at his original glass of port, and occasionally smoothing his bushy black mustache.

"It's one of those times when we have too many possible suspects," said Harris, swirling the ice cube with his index finger. "Outside of his 'family,' just about anybody in this community—including his wife—would be glad to see him dead."

"How about his mistress?"

"Mistress*es*," corrected Harris. "No, as far as we know, he kept them if not happy at least wealthy."

"Of course," Harris continued after a slight pause, "we have no cause of death."

"True," Koznicki responded, "but we must admit that even with Moellmann's eccentricities, we haven't given him much to go on."

"With nothing else to go on," said Harris, "I wouldn't mind going on the guess that somehow, somebody scared him to death. Think that's possible, Walt?"

Koznicki stared out the picture window across Jefferson Avenue and the unbroken black of the Detroit River at the blinking lights of Windsor. "Yes, I think so. Moellmann himself once told me of a young man who was trying to perform some stunt aboard a small prop plane. He slipped, and hung onto the landing gear for dear life. The pilot couldn't land for fear of crushing him."

"How about water?"

"There was no water reasonably near. The pilot finally

found a large haystack in an open field. He literally scraped the guy off into the haystack. But when they reached him, he was dead."

"Of fright?"

Koznicki nodded. "Moellman himself examined the body. Heart failure. No other apparent cause but fear. And he was a young man." The Inspector sipped at his wine. "But the unique element here, of course, is the Cardinal's red hat. Any leads there?"

"Not a one." Harris shook his head in bewilderment. "This morning, I got a crash course in red hats from a . . ." He paused to recall the name. ". . . a Dolson, Father Fred Dolson. He works at the cathedral—"

"He's probably an assistant pastor," Koznicki interrupted. "You really ought to brush up on your Catholic, Ned."

"Whatever. There's just no obvious reason for it, Walt. But whatever the reason, it had to be a damn good one. It was no easy trick to get that hat down from the ceiling— apparently, not too many even knew how to do it—much less pull it back up with the head in it."

"Well, that seems to narrow things a bit, doesn't it?"

"Narrows it to what? You think someone on the cathedral staff wasted Ruggiero?"

"Keep an open mind, Ned," Koznicki reminded. "Remember, you have a community full of suspects. That includes even the cathedral staff."

"O.K., but before I read some blue-haired housekeeper her rights, I think I'll check out some of Rudy's more natural enemies."

The two were silent for several minutes. They were nearing the bottom of the glass and the end of the evening.

"Ned," said Koznicki, "since this thing looks as if it's going to have some sort of 'Catholic connection,' have you given any thought to conferring with Father Koesler, just on a consultative basis? You know he was a vital help to us in those Rosary Murders a couple of years ago."

The friendship between Koesler and Koznicki that had

begun with the Rosary Murders had ripened over the years. It was not unusual to see the two lunching together or visiting each other at Koznicki's home or Koesler's rectory.

"It's a thought," said Harris, emptying his glass. "But it's early. Way too early."

"On the contrary, my friend," said Koznicki, checking his watch, "it's late and we've got a lot to do tomorrow."

"Would you like to know how big a Cardinal's hat is?" Harris asked in mock seriousness.

"Not big enough for your head." Koznicki picked up the check.

"Have you come up with anything in the Ruggiero murder?" Pat Lennon called from the bedroom.

"No," retorted Joe Cox from the living room, "we were left empty-hatted."

"What?"

"Forget it."

Lennon and Cox had been living together in a Lafayette Towers apartment for the past two years. Each had suffered through a disastrous marriage and messy divorce. Neither had children. Both were determined there would be no strings to their relationship. They were convinced a marriage license would be the death certificate to their life together. So far, all had worked well.

Lennon was changing into a Von Fürstenberg wrap dress for dinner at Schweizer's to be followed by a movie at the Renaissance Center. Lennon, like Cox, was a staff writer at the *Free Press*.

She entered the living room tying her dress at the side. As usual, lipstick was her only makeup. She needed no more to emphasize her attractive angular face and brunette hair that tumbled in curls.

Cox looked up from the latest issue of *Quest* magazine and smiled. The Von Fürstenberg clung to Lennon's voluptuous body, revealing pleasing curves.

"Do the cops have any suspects?" she asked.

"Yup." He selected a mint from the candy jar. "A veritable Who's Who of the dregs of Detroit's criminal society."

"Oh? They think it was one of Rudy's rivals?" Pat ran a comb through her hair.

"That's what they think." ·

"Which squad is on it?"

"Six."

"Six . . . Harris. Your pal Ned Harris."

"Yeah. The word I get is that they're going to drag out the throw net and begin interrogating just about every hood in Detroit. Maybe even Dearborn," he added, hoping to get a laugh. He got a fleeting smile. "But I have my own theory."

"What's that, Ellery Queen?"

He overlooked the sarcasm. "I don't think anybody on the local scene could've gotten close enough to Ruggiero to kill him, let alone decapitate him. He's just too closely guarded. And the goons who guarded him knew everybody locally, down to the corner pusher. It had to be somebody from out of town—maybe even a hit man from another country. Or, it had to be somebody from the inside. One of his own lieutenants." Cox, getting carried away by his own theory, was becoming excitedly animated.

Lennon smiled. "That's not at all bad, sweetie. But how does Cardinal Mooney's hat fit into your theory?"

"Beats me," he admitted. "It just plain flat out beats me. However," he added, "I am by no means alone in Baffleland. Nobody I know of has a single bankable theory. I suppose it's got to be somebody's idea of a joke. But wild! Whoever he is, he should give up murder as an occupation and become a comedy writer. TV needs him badly."

A look of seriousness, almost fright, passed over Lennon's face.

Cox noticed it. "What's wrong, honey?"

"That's not it, Joe, I don't know how to explain it . . . a premonition, I guess. Intuition, maybe. I just have a feeling that the answer to this whole thing is with the hat, that red hat, the Cardinal's hat. It's not a joke, Joe; it's the key to the whole thing."

Cox had too much respect for Lennon to dismiss, let alone deride, any feeling she might have. She had proven a most professional reporter many times over. He did not agree with her theory. From the center of his marrow, he did not agree. But hers was quite obviously a statement seriously made. And he would take it seriously.

"O.K., honey," he said. "But you won't mind if I follow MY theory and see if I can't find that out-of-town hit man or the invisible lieutenant from within, will ya? After all, if we were all to follow your theory and try to find the reason for the red hat, this might go down as one of the great unsolved mysteries of all time." He got her cape from the hall closet. "Now let's forget Rudy's red hat and sample the simple pleasures of beautiful downtown Detroit before the muggers get us."

"I confess to Almighty God..." Monsignor Terry McTaggart, pastor of St. Cecilia's parish, intoned the penitential prayer that begins the vernacular Mass.

McTaggart stood about five-feet-seven and was built like a rectangular brick house. Almost all McTaggart's clothing bore red piping shouting out his monsignorial rank. He wore his hair in a close-cropped crew cut—and so did his pet poodle. Though McTaggart was an anachronism, he was almost alone in being unaware of that fact.

St. Cecilia's was among the most relevant of inner city parishes. Monsignor McTaggart was among the more irrelevant of clergymen, inner city or suburban. That "Ceciliaville" remained one of the few vital and vibrant sections of the core city was due almost entirely to the work and presence of Ramon Toussaint. But no one had told McTaggart. So, he didn't know.

McTaggart had considered moving away with his friends. That he hadn't was due largely to that strongest force known to mankind: inertia. Now, he considered his presence at St. Cecilia's to be providential.

"Let us pray..." McTaggart adjusted his bifocals.

The usual daily congregation was present. Ramon Toussaint, wearing the long white alb and the stole that identified him as a deacon, stood near McTaggart and assisted him through the liturgy. Emerenciana Toussaint occupied her usual pew, front row center. Mr. and Mrs. Al Sapp were behind Mrs. Toussaint. Millie McIver, across the aisle, wore a babushka against the early morning chill of this Tuesday in September. Irene McNeeley was several pews back from Mrs. McIver. McTaggart was the only white person there.

". . . and he said to them, 'The Sabbath was made for man, not man for the Sabbath . . .'" Toussaint delivered the Gospel reading for that day. It was from the second chapter of Mark. He finished the reading and returned to his seat near where McTaggart remained standing. McTaggart regularly homilized following the weekday Scripture readings and, of course, at one or two of the Sunday Masses. Toussaint preached only at extremely well-attended Sunday liturgies. McTaggart never understood why Toussaint warranted such crowds.

"One of the greatest of the Ten Commandments is the one that tells us we've got to go to Mass on the Sabbath," began McTaggart, missing the point and erring simultaneously. "But that is not the only time Catholics must go to Mass. There are, as you all know, holy days of obligation when Catholics must go to Mass. But I'll bet that no matter if you attended parochial school or went to catechism classes regularly, I'll bet that not many of you can name all the holy days of obligation." He did not wait for a show of hands. "Well, I am going to give you some easy-to-remember letters that will make it possible for you to always remember the holy days of obligation.

"Just remember the three A's and the three C's." He seemed particularly pleased with himself. "The three A's and the three C's. All Saints, the Assumption and . . ." He drifted off. He had forgotten what the third "A" stood for. "All Saints, the Assumption . . ."

Perhaps if he went at it from the other side. "The Immaculate Conception, Christmas, the Circumcision, All

Saints, the Assumption . . . It will come to me . . . it will come to me later."

Irene McNeeley snickered audibly. Emerenciana Toussaint choked back laughter into her handkerchief.

Monsignor McTaggart rushed at it one more time. "All Saints, the Assumption and . . ."

"The Ascension," Ramon Toussaint stage-whispered.

"The Ascension!" cried McTaggart triumphantly.

McTaggart quickly terminated the homily. The remainder of the Mass proceeded almost without further incident. The only exceptions were when one of the congregation would fight to suppress a giggle that always proved infectious.

After Mass, the congregation left the church for the world. McTaggart knelt on a priedieu in the sanctuary, praying from his prayerbook. Toussaint cleared the altar of chalice, book, cruets, and dish.

He crossed to the side altar at the left of the main altar and sanctuary. He checked the votive lights and removed the remains of those that had burned out. He looked up, looked again, and stood transfixed. He moved quickly back to the main sanctuary. "Monsignor," he said, tapping McTaggart on the shoulder, "there's something you ought to see."

The two crossed to the Chapel of St. Cecilia.

Toussaint pointed.

There, atop the graceful statue of the parish's patroness, in place of the head of St. Cecilia, was the head of Stud Harding, the face contorted in its ultimate terror.

"Oh, my God!" cried McTaggart, "Oh, my God! Oh, my God!"

With the utterance of those three G's it was left to Toussaint to call the police—and the chancery.

Three

ST. ALOYSIUS

Lieutenant Harris had decided to spare the members of Squad Six any further encounters of an odd kind with the manic, explosive Chief Medical Examiner of Wayne County. Thus, it was Harris himself who arrived at the unimposing gray building on the corner of Brush and La-fayette, prompt for his eleven A.M. appointment.

He was greeted by the receptionist, who always appeared to be in a state of semi-bewilderment. Harris surmised her condition was the result of her daily, even if remote, contact with Willie Moellmann.

Her extensive and painstaking search through her appointment calendar failed to turn up Harris' name. But since he had police credentials, she advised him to go directly to the Chief's second-floor office.

There, Marge, the Chief's attractive, red-haired, recently-transplanted-from-Texas secretary, asked him to wait in the corridor.

Harris sat on a plain bench in the circular antechamber. Seated around an extremely large rectangular table pushed against the curved wall, a group of pathologists was discussing recent autopsies. One doctor looked as if he had escaped Nazi Germany just before final defeat; another, a middle-aged woman, appeared to have a similar background. There were also two very ordinary-looking WASP types; two Orientals and two East Indians, one light, the other dark, rounded out the group. They referred to their cases by four-digit numbers. Harris could discern little of their conversation, which was punctuated by laughter. Maybe, Harris thought, if you spend your days carving up rotting bodies, it helps to laugh.

His distraction ended when he peripherally caught sight of a sparrowlike figure staring at him from the adjacent doorway. It was Willie Moellmann, faintly resembling a Teutonic scarecrow, his glasses halfway down his nose.

"Do I know you?" asked Moellmann.

Harris sighed inaudibly as he stood. "Harris, Homicide, Squad Six."

"Have we met?" Moellmann persisted.

"Frequently."

"Then why don't I know you?"

"I'm black. We all look alike."

"That must be it." Moellmann led the way past Marge's desk into his office. Without formal invitation, Harris followed.

Moellmann sat behind his desk and looked up at Harris. "Well . . . ?"

"Lieutenant Harris."

"Well, Lieutenant Harris, what can I do for you?"

"I'm here about the head—Stud Harding's head. Were you able to determine the cause of death—or the time of death?"

All four of Moellman's extremities shot outward. For a moment, he resembled a Russian doing the kazatska. "Head!" he shouted.

Harris sighed again, this time audibly.

"Head!" Moellmann repeated. "What is this new custom with Squad Six of Homicide sending me heads!" He continued in a voice that could be heard throughout nearly the entire building. "It used to be you would send me more. But now? Just heads! I know what you're trying to do! You're trying to make me grateful for that inevitable day when you send me an entire torso!"

Harris fought back a sarcastic reply. Actually, he had always found it difficult to become angry with the Chief

Medical Examiner. He believed that when Moellmann had not taken to the stage, he had missed his true vocation.

"Then you don't know anything about that marvelous clue we gave you?" Harris asked, baitingly.

"Know anything? Know anything?" Moellmann began pacing between his large desk and the credenza that took up one entire wall behind the desk. "Marge!" he yelled. Marge could have heard him had she been standing on the corner of Brush and Lafayette, perhaps even farther. "Marge, bring in the folder on Harding!"

Marge ambled in. As she handed the folder to Moellmann, she remarked in her Texas twang, "Calm die-own, nay-oh, or yu'll jes' mike yorese'f ee-yul." She sauntered out.

Moellmann opened the file and consulted several typed pages. "The head—as was the case with Ruggiero's—was drained of blood. There was no mortal wound—to either head. Making it pretty well impossible to determine the cause of death. Your Mr. Harding died, as best we can determine, between four and eight P.M. yesterday." With an impish look, he added, "There's something more I can tell you."

His tone caused Harris to look up from the notes he was taking.

"I have ascertained that both heads were detached by a saw—a small handsaw—the same saw." Moellmann paused for effect.

"The same saw?" Harris straight-manned.

"The same saw. It has a defect. It is bent near the center. The same saw removed both heads. And one more thing . . ."

"Yes?" Harris wished Moellmann would drop the melodrama, at least occasionally.

"Your headsman is remarkably powerful. He needed only four to five strokes to cut through all that flesh, muscle and bone. And with a small, bent saw. Probably you're looking for an extremely well-built young man."

"That's it?" Harris closed his note pad.

"That's it! Oh . . ."

Harris assumed this device of a delayed reaction was borrowed from the "Columbo" TV series.

"Oh . . . one more thing: bring me a whole body sometime, and I'll tell you even more interesting stories."

"Thanks, Doc."

As Harris left, he nodded at Marge.

"Yawl have a nahss die," she drawled.

"You don't understand, Cox," Nelson Kane was explaining with dwindling patience, "I am trying to keep you two on separate assignments. Not make you into a team."

Kane, Joe Cox, and Pat Lennon were standing at one end of the city room near the oval slot desk, which, at this early time of the day, was unoccupied. Thus, the three enjoyed relative privacy.

"It's all right with me, Nellie," said Lennon. Basically, this was Joe's idea—"

"Damn right," Cox interrupted.

"Now listen," said Kane, "years ago, it was *Free Press* policy that married couples couldn't be employed here together, even if they worked in separate departments. Now I know the policy isn't enforced anymore, and I know you two aren't technically married. But you might just as well be. And there was a good reason for that rule."

"It's not like that with us. We're not tied by a piece of paper," said Cox. "Look at it this way, Nellie: I'm already on the story. But I'm convinced Pat has a better feel for it. Right off the bat, she realized the hat was more important than the head."

"The *what*?"

"The hat is more important than the head," Cox repeated.

"What I mean," Lennon explained, "is that the indication Joe gets from the police is that they're going after suspects who would be likely killers of both Ruggiero and Harding."

"And?"

"And I think a shortcut is to look for some reason why the heads are found in a Cardinal's hat and on a saint's statue. After the reason comes the person who placed them there, and at that point if you haven't got your murderer, you're probably breathing on him."

Kane mulled over the matter. "Well . . . O.K., we'll try it a while and see how it turns out. But I'm warning you, if I sense any foul-up or lack of progress you two will suffer a journalistic divorce."

Cox and Lennon departed almost as excited as kids. They liked living together, and they liked working together. They liked it all.

Kane watched them return to their desks. Shortly after arriving at the *Free Press*, Lennon had sealed her dead-end fate by rejecting the casting couch routine of Executive Manager Karl Lowell. From that moment, she knew she would do well merely to survive in the city room. There would be no promotions or merit increases even though she had proven worthy of both. Her moving in with Cox had rubbed salt on Lowell's raw id. Even with a Pulitzer in his pocket, Cox would be doomed by Lowell to tread water at the same level as Lennon.

Kane shook his head. He wondered how long he could keep them at the *Free Press*. A good paper with a fine history, but one that was being slowly destroyed by the infantile ego of a two-bit hatchet man. On second thought, Kane wondered how much longer he himself would last.

Once into September, it was never certain how much reasonably good golfing weather remained in Michigan. Today's was splendid. Sunny, warm, yet with just a hint of a breeze.

Two priestly foursomes had just gathered at the first tee of the course at St. John's Provincial Seminary. Located near the township of Plymouth, the institution was Michigan's major seminary offering theological studies to future diocesan priests.

The priests played this course because it was reserved

for the seminarians and Catholic clergy and thus relatively uncluttered. In addition, there was no fee. And, while a few private clubs asked no greens fees of the clergy, St. John's held the special attraction of being exclusively for the clergy. And if there was anything most of the clergy—at least the celibate Roman type—preferred, it was the company of fellow priests.

The eight swung their drivers, unlimbering muscles. With little conversation at the moment, the only sounds were the hum of the clubs moving through the air and the swish as the club heads passed through the grass.

"Did you fellows hear what they found in old St. Cecilia's this morning?" Monsignor Jasper Max, now in retirement at St. Norbert's parish in Inkster, was, though elderly, still powerfully built. Formerly one of the more active of jocks, he was truly a hail-fellow-well-met.

"Of course," Father Koesler responded. "By this time you'd have to be cloistered not to know."

"What?" asked Father Pat McNiff, who was not cloistered, just not very well informed.

"Another head!" Father Donald Curley answered. "To go with the one they found in the Cardinal's hat the other night. A matched pair." Curley, tall, paunchy, bald, myopic, acid-tongued, rummaged through his golf bag and discovered a new Spalding Dot. By the end of golf season, he had few if any unused balls. The source of the Spalding puzzled him.

"Well, hardly a matched pair," said Koesler, "unless you consider white and black, the top man in the rackets, and the top pimp somehow matched."

"Will someone tell me what happened?" demanded McNiff. He was abstractedly studying the wheels of Koesler's golf cart. Koesler had recently been given the cart by one of his sisters as a birthday present. Characteristically, he had not removed the plastic covering on the wheels, considering that an unnecessary gesture. Most of the plastic had worn off. The remaining clinging shreds were the object of McNiff's scrutiny.

"Found the head of Stud Harding on the shoulders of the statue of St. Cecilia," said Max.

"Was he dead?" McNiff asked absently, as he continued his study of Koesler's wheels.

"No," said Curley, brightly, "they were joining the two to get a black female saint who literally marketed virtue." He continued to study the Spalding Dot.

"Whoever did it, it's lucky for him he didn't do it to *my* statue," Father Ted Neighbors stated emphatically.

"Somebody do a statue of you?" Curley asked facetiously.

"You mean you haven't heard of the Ted Neighbors statue?" asked Koesler.

"It's not a statue of me!" Neighbors thundered. "It's a statue of St. Frances Cabrini!" Neighbors was pastor of the Allen Park parish whose patroness was Mother Cabrini.

"What's so special about it?" asked McNiff.

"What's so special about it?" Koesler repeated. "Ted, here, commissioned a local artist to do it for $50,000."

"$50,000!" Max whistled. "How'd you ever get your parish council to go along with that?"

"Monsignor," Neighbor's tone was autocratic, "when Pope Julius commissioned Michelangelo to redecorate the Sistine Chapel, he did not conduct a plebiscite!"

"Let's play a little shinny," invited Max, heading for the first tee.

"Koesler!" McNiff shouted, finally solving the mystery. "You didn't take the plastic covers off your wheels!"

"Couldn't do it," Koesler said, "it's against the Natural Law."

"There you go again, always making fool-around with holy things." McNiff shook his head and selected his driver.

After considering the matter briefly, Max hit his tee shot down the middle of the fairway, and short. From that position, he would tee off again. Max used tees constantly on the fairway, and picked up putts of up to twenty feet as "gimmies."

McNiff, after waggling his club and fanny incessantly, hit a duck hook. The ball flew powerfully from the tee, took a sharp turn to the left, and disappeared into the woods. "God, that felt good!" he said.

Koesler, who played golf virtually as a contact sport, swung from the heels. The ball faded in a sharp slice, cleared a large tree at the right of the fairway, hit on the cement handball court and bounded within reaching distance of the green.

"Lucky son-of-a-bitch," commented Neighbors, who would be in the second foursome.

Curley decided to use the new Spalding Dot. A better-than-average golfer, he teed the ball high. At the height of his backswing he remembered the origin of the Dot. Five months before, he had bought it at a novelty store, planning to slip it into Bob Koesler's bag. It was an exploding ball. Full realization hit as his club made contact with the Dot.

A crowd of students had gathered in the parking lot of Detroit's Cooley High School.

In the center of the growing ring of young people was a black girl, a Cooley sophomore. She lay prostrate on the asphalt. Kneeling next to her was a massive black police officer, who had spread his jacket over her body.

The girl was unconscious, her frail body racked by violent convulsions. She was salivating profusely. In an attempt to prevent her from drowning, the officer turned her head to one side so the saliva drooled from her mouth. Between soothing words that he hoped would penetrate her subconscious, the officer, Patrolman Lou Jackson, questioned the girl's frightened boyfriend, Willie Woods.

"What's her name?"

"Laura . . . Laura Gates," Woods blurted.

"It's gonna be all right, Laura," Jackson said gently but loudly. "It's gonna be all right. The ambulance is on the way. You're gonna be all right."

He looked up at Woods. "How'd this happen?"

"It must've been the pusher," Woods pointed to the corner of Fenkell and Hubbell, "the one who works the corner. She been playin' up to that dude for weeks," he added bitterly.

"So, what happened?"

"I do' know. She been tellin' him she used ever'thing. Tryin' to get him to think she worth him."

"Did she?"

"What?"

"Did she use everything?"

"Hell, man," Woods shook his head, "she never use nothin'. She just talk big to get him to listen."

"It's all right, honey." Jackson smoothed Laura Gates' hair. The convulsions were increasing in number and intensity. It seemed that if they got any more violent the girl's whole body would explode, or smash itself to pieces. Damn that ambulance, Jackson thought. Where the hell was it!

"Did you see what happened?" Jackson asked Woods.

"Well, from a far away. I think he gave her some horse. Shit, he had to show her how to take it. He shoulda known then that she din't know what she was doin'. He was laughin' when she snorted it."

"Then what?"

"Then she started shakin', shakin' all over. Then she fell over. She's been shakin' ever since."

"Know who the pusher is?"

"Naw, jes' he works this corner."

Jackson had been concentrating so deeply on getting information from Woods and caring as well as he could for the girl that he had not even been aware of the intensifying wail of the approaching ambulance. Suddenly it was there, backing toward the girl. The crowd parted at its approach.

The white-clad crew spilled out. Jackson removed his jacket from the girl's body as one of the attendants wrapped a sheet around her. Two others expertly lifted her onto a gurney.

"What've we got here?" one asked Jackson.

"One Laura Gates, age sixteen. O.D.'d on heroin most probably."

As they lifted the girl into the ambulance she was struck by a convulsion so powerful that her body would have hurled itself from the gurney if she had not been strapped in. Then, for the first time in several minutes, she was still. Her body relaxed. She did not move.

The attendants finished sliding the gurney into the ambulance. Two attached life support systems to her as the vehicle sped east on Fenkell. As it turned north on Schaefer en route to Mt. Carmel's emergency ward, Laura Gates died.

One could argue whether St. Aloysius Church was part of the Chancery Building or vice versa. Each had the same easy-to-remember address, 1234 Washington Boulevard.

The church's architecture was peculiar, if not unique. The chancel was set off by a parapet, which curved like a wide-mouthed horseshoe around a half-moon-shaped space similar to an open orchestra pit—except that this open space looked down into the basement, which had its own sanctuary and altar immediately beneath the main-floor altar. Thus, an event taking place at the main altar could be viewed not only from the nave and the balcony, but also by those in the basement. There were occasions when two separate events took place simultaneously in view of both those sitting in the balcony and the fore of the nave and those in the fore of the basement.

To the north of St. Aloysius, in the joined building, was the chancery, housing, among other departments, the Matrimonial Tribunal, the chancery offices, offices of the auxiliary bishops and, of course, the office of Archbishop Mark Boyle. The upper floors comprised a large dining room and kitchen, as well as residence rooms—most of which, once filled, were now empty.

One Dearborn priest bragged periodically, generally to the laity, that he had had "lunch with the boss." It was a feat any priest could achieve, though few cared to.

It required only that the priest appear about noon in St. Aloysius' dining room on the eighth floor of the Chancery Building. Far from being turned away, visiting priests were most welcome at the cafeteria-style luncheon. More often than not, Archbishop Boyle ate there at noon. And thus one had "lunch with the boss."

Usually, little was said at these meals. Few priests could think of anything that might interest the Archbishop conversationally. The tall, dignified, handsome, blue-eyed prelate was comfortable with silence.

One exception was Father Joe Sheehan, a particular favorite of Boyle's.

After Sheehan had received his doctorate in theology at the Angelicum in Rome and returned to Detroit, Boyle had Sheehan audition to be his secretary. To qualify for this position required little more than driver's training. It was, however, a position Sheehan did not want. His first and last test occurred when Boyle was to be chauffeured to St. Mary's of Redford for a confirmation service. Sheehan drove aimlessly and interminably. Finally, in desperation, the Archbishop turned to him. "Father Sheehan, do you have the slightest idea where you are going?"

"Not really, Your Excellency," Sheehan had replied. "But if you'll look at the street signs and read them off to me, I may find something familiar."

While Sheehan had not won the secretarial position, he had been appointed to head the Catholic Youth Organization.

Today, as Archbishop Boyle took his seat and carefully draped a napkin across his lap, he looked across the table to see the unpredictable Father Sheehan.

"Well, Father Sheehan," Boyle opened, "what is new at the Catholic Youth Organization?"

Sheehan looked Boyle straight in the eyes. "We've begun a program in coeducational judo."

Boyle shook his head and coughed.

Meanwhile, in the lobby, Father Thomas McInerny, pastor of St. Aloysius, paced among the seemingly endless racks of pamphlets. He noticed a woman who had just come out of the church. She looked extremely angry. He approached her.

"Excuse me," he said, "is there something wrong?"

She looked at him furiously. "I will never again go to confession in this church!"

"Why, what's the matter?"

"The priest, that's what's the matter. He gave me two thousand Hail Marys to say as a penance!"

"Two thousand Hail Marys!" McInerny repeated, dumbfounded. Then a thought occurred to him. "Wait a minute; there aren't any confessions scheduled now—"

Father McInerny moved quickly inside the church and looked at the confessional to the right of the main altar. Sure enough, the little red light above the central of three compartments was lit, indicating a priest was within prepared to hear confessions.

Puzzled, McInerny walked swiftly down the aisle and swung open the confessional door. There, smiling smugly, sat a derelict from Michigan Avenue.

St. Aloysius was one of Detroit's more interesting parishes.

"I gotsa git a fix!" Willie Monroe perspired profusely as he cruised along Riopelle in the direction of East State Fair. On the steering wheel of the '54 Ford, Monroe's hands trembled. It had been too long since he'd had his needed dose of heroin.

"Ain't you got no bread at all, man?" his partner, Harvey Murphy, asked.

"No, man. I got about enough to get me a Twinkie."

Monroe drove slowly, looking for something, anything, that would lead to money. Some victim. He knew from experience that he was in no condition to try to rob a store. He was too jittery. Either he would fumble such an effort badly or very probably he would shoot someone. He'd already done time for both such mistakes. In fact, most of his twenty-two years had been spent in prisons of one sort or another.

"Maybe we ought to knock over that supermarket up the street, man," suggested Murphy.

"No, man. This ain't the right time for that kinda scene. We gotsa hit on some*body*—and soon."

Several more minutes passed as the old Ford crossed East State Fair and cruised the quiet changing neighborhood.

It was Murphy who first spotted him. "Hey, looka that!" he said, pointing to a rather well-dressed man who had just come out of one of the old homes on Riopelle and was walking toward his car parked at the curb.

"That's the man," Monroe agreed.

He coaxed the Ford along the street. In this sort of endeavor, timing was everything. Just as the man came around his car to approach the door on the driver's side, Monroe gunned the old Ford. It shot ahead, the right fender hooking the man and catapulting him over the hood of his own car.

Monroe and Murphy leaped from their car and ran to the prostrate motionless victim.

"Lordee," Murphy whistled low. "Now you done it. Look at that collar: That's a priest you just wasted!"

"What's done's done," Monroe replied. "What's he got?"

Quickly, Monroe dug out a battered wallet.

"Five bucks! A lousy five bucks!"

"C'mon, man," Murphy urged. "We gotsa git outta here. The man gonna be on our ass for wasting a priest."

"Yeah, let's move it."

They quickly returned to the still running Ford, Monroe clutching the wallet containing little money and a couple of credit cards. Clearly, they were headed for a busy day if each of their victims carried so little cash.

As they sped away, the elderly lady the priest had just

visited took down their license number. First she called the ambulance, then the police.

The office of the Homicide Inspector resembled the proverbial jam-packed sardine can. Inspector Koznicki and Lieutenant Harris sat opposite each other in the room's only two chairs. One got the impression that if both had stood simultaneously, one of them would have been forced either through a wall or out the window.

"Can't you get any handle on this thing, Ned?" Koznicki asked, not without concern.

"No, dammit," said Harris. "Every lead has gone nowhere. I mean—" He tried to stretch a leg and succeeded only in barking his shin against the desk. "Damn!" he intoned softly. "I mean, it is within the realm of reality that the king of vice gets murdered by the king of pimps. And that the family of the king of vice then reciprocates. But, according to Moellmann, they were both wasted by the same guy—or at least both decapitated by the same guy. Now how do you figure that?"

Koznicki shrugged. "Maybe they don't know it. Maybe the killer is an out-of-town freelancer. Maybe the two gangs contact him independently. Then the only one who knows that he is playing both sides of the fence is the killer. It is his private joke."

Harris thought a moment. "That theory has possibilities. I mean, I've seen sicker dogs live. But Walt, what a coincidence! Can you imagine the odds against it?"

"I well can." Koznicki stretched his huge frame. Obviously, he was more acquainted with the confining dimensions of his office. "But it is nonetheless a possibility. And if true, the killer may end up wasting one hood after another alternately. If he was, say the top gun in Chicago, it's possible the odds against the killer's being the same man might drop a little."

Each allowed himself a small smile.

"You know, Walt, it's very tempting to step aside from

this affair and let 'em go loose at the O.K. Corral. Certainly would clean up Detroit nicely."

"Hell, Ned, I know it's tempting. But you don't get law and order by looking the other way when law and order is violated."

Harris smiled again. "I know, Walt, I know. I just had to get it off my chest with you so I could stay serious with the squad. It's hard to keep 'em enthusiastic when they know they're trying to solve a killing which, if they fail to solve, probably would at least diminish the city's crime rate."

"Are they holding well?"

"Yeah. They're a good bunch."

"By the way," Koznicki moved forward and so, naturally, did his desk, giving Harris even less room, "have you decided to call Father Koesler in for some consultation?"

"Yeah. This is his day off, but I've got a call in for him. Who knows, maybe he's got some idea of why we find one head inside a Cardinal's hat and another on top a saint's statue. None of us has a clue to that one."

"O.K., Ned. I'm glad you're calling him in. He has a fine, logical mind. And besides," Koznicki winked at Harris, "he does love playing detective."

Harris laughed, banging his hand against the table, and rose to leave.

"One more thing, Ned: Make sure the news media know we have evidence that indicates these two killings were perpetrated by the same person. If our theory is correct, this will seriously complicate the position of our hired gun. Even if our assumption is incorrect, the news should shake up Detroit's criminal world. And there's nothing we want more than a badly disturbed criminal world."

"But we keep to ourselves how we know—the bent handsaw, the powerful man."

"Exactly."

"Walt, you show promise."

* * *

In the emergency room of Saratoga General Hospital, Father Alfred Dalton, paster of St. Rita's, lay on a gurney. It was covered with blood—his blood. Though his eyes were open, it wasn't clear whether he was sentient. He had been given a pain-killer. Preparations for his examination continued.

"Ladies and gentlemen of the medical profession," he suddenly intoned, to everyone's surprise, "you have just cut away $195 worth of clothing and carefully removed a two-dollar pair of Jockey shorts." He was precisely correct.

"He's in shock," Dr. Sommerfelt diagnosed.

"No," Dalton responded, thoughtfully, "it puts me in mind of an incident that happened while I was bosun's mate in the U.S. Navy."

"His right leg is broken in three places." Sommerfelt continued his exploration.

"Well," Dalton resumed, his speech slightly slurred due to the analgesic, but clear enough to be understood, "we had this CPO who had a vocabulary of obscenities that just wouldn't quit. He could carry on for a full hour and more of pure vulgarity and never repeat himself."

"His left leg is shattered," said Sommerfelt, hardly daring to touch it.

"One day," persisted Dalton, "we had this drill. We were lowering a lifeboat filled with seamen over the side. I was working the davit at one end when the Chief shouted an order. I thought he meant to hold, whereas what he actually meant was that we should speed up. As it turned out, I was responsible for dumping a lot of sailors into the ocean."

"I think his lung is punctured," monotoned Sommerfelt.

"Well, sirs, that CPO looked long at that scene and finally said, 'Oh, dear!' It was so awful that nothing in his vocabulary of vulgarity was adequate."

"We'd better just try to keep him alive and see what starts healing first," Sommerfelt concluded.

"Well, sirs, that's just about how I feel now. To quote

my CPO, Oh, dear!" Dalton's eyes rolled back as he mercifully passed out.

Against his previous better judgment, Willie Monroe was about to rob a pharmacy. He needed drugs, money, or both. But he had been without the former too long. Not far from the agonies of withdrawal, he was not able to think clearly.

He and Harvey Murphy had selected a pharmacy tucked into a small shopping mall near Lafayette Towers. There were always clusters of shoppers in the area, which made escape slightly more certain.

Murphy, whose need was not nearly as advanced as was Monroe's, would keep watch outside the pharmacy while Monroe would carry out the actual robbery.

"You sure you don't want me to tap the man?" asked a worried Murphy.

"No, man. This is all downhill. They ain't nobody in this place hardly." Monroe was trembling, though not badly.

"O.K. But make it fast."

Monroe entered casually, fingering the small-caliber revolver in his jacket pocket. He moved slowly but deliberately toward the rear of the store.

The pharmacist pretended not to notice him. Actually, he never took his eyes off Monroe. Young and black, Monroe fit well enough into this racially mixed neighborhood, but there was something in his manner that, to the pharmacist's practiced eye, bore watching.

On his path down the left side aisle, Monroe picked up a number of items idly, handling each in turn, then replacing it. Finally, he reached the pharmacy's raised counter at the rear of the store.

It all happened quickly.

As Monroe ducked behind the counter, he pulled out his Saturday Night Special and aimed it at the pharmacist.

"Gimmee—" was as far as he got.

The man's right hand hit a button beneath the counter's

ledge. A loud bell sounded both in and outside the store.

Murphy swung the front door open and shouted, "Man, *move!*"

Monroe fired three times, hitting the pharmacist twice in the abdomen and once in the chest.

As his victim slumped to the floor, Monroe ran through the store and joined Murphy in a race to the car.

The store's single customer, a middle-aged nurse, nose coolly pressed to the glass door, took note of the auto's make and license number. Then she phoned the police.

Within a very short time, Willie Monroe and Harvey Murphy would be wanted by the law for felonious driving, assault with intent to do great bodily harm, robbery, attempted robbery, and murder. And an all-points-bulletin would alert the entire Detroit Police Department to be on the lookout for them.

Willie Monroe had badly injured one man and killed another. He still had neither money nor drugs.

The busboy was pouring ice water into the last empty glass on the table when Father Donald Curley stage-whispered to his three companions, "Now don't any of you let on that I'm the *Free Press*' Anonymous Gourmet!"

The busboy overfilled the glass, fumbled through an apology and retreated for a cloth to blot up the spill. The other three priests looked at Curley incredulously.

As the busboy left, Father Koesler said, "Don, are you out of your mind? You don't write a restaurant review column for the *Free Press*. You don't write anything for the *Free Press*!"

"I know, I know," Curley said, conspiratorially shushing him, "but watch what happens. Don't any of you look at the busboy now, but I can see him and I'll tell you what he's doing. He's gone directly to Mario, he's telling Mario something with a good bit of animation, and he's gesturing toward our table."

"O.K., O.K.," said Father Patrick McNiff, "but what's the idea?"

"The idea, my dear McNiff, is this: Suppose you owned a restaurant and you knew that someone who writes restaurant reviews for one of the town's major publications was eating in your place. Don't you suppose you'd go to a few extra pains to make sure everything was perfect?"

"Clever, damned clever!" said Monsignor Al Thomas. Thomas was head of the Tribunal, Detroit's Catholic marriage court. Of average height and slightly overweight, he had straight jet-black hair and a magnificent bass voice.

"Dishonest!" McNiff decided.

"Cute," said Koesler, "but how often do you try it?"

"Oh, not often. I keep track of which restaurants the Anonymous Gourmet has reviewed. It'd be disastrous to try this in a place that had recently been written up. And I pretend to be the Anonymous Gourmet only in the better places. Whoever he is, the Gourmet is not going to review a greasy spoon."

"I don't know about that," said McNiff, "but I do know *you're* not going to eat in a greasy spoon!"

At that moment, the busboy returned and wordlessly mopped up the spill. He was followed by a majestic, dark-suited waiter. Mario's, on Second Avenue, was a still fashionable eatery in an otherwise decaying neighborhood. All Mario's waiters were first, men and second, showmen.

"Fathers," the smiling waiter bowed slightly, "Mario himself would like to buy you a drink."

The smile on Curley's face was beatific. McNiff looked at him disapprovingly. Thomas decided Curley would have done well with a career in canon law. Koesler shook his head. It works, he thought, but you'd have to be a seller of snake oil to carry it off.

"Say," Koesler said, after the drink orders were taken and the waiter had left, "did any of you hear what happened to Al Dalton?"

No one had.

"Hit by a car," Koesler announced. "Heard it on the radio on my way here. He's in Saratoga. Pretty serious."

"Accident?" asked McNiff.

"No."

"Oh, my God," said Thomas, "I hope this isn't open season on priests and nuns again."

"No," said Koesler, "not that either. Some kid hit him on purpose, but the motive was robbery. Stole his wallet."

"Some hop-headed kid," said McNiff, correctly. "Probably wanted the money to get high on dope."

The drinks were delivered, but the foursome did not order. Curley had advised the delay to see if another complimentary round would be offered.

"I can't help it," said Thomas, "ever since those Rosary Murders, every time some Detroit priest or nun is even injured, I'm worried that it's starting all over again."

"That was two years ago, Al," said Koesler, "and it was such a special case it could never happen again."

"I don't know," countered Thomas. "There's those heads they've been finding in our churches. I just think it's peculiar that it's always the Catholic community that suffers."

"Now you know how the Jews have felt all these centuries," said Koesler. "But, yes, these latest incidents have certainly been strange. I haven't the foggiest idea of what it all means."

"Maybe," suggested McNiff, stirring his martini, "it's somebody's idea of a pun. You know, *caput* is Latin for 'head.' So you find a head in a hat and another on a statue where the head should be. Maybe it's a way of saying these guys committed capital crimes. See: capital—*caput*—head."

It made more sense to Koesler than anything he'd heard to date.

"I think it's hilarious," said Curley, who could not bear to be out of a conversation very long.

"You would!" said McNiff.

"Well, I mean," Curley continued, "you guys are all old enough to remember how fastidious Cardinal Mooney was. If you'll recall, those were the days of The Uniform. Diamond Ed Mooney dressed correctly and, by damn, so did his clergy." After a sip of his gin and tonic, Curley went on. "Remember the day Joe Marek went downtown all dressed in his clericals but without a hat? And as luck would have it, he bumped into Mooney outside the chancery."

The others nodded. They did not remember.

Curley warmed to his story. "Well, Mooney read Marek the riot act about how a gentleman always wears a hat and by an Act of God all priests are supposed to be gentlemen. So, in one of Mooney's grand gestures, he told Marek to go buy himself a hat and charge it to him, Mooney. So," Curley began to chuckle, "Marek goes right down Washington Boulevard into old A.J. Hickey's—the most expensive store on the street—and buys the most expensive hat in the place and charges it to Mooney!"

They laughed.

"I've always wondered," Koesler remarked, "why Marek's ecclesiastical career didn't bloom earlier."

"Imagine," said Curley, "how Mooney would have felt if he had known his hat was going to be worn by the biggest hood in town."

The waiter came. Their orders were taken. There would be no more free drinks. Nor would the dinners be complimentary. Mario's food was dependably good. Tonight it would be perfect.

"I wonder," McNiff said, "why it is that these murders and decapitations all take place in the city. Nothing like that has happened in any of the suburbs."

"It's a good point, Pat," said Koesler.

"Don't get me started," Thomas protested, wagging a bread stick, "on the inner city and inner-city priests!"

"Why?" asked Curley, "what did they ever do to you?"

"They don't use his Tribunal," said Koesler, smiling and looking directly at Thomas.

"Damn right!" said Thomas. "They think they're above the law. Why, hell, I know that just about all those inner-city people are involved in multiple marriages. But when one of them wants to become Catholic, do you think the marriage case is sent to the Tribunal?"

"No," said Curley, who enjoyed volunteering answers to rhetorical questions.

"No!" emphasized Thomas. "About the only cases we ever get down there are *Defectus Formae*—the easiest of 'em all."

"*Defectus* what?" Curley had nothing for or against the Church's marriage legislation. He just didn't pay much attention to Latin.

"*Defectus Formae*, Don," explained Koesler, who had a working knowledge of, and an active dislike for, most of the 2,414 laws in the Code of Canon Law. "A defect in the form of marriage. Like when a Catholic gets married but not by a priest. The marriage is considered invalid."

"And the worst offender of them all," averred Thomas, "is that black deacon, what's-his-name, over at St. Cecilia's."

"Ramon Toussaint," Koesler supplied.

"He's been there," Thomas resumed, "for what—five, six years. He's performed plenty of weddings. He's never sent us a single case. Can you believe that? Not one case. One of these days I'll get the bastard!"

"And then what?" asked Curley. "Nothing's going to happen to him. Everybody knows Boyle doesn't want to be told what's going on in the inner city."

"But," Koesler cut in, "that's reverse discrimination. Bad Church law can be discarded in the inner city but it has to be enforced in the suburbs."

"Bad law! Bad law!" shouted Thomas. The voices at the table had grown louder as the argument progressed. Many diners at neighboring tables had stopped talking and were listening to the priests. "Bad law!" Thomas repeated.

"Yes, bad law," Koesler returned. "Canon law is the only remaining reform ordered by Vatican II that hasn't been touched. If it was pronounced bad law more than a decade ago, it's got to be even worse now."

"Wait a minute, Koesler," said McNiff, "the Pope has told us we've got to use the present canon law until the revision is completed and approved."

"That's *his* opinion," said Koesler.

"*His* opinion! *His* opinion!" McNiff, his napkin crumpled in passion, almost rose from his chair. "What I want to know, Koesler, is, do you or do you not believe in the Holy Pope of God!"

"Sometimes," Koesler murmured.

"Sometimes! SOMETIMES!" McNiff, his voice crescendoing, was almost beside himself.

A man at an adjacent table leaned over and tapped Curley on the shoulder. "You know," he said, "if you guys talked like this on Sundays, I would seriously consider going back to church."

Harris was headed toward his far eastside apartment. This had been a long and mostly fruitless day. The only positive accomplishment had been the news conference, during which he had gotten the word out that due to one discovery in The Red Hat Murders, it had been determined that both decapitations had been perpetrated by the same subject. The *Free Press'* Joe Cox had fired several questions trying to get at the clue. But Harris had evaded every attempt. Outside of that one effective episode, Squad Six had spent the day exploring blind alleys.

Harris let the details of the case filter through his mind as he drove somewhat absently up Gratiot.

Gradually, he became aware that the black '54 Ford ahead of him was weaving ever so slightly. Not enough to cross lanes, but enough to suggest the driver might be having a problem. It could be a drunk driver.

Harris called dispatch, giving the license number and asking for a wants-warrants-and-registration check. Seconds later, his police radio crackled with the information on the hit-and-run, robbery, and murder. The suspects were considered armed and dangerous.

Harris asked for backup. He placed the portable flasher on the roof of his car, activated it and pulled alongside the Ford.

Willie Monroe, sweating profusely in the early stages of

drug withdrawal, looked to his left, saw the flashing red light and the black driver holding up his police ID and pointing to the curb.

Monroe floored the accelerator. The Ford leaped ahead, weaving through the sparse traffic, followed closely by Harris, who had now activated his siren.

Monroe ran the red light at Van Dyke, forcing Harris to do the same. This was not the way either of them had hoped to end the day. Harris stayed on the radio, tracing their course so the backup cars could keep track.

Abruptly, Monroe swung the Ford down the entrance ramp of the Edsel Ford Expressway and headed northeast.

Harris' siren was useless now. He was far past the point at which the siren's sound had been overridden by the car's velocity.

On the expressway, drivers who saw Harris' flasher in the rear-view mirrors pulled their vehicles to one side, the occupants watching fascinated as the two cars wove through the remaining traffic at speeds up to ninety miles an hour.

"Willie," Harvey Murphy pleaded, "face it, we bought it! I don' wanna be dead. Pull over."

"No way! I gotsa murder one with that guy in the drugstore. I ain't goin' down for that."

"But Willie, even if you can lose this guy, he's gotta called for help and he's givin' 'em directions now. Pretty soon we gonna have most of the Detroit cops on our ass."

Monroe thought that one over. "O.K.," he decided, "we're gonna cut out the middle man and I'm gonna waste me a black pig."

The Ford abruptly headed off the expressway at the Moross ramp. Harris almost missed the exit, but at the last second, veered onto the ramp. At the top of the ramp, Monroe slammed on his brakes and skidded sideways to a stop in the middle of Moross Road.

Taken by surprise, Harris hit his brakes even harder than Monroe had. His car spun out of control across Moross and stopped as it thudded into a street light.

Harris, stunned but still alert, was able to open his door and tumble out, drawing his service revolver as he fell.

He looked up to see Monroe standing beside the Ford, his gun pointed at Harris. Monroe fired. If Monroe's hands had not been trembling, Harris would have been hit. The bullet pierced the car door just to the left of his head. Monroe would not have another chance. Harris fired once. Monroe's body jerked backward as if he were a puppet whose string had been pulled. The bulled had passed through his heart. Never again would he go through the agonies of withdrawal.

Murphy, on the other side of the car, was on his knees, begging for his life.

Harris radioed for an ambulance and began to assess the damage. It was considerable.

Cox and Lennon had just arrived at their apartment. They were elated. Cox had two copies of the initial page proofs of their story on The Red Hat Murders. This was the first time the two had co-bylined a story. It would run in tomorrow's editions on page one. Cox had insisted Lennon's name should precede his. More than a chivalrous gesture, it was an acknowledgement that the story was more Lennon's work than his. Most of the ideas and leads had been hers.

They did not know what the headline would say; that was not their department. But the story was prefaced, "By Patricia Lennon and Joe Cox, *Free Press* Staff Writers."

Cox had done most of the actual writing, which was evidenced to the professional eye by the lean prose.

The lead began with Lieutenant Harris' announcement of the probability that both decapitations had been performed by the same person and that further details were being withheld. Other police were quoted as strongly assuming the deaths themselves each could have been caused by a different person. The very importance of the victims and the substantial protection they normally had seemed to indicate a gang effort that had to have been meticulously planned. The only explanation—and it was no more than a guess—for the church-related placement of the heads was that the killer—or killers—might be a religious fanatic.

Lennon had interviewed Dr. Joseph Markham of St. Joseph Mercy Hospital. Markham was easily Detroit's leading expert on the phenomenon of post-death experiences related by people who return to life after apparent death. Indeed, Markham taught a class on Thanatology at Wayne State University.

Regarding the look of terror on the faces of both heads, Markham pointed out that not all post-death experiences are delightful. Some of those who returned related experiences that could quite literally scare the hell out of you. Perhaps this might have been the case with these rather prominent if reputed criminals. Lennon, in writing this section, had managed to capture a sense of the macabre.

All in all, it was an excellent news analysis. The completed story had even triggered that rare event, Nelson Kane's publicly expressed pleasure.

Cox and Lennon finished reading the proofs and looked at each other with a mixture of pride, pleasure, and desire. They decided to treat each other to dinner at the London Chop House, the most expensive if not the poshest restaurant in town. But first, they would save on energy and shower together.

While Rudy Ruggiero was still among the living, there might have been some doubt about it. But now, everyone, from the law enforcement agencies to the depths of the underworld, was willing to admit that Dutch Strauss was kingpin of Detroit's drug empire.

A native Detroiter, Strauss came from a middle-class family on Detroit's southwest side. After graduating from Holy Redeemer High School, Strauss, never a very involved Catholic, had made a simple discovery that was to evolve into his raison d'être: entrepreneurs are the guys who give the other guys ulcers. A further prescient discovery was that drugs would soon cease to be an escape used almost solely by some of the black population. Strauss had been among the first to bring illicit drugs to the little white kids of Detroit and its suburbs. Ruthlessly, he had fought his way to the top of the drug market. He was now a millionaire many times over.

Surrounded by four bodyguards, Dutch now stood in the doorway of a room in which twelve nude women were cutting heroin with lesser drugs preparatory to street sale. The women were unclothed simply to insure that none of the stuff would leave with them.

Strauss was satisfied. The four men left the run-down apartment building on the corner of Clairmount and Byron. Strauss owned the building. Strauss owned the entire block.

It had been a busy day. Tomorrow, Strauss reflected, another dollar. Or maybe, he smiled, a hundred thousand.

Father Koesler had found the note when he returned to St. Anselm's that evening after his day off. Lieutenant Ned Harris would like his phone call returned. From experience, Koesler knew that when the police phoned, they did not do so without good reason. He had tried to call Harris several times, but the Lieutenant had left the station, and by the time Koesler retired near midnight there was still no answer at Harris' apartment.

Mornings were never kind to Koesler. He functioned through the early hours of the day, but not at his best. Given the opportunity to offer Mass in mid-morning, afternoon, or especially evening, Koesler was quite good at it. But in early morning, a satisfactory performance demanded an intense effort.

This morning, as he made his way from the rectory to the church, he was intercepted by Sister Marie Richard, who reminded him that the second graders would be attending this 8 A.M. Mass. They were preparing to receive their first holy communion, did he remember? Yes. And would he speak to that question? He would try.

For twelve years, Koesler had been editor of the *Detroit*

Catholic. For most of his nearly twenty-five years as a priest, he had dealt mostly with adults. He felt a particular sense of inadequacy when dealing with children on a formal basis.

The Mass began with a scattering of adults in the rear of the church and the small bodies of second graders needlessly packed like sardines in the front two pews. The children were singing something Koesler had not heard before. It didn't seem to be a hymn. Ah, the new, plastic church! Whatever seems relevant.

The inevitable moment for the homily came. Koesler began to speak to the children about communion and how they should prepare themselves for the event. Several minutes into the sermon, he knew he was going clear over the children's heads. In mid-homily, he switched to a few dozen words on the hylomorphic theory of matter and form. He decided as long as he was going over their heads, he would aim high.

Oddly, the children seemed to be paying attention. He could think of no reason they should.

Concluding his remarks, he asked if anyone had a question.

Oddly, again, one small boy raised his hand. Koesler could not imagine what possible question could come from his delivery. However...

"Yes?" Koesler invited.

"Father," asked the lad, standing, "what makes you so tall?"

The adults in attendance were rewarded with an unanticipated laugh.

After Mass, Koesler returned to the rectory. In the kitchen, he poured a glass of milk. As he returned the carton to the refrigerator, the phone rang.

"St. Anselm's."

"Father Koesler, please."

"This is he."

"Lieutenant Harris, Homicide." There was something

different in Harris' voice, a quaver Koesler had not noted before.

"I was wondering, Father, if it would be convenient for you to drop in and see me today."

His was a far different approach from that of Inspector Koznicki, Koesler reflected. Koznicki's invitation was a command; when Koznicki wanted you, Koznicki got you.

"Sure, Lieutenant. I have a couple of communion calls, but I can come down in an hour or two."

"Fine. Thanks. You know where we are?"

"Headquarters, fifth floor, right?"

"Right. Ask for Squad Six."

As Koesler returned the phone to its receiver, he began to wonder what the Homicide Division could possibly want with him.

Karl Lowell's head was filled with divergent thoughts. He didn't even notice the petite brunette who entered the elevator with him on the main floor of the Free Press Building.

They rode in silence. As the doors opened at the third floor, his fellow occupant asked, "What's the big bad wolf going to do today?"

Startled, Lowell experienced a rare indecisive moment. Should he exit at this, his floor, or light into her? He decided he was already behind in today's schedule. He shrugged and walked briskly toward his tastefully decorated office at the city room's far eastern end.

Who is she, he wondered. Familiar face. He'd seen her at meetings. Oh, yes; in the Women's Department. No, she's the head of it. Editor of the Women's Department. Now that he remembered her, he also remembered how, when their eyes met, she never looked away as most others did. He had to admire her fearless impudence.

He removed his black pinstripe suit jacket, tugged his vest down over his flat stomach, shot his French cuffs, smoothed his wavy black hair, and sat down at his large desk.

He swung his meticulously polished shoes up and rested his feet on the long credenza. He opened the morning edition of the *Free Press*.

He scanned the front page and immediately caught the headline, "RED HAT MURDERS LINKED," and the bugline, "Police Hold Secret Clue." And below the headline, "By Patricia Lennon and Joe Cox, *Free Press* Staff Writers."

Lowell clutched the paper so fiercely he almost tore it in half.

His feet hit the floor. He jerked the phone's receiver to his ear and punched two numbers.

"Kane!" he snapped, "I want you in here!" He slammed the receiver down.

In the city room, Nelson Kane's shoulders slumped almost imperceptibly. He had half-expected this.

The rest of Homicide Squad Six was out doing what detective work was all about—tracking down leads that regularly led to dead ends.

Lieutenant Harris, Inspector Koznicki, and Father Koesler sat in the otherwise unoccupied squad room. There was enough room for the three large men, never enough room for the complement of Squad Six.

Harris had asked Koznicki to sit in on this initial briefing of Koesler.

They reviewed their earlier association.

"... and so, Father," Koznicki was concluding, "because you were of such great help to us during that case and because the remains of these victims have been found in Catholic churches under most peculiar circumstances, we wondered if you might consent to assist again on a more formal consultative basis."

"It is even possible to arrange for a consultation fee," added Harris.

Koesler shook his head. "No, I don't want any money. For one thing, I don't need any money. And for another, if I were to accept a fee, I would feel bound to spend an allotted amount of time on the case. And I can't promise that."

"Besides," he continued, "the kind of help I was able to come up with was mostly a fluke. As it turned out, you would have solved those crimes with your police work."

Harris admired the honesty. Koesler's summation was accurate. But with the kind of publicity he had received at the time, it would have been very easy to develop a bad case of swollen head.

"You should not dismiss your contribution so quickly, Father," said Koznicki. "You discovered the ultimate clue and prevented a couple of murders."

"Believe me, Inspector," said Koesler, "I'm just a guy who likes to read mystery novels, knows more about Catholicism than the ordinary person, and got lucky."

"We," said Harris, leaning forward, "would like you to lay a little of that luck on us again."

"I'll be glad to do what I can, you know that. Just don't depend on the sort of luck we had before."

"Don't worry, Father," said Harris, "we'll be doing our job. But you may be able to help with this crazy Catholic angle."

"Yes," Koznicki said, "there are few similarities and many differences between these two cases. We are not now dealing with the murder of innocent men and women. We have here the apparent murders of two of Detroit's most notorious hoodlums."

"At this point," said Harris, "we have plenty of motives and plenty of suspects. Any number of hoods out there want guys like Ruggiero and Harding out of the way so they can move up in the rackets."

"What stymies us," Koznicki continued the thought, "is the heads being placed in churches, inside a hat, in the first instance, and on the shoulders of a statue, in the second."

"Any ideas?" Harris asked.

Koesler pondered a moment, twisting the ubiquitous toothpick between his lips. "Well, all I can think of is something one of my confreres said, that maybe it has something to do with a pun on the word 'capital.'"

"'Capital'?"

"Yes. The way my friend has it figured, *caput* is Latin for 'head.' It is also the source of our word 'capital' as in capital punishment. Thus, it would be appropriate for someone who is guilty of serious, or 'capital' crimes, to have his head, or *caput*, removed. And," Koesler rhetorized, adding a few thoughts of his own, "where better to put the *caput* than in a hat or on a body, even if the body is a statue?

"Plus," Koesler was warming to the subject, "you must remember, gentlemen, that it wasn't too many years ago that when criminals were executed, their heads were placed on poles or posts. And it wasn't too many years ago that this was a most common, if barbaric, practice."

"Not bad," Harris commented.

"But not much, I'm afraid." Koesler sighed, silently coming down from a self-induced high. "The hypothesis tells nothing of why Cardinal Mooney's gigantic red hat should be chosen for one head and St. Cecilia's statue for the other."

"That may be true, Father," said Koznicki, tipping his chair back against the wall. Both Harris and Koesler wondered how the chair's two rear legs could sustain all that weight. "But it remains the first solid theory we've had about the heads. So you see, you've made a contribution already." Koznicki smiled at Koesler.

"Tell me, Inspector—or Lieutenant," Koesler nodded at each man, "is it possible that this case is anything like the other one, The Rosary Murders? Remember, you told me, Inspector, that some killers, when there is a series of murders, want to be stopped almost as much as they want to complete their task. So they intentionally leave clues for the police."

"Yes, that's true, Father," Harris answered. "That sometimes happens. Like the 'Son of Sam' murders in New York a few years ago. The killer always used the same caliber revolver, sent notes to newspaper people, and established a pattern that allowed the police to tighten their surveillance until they caught him."

"It's a language the killer creates." Koznicki tipped his chair forward to an upright position. "The language—a shorthand of clues. The trick is to break the code. Once we understand what the killer intends these clues to represent, we've broken the code and should have our man."

"But you see, Father," said Harris, "we're not even sure that what we have in The Red Hat Murders is that classic conversation with clues. For all we know, the killer may be a maniac. Or someone who has some deep negative feelings about religion. Or both!"

The three were silent for a few moments.

"Well, Father," Koznicki stood, indicating the conversation was at an end, "what we'd like you to do is give this some thought. If you come up with anything—anything at all—please let us know. Here are numbers where we can be reached at any time, day or night."

Both Koznicki and Harris handed Koesler their business cards.

"All right." Koesler tucked the cards into his wallet. "I'll certainly do what I can, and I'll be praying for you."

"Please do," Koznicki called after Koesler as the priest left the squad room.

Koznicki and Harris looked at each other.

"Well, that's different," Harris commented.

"What's different?"

"Prayer added to police procedure."

"It couldn't hurt."

Harris glanced at an ashtray at one end of the squad room table. It contained several chewed-up toothpicks. "What," he asked, pointing to the pile, "is that all about?"

"Father Koesler recently gave up smoking," Koznicki explained.

"Someone will probably discover that toothpick chewing can be dangerous to one's health," said Harris, sardonically.

"Yeah, instead of dying from lung cancer, he'll probably

die of Dutch Elm disease," Koznicki retorted.

Koesler began the walk down the exit staircase, his thoughts mixed. He was trying to chance upon even a single reason why the heads had been found where they were. Nothing of consequence occurred to him. Finally, he decided to shop a bit at Hudson's and drop into St. Aloysius rectory for lunch. Have lunch with the boss! Koesler smiled as he thought of Father Brendan from Dearborn. Some people were actually impressed that Father Brendan was able to lunch with the boss. Almost at will. After all, how many of his Dearborn parishioners were able to lunch with Henry Ford II?

Nelson Kane drummed a pencil against his desk blotter. He felt something like a waiter forced to serve a dinner that has been badly prepared by a chef who is safe in the kitchen.

It was at times like these that Kane gave serious thought to chucking it all, retiring to an island off the Irish coast, and just writing.

However, becoming an author required not only skill, but a great deal of determination and, as frequently as not, a healthy dose of luck. Kane was not sure if he could count on all three.

Short of that, he was nearing fifty. And, he reflected, something happens to a man on reaching his fifties. Even with the growing phenomenon of the "midlife change," most people, especially men, who had a job where the pluses outweighed the minuses, held on. Even when the margin of difference was slight.

He'd given nearly his entire professional life to the *Free Press*. There had been many exultant times—chief among them when the paper, with him in the lead, had won a Pulitzer Prize for its coverage of the 1967 riots.

Now was one of the low points. Kane, his pencil drumming, his stomach churning, decided it was useless to further delay the inevitable.

"Lennon!" he called out. And, after a moment's hesitation, "Cox!"

The two reporters arrived at Kane's desk feeling very good. Finally,. they were able to work together and were proving they were good at it. The knowledge had brightened their already happy lives.

"Lennon . . ." Kane hesitated. "Lennon, you're off the story."

Lennon's smile dissolved into a look of disbelief. "Off . . . off what story, Nellie?"

"The Red Hat Murders." Kane, standing, dropped his gaze to his desk. He could no longer meet her eyes.

Lennon's lips began to tremble ever so slightly.

"For the love of God, Nellie, *why*?" Cox was livid.

"It's been decided," Kane looked at Cox, but without the accustomed animation in his eyes, "that this is a one-man story. We are not going to waste our personnel on something one man can cover."

"Bull!" shouted Cox. Several reportorial heads in the vicinity raised and glanced briefly at the three.

Lennon put her hand on Cox's arm. She was very near tears. "I know you can't say it, Nellie, but tell me if I'm wrong. It's Lowell, isn't it? He doesn't want me on this story."

Kane said nothing. He continued studying his desk blotter.

"Well, who's running this chickenshit outfit, anyway?" Cox looked as if he were ready to take on the entire administration of the *Free Press* one by one.

"Ease off, Joe," Lennon said. "Nellie, is it O.K. if I take the rest of the day off?"

Kane nodded.

"I'll go with you," Cox said.

"Like hell you will." Kane for the first time took the offensive.

"Shall we straighten this out in the hall?" Cox moved a step or two toward the glass partition. It was ridiculous. Although Cox had Kane by almost twenty-five years, Kane had Cox by nearly one hundred pounds. And Kane was still in sufficient shape to end an altercation with Cox decisively.

"Don't be silly," said Lennon. "I don't want you to come with me right now. I think I'll just go contemplate at Belle Isle for a while. See you later at the apartment, Joe."

She returned to her desk, picked up her tote bag, and left.

Cox and Kane stood riveted.

"Sorry, Nellie," Cox said finally. "It wasn't your fault."

"That's O.K., Joe. I know how you feel. If it were my woman, I'd feel the same."

"That guy," said Cox, motioning toward Lowell's office, "is going to make a shambles of this paper yet."

"I know," said Kane, sitting down behind his desk. "I know."

Father Joseph Sheehan had been the first to enter St. Aloysius' dining room for lunch. He had served himself some chicken broth and taken a seat directly across from the highbacked chair Archbishop Mark Boyle would occupy should he appear at this luncheon.

Sheehan had just begun to sip his soup when the ornate door opened and Father Bohdan Borucki entered. Borucki had just been appointed assistant to Sister Ann Marie Schultz, the Vicar for Religious. Thus, he was now Assistant Vicar for Religious.

Borucki was beginning to ladle some soup into his bowl, when Sheehan stood and, adapting the words of the popular spiritual, intoned, "Sometimes I feel like a vicarless nun . . ."

Borucki looked up, expressionless, paused a moment, then finished filling his bowl. He took a seat kitty-cornered from Sheehan.

At this point, Archbishop Mark Boyle entered and, as usually happened when the Archbishop entered a room, conversations either ceased or were reduced in volume.

Boyle selected several pieces of fresh fruit and took his

place. After saying Grace, his intense blue eyes briefly studied Sheehan and Borucki.

"Well, Father Borucki," Boyle said, "has there been any decision as to when the vicariate workshops for our religious should be held?"

"The other sisters and I feel as if the best time would be in May," said Borucki.

Sheehan guffawed. Boyle reddened slightly. Borucki stared at Sheehan briefly, then resumed spooning his soup.

Father Robert Koesler entered, nodded to those already seated, and created a hamburger sandwich. He seated himself next to the Archbishop. After several moments of continued silence, Boyle spoke.

"Have you been back visiting the *Detroit Catholic* lately, Father?"

"Not for several weeks, Excellency."

"What do you think of the job Irene Casey is doing?"

"First-rate. I think she's making the best possible use of the very limited space she is given. But how about yourself? After all, you are the publisher."

Father Adrian, a Jesuit who occasionally helped out with Masses and confessions in St. Aloysius, entered. He began with a glass of milk. The luncheon crowd was beginning to build.

"Oh," replied Boyle, "I am very pleased with Irene. The paper seems to have a nice balance. And I am especially pleased that she likes her job."

"I'm just glad you agreed to make her my successor," said Koesler, "there aren't very many lady editors-in-chief, especially in the Catholic press."

Father Paschal, a large round Dominican, who also helped occasionally at St. Aloysius, entered. He was vested in his black and white Dominican habit.

"I see," said Father Adrian, a bit more loudly than necessary, "that the Dominicans are still among us."

Paschal began to fill his plate with hash browns. "That's right, Father Adrian. *We've* never been suppressed."

Moments earlier, Sheehan and Borucki had begun a conversation that had steadily increased in volume. They were so loud now that the others stopped their own conversations to watch the two at the far end of the long table.

"What I'd like to know, Bohdan," Sheehan said, flourishing a stalk of celery like a crozier, "is how it feels under Ann Marie Schultz?"

"Basically, you see, Father," answered Borucki, ignoring or perhaps missing the double entendre, "we feel we are in parallel positions."

"I suppose," persisted Sheehan, "that since men wrote all the rules for nuns, it's only natural that they couldn't have just a woman vicar without having a man about?"

"It is generally felt," Borucki droned while tilting his soup bowl to scoop the last few drops, "in most dioceses that men are a stabilizing influence."

"Well, then," Sheehan was beginning to feel that he would never reach Borucki, "you are sort of convinced that you are, at least in the archdiocese, God's gift to nuns?"

Borucki stared across the table at Sheehan, a look of comprehension spreading over his face. "You're being sarcastic."

"You're being perceptive," Sheehan shot back.

"You did it again!" Borucki flung his napkin on the table.

Meanwhile, across the street from St. Aloysius, a black, late model Chevy pulled into the parking lot on the corner of Washington Boulevard and State Street. In the car were three deacons from St. John's Seminary. They had a 1:30 P.M. appointment with Bishop Arthur Kenny to receive their fall assignments. Each would be sent to a parish somewhere in the Archdiocese of Detroit where, for the next several months, they would act out their role as deacons and accustom themselves to parochial life. Unlike permanent deacons, these men were using the diaconate as a step toward ordination to the priesthood. Already attired as priests, each wore a black suit and clerical collar.

Unbeknownst to his two companions, Deacon Ed Landregan had prepared for this special day with intensive prayer and fasting. So severe had his self-imposed penance been that he was now physically very weak. But he resolved to conquer this weakness as he had subdued most demands of the flesh—by sheer will power.

As the three began to walk across Washington Boulevard, Landregan faltered, then almost collapsed.

"What is it, Ed?" asked a startled Deacon Mike Shanahan.

"What's the matter, Ed?" asked Deacon Dave Ballas, equally startled.

"It's nothing," Landregan said, "I'm all right." He focused all his energy on the door of the chancery, determined to reach at least that goal and not make a fool of himself in the middle of downtown Detroit.

They walked on. But, with each step, Landregan grew weaker.

As they reached the front of St. Aloysius, Landregan stopped and leaned against a light pole. His head was swimming. He fought the dizziness with dwindling will power. He knew he was about to faint.

"Don't you feel well?" asked Shanahan, now near panic.

Landregan slumped to the ground, unconscious.

Immediately, Shanahan knelt on the pavement and cradled Landregan's head in his arms.

A middle-aged woman coming out of St. Aloysius took in the scene of what was apparently one unconscious priest being cradled by another priest. She hurried to them.

"Can I do anything to help, Father?" she asked, with genuine concern.

"Yes!" Shanahan looked up at her and noticed the gathering crowd. "Get a priest!"

She was not sure she'd heard correctly. But, willing to follow any authoritative direction, she looked about and spied another apparent priest standing not more than fifteen feet away in frozen inaction. She rushed over to him.

"Father wants a priest . . . Father," she finished lamely, pointing to the clerical tableau on the sidewalk.

"I'll go get one," said Ballas, leaving her and entering St. Aloysius.

The would-be Good Samaritan walked away, muttering to herself.

St. Aloysius was one of Detroit's more interesting parishes.

If not for its location, the Summit restaurant undoubtedly would not have enjoyed its reputation as the place to see and be seen. The quality of the food was unpredictable, drinks were ample but on the whole weak, and service ranged from slow to nonexistent. But it was THE Summit, atop Renaissance Center, that cluster of buildings that had become a relatively safe enclave on the border of a high-crime area. The view, from the slowly rotating dining area, of Detroit, Windsor, and the Detroit River, was magnificent.

Three priests in clerical garb had just been seated near the center of the room. A very poor spot from which to enjoy the view. The trio studied their menus in silence as the busboy briskly poured ice water into their large glasses. He was filling the third and final glass when the balding, paunchy priest spoke.

"Now, don't any of you let on," stage-whispered Father Donald Curley to his two companions, "that I am the *Free Press'* Anonymous Gourmet!"

The busboy stopped in mid-fill of the third glass, and, as if carrying a message to Garcia, hurried from the table and headed toward the maitre d' at a brisk clip.

"Damn!" Monsignor Al Thomas intoned admiringly. This was the second such performance he had witnessed.

"Anonymous Gourmet!" repeated Father Ted Neighbors, wonderingly. "You're not the Anonymous Gourmet. I don't think you could even find the Free Press Building."

"Sure I could," beamed Curley, supremely self-satisfied. "It's the one beneath the great big sign that says 'The *Free Press.*' You can see it from almost anywhere in town. That's it over there." Curley stood and pointed. It was virtually impossible to see the sign from their table while seated.

"Now, Ted," Thomas addressed Neighbors in a conspiratorial tone, "just watch what happens after the busboy gives his message to the maitre d'." Thomas was enjoying this almost as much as Curley.

The three priests went back to studying their menus in silence. After some moments, a waitress came to their table.

"Fathers," she said in her brightest mechanical stewardess tone, "this is not a very good table. The management would like you to have a better view. Would you mind please following me?"

Curley could barely contain himself. Thomas, who admired Curley's wheeler-dealer qualities, wondered if there was any way he could lure him into joining the Matrimonial Tribunal, all the while knowing there was no way of prying him from old St. Joseph's, where Curley had found the best of all possible worlds.

Neighbors, for his part, was impressed. Any maneuver that could improve the quality of life was welcome in his world.

In total this afternoon, creating the impression that the Anonymous Gourmet was evaluating the Summit gained for the three clergymen an improved view, impeccable service, and better-than-average preparation of food. Nothing free. But it was enough to satisfy Curley and inspire him to future performances as the great Gourmet imposter.

Earlier, another threesome had been immediately seated at one of the best tables in the room. Two of the diners were top executives of the First Standard Bank and Trust. They might well have commanded this preferential seating. But the real reason for royal treatment was the presence of Mr. Alphonsus (Dutch) Strauss. His picture had been in the papers and on television frequently enough so that nearly everyone was familiar with his reputation as king of the Detroit drug empire. While that status classified him as allegedly one of Detroit's top criminals, it also guaranteed the fact that he was a millionaire many times over.

Seated at the neighboring table were four men who could have been professional football players or heavyweight wrestlers. Each seemed about to burst through his large but confining jacket. None seemed to have a neck. They were Dutch Strauss' bodyguards.

"We'd like to show you, Mr. Strauss," began the first banker, "some of the advantages of investment with us at this point in time."

A busboy removed the fourth place setting from the table.

"Whaddya think of them Tigers!" Strauss interjected. "If only they could keep The Bird healthy," he shook his head in dismay, "they'd be contenders, all right!"

A second busboy brought a basket replete with rolls, breadsticks, sliced rye, and pumpernickel. This three-some's status would ensure attention afforded few other tables.

"Oh, you're absolutely correct, Mr. Strauss," the second banker unhesitatingly agreed. "A healthy Bird and some heavier hitters in the infield. Oh, yes, indeed, contenders!"

A third busboy began pouring water in their glasses.

"So," said Strauss, gazing about the room and nodding perfunctorily as his eyes met those of important people he knew, "what's so special about investing now?"

The two bankers looked at each other and sighed inaudibly. This was going to be one of those follow-the-depositor business luncheons.

"Well," the first banker picked up the ball, "because there is an outstanding percentage interest rate now available on short-term certificates of deposit."

"Ouch!" Strauss cried out more in surprise than in pain. The busboy, while withdrawing the water pitcher, had apparently nicked Strauss' hand.

Instantly, the four bodyguards were on their feet. Two of their chairs clattered to the floor. The two nearest Strauss' table grabbed the now cringing busboy by the shoulders. Many nearby diners, fascinated by the sudden violence, stopped eating and talking to watch the scene.

"It's O.K., boys," Strauss reassured, "just a clumsy nigger."

The two released their grip on the busboy, and all the principals resumed their places.

"Nigger," thought the second banker; one rarely heard that racist insult these days. On further reflection, he decided Strauss could pretty well call anybody anything he wanted to.

"You were saying..." Strauss turned toward the first banker.

"Well, for instance, Mr. Strauss, a 180-day deposit of $100,000 brings a 10.42 percent increase." He looked expectantly at Strauss.

"One hundred thousand dollars." Strauss picked up a fork and began drawing lines on the tablecloth. He smiled a humorless smile. "One hundred thousand dollars!" Guys, I am talkin' three million."

The two bankers looked at each other. Their mutual expression of disbelief melted into a visage of greedy desire. Simultaneously, each removed a pencil-thin computer from his attaché case and began figuring furiously.

The early fall breeze pushed gentle waves along the surface of the Detroit River. Pat Lennon sat on a park bench in an otherwise deserted area on the south side of Belle Isle.

In the past, she had come many times to this beautiful island that rested midway between Detroit and Windsor. A bridge connected it with Detroit. Unspanned water flowed between the island and Canada.

Lennon sat, legs crossed, arms folded, facing Windsor and lost in thought. She had begun by trying to evaluate her position at the *Free Press*. She had been deeply embarrassed, hurt, and infuriated a few hours earlier when she had been removed from coverage of The Red Hat Murders.

There wasn't a single doubt in her mind that Karl Lowell was responsible. And there wasn't a single thing she could do about it. She had no intention of attempting to get into his good graces by climbing into his bed. Besides, Lowell's well-recorded history in such matters indicated that his invitation to couch was issued one time only. A determined refusal at such a time became conclusive.

Her future at the *Free Press*, at its brightest, promised little more than a continued existence in the stable of staff writers. She would get pay raises as the union negotiated them. Important assignments would be withheld from her. And this would continue until she slumped into the cobwebs of retirement.

At worst, she thought, she would be directed toward the worst assignments. Perhaps the night desk.

At best, Lowell would finally be fired. Perhaps he would die. Perhaps he would be murdered. A smile crossed her face. For the first time in history, almost every employee of a major metropolitan newspaper would be under suspicion of murder.

The smile was fleeting. It was all so depressing.

She freed her thoughts to float through her stream of subconsciousness.

A passing freighter caught her eye. Wasn't this the spot, she pondered, from which Prophet Jones, of happy memory, claimed to have received the divine inspiration to name his church?

She tried to recollect. The colorful prophet claimed to have been sitting somewhere near here, as she recalled.

He had been told, so he said, by God to watch the names of the passing freighters and be ready for instructions.

The first freighter had been named something like *Universal Transport*. God told the prophet, "You takes 'Universal' and drops the rest." That had been followed by a ship named *Triumph of the Seas*. God said, "Take 'Triumph' and drop the rest." The final ship had been named something like *Dominion of Canada*. God said, "Take 'Dominion' and drop the rest."

And then, according to the prophet, God concluded, "You gots 'Universal,' 'Triumph' and 'Dominion.' Now you adds 'of God' and YOU GOTS IT!"

And so was born The Universal Triumph and Dominion of God, Inc. The Very Reverend Prophet Jones its humble pastor and master.

The memory caused Lennon to laugh aloud. And that brought her out of her reverie.

As she began gathering her belongings preparatory to leaving, her eye was caught by an impressive yacht passing by. Quite evidently, there was a full-scale party going on aboard. The decks were filled with people, most of them young, most holding drinks. Loud disco music thrust itself over the waters.

Her eyes focused on the hull of the craft to its name.

Newport News.

She sat back on the bench. She could almost hear a voice saying, "You takes 'News,' drops 'Newport' and substitute 'Detroit.' NOW YOU GOTS IT!"

The shiny black Fleetwood glided to a stop at the side of an unlikely looking building on Alexandrine near Grand River. It was a dilapidated moderate-sized warehouse not far from downtown Detroit.

Five business-suited men grunted their way out of the car. Each was bulky. In a way, the scene was a macrocosm of the classic circus act wherein lots of midget clowns exit a midget car.

The unassuming building was headquarters for Dutch Strauss' drug empire. Wordlessly, the five entered the building. Inside the front door was an unfurnished, white-walled reception area. A one-way glass, a small counter area, and a door were all that broke the white monotony. Customers, after being scrutinized, identified and cleared, received their merchandise through the slot behind the counter. Never did a customer see who was behind the panel.

Strauss' four bodyguards disappeared through the door. Strauss pushed a button hidden behind a light switch. A stairway slowly lowered from the ceiling. He climbed the stairs, pushed a button on the wall just inside the upstairs room and the stairway returned to its former concealed position.

The room was something out of the Arabian nights. A basic decor of soft blacks and reds. Overstuffed leather furniture tastefully placed throughout. The light was indirect with one exception. In the far corner of the room was a mammoth round bed covered with a red crushed velvet spread. This area was illuminated by several spotlights and set off by mirrors on both walls and ceiling.

The smoothness of the velvet spread was disarranged slightly in one small area. Someone was in the bed.

Good, thought Strauss. He would use the girl, shower, and get back to work.

He dropped his clothes in a heap near the closet. They would be tended to later by one of his flunkies.

On his way to the bathroom, he glanced at the bed. Only the girl's head was visible. She had pulled the spread tightly under her chin. She was black. That was all right. Perhaps she was frightened. That was even better.

As Strauss entered the bathroom, he lost his balance and fell against the door. A wave of dizziness swept over him. For the first time, he was conscious that he had been perspiring more than usual. He tried to remember what he had eaten at the Summit. Nothing out of the ordinary. He shook his head and relieved himself.

He glanced in the mirror. Staring back at him was his father's face. The old-world, hard-working German looked at him from the mirror. An expression of unutterable sadness was on the old man's face. Confused, Strauss reached out and touched the mirror. His father was no longer there. But neither was Strauss. There was no reflection at all.

For the first time in his memory, he was close to panic.

At least the girl was there. She was real enough. She would bring reality back. If this got any worse, at least she could fetch help.

He staggered toward the bed, weaving almost out of control.

He threw back the spread. The girl was fully clothed.

"What's the idea?" He heard himself as if he were in a tunnel. "You're supposed to be naked."

She did not answer. She simply continued to stare at him.

He thought he recognized her. Hadn't he seen her picture in the paper the other day? Oh, yeah; she was the kid from Cooley who had O.D.'d.

"But . . . but . . ." Words were resisting him. ". . . you . . . you're dead!"

Laura Gates did not respond. She continued to stare without expression.

Behind the bed near the wall stood a young man. Strauss had been unaware of his presence until now. Nor had he any notion how the man had gotten in. Strauss more easily identified this stranger who had invaded his apartment. His picture was in this morning's paper. He had been killed in a gunfight with a policeman.

Willie Monroe bent down and touched the floor. A flame flashed up and quickly spread along the wall.

A powerful nauseating odor filled the room.

Strauss stumbled backward, trying to get as far from the fire as possible.

The room began to tilt toward the fire.

Strauss fell. He began to slide toward the fire, which now appeared to be coming from a vast cauldron of molten lava. Desperately, Strauss clung to the base of the closet door.

Willie Monroe on one side and Laura Gates on the other pried his fingers from the door.

Strauss clawed at the deep pile of the rug, but it did not provide sufficient anchorage to maintain his clutch.

He began to tumble toward the fiery pit.

He opened his mouth wide to scream his final terror. No sound was made. No sound ever again would be.

Joe Cox lay on the couch reading the current *Newsweek*. Outside Lafayette Towers, the sun had almost set. The days were getting shorter. Soon it would be winter and Detroiters would again wonder what to do with all that snow.

Cox checked his watch. 7:30. If it got much later and Pat still was not home, he would begin to worry.

He heard a key turn in the lock. "That you, Pat?"

"Yeah!" There was a trace of barely concealed excitement in her voice. "Have you eaten?"

"No. Been waiting for you."

Pat Lennon entered the living room and began to pile parcels on the coffee table. She removed her coat and sat in a chair near the couch. "Let's have a treat and go out for dinner tonight." Her cheeks were slightly flushed.

"Sure." Cox laid down the magazine and for the first time took careful note of her emotional high. "What is it with you? Where've you been?"

"Oh, I've been talking to a nice man named William Gilbert."

"That's nice . . . and I suppose a man named Sullivan was humming along." Cox returned to *Newsweek*. Suddenly he dropped the magazine and stared at Pat. "Gilbert? William Gilbert of the *News*?"

"The very one." Pat was smiling broadly.

"Why were you talking to Bill Gilbert?" Cox's astonishment threshold was high, but he was obviously reached by this news.

"I was talking to Billy Gilbert about a job."

"A job? At the *News*?"

"At the *News*."

"And?"

"I got it."

"I don't believe it!"

"Don't I look a bit different? A little more conservative?"

"But . . . why?"

"Joe, this morning was as good a description of my future at the *Free Press* as anyone could draw. I'm going nowhere retroactively. As long as Lowell is around, I can't even work on a major story." Recalling this morning's incident angered her all over again.

"But Lowell isn't eternal. Sooner or later he's got to go."

"Joe, I just decided that I'm not about to wait for that silver lining. Although," she smiled, "I did reach my decision rather peculiarly. I'll tell you about it over dinner."

"Well, O.K.," he said, glumly, "but I really feel rotten about it."

"Don't feel bad, Joe. It's for my own good. We'll probably get to see more of each other now than when we were at the same paper."

"I didn't mean that."

"Then what did you mean?"

"I meant I'll feel kind of bad now when we beat the *News*."

"You forget, Sweetie, I'm with the *News* now."

"I haven't forgot!" It was Cox's turn to grin from ear to ear.

"You!" she shrieked, and launched herself at him, laughing.

They rolled off the couch onto the floor.

Gradually, their wrestling took on more tender tones. Then there was no more wrestling. It had segued into love-making.

Dinner would be delayed.

Although the temperature was in the high forties, it felt colder this rainy Thursday morning. Quite possibly, one of the chilliest spots in Detroit at such times was Washington Boulevard, where the wind whistled in off the Detroit River and whipped along the wide street in the canyon formed by large buildings on both sides. Girl-watchers occasionally referred to that windy stretch of downtown Detroit as Thighland.

Inside St. Aloysius, in the 1200 block of Washington Boulevard, Father Thomas McInerny was offering Mass, trying as best he could to avoid distractions.

Avoiding distractions was no easy task in St. Aloysius. It had been easier before the Second Vatican Council, with the great high altar against the church's rear wall, his back to the congregation mumbling along in Latin. The altar now was a table flush against the railing at the edge of the opening in the first floor revealing the basement church; he was facing the congregation; the Mass was in English and, worst of all, he not only could hear the almost constant racket, he could see the constant movement that went on.

Both the upper and lower levels of the church had many shrines here and there against the walls. Many of those shrines had stands holding as many as fifty votive candles. Incessantly, worshippers would visit the shrine of their choice, noisily drop a coin or two or three into the metal container, and light a candle.

Added to this was the regular changing of the guard as downtowners stepped into the church, knelt, said a few prayers, then continued on their way to the office or store.

Because it was a centrally located downtown church and because it was almost in the middle of the business section, but only a few blocks from skid row, St. Aloysius frequently was reluctant host to some strange characters.

There was the lady who, on entering, always removed the sopping sponge from the holy water container and threw it against the wall. Or, Father McInerny reflected, the bum sitting in the confessional distributing outrageous penances. Or the woman who, at this moment, and many times previously, moved seemingly aimlessly through the church endlessly crossing herself.

Actually, very few of the considerable number who visited St. Aloysius Mondays through Fridays stayed long enough to attend an entire Mass.

One of the few who occasionally dropped in to attend the 7:30 morning Mass, and who was in attendance now, was Inspector Koznicki. Ordinarily when Koznicki attended Mass—or for that matter a movie or a concert—he tried to find a place in the rear of the church or theater. Conscious of his size, he was considerate enough to avoid blocking the view of others. However, at St. Aloysius, so few came to attend weekday Mass that he would be an impediment to another's vision only if the other were to plan it that way.

This Thursday morning, he was kneeling in the second pew, thus purposely missing most of the distractions behind him. But he was unable to avoid the self-made distractions that buzzed through his brain.

For a brief time as a boy, Koznicki had toyed with the idea of becoming a priest. That plan had quickly given way to the desire to be a policeman. From that time on, he had never swerved. After becoming a policeman, he had wanted to be part of the Homicide Division. When he became a homicide detective, he had hoped he would one day become Inspector of Homicide. Now that he was, he wanted nothing more.

Koznicki was never sure of all the reasons that contributed to his love for homicide detection. He prized life, all life, especially human life. When human life was taken by violence, he always experienced an insatiable curiosity to learn who had done it and why. He was good at his work. Many would claim that if he were not the best there was none better.

While Detroit probably suffered unjustly from its popular description as The Murder Capital of the World, there was no serious lack of homicide within the corporate limits of the city. Morticians would not run out of customers, and Homicide would not run out of cases.

Koznicki's thoughts turned to some of the current cases being investigated by his seven squads. The most intriguing, currently, was the killing of two of the city's most notorious criminals. The special problem here was keeping a serious attitude toward the solution of the murders. The most natural reaction of most law enforcement officers when a known criminal was killed was relief. Even euphoria. But these cases easily deserved as much serious work as any other homicide.

Besides, if there was no breakthrough soon, the public might be led to believe, mostly by the news media, that the police were uninterested in solving the case. It was never good to allow the reputation of police unconcern to be established.

Father McInerny was nearing the Greeting of Peace.

Koznicki consciously drew his attention fully to the ritual.

"The peace of the Lord be with you always," Father McInerny intoned.

"And also with you." The response came cacophonously from isolated sections of the church.

"Let us," McInerny said from memory, "offer each other a sign of peace." He turned and shook hands with the little old man who was acting as altar server.

Koznicki looked about. There wasn't anyone within even his wingspread to shake hands with. So he kept his peace to himself.

"Lamb of God," McInerny continued, "who takes away the sin of the world, have mercy on us."

Some movement in the basement of the church caught Koznicki's eye. A small blue-haired woman was dropping coins in a votive receptacle. Her attempts to light a candle were so awkward that Koznicki couldn't take his eyes off her. She knelt before the shrine of St. Raphael the Archangel and made the sign of the cross over and over and over.

Koznicki smiled at the varieties of human idiosyncrasy.

About to return his attention to the altar in front of him, he became aware of something amiss. He looked again at the crossing lady, then at the shrine, then at the life-size statue.

It indeed resembled the popular artistic rendering of St. Raphael, except for the head. A real human head rested on the statued saint's shoulders.

The lady continued to cross herself.

For once, in this series of crimes, no one had to phone and inform the Inspector of Homicide about a suspicious death.

Four

ST. FRANCES CABRINI

It was one of those rare mornings in the city room. No one at the coffee machine, no one at the water cooler, no clusters of people standing around in idle conversation.

The three exceptions to this scene of unrelieved labor were Nelson Kane, Joe Cox, and Pat Lennon. They were standing around Lennon's desk, which she was cleaning out.

"Lennon," Kane was saying, "don't you think you're being precipitate?"

"Nope!"

"I mean, you've been here—what is it, five years now? You're at top scale. This is no time to let some personal problem interfere with your work here. And besides, you haven't given the customary two weeks' notice."

"Nellie..." Lennon continued fitting her personal belongings into a cardboard box, "My 'personal problem,' as you so winningly understate it, is practically a denial of the First Amendment as far as I'm concerned. I could continue to work here at scale and not a dollar more, writing nice fluffy stories and here and there an obit until I don't mind the cobwebs growing between my ears.

"As for your 'notice,' I have four weeks of a long-overdue vacation due me. I am taking it starting today, and you are herewith formally informed," she bowed in Kane's direction, "that I am thereupon terminating my employment with Knight-Ridder's *Detroit Free Press*. There," she straightened up, "you now have *four* weeks' notice!"

"But—"

"It's no use, Nellie," Cox said, dejectedly, "I spent all last night trying to talk her out of it. I couldn't. In the end," he added, "I can't say I blame her."

"Nellie," Lennon's voice was insistent, "they offered me more money. Loads more money. Scale is higher there than it is here anyway. And, on top of that, they offered me a merit increase before I even start. And I've got practically carte blanche on the stories I want to develop outside of regular assignments."

"And," she added triumphantly, "that includes The Red Hat Murders!"

"Yeah, yeah, I know, but this is where you cut your teeth. The *Free Press* will always be home to you." Kane was not known for giving up easily.

"Your argument would've made more sense a few years ago," Lennon said. "Then it wouldn't have made any difference what the *News* had offered, I would've had enough loyalty and esprit de corps to stick it out here. But that's all changed now." She tossed her head in the direction of Karl Lowell's office.

Nelson Kane's broad shoulders slumped slightly. He suddenly felt older than his years and tired.

The phone on Kane's desk rang.

"City desk!" he barked. His voice and whole being became suddenly animated. "What? Where? When? Who?" Furiously, in his own peculiar shorthand, he was taking notes.

He's asked just about all the questions they teach in basic journalism class, Cox thought.

Kane slammed the receiver to its cradle. "Cox," he turned to the reporter, "they found another one—another head—another Red Hat Murder! In St. Al's up the street. Preliminary identification says it's Dutch Strauss—"

"Dutch Strauss!" Cox whistled.

"Looks like the same M.O. Drag your ass over there right away!"

"Breslin! McNaught!" Kane called out to two more of his best staff writers, who had been working at their desks, but who now looked up ready to move. "There's been another Red Hat Murder. Breslin, check with the Medical Examiner. McNaught, check in with Homicide Squad Six —what's his name?—Harris. And see if you can talk to Koznicki. Go!"

The two jumped from their chairs, grabbed their coats, and left the city room at nearly a run.

There was nothing, thought Kane, to get the old adrenaline going again like a lurid murder—unless it was a series of lurid murders.

Cox had already reached the rack of elevators.

Lennon fished through the box she had packed, found her notebook, and turned to leave.

"Where d'ya think you're going?" Kane almost roared.

"To cover the latest Red Hat Murder," she said over her shoulder.

"But . . . you got that lead from me!"

"Thanks! You owed me several!" As she turned toward the elevators, she gave an elaborate wink and a toss of her hip in the direction of Lowell's office. She knew he'd been watching from behind his venetian blinds.

In his office, behind the blinds, Karl Lowell recoiled as if a bucket of ice water had been thrown on him.

Lieutenant Harris was cooling his heels aboard the bench outside Dr. Wilhelm Moellmann's office. The Medical Examiner was doing just that—examining the remains of the decapitation that had been delivered a short time earlier.

Harris had divided his squad. One group he had sent to St. Aloysius, the other to Strauss' headquarters.

While Harris waited for Moellmann's findings, Marge, the Medical Examiner's red-headed Texas transplant, first offered Harris coffee, which he politely declined, then regaled him with the tale of her latest tribulation, an offering impossible to politely decline.

It seemed that earlier in the week, the small dog owned

by Marge's small son had managed to squeeze under the fence into her neighbor's yard, where, according to Marge, little damage had been done. The neighbors, however, had called the police, who then ticketed Marge. Now she had a court date.

Harris was sure her story would culminate in a request to fix her ticket. He was therefore pleasantly surprised when Marge concluded what was literally and figuratively a shaggy dog story with the simple comment, "Ah jes' thank it wuz dawnrot tacky of mah naibuhs to call the fuhzz!"

Harris admitted it was indeed tacky and admired her figure as she returned to her office.

Ned Harris was more than a police officer. He was a student of his profession. He read all the law enforcement publications and studied the serious literature and texts on the subject. He never read mystery novels. Mistakes in police procedure, common in novels, disgusted him. He was even more angered by the macho big city cops who single-handedly solved even the most difficult mysteries, invariably bringing in either a dead malefactor who should have been taken alive, or a live one whose case would never stand the test of trial.

Harris could not remember a time when he had not wanted to be a police officer. His constant state of physical fitness and his lively, inquisitive, and retentive mind had pushed him through the ranks at far greater than average speed. Like many others, his prime goal after being inducted into the force had been to become a member of the Homicide Division. This he had achieved, leapfrogging many other candidates.

Once in Homicide, it had been his great good fortune to become the partner of Walter Koznicki. The two had operated almost as Damon and Pythias, becoming the best of friends. Harris was proud that he was a lieutenant in Homicide and almost equally proud that his close friend was the Inspector.

From time to time, Harris tried to pinpoint the reasons for his strong attraction to this division. There were almost as many reasons as there were occasions devoted to trying to ascertain them.

Danger surely was high among his motives. All law enforcement involved a certain level of danger, from the precinct desk to traffic control to the classic domestic disturbance to the ultimate gun battle. But in murder, the highest stakes had already been established. A murderer had already committed the ultimate physical crime. Having done so, he usually had little hesitancy in repeating the act, even against a police officer.

Harris' reverie was interrupted by the appearance of Dr. Wilhelm Moellmann. Moellmann startled him. Harris had no idea how long the Medical Examiner had been standing there, only that he suddenly was aware of a vulturine shape, slightly stooped, hands locked behind his back, glasses nearly ready to fall from the edge of his nose.

"Were you waiting to see me?" Moellmann asked, needlessly.

"Yes." Harris sighed softly. "Lieutenant Harris, Homicide Squad Six." He decided to obviate the usual routine of repetitive identifications.

"Ah, yes." Moellmann's tone might have indicated he was recalling an old friend. "Homicide Squad Six. Or the Head Squad, as we refer to them in the autopsy room."

Moellmann strode through the anteroom that was his secretary's office and into his own spacious office, hands still clutched tightly behind his back. He did not invite Harris to follow. The Lieutenant took the invitation for granted and followed. As they passed through Marge's office, she dramatically raised her eyes heavenward. Only Harris noticed. He grinned.

Moellmann sat in the straight-back leather chair before the desk. Harris settled into the overstuffed leather couch. He waited for the explosion. Everything was going far too urbanely. Still, Moellmann was ever the histrionic, and master of the unexpected.

"So, Lieutenant Harris, you found another head. How interesting." He might have been speaking to a grade school pupil who had handed in a satisfactory paper.

There was a long, pregnant pause.

"Uh," Harris determined he might just as well break the ice, "did you find anything new?"

"No! No! No! No!" Moellmann shouted, throwing his head back and covering his eyes with both hands. "No! No! No! No!"

Outside the office, Marge could barely be heard. "Y'all jes' gonna rise your timpercheer."

Inwardly, Harris enjoyed the exhibition. But he needed to plow ahead. "Well, then, did you find anything old?"

"Old? Old? *Old?*" Moellmann was taken slightly off balance.

"Is it the same M.O.?"

"Ah." Moellmann rubbed his hands together. "Yes, it is the same M.O. The neck was severed at shoulder level; the same bent handsaw was used; despite the decedent's rather thick muscular neck, it was severed in four or five strokes, and there was a genuine look of horror on the mask. The head was drained of blood."

"Have you established a time of death?"

"Between two and five P.M. yesterday."

"Anything else, Doc?" The interview, all things considered, was going quite well.

"Yes!" Moellmann shouted, flinging his arms wide as if to embrace the world with all its problems. "My colleagues and I at the Wayne County Morgue have a question. Has it occurred to the Homicide Division that those heads you've been bringing us originally had bodies attached to them? We *can* work on the bodies even if you bring them in after you bring us the heads. Is anyone out there looking for those bodies?" Moellmann's volume had been rising throughout this tirade. The last sentence rose in a crescendo worthy of Richard Wagner.

"We're trying, Doc," Harris said mildly. He tipped his finger to his forehead in semblance of a salute, got up and left.

"Verdammt!" Moellmann shot after him.

As Harris passed through the outer office, Marge beckoned. Stopping at her desk, he leaned over it since it was apparent she wanted to whisper.

"Ah'd 'preciate it if y'all would brang him an *in*tahr body. He's gettin' to be a certifahd bastard to work with."

Harris winked broadly and, once again, rendered his version of a salute.

Detective Fred Ross' blue pinstripe was spanking clean and sharply pressed. "Can you give me any reason why the head was not found earlier?" he asked.

"You've got to understand St. Aloysius," explained Father Thomas McInerny, the pastor. "This place, especially on weekday mornings, is a madhouse. The janitor opens the church at six. We have a six-thirty Mass, then a seven-thirty Mass."

"I understand that, Father." Ross was recording times and events in his note pad. "But my question is why the head wasn't discovered until almost eight o'clock. And possibly would not have been discovered even then if it hadn't been for the presence of Inspector Koznicki."

"Well, see, when the janitor opens up, he lights the church and arranges things for Mass. But he hardly ever goes into the basement church until later in the day. Nor, generally, does anyone else, since the two morning Masses are offered on the main level. Then there is a constant flow of people, just hundreds of distractions. You're probably right: if it hadn't been for Inspector Koznicki, we might not have found the head even now."

Although the doors at St. Aloysius had been locked and the general public excluded, the church was living up to its reputation for bedlam. Six members of Squad Six were interrogating various functionaries, from the janitor to the pastor. Other specialists were taking pictures or dusting for prints. In addition to Lennon, three reporters from the *News* and one—Joe Cox—from the *Free Press* were interviewing everybody but each other. Television and radio crews were busy filming the story.

Ven Marshall, longtime reporter for TV's Channel 7,

flagged down Father Bohdan Borucki, who was en route to his office. After a few words, Marshall nodded to his crew. The lights made the scene stand out in unreality as the cameraman began filming.

Marshall: I have with me Father Bohdan Borucki, who is Vicar for Religious—

Borucki (interrupting): Actually, I'm *Assistant* Vicar for Religious.

Marshall: Damn—sorry, Father. (To his crew): Let's take it from the top.

Marshall: I have with me Father Bohdan Borucki, Assistant Vicar for Religious.

Borucki smiled.

Marshall: Father, your offices are in the adjoining Chancery Building, but you say Mass here in St. Aloysius regularly, isn't that right?

Borucki nodded. Fortunately, they were not on radio.

Marshall: Tell me, Father, we have learned that the deceased, Dutch Strauss, was a Catholic—at least nominally —and that he graduated from Holy Redeemer High School here in Detroit. Did you ever see him in attendance here at St. Aloysius?

Borucki: Oh, I wouldn't know about that. There are so many coming in and out here all the time I have trouble remembering the few regulars we have.

Marshall: But you must discuss with the other priests who comes to Mass here, particularly if it is someone as notorious as Dutch Strauss.

Borucki: Well, not really. You see, I'm into heraldry.

Marshall (somewhat confused): What?

Borucki: Heraldry. You know, making coats of arms, things like that.

Marshall: Uh, well, yes, well, thank you, Father. (Camera full on Marshall. He turns to camera.) This is Ven Marshall, Channel 7 Action News, at St. Aloysius Church, Detroit.

(Camera off. Lights out.)

Marshall turned to his crew. "Would you guys see if you can find me a normal priest?"

Joe Cox had been moving swiftly from one group to another, listening to conversations and asking questions. Periodically, he glanced at Pat Lennon.

Throughout this entire period, she stood motionless, contemplating the headless statue of St. Raphael the Archangel.

Larry Delaney, film critic for the *Detroit Free Press*, sat at his desk searching his mind for just the right phrase. He was reviewing the Americana's latest offering, a return engagement of "Claire's Knee."

Besides writing matchless reviews of local cinematic offerings, Delaney periodically was sent to cover such foreign delights as the Cannes and Venice Film Festivals, and that made-for-media event, Hollywood's Oscar presentations.

In addition, Delaney was the original Anonymous Gourmet, a secret so well kept that even many *Free Press* staffers did not know the A.G.'s identity—though a true investigative reporter would have had little trouble ferreting out the truth.

Steady surveillance over Delaney's shoulder would have revealed, in place of the usual press kit for consultation near his typewriter, a menu.

No matter which was there, press kit or menu, Delaney would sit lost in reflective thought until just the proper phrase emerged into his consciousness. This emergence, once transmitted into deathless black and white, was occasionally greeted by its author with brief delighted applause.

On the neighboring desk, belonging to Donna Halliday, the *Free Press* book editor, the phone rang. She answered it: "Features Department."

Donna, petite, pretty, and preoccupied, was one of the staffers least recognized by the reading public. Generally, she was hidden from view by stacks of books. The books were heaped high on and around her desk, on nearby filing cabinets and under tables. The tables were also heaped high with literary journals and newsletters, as well as the outpourings of publicists' flackery, each proclaiming their latest offering to be another *Roots* or *Gone With the Wind*. The majority of these books were doomed, for sheer lack of editorial space, to remain stillborn as far as a possible *Free Press* review was concerned.

After listening to the party on the other end for a few seconds, Halliday, covering the mouthpiece with her hand, stood on tiptoe. Like an attractive version of Kilroy, she peered over the pile of books sandbagging her desk. "Larry, it's the general manager of Mario's restaurant on the phone. He wants to know when the Anonymous Gourmet is going to run the review of his place."

Delaney pushed aside the press kit and pondered the question as he gazed absently across Lafayette Boulevard into the maze of skyscrapers. "Not in the foreseeable future. I haven't been there in a while."

Quietly, Halliday relayed this information. Seconds later, she returned to her tiptoes, once more peered over the books and said, "Larry, he says you were there just the other night. You were masquerading as a priest."

Delaney's fingers stopped in mid-type. He thought this allegation over carefully. Finally, he returned to his review, commenting over his shoulder to Halliday, "He's out of his mind."

Halliday spoke calmly into the receiver. "He says you're out of your mind!" With that, she hung up and wondered what on earth she was going to do with all these books.

After receiving Moellmann's verdict on the latest head, Harris drove to St. Aloysius and added his car to the many other marked and unmarked police vehicles at the scene. He checked with Fred Ross and several others of his squad, dodged Ven Marshall, who was not having a particularly good day, and proceeded to the clandestine headquarters of the late Dutch Strauss on Alexandrine.

In the whitewashed foyer, Harris met Detectives Charlie

Papkin and Dietrich Bernhard. Harris glanced into the interior of the back room. It was outfitted like a relatively small warehouse, except that its one commodity was illegal drugs. In one corner, seated uncomfortably on straight-back chairs, were four oversized men, erstwhile bodyguards of the late king of the drug empire.

Nodding in the direction of the four, Harris asked, "The goons give you any trouble?"

"They are completely bewildered," said the precise Bernhard.

"At the moment," continued Papkin, doing the color commentary, "they couldn't lean on Mary Tyler Moore."

"They have no explanation for what happened," said Bernhard. "Everything went according to routine to a point. They had a late lunch at a prestigious restaurant; yesterday it happened to be the Ren Cen's Summit—"

"Did they eat with anyone in particular?" interrupted Harris.

"Well," Papkin consulted his note pad, "the four stooges usually ate together. Sort of a floating pigsty. But Strauss' companions were a couple of high-ranking bankers from," he turned a page, "First Standard Bank and Trust."

"Anyone checking them?"

"Pat Karnego is over there now."

"Go on," Harris said, addressing Bernhard.

"They returned to this address at approximately three in the afternoon. The four bodyguards went immediately to the workhouse."

"You mean," Harris interjected, "they left Strauss alone?"

"It was part of the routine," Bernhard answered.

"Hidden behind that light switch is a button that lowers this staircase." Bernhard indicated the exposed button and the now lowered staircase.

"You won't believe what's up there!" Papkin enthused.

"In any case," Bernhard continued, "according to routine, a girl is waiting for Strauss. They have a quick sexual encounter, and Strauss returns invigorated."

"Except that yesterday," said Papkin, "before Goldilocks and his four bears got back from lunch, someone called the caretaker, using the secret code, and told him Strauss wanted no girl today and that the others knew it."

"But what happened to Strauss?" Harris asked.

"Well," Bernhard responded, "after about three hours—which was about two hours more than usual—the bodyguards decided to investigate. They went upstairs cautiously, since Strauss was furious when interrupted. They found no one.

"They didn't know what happened or where to look until they heard on the radio this morning about Strauss' head at St. Aloysius."

"I see," said Harris. He started up the staircase, followed by Bernhard and Papkin.

As Harris' head cleared the floor level, he stopped in his tracks, his eyes widened in surprise. Somebody was in the large circular bed in the room's far corner. Surprised eyes relaxed into laugh lines. The slim, subtly undulated form belonged to Detective Colleen Farrell.

"Lying down on the job, Sergeant?" Harris asked with mock severity.

Farrell was out of the bed and on her feet as if catapulted. She smoothed the wrinkles in her skirt. "I was just checking out the male chauvinistic pig side of life," she said, but there was heightened color in her cheeks.

"And what did you find?" pursued the broadly smiling Harris.

Farrell looked back into the mutually reflecting mirrors. "I feel sorry for anybody who needs all that to turn on."

"Not much here," Papkin commented. "No sign of a struggle, no broken or overturned furniture, no blood."

"Latent prints don't give us much," said Bernhard. "Most we've lifted appear to be Strauss' or one of his attendants."

"There is something," said Farrell, indicating the molding at the closet's corner. "I just happened on it before you came up, Lieutenant. See these marks on the molding . . .

as if someone were hanging on for dear life. And then," she moved slowly across the room toward the opposite wall, "there seem to be fingernail marks along the carpet, as if a reluctant body had been dragged across it. But the marks stop here, just a little beyond the middle of the room."

The three men examined the marks Farrell had indicated.

Harris scratched his chin. "If there had been any kind of struggle, if there had been any shouting or screaming, wouldn't Strauss' goons downstairs have heard it?"

"Negative," Bernhard answered. "Room's entirely soundproof. Strauss was frequently pretty rough with his playmates. He felt more comfortable if no one could hear their cries for mercy."

Farrell grimaced.

Harris wandered toward the wall leading to the bathroom. On a small nightstand was an ordinary copper ashtray.

Harris picked it up and examined its contents. He stood silent for so long that the other three came over to see what was holding his attention. All four stood gazing into the ashtray.

"Do any of you," asked Harris, finally, "know anyone who has a habit of chewing toothpicks?"

The three looked from one to the other. Each shrugged negatively.

"Well," sighed Harris, "I do." He handed the ashtray to Bernhard. "Take this downtown and see if the toothpicks can be checked for fingerprints or tooth imprints."

Bernhard draped a clean cloth over and around the ashtray and its contents, picked up the bundle, and departed.

"This case," said Harris ruefully, "has taken a sudden turn of my stomach."

"Hey! Ain't Malcolm ever gon' be back?"

"No, man. You know better than that. Malcolm got hit on a big number and he took the money and run."

The verbal transaction was taking place on the corner of West Grand Boulevard and Bagley in the midst of a large Chicano community on Detroit's near southwest side. Juan Gonzales was making his daily numbers bet.

"Well, you know, man, Malcolm was on these streets lots of years. We come to trust him, man. You sure he ain't never gon' be back?" Gonzales was one among many, mostly minorities, who for various reasons preferred continuing to do business with illegal numbers runners rather than playing the legal Michigan lotteries.

"No, man. You can be sure Malcolm ain' gonna be back. First off, he owed Martinez twenty-two hundred, which he ain't got and which, if Martinez ever catches him, he will take out of Malcolm's hide. You guys oughta know by now you can't do business with them niggers!"

As far as that goes, Gonzales thought, he'd just as soon do business with a black as a gringo. He left the thought unarticulated; Gonzales was thoroughly convinced there was no sense in this short life in making enemies needlessly. And not only was Scott Duprie, with whom Gonzales was now doing business, a large gringo with a short fuse, but Duprie was a runner for the Fitzgerald syndicate. It was common knowledge that one did not stir up the Fitzgerald gang. Or one was leaned on until crushed.

"Well, Juan, what's it gonna be?" Duprie was eager to get by Gonzales, a notoriously small bettor known to wager as little as a dime, and get on to bigger fish.

"I want," Gonzales wore a rare look of confidence, "number 315!" Duprie smiled as he wrote out the slip. 315 had been a popular number this day. This was about the forty-fifth customer who had picked that number. Evidently, it was based on the fact that the Tigers were in third place in the American League's East division, with fifteen games remaining to be played. One thing Duprie was sure of: if 315 came in this day, the winning number would be changed. The syndicate would never pay off on such a popularly played number.

"O.K.," Duprie said, "how much you gonna lay on it, Juan?"

Proudly, Gonzales displayed fifteen one-dollar bills and one ten.

Duprie didn't care how Gonzales had come up with twenty-five dollars. He could have stolen it from one of the local Ma and Pa groceries or from the sugar jar at home. In any case, Gonzales was about to lose twenty-five smackers.

"O.K., Juan." Duprie tucked Gonzales' twenty-five dollars away. "I hope this is your lucky day."

"Oh, this is my lucky day, O.K. I'm gon' hit it big just in time. Maria gon' have another kid pretty soon. And this money, it's gon' get her in big safe hospital instead of clinic this time. You see!"

"Yeah, Juan." Duprie tipped his finger against the brim of his hat. "See you 'round."

The doorbell rang at St. Anselm's rectory. An event that had lessened in frequency over the parish's nearly twenty-five-year history.

In the past quarter-century, the Catholic rectory, particularly in the suburbs, had evolved from being the hub of neighborhood activity to being, as some wags insisted, a home for unmarried fathers.

Especially in a parish such as Anselm's in affluent Dearborn Heights, the parish priest was no longer the only—let alone the best—educated person in the community. St. Anselm's could number among its parishioners college presidents, school supervisors, Ph.D's, M.D.'s, dentists, and auto executives. When they were under psychic stress, they saw a psychotherapist—another professional. When they were under financial stress, they saw a broker or banker. Seldom, particularly since the de-emphasis on confession after Vatican II, did they search out their friendly parish priest. Unless they needed a fourth for bridge or tennis.

Mary O'Connor, the parish secretary, opened the door.

Her eyes focused first on an open wallet containing the police shield and I.D. of Detective Dietrich Bernhard. Her focus widened to encompass Bernhard's tall blond Teutonic figure.

"I'm here to see Father Koesler, Ma'am." Bernhard bowed, and almost clicked his heels. "I called earlier. I believe Father expects me."

"Oh . . . well, won't you come in?" Mary stepped back from the door, opening it to allow the officer's entry. No one had told her a policeman was expected. That was odd; Father Koesler usually kept her well informed. She buzzed his room on the intercom and announced the official visitor.

In no time, Koesler reached the hallway, greeted Bernhard, and invited him into the living room, which, along with the dining area, had been decorated by a predecessor with scenes from *The Canterbury Tales*.

"What can I do for you, Officer?"

Bernhard consulted his notes. "I wonder, Father, if you could account for your whereabouts between two and five P.M. yesterday?"

Koesler bristled. "May I ask why I must account for my whereabouts yesterday?"

"Part of a routine investigation, Father." Bernhard's tone was calm, low, and conversational.

Koesler recollected briefly. "Yes, as a matter of fact." There was an edge of anger in the priest's voice. For some strange reason, he was under investigation for some crime. He felt insulted and deeply resentful. "I spent the afternoon with Irene Casey, editor of the *Detroit Catholic*."

"She can corroborate this?"

"Of course."

Bernhard was writing in his note pad. "Would anyone have seen the two of you together?"

"Well . . ." Koesler hesitated, trying to recall the details of his visit with his successor at the archdiocesan newspaper. "Oh, yes, of course. The door to her office is always open, and members of the editorial staff are constantly passing by. Jim Pool, the managing editor, interrupted us pretty regularly."

"And your visit extended from two until five?"

Koesler sighed. "Actually, I arrived a little before two and stayed through the afternoon. We talked, mostly about business matters, then I took Irene to dinner at Carl's Chop House about five-thirty. Carl himself was there to greet us."

"Do you frequently drop in at the *Detroit Catholic* for a visit?"

"No. Yesterday I had lunch with Archbishop Boyle." Koesler reflected once more on how pompous that sounded when the act was so easily accomplished. "During my conversation with the Archbishop, formerly my publisher, Irene's name came up. It occurred to me that it had been too long since I had visited with her and since I had a rather undemanding afternoon I decided to visit her."

Bernhard finished his notes, closed his pad, and pocketed his pen. The interview seemed at a close.

"Now," said Koesler, "may I ask what this is all about?"

Bernhard seemed momentarily uncertain whether to answer the direct question. "You have heard about the probable murder of one Dutch Strauss and the discovery of his head at St. Aloysius Church?"

Koesler nodded.

"Well, so far there are very few clues for us to work with. But at Strauss' headquarters we found an ashtray containing several well-chewed-over toothpicks." Bernhard glanced significantly at the ashtray on the nearby coffee table. It contained several mangled toothpicks that the priest had masticated during their interview.

Koesler was speechless.

"Have you any objections," Bernhard asked, gesturing toward the gnawed toothpicks, "to my taking these for toothprint analysis?"

Numbly, Koesler assented to the request.

Bernhard took a white envelope from his inside jacket pocket, gathered up the toothpicks, deposited them in the envelope, rose, excused himself, explained that he could let himself out of the rectory, and left.

Ordinarily, Koesler would have accompanied his guest to the door. But in this instance, he remained seated, his eyes fixed on the now-empty ashtray, his thoughts a jumble.

Resentment over this interrogation drained from him as he pondered the fact that, even briefly, he had been a suspect in a murder.

He had always imagined murderers, at least the type who methodically and cleverly carried out a series of meticulously planned crimes such as The Rosary Murders or, now, The Red Hat Murders, as having fascinating if not unique backgrounds. At least this was true in the mystery novels he was forever reading.

Koesler considered his own history to be ordinary to the point of dullness. He'd had an unexceptional career in the seminary. He had been given a series of ordinary appointments as assistant pastor at several Detroit parishes. His one out-of-the-ordinary assignment had been as editor-in-chief of the *Detroit Catholic*, a position he had held for twelve years. It was during this time that the Second Vatican Council had taken place. Vatican II, for the first time in many centuries, had openly invited Catholic clergy and laity alike to ask questions regarding their faith.

For Koesler, this had been a mind-opening event. He found there were few legitimate answers to the legitimate questions theologians were asking of canon law that had been codified some sixty years before. Even the Church acknowledged the dated quality of its law, and Pope Paul VI had established a committee to reform that very law. To date, almost twenty years after its establishment, that committee had come up with nothing more than equally unacceptable law.

That this acknowledgedly antediluvian law was still on the books with the ecclesial presumption that it be enforced, disturbed Koesler. He was grateful he was no longer at the *Detroit Catholic*. He no longer had the duty of expressing his opinions publicly for all to read. It had been a duty that had gotten him into trouble many times.

He enjoyed being pastor at St. Anselm's. The tall, slender, blond, soft-spoken, bifocaled priest loved to mingle with the everpresent parochial school children and offer friendship, advice, encouragement, and consolation to the adults. From time to time, he experienced a strong spiritual call to inner-city ministry. At such times, Archbishop Boyle would assure him that his place was at St. Anselm's. That reassurance was sufficient for Koesler. He admired and respected Boyle. Now, Koesler and St. Anselm's parish were preparing to celebrate their twenty-fifth anniversaries, which, coincidentally, fell within the same month.

But celebration was far from his mind now. He was busily pursuing the possibilities presented by masticated toothpicks at the scene of a probable murder.

He was, of course, certainly not the only person who chewed toothpicks. His mind filtered through a montage of restaurants, rectory dinners, picnics, all the eating experiences he could evoke. Toothpicks were, indeed, a common implement.

But away from the table, long after the meal was finished? Now it was more difficult to recall anyone's using a toothpick. Surely some people must. However, he could not, at this moment, think of anyone but himself. A stupid habit, he reflected. Only slightly less stupid than the cigarette smoking his toothpick-chewing had replaced.

He suddenly became aware of the presence of Mary O'Connor at the archway of the living room. He had no idea how long she'd been standing there.

"Yes, Mary?" He stood and faced her. He was easily a foot taller than she.

"I'm going now, Father." Her voice carried the usual sense of hesitation as though she was never certain that what she was doing or saying was quite correct. But she was a gem. Koesler knew that if canon law had permitted, Mary could run this parish well with no help from him.

"The printer was here earlier and collected this week's

copy for the *Anselmeter*. Evelyn called. Her car won't start, so she can't be here to get supper. Do you want me to get something for you to eat before I leave?"

"No, Mary. Thanks a lot. I'll try some original potluck. I think there's some food in the freezer. I'll get along fine. You go on home."

"Thank you, Father. I'll see you tomorrow."

Koesler heard the front door close behind her.

He found a package of frozen chicken and a plastic bag of mixed vegetables. He put the vegetables in to boil and the chicken in the oven.

In many of the mystery novels he had read, he thought, it was a common stratagem on the part of the murderer to try to throw the police off the track by tossing a red herring or two into the picture. What if the murderer had deliberately planted those toothpicks at the scene of the crime? According to that detective, there were few other clues. Which probably meant no fingerprints. Why would a murderer leave no clue, not even a fingerprint, and yet leave chewed toothpicks?

If the toothpicks were planted, if someone were trying to implicate him, it would have to be someone who knew of his recent surrogated habit. Who knew? Just about everyone who was familiar with him. The parishioners. The entire staff of the *Detroit Catholic*. Many of the Detroit police. All his clerical and religious friends.

If there were any truth to this unlikely supposition, it meant that Koesler would actually have met the killer. His mind was now racing, going through the hundreds of people he knew, discarding one after another as being incapable of such crimes.

He smelled smoke. He opened the oven door. He had forgotten to remove the box when he put the chicken in to bake.

With his finger, Father Ted Neighbors thoughtfully stirred the ice in his martini. He sat upright in a reclining chair in the living room of the rectory of St. Frances Cabrini. Opposite him, on a tan sofabed, sat Father William Moloney, director of the Office of Education for the Archdiocese of Detroit, and resident of Cabrini's rectory. Moloney's office was in the Chancery Building downtown. His principle responsibility was the supervision of all Catholic education and educational institutions within the archdiocese. In return for his room and board, he helped Neighbors with confessions, as well as weekday and weekend Masses.

Moloney was drinking a light but rare Chablis. He studied his Waterford wineglass with interest, took another small sip, and rolled the liquid gently over his gums. "Pleasantly disturbing, appealingly provocative, yet assuming little."

"What?" Neighbors' mind had been lost in plotting this evening's parish council meeting, while his index finger was lost in a glass of gin over which had been pronounced the word Vermouth.

"The Chablis. Very interesting. What year?"

"Uhmmm . . . '73."

Moloney, pausing to recall, "A good year!"

"Ah . . . a good year . . . yes, a good year."

Smiling, Moloney placed his glass carefully on a coaster on the end table. "What is it, Thomas Aquinas? Are you puzzling out the ultimate response to the Albigensian heresy?"

"What?"

"You've spent our entire preprandial period lost in thought. You've even passed lightly over my sincerely expressed compliment to your excellent wine. And your index finger must be cryogenically wed to that martini."

"The parish council," Neighbors explained.

"The parish council?"

"Yes, they're meeting tonight. It's their first meeting since the solemn installation of St. Frances Cabrini's statue."

"The $50,000 wonder of the world! And," Moloney continued, "they've never even had an opportunity to express their opinion on the outlay of parochial funds for that enterprise."

"Listen," Neighbors spoke, head thrown back, square jaw jutting, "when Pope Julius—"

"I know, I know; when the Pope made Michelangelo an interior designer, he did not conduct a plebiscite."

"Exactly!"

"Well, my dear Teddie, I think you are going to learn tonight that you are not Pope Buster the First and that Pope Julius never had to face a parish council."

Neighbors slumped slightly and took a long gulp of his drink. "What makes it worse is we have five excused absences. All five generally back me blindly. That leaves us with seven—unfortunately, a quorum—and all but one are troublemakers."

"Looks bad for the home team." Moloney resumed sipping his wine.

"I'll make them see!" Neighbors vowed. "By damn, I'll make them believers in true art!"

"We'll see. Numerically, they've got you."

"Quality will out." Neighbors finished his martini with a flourishing bottoms-up.

At that, a shy Mrs. Bovey, the housekeeper, lightly touched the bell at the dining table. "Dinner is ready, Fathers," she softly announced.

The two rose and started toward the dining room.

"And what will the condemned man have for his final meal?" Moloney asked.

Neighbors beamed. *"Truite au Bleu!"* He shivered in gastronomic anticipation.

Moloney raised his partially empty glass of Chablis. "Speaking for the faithful seven who will confront you this night, *morituri te salutamus!"*

Harris and Koznicki were once again tucking in a workday sitting near the bar on the second level of the nearly empty Code 30.

Much of the time they were reflectively silent. Koznicki

toyed with a small glass of port. In his huge hands, the glass resembled a miniature. Harris had ordered a gin and tonic, an unusually light drink for him.

"I meant to talk to you yesterday," Koznicki said. "You really should have taken at least a couple of days off."

"Can't, Walt." Harris swirled his drink. "I've got to stay with this Red Hat crime wave. The killer shows no signs of letting up. Neither can we."

There was a pause.

"That was your first, wasn't it?"

"Yeah," Harris replied, "it was my first. Been on the force all these years and never killed anyone until the other night. I don't mind telling you, I was shaking pretty bad and for a long time."

"I know. I've had three. It's always them or us. But I don't think you ever get over taking a human life, no matter how low the guy may be. Killers, especially the pros, come to look at it as just a day's work. Something like circus performers where there's a certain amount of danger but they just don't think of the risk after a while."

"Well, anyway, I'm over it now." Harris was nearly finished with his drink. "What makes it a little easier to live with is that if that kid hadn't been nearly freaked out on drug withdrawal, he'd have got me for sure. Even with trembling hands, he missed me by only inches. If he'd been able to squeeze one more off, you'd be playing solitaire this evening."

There was another lengthy pause. Harris ordered a second gin and tonic. He began to fold the paper napkin into odd shapes.

"Somehow, Walt, I feel as if I should apologize for checking out Koesler. After all, he *is* your friend."

Koznicki didn't raise his eyes from his diminishing port. "Not at all. You and I both know the man has taken to chewing toothpicks. I have no idea how many people chew toothpicks, but there can't be that many who practically destroy the toothpicks they chew."

Koznicki smiled briefly at the memory of his friend's

odd choice of a surrogate oral satisfaction. "I can tell you this, though: very few things in life surprise me, especially after all these years on the force. But if Father Koesler had been in any way involved in murder, I would have been genuinely surprised. Flabbergasted!"

Bernhard had turned the toothpicks collected from Father Koesler's ashtray over to a forensic odontologist. That meticulous specialist had compared them with those found in the ashtray next to Dutch Strauss' bed. The teethmarks had not matched.

There was another period of silence. Harris ordered another small glass of port for Koznicki. The Inspector did not object. His oversize metabolism could absorb, without adverse effect, even more than Harris'—if pressed.

"However," Harris' tone of voice gave every indication this would be, for him, a delicate turn of conversation, "the investigation into Koesler's alibi led me to a related train of thought."

"Yes?"

"So far, we've been operating under the assumption that these top crime figures are being wasted if not by rival hoods, at least at their order, maybe by outside talent."

"Yes?"

"Well, after giving the order to have Koesler checked out, it dawned on me. I mean, before I saw those chewed-up toothpicks it wouldn't have occurred to me in a thousand years to suspect a priest of cold-blooded murder. But now, all of a sudden, the impossible becomes possible."

"Yes?"

"See, once you open up the possibility that a priest could conceivably waste somebody," Harris, becoming animated, emphasized his words with expansive gestures, "maybe in this case, for what a priest might regard as the best of motives—I mean, getting rid of the worst criminals in the community—it begins to make sense. Doesn't it?"

"Go on."

"The 'inside job' factor. These guys' heads—we've been finding them exclusively in Catholic churches. One in the cathedral, where the guy who tucked it into the Cardinal's hat had to know how to lower and raise the hat. Information that, allegedly, few people had.

"The next is found in a church that, because it's in a high-crime section, is pretty securely locked.

"Finally, a head is found in a downtown church that is not only particularly well secured but, during daytime hours when it *is* open, is pretty well filled all day."

"So?"

"So who would have easier access to these secured places than a priest, who could pretty well come and go without attracting special attention? I mean," Harris was almost pleading, "it's possible, isn't it?"

Koznicki tossed down the remainder of his port. "If I were you, Ned," he smiled, gathered his hat from the empty chair next to him and rose to leave, "I'd pursue that."

Six of the seven St. Frances Cabrini parish council members present for the September meeting seemed intent on returning at least their parish, if not the Church, to the Thirteenth, what they considered the Greatest of Centuries. The seventh, Mrs. June McAvoy, was of the dual opinion that "Father knows best," and "Nothing is too good for Father."

Basically, Father Ted Neighbors was in agreement with Mrs. McAvoy. He would have been more comfortable in the nineteenth or early twentieth century. A time during which pastors grabbed for and secured more and more parochial power. A time during which a pastor, outside his parish, was a figurehead worthy of sometimes obsequious honor, while within his parish he was the macho honcho of all he surveyed.

Unfortunately, everyone now seated at the large round table in Cabrini's rectory basement was on the verge of the twenty-first century. And none of them was ready.

"The September meeting of the parish council of St. Frances Cabrini will come to order," Steve Dowd, council president, intoned. "Father Neighbors will open the meeting with a prayer."

All heads bowed.

"Bless us, O Lord, and these Thy gift...uhh..." Neighbors, for no apparent reason, had inadvertently begun the traditional before-meal grace. "Uhh...Hail Mary, full of grace, the Lord is with thee. Blessed art thou among women and blessed is the fruit of thy womb, Jesus."

"Holy Mary," came the chorus, "Mother of God, pray for us sinners, now and at the hour of our death. Amen."

"St. Frances Cabrini..."

"Pray for us."

There was a general and self-conscious adjusting of chairs and shuffling of papers.

"Correspondence?" Dowd asked.

Mrs. Nowicki fumbled through her folder, found and read the thank-you note sent by the missioner who had preached at all the Masses one weekend the previous month and who had received a special collection for his missionary order.

"I move," moved Charlie Korman, a wispy fellow who always seemed to be looking for a bone to gnaw, "that Father's letter be published in our parish bulletin."

"I second the motion," moved the trim, attractive, agreeable Mrs. McAvoy.

"All in favor?" asked Dowd.

Grunts, groans and ayes.

"All opposed?"

Silence.

Mrs. Nowicki recorded the vote.

"Old business?" Dowd asked.

"I'd like to bring up that Folk Mass for the parochial school children that opened the school year," offered Mrs. Ann Kurlick, a strikingly handsome woman gracefully approaching middle age.

"What about it?" asked Dowd.

"It was a disgrace! I may be old-fashioned," Mrs. Kurlick began nearly all her conservative statements with those words, "but I don't think there is any place for guitar playing when we have a perfectly good organ."

"They played guitars?" Korman inched forward.

"Yes," Kurlick continued, "and the closing hymn... well!"

"What was it? What was it?" In his eagerness, Korman almost fell off his chair.

"'Blowin' in the Wind'!" Kurlick identified triumphantly.

"'Blowin' in the Wind'! 'Blowin' in the Wind'!" Korman needlessly repeated. "That's no hymn! That's no hymn! That's a barroom song!"

"It's not a barroom song," Neighbors interjected as quietly as possible. "It's a very legitimate song that the children find relevant."

"I think Father should be able to schedule any song he thinks appropriate," said Mrs. McAvoy supportively.

"If you have any further questions," Neighbors said firmly, "you may refer them to the liturgy department of the archdiocese."

That seemed to end the "Blowin' in the Wind" controversy. Tempers seethed perceptibly, but there were no further words on the subject.

"New business?" Dowd's smile was conspiratorial.

"The statue! The statue!" Korman loudly observed.

"Which statue?" Dowd well knew which statue.

"St. Frances Cabrini!" whooped Korman. "I understand that you, Father, paid somebody $25,000 to build that statue!"

"Fifty-thousand," Neighbors corrected. "And the artist didn't *build* it; he sculpted it."

There was an audible gasp.

"Fifty-thousand dollars!" Dowd exclaimed. "You have no authority to spend that kind of money without the advice and consent of the parish council!"

"When Pope Julius commissioned Michelangelo to paint the Sistine Chapel, he did not conduct a plebiscite!"

Neighbors' delivery was improving with each repetition.

"Conduct a what?" Korman asked.

"Vote," McAvoy explained.

"You are not a Pope!" Dowd noted.

"And you are not a College of Cardinals," Neighbors noted back.

"I think Father should be encouraged to do what he thinks best for the parish," said McAvoy, supportively. "After all, he has the overall view of the parish."

"I want to go on record as being totally opposed to the statue!" Korman was standing and pointing at Mrs. No-wicki's pad, encouraging her to record his opposition in the minutes.

Mrs. Kurlick pounded her small fists on the table. "I may be old-fashioned, but—"

Neighbors removed his glasses and buried his knuckles in his eyes. He wished he were able to return to the infant defense mechanism of denial and pretend none of this was happening. But he wasn't. And it was.

She hit him with the large frying pan. He howled. She had aimed at his head but he had raised his arm in time to take the blow on his elbow. The only possible good news was that if she had connected with her target, he would now be unconscious.

The weather was unpleasant this early Friday morning in September, and so was Margarita Gonzales' disposition.

"Juan Gonzales!" She stamped her foot on the kitchen's tile floor. She was furious. "You stupid man! We owe two months' rent! The kids need clothes to go to school without wearin' rags! We are eatin' the cheapest food in the market! We are eatin' leftovers so often it might as well be garbage! And you try to take our welfare money and give it to that loafer Malcolm to play a number!"

She had caught her husband with his hand literally in the cookie jar. He hadn't even had time to remove the remaining few dollars.

"That's all you know, old woman." Gonzales was vigorously rubbing his elbow. "Malcolm ain't even here no more."

"He's dead, ain't he? Somebody knife him? It's about time!"

"No, he ain't dead. He . . . he left town." Gonzales was unwilling to volunteer the information that Malcolm had fled, taking with him their neighbors' winnings. He was certain his wife would only use the knowledge as an additional argument against his playing the numbers.

"That don't make no difference. You still was gonna take our money and play the numbers, wasn't you? If Malcolm's gone, there's gotta be somebody else on the street. You was gonna do it, wasn't you? After all your promises!"

"Oh, old woman, leave me alone. I wasn't gonna take any money. I was just gonna see how much we got, is all."

"That's a pretty good idea. I shoulda thought of that myself."

She reached in front of him, took the cookie jar from the shelf and placed it on the kitchen table. Removing a small roll of bills from it, she quickly counted them.

She turned on him with the frying pan again raised on high in righteous vengeance.

"Damn you for a thief! You took twenty-five dollars from here! You musta done it yesterday!"

Again she swung at his head. Again he was able to raise his arm in time to absorb the blow with his elbow.

He screamed in agony. It occurred to him that if she swung again, he might well take the blow with his head. Otherwise, he might lose his arm.

Besides, by now he could use the anesthesia.

It was Pat Lennon's first full day of employment at the *Detroit News*. There was a lot of getting-used-to to be done.

Least among these was a transfer of allegiance from the *Free Press* VDTs (video display terminals) to the *News* CRTs (cathode ray terminals). A terminal, Pat thought, is a terminal is a terminal. In either case these were the computer instruments that staff writers were expected to master. The VDTs and CRTs had replaced the Linotypes and their operators. The introduction of these computer machines also marked the transition from "hot" to "cold" type. A transition that Lennon, among other print purists, regretted.

At that, she was fortunate she had, on her own accord, learned to operate the VDTs in the *Free Press* feature department. *Free Press* city room staffers were not yet using terminals, though there were terminals in their future.

It was strange, she thought, with these two major media competitors separated by only a couple of city blocks, that there was so little visiting done. Today was only the second time she had ever been in the *News* building. She had been very surprised at the security measures in the main lobby. No one got past the guard without an appointment with or approval of staff personnel. Only the *Minneapolis Star* and *Tribune*, in her experience, had tighter security than the *News*.

This was quite a shock after the *Free Press'* open entrée. There, anybody could go anywhere, and frequently did. That, in her opinion, was how a newspaper should be run.

Although such openness did occasionally lead to peculiar incidents: she recalled a story regularly told by Nelson Kane about a man who showed up in the city room one day. The stranger explained to one of the staffers that years previously the *Free Press* had run a front-page story reporting he had been declared criminally insane. Now, he said, he had a doctor's certificate stating he was sane, and he wanted the paper to publish that fact—again on the front page.

The then city editor had told the staffer that the *Free Press* would not comply but added that the man should be treated with the utmost respect because, of all the people in the building, he was the only one who could *prove* he was sane.

Pat smiled as she thought of the story but then became

serious again at the thought of Nelson Kane. She had become sentimental over the old bear. Now he was on the enemy's team.

One more thing she'd have to get used to. The *News* didn't have a city editor. Years before, they had abolished that title in favor of news editor. She and the other reporters did not have direct access to the news editor. She was assigned to an assistant news editor, Bob Ankenazy. A nice enough man, about ten years her senior with plenty of reportorial experience and, seemingly, an open attitude toward new ideas. She felt she would work well with him.

Pat Lennon, thirty years old, was a graduate of Mercy High School and College, both Detroit Catholic institutions. Shortly after college, she had entered into a disastrous marriage that had been doomed from the honeymoon on. However, it had been officially witnessed and blessed by the Church. She knew enough of Church law to realize she had no chance of ever having her marriage declared null.

As frequently happens in such cases, she had drifted away from Mass attendance. This caused her mother grief and her father to wonder why he had spent so much money on a Catholic school education.

For the past two years, she had been living with Joe Cox. This was the first long-term relationship with a man since her divorce. So far, it was working well. Only, she figured, because neither she nor Cox had attached any strings. She was certain that if they joined the paper chase, the wedding license would be tantamount to a death certificate.

Like many other nonpracticing Catholics, Lennon was unable to shake her Catholic past. She still attended Mass at Christmas and Easter. If asked her religion, she automatically admitted to being Catholic.

It was a combination of her Catholic background, her inquisitive mind, and her usually dependable intuition that had drawn her attention to the sites where the heads had been found in The Red Hat Murders. A Cardinal's hat and two statues, each in a Catholic church. She was convinced that if she could crack the mystery of the placement of those heads, she could go a long way toward solving the mystery of the actual murders.

But she would not get anywhere daydreaming.

As she searched the Yellow Pages for a phone number, she was conscious of the guarded stares of several of her new confreres. She thought she knew what they were thinking. The latest refugee from the *Free Press*. The first general reporter from that paper who knew how to operate a CRT. Has her own special desk on her first day. Already working on an important story. If, she thought, they knew what she was being paid, their noses would really be bent. She dialed.

"Father Koesler, please."

There was a pause as she was put on hold while Mary O'Connor located Koesler in his study. Each of the few times Pat had talked to priests in recent years she had felt a twinge of guilt. Perhaps, she had thought at one point, that was because she had not paid her dues lately.

"Koesler."

"Father? My name is Pat Lennon. Maybe you remember me? I was with the *Free Press*, now I'm with the *News*."

Koesler thought a moment. The only image that came to mind was curves. As they assembled themselves to his appreciation, he recalled meeting her some years back at the Press Club and enjoying her beauty from afar several times since.

"Yes, I do remember you. So you've gone to the *News* . . . is it true they make you promise to vote Republican?"

"No." She smiled. "Only that you never again will make a left turn."

He laughed. "What can I do for you, Pat?"

"I'm calling about The Red Hat Murders, Father. I'm trying to get a line on why the heads were left where they were."

"I'm afraid I'm not going to be much help."

"Well," she persisted, "let me ask you, for instance,

about Rudy Ruggiero. Do you have any idea at all why his head would be attached to Cardinal Mooney's ceremonial hat?"

Without reflection, merely in a spontaneous effort to be helpful, Koesler began explaining the hypothesis that had originated with Father McNiff. Midway through the explanation, it occurred to Koesler that perhaps he should not be sharing this with a reporter. But he quickly dismissed the caution. It did not seem important to keep the hypothesis secret and, besides neither Inspector Koznicki nor Lieutenant Harris had so admonished him, and he knew from experience both officers were inclined to be specific about information they wanted withheld.

". . . so you see," he concluded, "the reason for using the Cardinal's hat may spring from a pun on the root meaning of 'cardinal' as well as the Latin derivative of the word for 'head.' And thus the intent could be a statement that this is 'capital' crime or 'capital' punishment."

There was a pause while Lennon, who had been taking notes furiously, caught up with the conclusion of Koesler's explanation.

"That's a marvelous lead, Father." She continued to write with the receiver pressed between her shoulder and ear. "Now, how about Saints Cecilia and Raphael?"

Koesler chuckled. "I'm afraid that's out of my league. Maybe it would help if you talk to someone who specializes in, or at least is more familiar with, saints and hagiography and the like."

"Any suggestions?"

Koesler thought. "Maybe . . . maybe Father Leo Clark out at St. John's Seminary in Plymouth. Basically, he's a moral theologian—"

"What's that?" she interrupted.

Koesler laughed. "Well, love me, love my jargon. I keep forgetting not everybody is plugged into things Catholic. What I meant is that Father Clark's specialty is morality— moral law. But he also teaches Scripture, about the Bible, and, on top of all that, he has an abiding interest in the lives and legends of saints."

"He must have a mind that doesn't quit."

"That's about it. If Leo Clark can't tell you more than you ever wanted to know about almost any religious subject you could think of, then don't bother looking it up. It probably hasn't been written."

"Thanks, Father. You've been a big help. I'll get in touch with Father Clark right away."

They hung up. Koesler fished a toothpick from his shirt pocket and began chewing on it absently. St. Cecilia. Raphael the Archangel. He decided to walk over to St. Anselm's school, visit the library, and see what he could find on those two very disparate creatures. What possible connection, he wondered, could there be between a martyred woman, an archangel, and a Cardinal's hat?

It was the kind of fickle weather that Michiganders are accustomed to. A light rain combined with a steady strong breeze chilled the pedestrian to the bone. It seemed that winter had arrived out of due time. However, the natives knew that in mid-September there was plenty of summer remaining. Not to mention the anticipated and especially desirable Indian Summer that had been known to linger even into November.

The white Eldorado glided into the Machus Red Fox parking lot as if eager to escape the pell-mell traffic of Telegraph Road.

There were those who thought the Red Fox's enormous popularity would be diminished if not destroyed when it became known as the scene of Jimmy Hoffa's abduction. Such people were mistaken. Reservations at the Red Fox continued to be coveted as unabatedly as if Hoffa had never made his last public appearance there.

A tall, distinguished figure emerged from the Cadillac. He stood a minute to let his expensive three-piece gray suit settle into shape, then ran a manicured hand through his wavy black hair as a parking attendant sped to raise an umbrella over his head protectively.

"I'm just having a quick lunch, Henry. So keep my car up front, ready to go."

"Yessir, Mr. Fitzgerald!" The attendant accompanied Fitzgerald to the restaurant's entrance, all the while being careful to keep the umbrella directly over his charge's handsome head.

"I hope you don't mind, Ray," said Father Koesler. "I mean, I thought a good night's sleep would take care of it—the embarrassment—but I didn't get a good night's sleep and I'm still angry."

Ramon Toussaint lowered himself gingerly into a worn chair opposite Koesler. "That's all right, Bob; every once in a while everyone needs to talk to someone. I am fortunate I have 'Ciane, and," he added with a touch of diplomacy, "you and I are fortunate we have each other as friends."

Emerenciana entered the living room carrying a tray of coffee servings. "But why would the police question you, Bob?" she asked.

"Apparently because the only clue or unaccounted-for evidence they uncovered in Dutch Strauss' bedroom was an ashtray filled with chewed-up toothpicks." Koesler felt himself reddening. He knew his was a ridiculous habit.

"Bob," said Toussaint, "you cannot be the only person in Detroit who worries toothpicks to death. They must be among the most available instruments, or playthings, in the world. Why, some of them are even flavored. And that alone would tempt people to keep using them—at least as long as the flavor lasts."

Toussaint was trying very hard to stay serious. In reality, he found it difficult to understand Koesler's concern. After all, the priest had neither been arrested nor even accused of any crime, merely questioned.

"I know, I know," Koesler said. "I've gone over all those rationalizations and more. But nothing like this ever happened to me before. I guess I resent even being suspected of a crime."

"Why don't you look at this as a learning experience, Bob?" Emerenciana handed the priest a cup of black coffee.

"A learning experience?"

"Yes. This, at least in part, is what it is like to be black or sometimes just poor."

Koesler looked at her uncomprehendingly.

"It's not as bad in Detroit as it used to be," Emerenciana continued, "because now the police department is nearly fifty percent black. But in the old days, if something went wrong or there was a disturbance, it was always the black community that suffered."

"The police," said Toussaint, "would round up all the usual suspects. All of whom would be black." He grimaced wryly. "The 'nearest-available-nigger' school of police philosophy.

"Then, after scaring the black neighborhoods half to death, the lawmen would drive out to their nice white suburbs for a pleasant night's sleep."

"So you see, Bob," said Emerenciana, "you've had just a small sample of what less fortunate folk have had to suffer over the years."

"I hadn't looked at it that way," Koesler confessed. "But now that you point it out, I can see it more clearly. All of a sudden, I begin to feel grateful to the police department for humanizing me."

All was quiet as the three sipped coffee.

"Why don't you get out?" Koesler asked at length.

"I beg your pardon?" Toussaint seemed puzzled.

"Why don't you get out of the inner city?" Koesler clarified. "You two would be accepted anywhere in this archdiocese: Grosse Pointe, Rochester, Bloomfield Hills, Birmingham, Dearborn, you name it. Any parish would be happy to have you. And think of the good you would accomplish among the suburbanites. You two would be excellent at consciousness-raising!"

"And why," Toussaint countered, "don't *you* stop trying to get assigned to the inner city, Bob?"

Koesler smiled self-consciously. "That's different, Ray. I believe I'd feel more comfortable in the city. I just haven't been able to convince Archbishop Boyle yet. Besides, if there was ever a good argument for an unmarried clergy, it's a core city ministry. If I make a commitment to the city, it involves only my choice. You have 'Ciane to consider."

Emerenciana spoke up. "Don't you think we have shared our decision to remain, Bob? This is where we belong. This is where our people are."

"From our experience," Toussaint continued, "we regard the constant race consciousness of most people in this country as somewhat backward and uncivilized. We are more amused at it than outraged by it."

"And it is really not as much a risk as it seems." Emerenciana, who had been sitting on the arm of her husband's chair, let her hand drop across his shoulder. "The people here in Ceciliaville have accepted us and our ministry. We are as safe here as we would be anywhere."

"And," said Toussaint, "we are nobody's token."

The three were quiet again with a silence that could be shared unembarrassingly only by close friends.

Koesler looked at the couple. "Thanks," he said simply. "Thanks very much. As usual, you two have been a big help." He rose, picked up his hat and prepared to leave.

"Can I get you anything to eat on your way back to Dearborn Heights?" asked a seemingly solicitous Emerenciana. "A toothpick?"

Both men broke up in laughter.

"No," said Koesler, recovering, "I think I'll be able to make it. But if worse comes to worst," he reached into his shirt pocket, "I always have these." He pulled out several rounded wooden toothpicks.

At the door, Koesler turned back, a questioning look replacing his smile. "Say," he said, sniffing, "Is that incense I smell? Are you two running a family-style religion?

Isn't St. Cecilia's big enough for you anymore?" he added, half in jest.

"Another fact of life you'll learn about if you ever do get your inner-city assignment, Bob," said Toussaint. "The pest control people come and fumigate and give us temporary relief from the cockroaches. But it's anybody's guess which is worse, the roaches or the odor left by the fumigators. So, we burn a little incense."

"Oh, I'm sorry." It was all Koesler could think of to say as he left and drove with an added measure of discomfort toward his virtually pest-free Dearborn Heights rectory.

Garnet Fitzgerald was a big man, physically and in the numbers racket. And he was rapidly getting bigger in the rackets. It was a simple matter of invasion: invading a numbers territory once completely controlled by Muhammad Yaphet and his cohort. The method was direct. Fitzgerald's men would discredit, threaten, or physically abuse Yaphet's runners. As Yaphet's men disappeared, Fitzgerald would send his own runners in to replace them. In only a few months, Fitzgerald had made great inroads into Yaphet's kingdom.

Fitzgerald had finished lunch at the Machus Red Fox. He had eaten with and gotten reports from three of his top lieutenants. All was going well. Nothing had been heard from Yaphet. Evidently, he was absorbing the financial beating he was taking.

Fitzgerald expected no more trouble from the man he had once known as Tyrone Jones. Only a few years before, there had been no one tougher or meaner than Tyrone Jones. But Fitzgerald had sensed a soft underbelly when Jones had gotten religion. Religion—any religion—did not mix with the toughness needed to advance in the rackets.

After being assured that it was only a matter of time before he would have the entire Detroit numbers scene sewn up, Fitzgerald signed the meal check, left his men to finish their drinks, and emerged from the restaurant. He was careful to stay under the brief canopy. It was still raining. Not hard, but enough to discourage him from dampening his suit or shoes. He tugged at his vest, making sure it covered his ample middle, as he waited for Henry to fetch his car.

Henry hit the brakes and the Eldorado rocked gently to a stop in front of Fitzgerald. Henry solicitously kept the umbrella over Fitzgerald's head as they circled the car.

"Here ya go, Henry." Fitzgerald slipped a five-dollar bill into the young man's free hand.

"Oh, thank y'all, Mistah Fitz," said a grateful Henry.

Fitzgerald slid in behind the wheel and swung the Cadillac into Telegraph Road traffic.

As he drove, he was conscious that something was not quite right. He couldn't put his finger on it, but there was definitely something strange going on. There was an added scent in the car, something that clashed with his Brut.

In his haste to get out of the rain, he had failed to check the back seat. Damn! Someone was in the back, he was sure of it. He scanned the rear-view mirror for some sign of whomever was crouched on the floor behind him. His right hand eased toward the glove compartment.

"It ain't there," a soft, menacing voice declared.

Sweat began to flow down Fitzgerald's armpits and back. He could feel the moisture seeping into his white-on-white shirt. Something cold and round was pressed against his neck. He checked the rear-view mirror again. This time it reflected the image of a black man wearing sunglasses and a dark hat. He held a revolver against Fitzgerald's neck.

"It used to be there," the man said, referring to the glove compartment, "but now I got it! So suppose you keep both hands on the wheel and just drive."

"Where we goin'?" Fitzgerald wished he could make his voice sound more confident, but he couldn't mask a slight tremor. He was frightened. And with good reason.

"Never mind, you jive turkey. Just drive. Hang a right on Northwestern. You got a date with Muhammad."

There was no doubting it, Fitzgerald had bought a lot of trouble. How much, he was at this moment unable to predict. His only hope was that he would emerge from this plight alive.

Father Leo Clark was concluding a class in Sacred Scripture at St. John's Seminary. He saved the last few minutes of the allotted time to review the answers to a test he had recently given his students.

Clark, of medium build, with receding dark hair, was bespectacled and usually bemused. A good teacher and a genuine scholar, he was not happy when his students gave incorrect answers. But when they were bizarrely wrong, he couldn't help enjoying and sharing the more humorous aspects of their efforts. He was doing just that as he wrapped up this mid-afternoon class.

"Gentlemen," he said, adjusting his glasses and peering at one test paper, "Paul *circumcised* Timothy; he did not castrate him!"

Laughter. Except for the student who had authored the surgical blunder.

"And," Clark continued as the laughter subsided, "the Red Sea is not red because of the *orgasms* on the bottom!"

Again, general laughter, except for one red-faced student.

As the hilarity subsided, a bell sounded, signaling the end of class. Clark gave the students the assignment for Monday, led them in prayer, and dismissed them.

En route from the classroom to his suite, Clark stopped at the switchboard and picked up his messages. He noted a request for a return call from one Pat Lennon of the *Detroit News*. Scribbled on the slip was, "Wants to know about Saints Cecilia and Raphael." He mulled that over as he walked slowly through the cloisters.

On entering his study, he went directly to one section of the bookshelves that lined the walls. Having occupied this same room for the past thirty years, he knew the exact location of every book, much as he would the whereabouts of many good friends. He selected one specific volume, made his way to his desk and dialed Lennon's number.

"Mr. Lennon, please."

There was a slight hesitation. Then, "This is Pat Lennon."

"Oh, I'm sorry. I simply assumed you'd be a man. This is Father Clark at the seminary returning your call."

Lennon smiled. If there were any question of whether a man or a woman was doing important work, such as reporting for a major newspaper, the assumption favored the former.

"Oh, that's perfectly all right, Father. Think nothing of it," she lied lightly. "Did you get my message and what I called about?"

"Yes. You want to know something about St. Cecilia, and Raphael the Archangel."

Lennon explained the purpose of her call. Fortunately, Clark had read about The Red Hat Murders, so she did not have to go into undue detail. She merely explained the theory Father Koesler had given her earlier regarding the Cardinal's hat.

"Bob came up with that theory all by himself?" Clark asked, in an incredulous tone.

"I suppose he did. I didn't think to ask him."

"Well, that just proves that behind that bland expression all those years in class, there was something going on after all."

"You taught him?" It was Lennon's turn to be incredulous.

"That's right! I'm a crazy old duck, huh?"

"No, not at all, Father," she said, recovering.

"By the way, if I may ask, are you a Catholic? You're 'fathering' me to death."

Lennon sighed and wondered if all priests dabbled in detective work.

"Yes, uh, no, Father," she said. Then, correcting herself, "Well, not anymore anyway. Old habits are hard to break. But can you tell me anything about Cecilia and Raphael?"

"Oh, yes. Indeed I can. The trouble is that I may tell you more than you want to know. Please feel free to cut off my water at any point during the flood."

Lennon tucked the receiver between her shoulder and ear and prepared for vigorous note-taking in her own version of speedwriting.

"Regarding Cecilia," Clark began, "I thought I would read you a paragraph from one of my favorite little books. It's *St. Fidgeta and Other Parodies*, written by John Bellairs and published by Macmillan. The paragraph explains the sanctity of a fictitious St. Pudibunda, who, on her wedding night, decided that God had called her to a life of spotless virginity, and I quote: 'The causes of her death that very night are not known, but the pious may guess at them.'"

Lennon was laughing uncontrollably. Clark waited for her return to sobriety.

"Well," he continued, "that's pretty much the way it was with Cecilia. She let her husband in on her rather unusual calling somewhat earlier and she wasn't martyred until many years after her marriage ceremony. But her husband could go around introducing her as 'my wife, the Blessed Virgin Cecilia.' She gave much to the poor, but is probably somewhat more famous for living what many would call an extraordinary life of sublime purity. Is that enough?"

Lennon acknowledged that it probably was.

"Now, as to Raphael. He is a bit of Midrash, a bit of myth. He appears in the book of Tobit in the Old Testament. He leads Tobias to Sarah, who has lost her seven previous husbands on seven consecutive wedding nights."

Clark paused. "Now that I think of it," he said, "that could well be the connection. There was not an awful lot of what you'd expect going on during either Cecilia's or Sarah's wedding nights."

Lennon said nothing, merely continuing her note-taking as she underlined Clark's latest point.

"In any case, Raphael urged Tobias to marry Sarah. He did and, to make a long and fairly interesting story short, they lived happily ever after. Is that enough?"

Lennon, running a couple of phrases behind Clark, caught up to his conclusion.

"I think so, Father. If I need to call you again, it will be all right, won't it?"

"Certainly. Oh, by the way, it just occurred to me: Raphael is the patron saint of apothecaries."

"Druggists? Why? What's the connection?"

"I forgot to tell you. On the journey to meet Sarah, Tobias is attacked by a huge fish while he bathes. Raphael tells Tobias to remove the fish's gall, heart, and liver because, according to Raphael, they make great medicines. Well, Tobias drives the evil spirit away from the nuptial bed with the heart and liver. And he cures his father's blindness by rubbing the fish's gall on the old man's eyes."

"Is that all, Father?"

"Yes, that's all I can think of at the moment." He hesitated. "You're trying to figure out why those heads are being left where they are and you hope to establish the identity of the killer by knowing why he is doing this. Is that correct?"

"Yes," Lennon admitted, "that's right. Why do you ask?"

"Because I think you're on the right track."

Lennon drummed her fingers on the desk. She thought she might take a quick trip to Belle Isle and contemplate all those wasted wedding nights. And, perhaps, study the names of passing ships.

The doorbell rang in the trim two-story house on Stoepel Avenue.

A minute or so after the single ring, Emerenciana Toussaint opened the front door. Two well-built, well-dressed white men stood on the porch. One, who looked as if he had stepped out of a World War II Nazi recruitment poster, showed police credentials as he introduced himself and his partner.

"I am Detective Dietrich Bernhard of Homicide Squad Six. This is my partner, Sergeant Fred Ross. Is this the residence of Ramon Toussaint?"

"It is."

"Is Mr. Toussaint at home?"

"He is."

"May we speak with him?"

"You may."

Emerenciana turned and called her husband.

Toussaint came from the kitchen area. After the officers again identified themselves, Toussaint invited them into the living room. They declined Mrs. Toussaint's offer of coffee and came right to the point of their visit.

"Mr. Toussaint," Bernhard asked, "can you account for your whereabouts between the hours of two and five P.M. on Wednesday, the day before yesterday?"

The Toussaints looked at each other, a hint of amusement in their eyes. Apparently, Bob Koesler was not the only clergyman to be questioned by the police. It was now Toussaint's turn to come up with an alibi.

The building on East Columbia near Beaubien was quite close to the periphery of Detroit's downtown. It had housed everything from vaudeville to legitimate movies to skin-flicks. Now to all appearances vacant, it blended well with the block's other ancient, dusty buildings. Very few Detroiters knew it was headquarters for Muhammad Yaphet. Even fewer knew of the room directly beneath the old stage that had been especially outfitted to dispense punishment to Yaphet's enemies.

The current scene inside this room was not pretty.

Garnet Fitzgerald's inert body lay in a metal tray that was tipped at a thirty-degree angle. Rivulets of his blood trickled down the tray, emptying into a tank of fetid water.

Borrowing their skills from the executioners of yore who would hang, draw and quarter their victims, Yaphet's henchmen were expert at sensing the point at which the subject of their torture was about to pass from this life to the next. And, as often as they wished, they would cease afflicting the subject, allow time for sufficient recovery, and then recommence, usually alternating tortures.

All of which had happened to Fitzgerald throughout this afternoon. Several times he had wished to die, indeed had tried to die. Each time he had been revived.

For the past forty-five minutes, his torturers had been pumping sodium pentothal into him. The so-called truth serum had finished the job of eliciting from Fitzgerald the names of the top men in his organization as well as the location of the key documents detailing his numbers empire.

It seemed near the end now. Yaphet had been summoned from his executive office elsewhere in the building.

Yaphet viewed the scene dispassionately. So, Fitz, he thought, you figured old Tyrone Jones had gone soft when he got religion. Well, Fitz, you never were long on brains. Tough, but not much gray stuff. Too bad. If you'd stayed in your own back yard, if you hadn't invaded my territory, you'd be healthy and gettin' fatter instead of lyin' in that tray like a stuck pig.

"We got the names and places from him, chief." Yaphet's number-one aide stood just behind Yaphet and spoke just loudly enough to be heard only by his employer.

"Can you get anything else?"

"Nah. He's been doin' nothin' but vomiting and hallucinating for the past half hour."

Yaphet nodded. The aide glanced meaningfully at two of his men. They flipped Fitzgerald's bulky body over. His head turned from side to side as if fighting off a bad dream.

The aide stepped forward, calmly removed a .38-caliber revolver from his holster and fired five shots into Fitzgerald's chest. Fitzgerald's body jerked with each impact. Then it lay still.

"Take him over to Billy Bates' Funeral Home on West

Vernor," Yaphet ordered. "He'll know what to do with him."

Yaphet turned and left the room. He would sleep well this night. The integrity of his empire had been restored.

All twelve members of Homicide Squad Six were assembled in their squad room. Adding measurably to the sardine can configuration was the presence of the entire person of Inspector Koznicki.

Those officers who had spent the major portion of this Friday questioning designated clergymen had just completed their reports.

"So," Lieutenant Harris summed up, "it seems that each of our clergymen has an established alibi for the times at least one or more of these men were murdered."

"Yes," said Sergeant Ross, glancing again at his note pad, "Monsignor McTaggart was visiting his sister in Lansing all day Monday. And the deacon," he checked the name, "Ramon Toussaint, was with his wife on all three occasions, one of them corroborated by a neighbor."

"I think," Detective Bernhard added, "we can pretty well forget about that monsignor from here on out. He doesn't seem to know what's going on."

There was scattered laughter. Since neither Koznicki nor Harris had joined in, it was short-lived.

Sergeant Dean Patrick concluded for himself and his partner, Sergeant Bill Lynch. "Father Fred Dolson, over at the cathedral, was giving instructions to a prospective convert during the critical hours on Wednesday. The rest of the cathedral staff are all accounted for during at least one of the times of death on Saturday, Monday or Wednesday."

Patrick, nearly six feet tall, was strikingly handsome, with a heavy head of salt-and-pepper hair, sooty eyebrows, and deep blue eyes. Lynch, angular, well over six feet tall, sported a dark brown mustache and, generally, a bemused expression.

"It's the same at St. Aloysius," reported Sergeant Dan Fallon, brushing cigarette ashes from his shirt. "Father

McInerny, the pastor, was in the church, and seen by many, practically all Saturday afternoon and evening. The priests who work in the chancery all were in their offices, each with an appointment for at least one of the times in question."

"Well, that pretty well wraps it up, doesn't it?" asked Charlie Papkin. "Since we're dealing with identical M.O.s in the three killings, one rainout and there's no ball game."

"Yeah, that's right. But," Harris grimaced, "it leaves us with maybe the biggest hole to fill in this entire case. Why the Catholic churches? Why that damn red hat and those statues? And how is the killer able to enter these places without breaking in? And how did he know about the pulley that lowered and raised that damn hat?"

"Maybe," Koznicki interjected, "we are presuming too much."

"What do you mean, Walt?" Harris asked.

"We seem to have eliminated all these clergymen as murder suspects. But before we leave this point, we must remember that an alibi only makes it more difficult to prove guilt. It is not a guarantee of innocence. We are all familiar with alibis that have not stood more careful examination."

He paused to let his words have their effect.

"Even granting," he continued, "that the murders were not committed by a clergyman, what if a clergyman were in collusion with the murderer?"

It was obvious he had raised a hypothesis that had not previously been considered. The officers shifted to renewed attentiveness.

"What if, after each murder, a clergyman takes the severed head and, using the knowledge and special access he has, places the head in the hat or on the statue?"

There were several moments of silence.

"That," Pat Karnego protested, "is creepy."

"What?" Koznicki asked.

"Imagining that a priest could be guilty of conspiracy in a crime like this."

"There are all those very relevant questions of Lieutenant Harris' that need answering," said Koznicki.

"And remember," added Harris, "whoever is doing this isn't rubbing out Detroit's High Society."

"That's right," said Colleen Farrell. "If a clergyperson is mixed up in this in any way, even by conspiracy, he or she could be doing it on the basis that it's God's will."

"Colleen," Karnego reminded, "there are no female clergypersons in the Roman Catholic Church."

"Not yet," Farrell admitted, "but there should be. And," she concluded defiantly, "there will be."

Almost reflectively, Sergeant Patrick tapped his front teeth with his index finger. "You know," he said softly, "that Dolson fellow at the cathedral has a small-caliber revolver. Did you notice it, Bill?"

"Yes," said Lynch, "now that you mention it, Dean. It was in a holster on his nightstand."

"And that deacon, Toussaint," said Ross, "he seemed to have his alibis right on tap—like he was ready and waiting with 'em."

"And I thought that Father Koesler was too defensive," said Bernhard.

"That's the spirit," Harris enthused, "nothing better for detectives than a healthy dose of mass suspicion."

"If we're dealing with a case of conspiracy," Farrell said, "then the fact that these people had alibis for the actual times of death wouldn't matter. Whoever it is would be affixing the heads at some convenient time after the murders."

"That's right," Karnego agreed.

"So, it's back to the drawing board," Harris said.

"Before we go back to the drawing board," Koznicki said, "and I don't for a moment suggest that is not where we should be going, but there is an added consideration that hasn't been mentioned."

Everyone looked at the Inspector expectantly.

"We have," Koznicki continued, "three places where the heads have been found: the Cathedral, St. Cecilia's, and

St. Aloysius. We have considered the possibility of involvement of the clergy who are in any way connected with these parishes, and we may consider their possible involvement again, this time under a different aspect of the case."

"A different aspect?" asked a puzzled Patrick.

"What if there are more?" Koznicki asked in reply.

"More?" Patrick repeated.

"Yes," said Koznicki. "More. We have no reason to assume that three victims are all the killer intended."

One could almost hear the gears grinding in the minds of his listeners.

"What if there is a fourth victim? A fifth? What if, before we can find the murderer and stop him, more heads are left in more churches? Each new parish will have new possible suspects, either of murder or conspiracy, every bit as suspectable as the few clergypersons," he inclined his head toward Farrell, "whom we will be reinvestigating.

"If, in other words, we now had four, instead of three, murders in this sequence, we would be considering additional clergy—the number depending on how many clergy were associated with the fourth parish."

The group was silent again.

Finally, Harris spoke. "Saturday, Monday, and Wednesday," he said, enigmatically. "The killer has acted last Saturday, Monday, and Wednesday," he amplified. "Every other day. We have found the heads on Sunday, Tuesday, and Thursday. Every other day. If there are to be more victims, someone should be killed today. And if we're in luck, we should find a head in some Catholic church tomorrow."

Koznicki nodded. "You could be right, Ned. It is the logical move."

"Well," said Harris, "it would be professional suicide to wait around for the killer's next move. We've got to try to get ahead of him. Let's make our plans for tomorrow. It goes without saying, all time off and leaves are canceled until we crack this case. There's every indication the killer is working overtime on this. We've got to, too."

The announcement was greeted with a mixture of determination, resignation, and resentment. But work overtime they would.

The number of Mass attenders at St. Frances Cabrini on Saturday mornings was even fewer than on weekdays.

It was the habit of Father Bill Moloney to offer the Saturday morning Mass and let his confrere, Father Ted Neighbors, sleep in.

The seven nuns who taught at St. Frances Cabrini's parochial school were present for the 8 A.M. Mass, along with ten parishioners. Seven was a rather large complement of nuns to have in one parish, considering the scarcity of nuns. In appreciation of their presence, many events in the parish were scheduled for the nuns' convenience. For instance, the 8 A.M. starting time for Saturday's Mass gave the nuns a little extra time to sleep in and still accomplish all that needed doing in preparation for the heavily attended Saturday evening and Sunday morning Masses.

There was no saint's feast day today, so Moloney had selected a votive Mass honoring the Blessed Mother Mary. Now halfway through the Mass, he began the preface that would lead to the most important moment, the consecration.

The preface for this Mass was dedicated to Mary. Near the beginning of the preface were a number of options. One could salute Mary "on this your feast," or "on this festive occasion," or "as we honor your Son, Jesus."

Moloney began the preface with the series of antiphons and responses that lead into all prefaces, all the while trying to determine which of the options he would choose.

"The Lord be with you," he said.

"And also with you," they responded.

He decided he would use "on this your feast." With that in mind, he stumbled into the next antiphon.

"Lift up your feet," he said, instead of the proper "Lift up your hearts" that he should have said.

132

Fortunately, the nuns were alert. They burst out laughing. Had they been more somnolent, they would have responded, "We have lifted them up to the Lord."

The image of the congregation lifting up its collective feet to the Lord was hilarious enough to keep its various members snickering from time to time through to the end of the Mass.

At the conclusion, Moloney lamely attempted to explain how he had confused 'feast' with 'feet.' But he only caused more laughter. He gave it up, at last, as simply a bad way of beginning this Saturday.

Moloney was divesting in the sacristy when he thought he heard screams. Still wearing alb and cincture, he tentatively approached the door. Yes, those were definitely screams. And coming from more than one person.

He followed the sound until he reached the arch leading to the shrine dedicated to St. Frances Cabrini. Two of the nuns were standing before the new statue of St. Frances. They were screaming determinedly.

Moloney noticed first the man's head that had replaced the statue's head. It was horrible. The face was unnaturally white and contorted in terror. Moloney thought he was going to be ill.

Then he noticed what had been the marble head of the statue. It had been smashed into hundreds of pieces. The shards lay on the floor near the base of the statue.

Strangely, all Moloney could think was, Poor Ted, the parish council will tear him apart. The poor bastard hasn't even paid for the damn statue yet.

This, Moloney reflected, is indeed a bad way to begin a Saturday.

St. Frances Cabrini Church had not been this crowded on a Saturday morning since the previous Easter Saturday. And that crowd had come with food—Easter food—to be blessed. Basically a Polish custom, the Easter blessing of food had been adopted by most other Catholics as well.

Now, instead of being redolent of pungent sausage, the

church was swarming with police and news people.

Lieutenant Harris was directing the investigation. He had already dispatched Sergeants Patrick and Lynch to the headquarters of Garnet Fitzgerald. He had also assigned Patricia Karnego and Fred Ross to act as liaison with the Organized Crime Division, since Fitzgerald's numbers racket fell under their jurisdiction.

Harris responded to the repeated questions, initially from the television and radio people, who were always first to begin and end their stay at a news scene, then from the print people.

Yes, this appeared to be another in the series of Red Hat Murders, if you've got to keep on calling them that. But the investigation is not completed. No, the police have no further solid leads. Yes, there are some possible suspects but he was not at liberty to reveal any names. No, dammit, the police department was not looking the other way while Detroit's criminal element was wiping itself out.

As was his wont, Joe Cox stood apart from the madding crowd of reporters. He was aware of the questions and answers, but his eyes alertly scanned the assemblage. He relied on what frequently proved an unerring instinct that led him to the soft underbelly of a story.

Right now, his intuition was leading him in the direction of Father William Moloney. Cox knew that Moloney was director of education for the Detroit archdiocese. He hadn't known of Moloney's residency here. After being questioned by the police, Moloney had stood about the fringes of activity and was attended by no one. Cox moved across the church to stand next to him.

"Hi, Father, I didn't know you lived here."

"Oh," the surprised Moloney replied, "hello, Joe."

They had met many times at news conferences where Moloney had played the role of Official Archdiocesan Spokesman.

"Can you tell me anything about this statue?" Cox nodded toward the literally defaced St. Frances Cabrini.

"On or off the record, Joe?"

"Whichever way you say."

"Off."

"O.K."

"Only that the pastor here has been carrying his ass in a sling because of it."

"How's that?"

Moloney explained the prodigality and the parish council's reaction.

"Then," Cox asked, "this statue is a rather recent addition to this church?"

"Oh, yes," Moloney said. "Father Neighbors had pretty well kept it under his hat, I think for fear of the parishioners' reaction. And judging from the reaction of the parish council, he was correct in his foreboding of doom."

"Until the statue was placed in the church a couple of weeks ago," Cox persisted, "who would you say knew of its existence?"

"Oh, I'd say the artist, Ted Neighbors, and, as one born out of due time, he let me in on it. That's about the size of it."

"Thanks, Father." Cox shut his notebook and tucked pen in pocket.

"You mean that was a help?" Moloney asked.

"You don't know how much," Cox said, as he turned to leave.

As he walked down the aisle, he glanced back at the fated statue. For the first time, he noticed Pat Lennon standing motionless before the statue, staring at it. Poor girl, he thought, she's going to have to abandon her hypothesis about the relevance of the hat and statues to the solution of these murders. He was about to blow that line of reasoning out of the water. Since no one had known of the existence of the Cabrini statue until a couple of weeks ago except three people who couldn't possibly be involved in these murders, no one could have made the necessary plans long enough in advance to use this statue as a statement of any kind.

He would use this in the lead of his article on the Red Hat murderer striking again.

He'd have to talk to Pat tonight. She would undoubtedly feel down in the dumps after she read his piece.

The scene inside St. Frances Cabrini rectory was not as confused as that in the church, but it was no happier.

Since Father Moloney had been scheduled to offer morning Mass, Father Neighbors had not expected to be needed until at least early Saturday afternoon. Armed with this assurance, Neighbors had put away a bit too much wine before going to bed Friday night. As a result of all that wine and the unexpected discovery of the decapitated statue and the severed head, Neighbors was nursing an impressive hangover.

Which was nothing compared with his anguish at the iconoclasm that had been committed in his church.

Moloney had wakened him, after much effort, just before nine this morning to give him the sad news. At the time, he had treated it as a nightmare and had pulled the covers back over his head.

He had been unable to extend this defense mechanism to the police investigation. Fortunately, since the police had gotten most of their information from Moloney, they had blessedly few questions for him. Since the time he had decided to face reality, he had been steadily drinking the coffee Mrs. Bovey kept pumping into him. It was not helping much.

The doorbell rang. More loudly in his head than at the chimes in the kitchen. Though it was painful, he shouted to Mrs. Bovey that he would answer the door.

It was Sergeant Farrell, that abrupt young woman who had called on him earlier.

"Yes?" He tried very hard to concentrate.

"Lieutenant Harris," she said, "wants you to know that the lock on the side door of the church has been broken."

Wordlessly, he shut the door. Woe upon woe. His precious statue was ruined. That nasty situation would have to be faced and handled eventually. Now the door lock was broken. That would have to be faced immediately. He wondered if he could enlist Moloney's help.

This was indeed a poor way to begin a Saturday.

Pat Lennon had convinced her assistant news editor, Bob Ankenazy. Now both were making their case with Leon London, managing editor. London was empowered to make a final decision. And a final decision would have to be made very soon.

Lennon explained her hypothesis for the third and, she hoped, final time.

The Red Hat was an outrageous pun for capital punishment. St. Cecilia's storied purity was an outrageous travesty on Detroit's premier pimp. St. Raphael, as patron saint of druggists, was symbolic of phencyclidine, more popularly known as PCP, or in street parlance, angel dust.

Pat had checked all this with her expert source, Father Leo Clark, who had agreed with her hypothesis.

From the moment she had heard that Garnet Fitzgerald's head had been found on the statue of St. Frances Cabrini, she had been unable to draw any connection between them. She had called Father Clark again, and again he had agreed with her.

Mother Cabrini, Clark reported, was an Italian immigrant who became a naturalized citizen. She had worked among the poor in New York and, he had been positive, there was no possible connection between the saint and the operator of a numbers racket. Not even in travesty.

Pat's conclusion: Fitzgerald's was not one of The Red Hat Murders.

As if to bolster her rather flimsy evidence, *News* reporters still on the scene reported that the police were taking an unaccountable amount of time confirming that this was one more in that series.

Soon the *News* would have to go with something. But what?

The style that most readers had become accustomed to

from the *News* was a conservative approach with a great deal of hedging language. If the *News* ran Lennon's hypothesis and she were wrong, there would be little egg left for anyone else in Detroit. All of it would be on the *News'* corporate face.

The explanations and rationalizations were over. London pondered and paced. "What the hell, Lennon," he finally growled, "we didn't hire you because you were a cub. We'll go with your story. Write it and damn the torpedoes!"

Wayne County Medical Examiner Wilhelm Moellmann trudged up the staircase toward his second-floor office. As he reached the top step, he paused, momentarily overwhelmed by the unexpected sight of Inspector Walter Koznicki. Koznicki was seated on the wooden bench outside Moellmann's office.

"Well, well, well!" Moellmann extended his arm widely in an exaggerated gesture of welcome, while a large smile lit his face. "If it isn't the *head* of the entire operation!"

Koznicki, ever the gentleman, rose, removed his hat, and said, "Good morning, Doctor. I hope I am not calling on you too early." As he greeted Moellmann, he took a step toward the doctor, who recoiled involuntarily. Koznicki, it seemed, could have eaten the wiry little man and not known he'd had a meal.

"No, no, not too early." Moellmann recovered quickly and went staunchly on the offensive. "We received the present sent us by Squad Six of your homicide department. Or," he moved close to Koznicki, thus enhancing the disparity in their proportions, "the Headhunters, as Squad Six is known to us in the trade."

Koznicki resisted several urges to respond in kind. "Well, good doctor," he said instead, "have you any news for us?"

"Indeed I do. Oh, indeed I do." Moellmann found it necessary to walk around Koznicki in order to enter his own office. The extra motion destroyed his planned distracted attitude. People shouldn't be allowed to grow that large, he thought, as he led the abbreviated procession into his inner office.

As they passed through the outer office, Koznicki tendered Marge a semi-bow.

"Hawr y'all this dye, Inspectah?" she asked, with little evident interest.

"Just fine, Marge. And how are all of you?"

She blushed becomingly.

Moellmann seated himself in the straight-back chair in front of his desk. Koznicki lowered his bulk onto the couch, which made a groaning sound. They stared at each other in silence.

"Well?" Moellmann opened.

"Well?" Koznicki countered.

"I suppose you believe you have one more of those Red Hat Murders on your hands, don't you?"

"Unless you provide me with a good reason, I have no reason not to believe it."

"Oh, I have some reasons that may make you want to believe that this one will not fit in your red hat."

"Marge!" He yelled loudly enough to be heard throughout the second floor. "Marge! Bring me the Fitzgerald file!"

Marge's sigh was highly audible.

As she handed Moellmann the file, she nodded toward the black blood pressure sleeve resting on the corner of his desk. "Have y'all tiken yore bluhd pressure with theyat thang lately?"

"No, not lately," Moellmann replied. Marge remained about the only person who could put him on.

"Way-ell," she continued as she languidly returned to her office, "if y'all don't quee-ut usin' theyat tone a voice with me, youre gonna haftuh tike mahn."

Koznicki could not suppress a chuckle.

Moellmann, pretending it was still a scoreless tie between him and Marge, carefully studied the contents of the Fitzgerald file.

"You were saying, Doctor..." Koznicki returned the conversation to a professional level.

"Ah, yes." Moellmann used his index finger to shove his glasses back to the bridge of his nose. "Well, there are several differences between Fitzgerald's head and those of the previous victims, namely, Ruggiero, Harding, and Strauss."

He paused to make certain he had Koznicki's attention.

"Chief among these differences is that Fitzgerald's head has been embalmed."

"Embalmed!" Koznicki did not attempt to mask his surprise.

"Yes, embalmed. I would hazard a guess that Mr. Fitzgerald died without the appropriate expression on his face. And so, to effect such an expression, it was necessary to embalm him."

"I don't believe I understand—"

"You see," Moellmann said, "the others, Ruggiero, Harding, and Strauss, seem to have died in the grip of intense—no, intense is not a sufficiently powerful word—*supreme* fright. It was evident on their death masks. Do you remember?"

Koznicki nodded.

"Their eyes and mouths were the embodiment of stark terror."

"But Fitzgerald's death mask looked just like the others," objected Koznicki.

"Yes, it did, my dear Inspector. But each of the first three clearly died with that expression on his face. Terror became an intrinsic characteristic of their death masks. It was their natural, if final, expression. No embalming fluid was used in their heads."

"But Fitzgerald?"

"Fitzgerald evidently needed help to achieve that expression of ultimate terror. His head was embalmed and the expression was artificially formed, built, created, probably by a skilled mortician."

"But what if," Koznicki protested, "what if Fitzgerald

were killed by the same person who killed the first three, but for some reason he did not manage to frighten Fitzgerald as he had the others?"

"Ah, my dear Inspector, that brings us to the manner of removing the heads!" Moellmann was enjoying this moment of drama to the hilt.

"Yes?" Koznicki prodded.

"You may be familiar with my findings regarding the first three heads in the series," Moellmann rhetorized.

Koznicki nodded.

"It is my opinion that all three heads were removed by a very powerful, probably young, man who used the same slightly bent saw in each instance."

"I am familiar with those findings, Doctor."

"Well . . ." Moellmann's denouement was handled with flair. "Fitzgerald's head was removed very carefully with a surgical instrument. It is my opinion that a scalpel was used on the outer fleshy and muscular tissues, and then a saw—but not the flawed instrument used in the other beheadings—finished the job."

Moellmann settled back in his chair, extremely pleased with himself.

Koznicki smiled. He appreciated working with someone like Moellmann. Certainly not because of his histrionic tendencies, but because he was a professional who was very good in his scientific field.

The phone rang. In a moment, Marge stood in the doorway. "It's for yew, Inspectah."

It was Harris, calling from St. Frances Cabrini rectory.

"Walt, we're uncovering a bunch of details here that don't seem to fit into the established M.O."

"You tell me your good news," Koznicki said, "and I'll tell you mine."

Taken slightly aback, Harris continued. "First of all, this was not a clean entry like the other three. This was a clear case of breaking and entering. The lock on the side door of the church was jimmied."

"Go on."

"Then, the head of the statue was not cleanly removed like the other two. This one was smashed off and pretty well demolished."

"Is there more?"

"Yeah, one more. There are some pretty clear prints on the door, on the plinth and on the statue itself."

"That it?"

"Yeah, that's it. Either our killer got awfully sloppy for some reason, or this is just not one of The Red Hat Murders."

"The latter, Ned."

Koznicki related the Medical Examiner's findings. As he finished, Harris gave a long, low whistle.

"I'll be damned, Walt, some damn fool turkey has tried to get in on The Red Hat Murders! I think we're gonna burn some asses."

"I couldn't agree with you more."

The phone conversation concluded, Koznicki turned back to Moellmann. "I think very shortly I will be able to present you with something you've wanted and deserved for too long a time."

Moellmann looked up at Koznicki quizzically.

"A body," said Koznicki, "to go with the latest head."

As it happened, only Pat Lennon's account of the murder was correct. But no one in the news media knew this until a hastily called news conference was held at Detroit Police Headquarters at 8:15 Saturday evening.

At this gathering, Koznicki and Harris, without revealing any of the details they wanted kept from the public, explained that Garnet Fitzgerald's apparent murder was not another in the series of Red Hat Murders. They admitted there was a resemblance to the other murders and that the resemblance had undoubtedly been intended. However, they concluded, there were enough discrepancies in the method of operations that there was no doubt that Fitzgerald's head had been placed in the church by someone other than whoever had placed the first three heads.

This information had surprisingly little effect on the television and radio newscasters. They had been incorrect at 5:30 P.M. They would be correct at the eleven o'clock wrap-up. Perhaps their relative indifference was due to the ephemeral nature of their media. News was carried over the air and promptly became equally invisible.

This was not the case with the print medium.

Joe Cox had written an erroneous story. It was too late to catch the first Sunday edition. He returned to the city room to rewrite the story for a later edition, but his initial error was there in black and white. Neither he nor his editors would quickly forget the error. Should there be a chance they might forget, the other news media would find subtle ways of reminding them.

Pat Lennon returned to the *News* to add details to her story, which was not only accurate, but filled with many more particulars than the police had disclosed at the news conference.

She returned to the Lafayette Towers apartment about 10 P.M. and waited for Cox.

He did not come home Saturday night or Sunday morning.

It had been a most busy but satisfying weekend. Now, late Sunday evening, three large men sat around Inspector Koznicki's kitchen table reminiscing and eating the sandwiches and beer snack prepared by Koznicki's wife, Wanda.

"I can think of a few reasons, but not many," Harris said, "why anybody would go on playing the numbers when there are legal lotteries in Michigan."

"Especially," Koznicki added, "when the lotteries are on the up and up. If you win, you win. There is no shifting the winning number if too many hit on it."

Inspector Frank Thompson, head of the DPD's Organized Crime Division, sighed. "Well, there's lots of reasons." Thompson, black, with a seemingly perpetual quizzical expression, was the only one of the three in uniform. "First and foremost for lots of these people, it's a habit. They've been doing it for years, sometimes doing business with the same runner, and they're simply not going to break it. Some establish such a close relationship with the runner that they'd sooner leave home than stop doing business at the same old corner."

"Then too," Thompson added as he applied horseradish liberally to a colossal corned beef, roast beef, ham, and chicken sandwich, "in the numbers, a person can invest as little as a nickel."

"And you must remember, Ned," said Koznicki, his eyes riveted on Thompson's first bite of his super sandwich, "if a person happens to hit a number, the winnings are tax-free."

"Yes," mumbled Thompson as he fought through his first bite, "and, unlike the lotteries, the numbers can be played on credit."

"And that," Harris said, "can lead to trouble. When the mob's collection agency comes calling, they sometimes literally take a pound or so of flesh."

"Another spot of trouble," Thompson said, "comes when one numbers king invades another's territory."

"That," said Koznicki, "brings us back to Fitzgerald."

"It may have been stupid of Fitzgerald to step on Yaphet's toes," Harris said, "but that can't begin to touch the stupidity of Yaphet's boys. Imagine," Harris popped the top of a Stroh's can, "using Sugar Lemon!"

"Yes," said Koznicki, "it was good of Lemon to leave his prints all over St. Frances Cabrini Church. But, then, doing unwise things like that is the way Sugar built his impressive record of arrests and convictions."

"Likewise," Thompson paused in the destruction of his sandwich to swallow some beer, "it was kind of Billy Bates to hire Lemon at the funeral home. Even if he did hire him as a bodyguard and use him to plant Fitzgerald's head because Lemon, being a felon would, of course, know how to do it right!"

All three laughed.

"And," said Harris, "wasn't Bates cooperative in telling us just where and from whom he got the head."

"One thing, though," Thompson became serious, "we'll never get Yaphet on a charge like this. We will slice nicely into his numbers game for a while and pick off a few of his prized lieutenants, but, you'll see, when we catch up with Yaphet, he'll have an air-tight alibi. And no one will dare squeal on him."

"Well," said Harris, "at least we finally got Doc Moellmann a body complete with bullet holes."

"That's true," Koznicki scratched his head. "But we're back to square one."

"How's that?" Harris asked.

"Who committed The Red Hat Murders?"

The three silently finished their sandwiches.

No doubt about it, Father Koesler thought, it was easier in the good old days. Weekdays, back when there was a daily high Mass, had involved nothing more than being sufficiently awake to sing the notes and read the words in the *Missale Romanum*.

Those *were* the good old days, he thought. Although he had reluctantly joined the movement for liturgical reform, at one point he had found himself in the vanguard in defense of the new vernacular liturgy. As editor of the *Detroit Catholic*, he had written scathing attacks aimed at those who were dedicated to the preservation of the Latin Mass. In response to their argument that Latin was a sign of universality in that one could attend a Mass offered similarly throughout the world, he had written that the Mass was equally unintelligible, at least to the majority of the laity, no matter in which country one found oneself.

However, he now had to admit, the baby had been thrown out with the bath water. Most of the English liturgical texts lacked literary quality; the mystic mystery of carefully worded Latin was gone; the glory of Gregorian Chant was a misty memory; and the music that had been composed to replace Chant was, by and large, puerile.

As mistaken as he now thought himself to have been about liturgical change, Koesler was far more repentant over his original stand regarding Church law.

He recalled attending a lecture given by the famous theologian, Father Bernard Häring, a few years before Vatican Council II. There had been standing room only in Sacred Heart Seminary's auditorium. Most of the priests attending the lecture had been younger than Koesler.

He had found Häring's easy familiarity with the Bible most impressive. When it came to the question and answer session, one bearded young priest rose to ask Häring what connection there was between canon law and the law of Christ. After a moment's reflection, Häring had responded, "There isn't any."

The response had elicited laughter and applause from the young priests. Koesler had been infuriated. However, ensuing years of experience and thought had convinced him that it was not quite true to claim there was no connection between the 2,414 laws of the Church and the law of Christ. Actually, one was the antithesis of the other. While the law of Christ centered around selfless love, all canon law's presumptions favored the institutional Church.

On January 25, 1959, Pope John XXIII called for the convening of a Vatican Council *and* the reform of canon law. The Council had come and gone, but canon law remained about as welcome as the man who came to dinner.

In practice, Koesler bent Church law as far as he feasibly could to serve the needs of individuals.

One of the nicer things about the new liturgy, he thought as he rescued his mind from this stream of consciousness, was its fresh emphasis on the presence of God through Sacred Scripture.

In weekday Masses, now, there were always two readings from the Bible, one usually from the Old Testament, the other always from the Gospels. The priest was urged to deliver a brief homily. Koesler enjoyed working on the three- to five-minute daily sermon. It kept his mind actively involved with the Scriptures. More than that, he enjoyed finding the connection, vague as it sometimes was, between the two Bible readings. It reminded him of the mystery novels he was forever reading. He simply enjoyed solving puzzles whether they might be the reasons some liturgist thought two readings could complete one message, or the more traditional whodunit.

The readings for this Monday morning's Mass were from Isaiah, Chapter 40, Verses one to eight. The Old Testament reading promised the arrival of someone who would prepare the way for another. The Gospel reading recounted the story of John the Baptizer preparing the way for Christ. The connection was clear and the message, clearly, was an invitation to prepare for the presence of Christ in our lives and in the lives of others.

Now if only he could think of some homey illustrations in which to couch the message. But he was not to have that opportunity. The phone rang.

Before lifting the receiver, Koesler breathed a quick prayer that the caller not be Mrs. Lester, who was one-half of a sadomasochistic couple—a twosome present in almost every parish. Mrs. Lester regularly wasted Koesler's time with lengthy phone monologues detailing her husband's sadistic behavior. She did not lie. Koesler had seen the bruises on her face and arms. It was useless advising her either to leave her husband or force him to move. They needed each other in very sick ways—like the cliché, Koesler thought, the rocks in his head fit the holes in hers. And neither would agree to accept the level of psychic aid that in any event was beyond Koesler's ability to offer.

Fortunately for the 8 A.M. Mass' chance of beginning on time, the caller was not Mrs. Lester. It was Koesler's old friend, Inspector Koznicki.

"Congratulations, Inspector," Koesler greeted him warmly. "I see by this morning's *Free Press* that you had a very speedy and successful investigation this past weekend."

"Thank you, Father," said Koznicki. "But it wasn't all that difficult."

Partly because there was a little of the Old World in both Koesler and Koznicki, each invariably accorded the other his respective title of 'Father' and 'Inspector,' even in casual conversation.

"It's not like you to be modest, Inspector." Koesler took a toothpick from his shirt pocket and contemplated it.

"It's not modesty, Father. The executioners of Garnet Fitzgerald left a trail that could have been followed by a Cub Scout."

The word "executioners" brought to Koesler's mind the gory details of Fitzgerald's death. Details that one of the daily papers, he couldn't recall which, recounted all too explicitly. What does violent death do? It sells newspapers.

"And did you see, Father," Koznicki continued, "that the Fitzgerald killing proved to be an unsuccessful imitation of The Red Hat Murders?"

"Well, yes, though it was a bit confusing. I got an early Sunday edition of the *Free Press* that carried a story—I think it was Joe Cox's byline—that claimed it was another Red Hat Murder. Then I read a *News* story that claimed it wasn't. This morning's *Free Press* appears to agree with the *News*' account."

Koesler pronounced Cox's name with the reverence due a Pulitzer Prize winner mixed with the sense of amazement appropriate to the phenomenon of the prize winner's having been dead wrong. Koesler, mostly out of habit from his editorial days, was one of some few Detroiters who read both *News* and *Free Press* daily.

"Yes, all of that is correct, Father." Koznicki caught the emphasis given Cox's name. "It just proves that even the mighty sometimes fail."

"Quo modo ceciderunt fortes."

"I beg your pardon, Father?"

"Nothing. Just the Latin form of your comment about Joe Cox's failure." The Latin must have surfaced as a result of his recent bout with nostalgia.

"What I'm calling you about, Father, is the other story,

the one in the *News* written by Miss Lennon . . . you *have* read it?"

"Yes."

"What did you think of it? Specifically, I am interested in the reasons she enumerated for the placement of the heads."

Koesler chuckled. "I agree with her completely."

"Why did you laugh?"

"Because Miss Lennon called the other day to ask just those questions. I gave her Father Clark as a source. I have complete confidence in Father Clark. Besides, after she called, I did a little research myself and came to the same conclusions. I was about to call and offer you my hypothesis when I read Miss Lennon's story. Then I felt the call was unnecessary."

"It is an interesting hypothesis and I felt it had the ring of truth," Koznicki agreed, "but, at the moment, I don't know how it will help find the murderer."

Koesler hesitated. "Inspector, do you ever get the feeling that he—whoever he is—is doing Detroit a favor?"

"Oh, he is doing Detroit a favor! I have never seen organized crime so disorganized. Most of the major crime figures are openly confused. But the day of the vigilante is over. We cannot condone murder, even of known criminals. However, our greatest problem now is that the murderer may be finished."

"Finished?"

"Yes. He killed three people last week, on Saturday, Monday, and Wednesday, every other day. There have been no more, that we know of, since last Wednesday. Homicide considers it very possible that the murderer has accomplished what he set out to do—badly rattle the criminal community. And now he is done."

"Fascinating!"

"But it also means we will likely be provided with no further clues. And we have precious little to go on. For one thing, I dearly would like to find the bodies that belong with those heads. Meanwhile, Father, I would appreciate your giving additional thought to those statues and that hat. It is very possible the hypothesis you and Miss Lennon have arrived at may be accurate. But we must know how it fitted into the killer's scheme of things.

"And thank you, Father, for your time."

"Not at all. Should I come across any headless bodies, I'll let you know."

"Or headless statues, for that matter, Father."

The morning homily, due to unforeseen circumstances that caused lack of sufficient preparation, would be very brief.

It would be inaccurate to state that Joe Cox had been humbled by his blunder. He had been, and still was, angry at himself.

On his return to the city room Saturday evening to correct and rewrite his story, he had been well chewed out by a Nelson Kane fortified with righteous anger. Thereafter, he had conducted a one-man tour of interesting bars, each sleazier than the one before. He had gotten falling-down drunk and wakened Sunday afternoon in the bed of a female who was not Pat Lennon. By the time he returned to the Lafayette Towers apartment, Pat Lennon was not talking to him. Counting his monumental hangover, by and large it had not been a weekend worth enshrining.

Now, this Monday morning, he did not wish to appear at work empty-handed. So, en route to the *Free Press*, he stopped off at Police Headquarters.

Later, arriving at his desk, he was about to be seated when he heard a familiar voice.

"Cox!" Kane bellowed. "You're late!"

The nice thing about Kane, thought Cox, is that he did not hold a grudge. If he was angry, he let you know it. But that was that. Grudges were the department of Karl Lowell and he held them as a miser holds his coins.

However, if you were tardy arriving for work, as Cox indisputably was, Kane would not overlook it just because he'd read you the riot act at the latest previous encounter.

Cox approached Kane's desk warily, pinching his forehead between thumb and index finger.

"Easy, Nellie," he implored, "I took a Bromo this morning and pleaded with it not to fizz."

Kane nodded. He knew the feeling.

"How's Lennon?" he asked.

"I'm not sure. She is deciding whether to talk to me ever again."

"She did a good job with her story Sunday."

"Damn right," Cox agreed. "I told you I had the feeling this was her story."

"'Her story' and twenty cents will get you a *Free Press*." Kane tended to discount intuition in the gathering of news. "It doesn't surprise me that Lennon did a good job—she's a good reporter. And," he reminded needlessly, "we trained her.

"What does surprise me is that the editors at the *News* gave her her head."

"Yeah, that's not like them. Maybe they were inspired."

"We could use a little of that inspiration."

"Maybe not." Little by little, Cox's head was clearing. If only he could survive the day. "I was just over at headquarters. The cops think the Red Hat murderer is finished."

"Really? Are you sure? Are *they* sure?"

"Got it from Harris himself. They figure the guy hit three times last week on alternate days. But nobody's heard from him since last Wednesday. They figure he's made his statement. He set out to get the attention of Detroit's top hoods, and he got it!"

"So they'll be working with the leads they've got?"

"So they say."

"O.K. I'm going to put McNaught on The Red Hat Murders. I want you to get on the city's Community and Economic Development Department."

"The C&EDD? What've they done wrong now?"

"It's what they haven't done. I want a nice balanced series, maybe a four- or five-parter, all about the time it takes them to complete a project. This will be a good spot to highlight bureaucratic bungling."

"Why do I have to go all the way over to the City-County Building to do a story on bureaucratic bungling?" Cox asked. "Why don't I just visit the neighboring office and interview Karl Lowell."

"Get the hell out of here," Kane snarled.

Pat Lennon huddled with her assistant news editor.

In the age-old rivalry between the *News* and *Free Press*, each had had its share of awards, glory, and scoops. But when one beat the other as clearly as the *News* had beaten the *Free Press* on the latest Red Hat Murder, it was a cause for special pride. An air of exhilaration seemed to be flowing through the Old Grey Lady, even on this dark and damp September Monday.

"But," said Bob Ankenazy, "you said the cops think it's all over. That the Red Hat killer is not going to hit again."

"That's what Colleen Farrell told me on the phone half an hour ago," Lennon replied.

"But you don't buy it."

"No, I don't." Lennon turned in her chair to directly face Ankenazy. "I'm convinced we've found the motives for the murderer's putting the heads in the hat and on the statues. It makes a logical statement. But, as of now, there is no logical conclusion. And a logical statement, it seems to me, demands a logical conclusion. I don't know what objective point we've reached in the plans of the killer, but I am positive we're in the eye of the tornado."

Ankenazy thought a moment. He considered Lennon's hypothesis mostly the product of intuition. And he, like Nelson Kane, thought intuition had no place in a newsroom. Yet, oddly, he was comfortable about following the course he was about to take—and play a hunch.

"What do you want to do, Pat?" he asked.

"I've got an excellent contact in Homicide's Squad Six —Sergeant Colleen Farrell. She's deeply into the women's movement so she's on my side. I want to stay in touch with the case through her and follow a couple of leads I've developed."

"O.K., follow through," Ankenazy advised. "But there's something else I'd like you to work on too. Edward Hines Parkway is slowly being destroyed each summer. I'd like you to start working up a series on the Parkway. It's the ideal time now that we're concluding the season. You can play on the juvenile delinquency angle along with the early drinking age. Obviously, the big hook is the easy availability of drugs throughout the Parkway."

Lennon could spot a hedged bet when she was the victim of one. But if she were going to stay on The Red Hat Murders she saw no alternative.

"O.K.," she agreed. "From the sublime to the ridiculous. But when the leads get hot and/or the killer strikes again, Edward Hines Parkway gets the back seat."

"You got it," Ankenazy agreed.

Lennon parked this agreement in her subconscious. She had no experience in verbal agreements with the *News*, but she was willing to make an investment in trust at least this once.

"I have this plan that I think will work, or at least help us," said Detective Colleen Farrell, "and Papkin here has agreed to cooperate with me on it."

Farrell was addressing Lieutenant Harris. Sergeant Charlie Papkin stood beside her. The three were alone in the squad room after a general Monday morning meeting of Squad Six.

"O.K., Farrell," Harris said, "I'm listening."

Harris, along with the other members of Squad Six, had to almost deliberately slow the adrenaline after the past weekend's breakneck pace of events.

It was by no means usual to close an investigation of a major murder case successfully in little more than a single day. But the Fitzgerald case had renewed their confidence in their ability to wrap up homicides. After a week of drifting with almost no clues to The Red Hat Murders and traveling up one blind alley after another, their self-confidence had been suffering to some degree.

"Well," Farrell explained, "one of our theories involves a possible conspiracy between the killer and one of the clergypersons attached to one of the parishes involved."

"Yes?" Harris sat down as did the two detectives. Never as cautious as his friend Inspector Koznicki, Harris, at this point, was open to any possible lead.

"It seems to me," said Farrell, "that if any of our clergypersons is involved even in a conspiracy, he or she would have to have a pretty casual attitude toward the law."

Harris thought a moment. "Yes, I guess I'd have to agree with that."

"My next assumption," Farrell continued, "is that *if* we are dealing with such a person and *if* that person has a disregard for civil law that permits collaboration with a murderer, this same person probably will have a very similar attitude toward canon law, the law of his or her own Church."

"Now hold on a bit," Harris objected. "I don't see the connection. I can see the possibility of a priest's thinking he was doing a good deed in a sort of passive cooperation with somebody who was killing known criminals, but I don't see how that attitude would spill over into his own Church law."

"Trust her," said Papkin, who had been smiling through nearly all the exchange between Farrell and Harris.

Harris reflected that he might, indeed, invest a measure of blind trust in Farrell. He knew she was so deeply involved in Catholicism that she had taken courses in theology at the University of Detroit.

"Yes, trust me," said Farrell. "In the eyes of not a few Catholic clergypersons, there are far better reasons to respect American civil law than Catholic Church law."

"There are?" asked Harris.

"Yes, indeed," she answered. "Supposing the United States Supreme Court, some twenty years ago, had declared our whole system of civil law to be outdated and had ordered it to be revised. And then, suppose in these twenty years, nothing had been done about it."

Harris whistled softly. "You mean that's the shape law is in in the Catholic Church?"

"Yup," she said. "So it is not all that rare to find a priest who is very discouraged with Church law and resentful of it. I think that if we are dealing with a priest who is willing to collaborate with a murderer, after the fact, for what he considers to be a noble cause, then I think we must also be dealing with a man who will be selective in the enforcement of certain laws of the Church that are badly in need of reform."

"Like what?" Harris asked.

"Like the laws regarding remarriage," she answered.

"O.K., Farrell, what's your idea?" Harris felt he was learning more about the Catholic Church than he had any need to know for the investigation of any case besides The Red Hat Murders.

"This is where Charlie comes in," Farrell said, gesturing toward the still-smiling Papkin. "Posing as a couple who want to get married, we will go to consult certain clergy-persons. Charlie will pretend he has been divorced from a wife he married in the Church. Both he and his first wife will have been Catholic, and there will be no way Church law would grant them an annulment. And, of course I will be a Catholic. I might even have been married and di-vorced—from a bad, bad husband.

"We'll just get the reaction of these clergypersons to our plight. Will they ignore Church law and help us for the good reason that we need help? Or will they insist on fol-lowing the letter of the law? If they enforce canon law, it should at least reduce the possibility of their being involved in a conspiracy."

"What do you think?" Harris asked Papkin.

"It's better than anything I can think of." He shrugged. "It may eliminate some of the people we're thinking about."

"It's at least as good as anything I can think of," said

Harris. "O.K., Farrell, how long do you think this will take?"

"A couple of days at most."

"Who do you plan to visit?"

"Dolson, that guy at the cathedral who is so fond of guns. Sheehan, the one who heads the C.Y.O. and seems to have too flip an attitude toward regulations. And the deacon, Toussaint, whose alibis I and several others on the squad consider too pat."

"I didn't know deacons could perform marriages," said Harris.

"Sure they can," said Farrell. "They can do anything priests do except say Mass and hear confessions."

Harris stood to leave and let Farrell and Papkin finalize their plans. "One last thing, Colleen," he said. "Make sure you and Charlie don't bump into too liberal a *clergyperson*," he emphasized the word, "or you might *have* to get married."

Five

SACRED HEART SEMINARY

The squat one-story brick building stood on Antietam, a winding street on the eastern fringe of downtown Detroit. The building, bearing the sign, "Services, Inc.," was an abortion clinic. It had been built a decade before when, as part of the women's movement, abortion came out of the closet and began to be accepted by many as a legitimate method of terminating pregnancy.

Those familiar with Services, Inc. knew it to be among the worst of its ilk. It was an abortion mill. There was neither consideration nor concern for the clients. It was popular—very popular—for one reason: it offered relatively inexpensive abortions while maintaining an image slightly better than the back-alley clothes hanger approach. What was lost in higher fees at Services, Inc. was more than compensated for in volume of trade.

Diane Garson stood on the sidewalk near the entrance to Services, Inc. From where she stood she could see the blue and white sign of Detroit Memorial Hospital, where she would have received much better but higher-priced treatment. She also stood in view of Lafayette Clinic, which offered the type of psychiatric services that many clients of Services, Inc. would eventually need.

After fidgeting with her purse for several minutes, she determined to go through with it. She entered the clinic.

The waiting room was not large. Twelve straight-back chairs were tucked tightly against the walls with very little space between them. Only one chair was vacant.

Diane approached the receptionist's small desk, behind which was seated a woman in a nurse's uniform.

"Yes?" The woman looked up from her writing. She gave the impression of being angered by the interruption.

"I . . . I'd like to see about having an abortion." Earlier in her young life, Diane would have wagered she would never make that request. It was in conflict with everything in her Catholic upbringing. But she and her boyfriend had had intercourse, awkwardly, in the back of his van, and now she was late.

"What makes you think you're pregnant?" the woman asked.

Diane wished she would use a lower tone of voice. She glanced around. Several women had looked up from their magazines and were openly listening to the conversation.

"I . . . I'm two weeks late."

A hint of a smile crossed the woman's face. This clinic handled everyone from those who used abortion as a routine method of birth control to kids as naive as this one. A girl like this, she thought, might not even know one had to have intercourse to get pregnant.

"How old are you?"

"Eighteen."

"So you have medical insurance?"

"I'm covered by my dad's insurance. He works on the line at Ford's. But I'm going to pay for this myself."

"For someone at your term, that will be one hundred dollars for the procedure and twenty dollars today for the test. Both must be paid in advance."

Diane gulped. She had not expected there would be this much expense. She had checked with other, more reliable clinics and learned that the going rate for the procedure was one hundred and sixty dollars. So she was saving money even though this would nearly wipe out her bank account.

"All right," she agreed, "what do I have to do?"

"First," said the woman, "you pay the twenty dollars and then you fill out this form."

Diane laid on the desk a ten-dollar bill, a five, and five ones. She accepted the form from the nurse and took the only empty chair. She was aware that the women on either side of her were reading her answers as she filled out the form. Some of the questions were distinctly personal and she was embarrassed.

She returned the completed form to the nurse and waited expectantly. The nurse removed a small clear bottle from a desk drawer.

"You did not bring a specimen with you?"

Diane shook her head. A look of impatience crossed the woman's face.

"Take this," she said, handing Diane the bottle, then indicating by glancing at a door, "and go in there. Once you've put your specimen in this bottle—you do know what I'm talking about, don't you?"

Diane nodded.

"—bring it back to me."

Diane entered the other room. Like the reception room, its walls were stark white unrelieved by a single work of art. In the room were four gurneys, each bearing a woman draped with a white sheet. This had to be either the waiting or the recovery room. Diane felt a sense of an assembly line.

There were no curtain separations or modesty shields. There were two toilets, in separate open cubicles. In these surroundings, it took Diane a while to produce a specimen. She did so awkwardly, spilling a small amount of urine on the outside of the bottle. Only then did she notice the empty tissue roll. There was nothing to dry either the bottle or herself.

She returned to the reception area and handed the bottle to the receptionist, who received it with evident disgust, adding immeasurably to Diane's embarrassment.

"When will you know?" Diane asked softly.

"We'll call you in a day or so," the woman said in her matter-of-fact tone.

"I'd rather you didn't. I'll be glad to call you."

"Then call late tomorrow."

Thoroughly mortified, Diane left the clinic.

That's odd, she thought, nobody once mentioned the possibility that I might not be pregnant.

Sacred Heart Seminary is an enormous basically Gothic structure in west central Detroit. It is very near the area that suffered the greatest destruction during the 1967 riot. Fundamentally, the seminary is built in the form of a square. In the central courtyard is the chapel. At each of the four corners is an added wing. At one, residence halls; at another, a gym and recreation facility; at a third, an auditorium, and at a fourth, a nuns' residence and infirmary.

Only a few nuns still lived at the seminary. They were all elderly and did little but help prepare the meals, mend and iron the seminarians' clothing when it returned from the laundry, and pray.

Many sections of the rambling building were used for non-seminary purposes or simply closed off. There were not many candidates for the priesthood in this college seminary.

At one time, some twenty years before, the walls had bulged with seminarians.

Now, late this Tuesday afternoon, four seminarians had just completed a vigorous game of handball and were preparing for dinner. All four were college freshmen and, like all the seminarians, were residents of the institution.

"I have my own theory about those Red Hat Murders," said Vito Lombardo. He stood naked before a small mirror. The towel he had used to dry himself after the shower was draped over his shoulders. He was carefully combing his thick black hair.

"What's that?" asked Joe Smolenski, getting into his underwear.

"I figure it's a religiously oriented sociopath with homicidal tendencies." Lombardo fancied himself a budding psychologist. He had read two textbooks on psychotherapy.

"Oh, I don't think so, Vito," said Dick Kiefer, struggling into trousers that fit like a glove. "My pastor says it's probably members of the mob rubbing each other out."

"What about the Catholic churches?" asked Kevin Dunne, tying his shoelaces.

"The Mafia," Kiefer clarified. "Italian gangsters."

"Watch that!" Lombardo warned.

"I've been meaning to ask you, Vito," said Smolenski, "why is it the first thing you do after a shower is comb your hair?"

"In case of fire," Lombardo replied.

"Well, I think," said Dunne, "that it's somebody on a lower level of the criminal community of Detroit who is simply clearing the way to the top for himself."

"Why the churches?" asked Smolenski.

Dunne glanced at Lombardo. "Irish Catholics," he said.

"Will you look at this?" cried Kiefer. "This takes the cake!" He had taken a white, long-sleeved shirt from his laundry box.

He now held it by the collar and let it hang out. "Remember last week?" he demanded. "Remember I had just one button left right here in the middle?"

The others nodded.

"Well, it's gone," Kiefer declared. "And look what those crazy old nuns did: they sewed up all the buttonholes!"

It was true. Each buttonhole had been stitched shut with white thread.

"That," said Dunne, "is the *bad* news. This," he said, holding up a pair of undershorts, "is the *good* news."

It was anyone's guess whether the exhibited undershorts contained any of the original cloth. They had been patched that often.

"Personally," Smolenski said, "I tend to agree with Vito. It's got to be a religious fanatic."

"Vito," said Dunne, pointing at an article of athletic garb

hanging in Lombardo's locker, "why in hell don't you wash that jockstrap? If it had legs it would walk away."

"Yeah," Kiefer echoed, "that thing might spread jock itch to all of us by osmosis."

They laughed.

"Man," explained the macho Lombardo, "was not made to wash clothes."

"Yeah, I've been wondering," Smolenski mused, "why we're not supposed to send our jockstraps in the laundry with the rest of our clothes."

"It's the nuns," Dunne explained.

"The nuns?" Smolenski asked.

"Yeah," said Dunne, "the nuns don't know what a jockstrap is for."

"And," Lombardo added, "Holy Mother Church don't want 'em to find out."

They laughed, closed their lockers, and headed for a dinner whose piece de resistance would be bread and peanut butter.

"Was it because I got it right and you didn't?" Pat Lennon asked.

Joe Cox had returned to the apartment late Monday evening. Lennon decided it was time to bury the hatchet.

"No, no! Hell, no!" Cox replied. "It wasn't that. I wasn't jealous. And it wasn't because you got it right. Good for you for getting it right. No, it was because I got it wrong. I was just sore at myself for blowing it."

"Excuse the lack of modesty," Lennon moved into the kitchen to put a couple of frozen dinners in the oven, "but without my formula for putting the heads and the hat and the statues together, you couldn't have gotten it right. It appeared to be another Red Hat Murder and the cops didn't call their news conference until it was too late to catch the first edition."

"That's not what I mean." Cox called out more loudly so he could be heard in the kitchen. "It was the angle I took in that first edition. Claiming there was no rhyme or reason to the selection because Cabrini's statue was too new to be part of any long-range planning. That's what I got upset about."

"It wasn't too bad, Joe." Lennon returned to the living room and sat near Cox on the sofa. "It was only in the first edition."

Cox shook his head. "You haven't been listening to the radio, watching TV, or even reading your own paper, have you?"

"What do you mean?" She was genuinely surprised.

"They're not going to let me—or the *Free Press*—forget it. The prize-winning boy blew a big one."

"You'll get over it, Joe. You'll ride it through. You're too good not to."

"That's not all. Not only did I have a lost weekend, I didn't do a damn thing today. Just went through the motions, nursing the all-time winningest hangover I've ever had."

"Pretty well gone now?"

"Yeah." He shrugged. "Well, maybe I'll get lucky tomorrow."

Pat leaned toward him and winked. "Maybe you'll get lucky tonight."

Colleen Farrell wound up her fictional tale of broken marriages and Catholic backgrounds.

Father Fred Dolson made a few more notations on his pad and slowly shook his head.

"I fail to see any canonical reason to question the validity of either of your marriages," Dolson concluded.

"But Father," Farrell protested, "my husband was almost never home. And when he did come home he beat me. My God, the marriage—if you could call it that—lasted only a few months."

"And my wife," said Charlie Papkin, entering into the spirit of things, "drank, refused to care for the kids, and went out with other men. It's a miracle we stayed together as long as we did. And we did that only for the sake of the kids."

"Now, you see," Dolson used his most conciliatory tone, "you still refer to these people as your 'husband' and your 'wife.'"

"Semantics!" Farrell interjected ruefully.

"Isn't there some way of getting you all back together again?" asked Dolson.

"No way whatsoever," said Papkin. "We're in love and we want to be married."

Dolson tapped his pen against the desk top for a few moments. He was uncomfortable. He did not like to be in the company of people with terminal illness or people with insoluble problems.

"Why don't you go talk to your own pastors?" Dolson temporized.

"We did," said Farrell, "but they said they couldn't help us. Then someone told us about you and recommended we see you."

That, thought Dolson, is unique. No one had ever been referred to him for help by anyone.

"Well," Dolson tried to bring this unpleasantness to an end, "I'm afraid I'm in the same position as your pastors. I'm unable to do anything. The canon law on this is quite clear. Drunks and adulterers can contract valid marriages," he said to Papkin, then, turning toward Farrell, "as well as wife-beaters and deserters."

"Thank you for your trouble, Father," said Farrell, rising and starting toward the door.

"Not at all," said Dolson, ushering them out. "I'll keep you in my prayers."

Papkin and Farrell paused on the sidewalk outside Blessed Sacrament Cathedral rectory.

"We can forget about him," said Farrell. "That's Mr. Noninvolvement."

"Yeah," Papkin agreed, "pretty rigid on the law, too."

"That's not at all unusual among priests," Farrell said, "at least among the ones who are left. But the man we're looking for, I'm convinced, would be willing to bend, or even break this canonical barrier to true love." She smiled self-consciously.

"Well, there's one nice thing," said Papkin as they got into his car.

"What's that?"

"Father Dolson will pray for us."

"Tell me about it," said Farrell.

The faculty dining room in Sacred Heart Seminary had formerly been an open porch at the rear of the building's second floor. Meals, of average quality, were served cafeteria-style in the now glassed-in and remodeled room.

The faculty, once entirely clerical, was now about equally divided between priests and laypersons. Usually, nearly all the faculty and staff were present for luncheons. Such was the case today.

There was no seating prearrangement. Faculty and staff filled the tables in the order of their arrival. Today, at lunch, three priests happened to be seated at the same table as the rector, Monsignor Albert Martin.

"I just don't know about this new kid," commented Father Donald Osborn, registrar, and professor of Greek.

"Who's that?" asked Father Paul Burk, professor of philosophy.

"Vito Lombardo," said Osborn. "He looks to me as if he'll be a troublemaker."

"Probably nothing wrong with the kid," said Burk, whose premature baldness had been arrested by hair transplants. "He probably just needs a tin can tied to his tail and every time he stops running, somebody should drop-kick it." Burk laughed in spasms, as was his fashion.

"I tend to agree with you, Don," said Father Ed Harkins, professor of English and director of vocations for the archdiocese. "He doesn't show much respect for The Rule."

"Keep The Rule," Martin intoned, "and The Rule will keep you."

"Remember the kid we expelled last year?" asked Harkins. "The one who ran a hose up three flights and attached it to a water sprinkler that he put on top of the dormitory stalls and then at midnight turned on the water?"

"That kid showed a lot of spirit and imagination," Burk remonstrated.

"Well," Harkins continued, ignoring Burk, "Lombardo reminds me of him."

"What's the lad accomplished so far?" asked Martin, adding, "the season's young."

"The other night," Osborn warmed to his story as he buttered a slice of bread, "Lombardo decided to scare his buddy, Smolenski. So, while the boys were washing up before bed, he waited till Smolenski was shaving. Then he climbed up on his sink, peered over the partition, and whooped at Smolenski."

Burk began to laugh.

"Did Smolenski cut himself?" Martin asked.

"You know," Osborn confessed, "I didn't think to ask. But, you know, Lombardo is a pretty big kid. So, the sink gave way. Ripped right off the wall. Water everywhere."

Burk was about to say something when Harkins touched his arm.

"That," Harkins reminded, "didn't take much imagination."

"By the time the janitor arrived with a wrench, all Lombardo could say was, 'My ass is in a sling!'"

"I trust it was," said Martin.

"It was," said Osborn.

"You know, if we're not careful," said Burk, "all we'll send out into the world as priests will be automatons. They won't have any spirit or leadership qualities."

"I don't think that's possible," Martin said, "but if it were possible to produce automatons, I think Archbishop Boyle would be grateful."

"You know," said Burk very seriously, "I don't think he would."

"You may be right," Martin admitted, "maybe the Archbishop can live with a measure of ambivalence. Maybe I can't."

The checkout clerk requested and received a fifteen-minute relief.

Wearing her A&P uniform, she left the Highland Park supermarket and walked quickly to the pay phone near Second Avenue. She looked in all directions before entering the booth. No one seemed to notice her. She consulted a card, then dialed.

"Services, Incorporated," an emotionless voice announced.

"Is this the nurse?"

"Yes."

"This is Diane Garson. I was in to see you yesterday. You said I could call today—about my test."

"Oh, yes. Just a moment."

There was a pause while the nurse consulted her files.

"Yes, Miss Garson," she stressed the 'Miss.' "Your test turned out positive. You are pregnant," she lied.

Diane said nothing. It was as if her world had come to an end.

"Miss Garson? Miss Garson?"

"Yes."

"Do you want to have that taken care of? I can schedule you for tomorrow."

"How long will it take?"

"For someone in your condition and age, not long. A couple of hours. If you can arrange to take the morning off . . ."

Diane thought of all those women in the reception office and the four in the next room, and mentally placed herself in the lineup. It was not a pleasant prospect.

"Miss Garson? Miss Garson?"

"All right. What time do you want me there?"

"The earlier the better. We open at seven."

Diane silently vowed she'd be there when the doors opened. "One more thing . . ." She hesitated.

"What?" The nurse's tone left no doubt she wanted this conversation concluded.

"Is . . . is it really safe?"

"You have nothing to worry about."

Colleen Farrell and Charles Papkin sat opposite Father Joseph Sheehan in his Spartan office in the Gabriel Richard Building.

It was late in the afternoon and Farrell and Papkin, for the second time that day, had told a priest every lurid detail of their made-up marriages. Marriages that could be described only as unqualified disasters for both.

Early in her narration, Sheehan had busily taken notes. About halfway through her delivery, he had stopped writing and simply leaned back and listened.

Now he leaned forward, elbows on the desk.

"My gracious," he exclaimed, "you people have been to hell and back, haven't you? I suppose the divorces were messy?"

A bit taken aback by the priest's sincere sympathy, both Papkin and Farrell agreed that yes, their divorces had indeed been messy.

"I'm afraid the Church is not going to be much help to you now, either. You haven't got a prayer before the Church court. After all you've gone through, I wouldn't want to send you to the Tribunal. It would be messy, costly, almost interminable, and in the end futile.

"But that's neither here nor there. You intend to get married anyway, don't you?"

They nodded that, yes, that was their intention.

"Well then, why don't you? Your consciences tell you your previous attempts at marriage were nice tries but no good. Your consciences tell you you are free to marry, right?"

They nodded.

"Then get married in some appropriate fashion. A minister, a judge. Then, if you wish, just continue living as Catholics. Go to Mass, communion, the works. You may be tempted to mention your civil marriage in confession—just to clear the decks. Don't! It's not a sin if you follow your conscience. And that's what you're doing."

"And that's it?" Papkin asked.

"That's it," said Sheehan, "unless you want to stay to dinner. If you do that, you may meet the Archbishop. And that has a habit of stifling conversation at table."

"No, no," said Papkin as they all rose, "thank you ever so much."

"I'd appreciate it if you'd say a prayer for me," Sheehan said as Papkin and Farrell left his office.

"I think we've got a hot prospect," Papkin said as he and Farrell walked up Michigan Avenue toward the parking lot.

"No, we haven't," Farrell said, shaking her head. "He's just not the technical bastard that Dolson is. He handled it perfectly. That's the 'Pastoral Solution' where everything is kept in the internal forum."

"The what?"

"In a person's conscience. Catholic teaching is that everybody must form his or her own conscience and then follow it. That's what Father Sheehan just told us to do. It's the way most smart priests, at least the ones who want to stay priests, handle canon law now."

It was Papkin's turn to shake his head. "God, Coll, I'm a born-and-raised Catholic and I didn't know that. You ought to be a priest."

"No, I'm content to be a police officer. Besides, they'll get around to letting women be priests about the same time they revise canon law—or better, get rid of it."

They reached the parking lot.

"There's one thing I'm going to do before I go to sleep tonight," declared Papkin.

"What's that?"

He smiled charmingly. "I'm going to say a prayer for that guy."

* * *

Wednesday morning at seven sharp she was at the entrance to Services, Inc. Still, Diane Garson was seventh in line.

She sat for about an hour in the reception room. She tried to get interested in an old copy of *Sports Illustrated* but was too distracted. From time to time, a small voice within urged her to leave, but she could not.

For one thing, the nurse already had her hundred dollars. That had been paid even before she had removed her coat. And besides, there was no possible way she could care for a child. Since she was pregnant, an abortion would have to be performed sometime. Better that it be done now, early in the term.

There was no conversation among the waiting women. By now, all the chairs were filled; and two women stood leaning against the wall. No one looked very pregnant. The law required that after fourteen weeks, abortions be performed in hospitals. Even Services, Inc. observed that law.

"Garson!"

Finally. Diane rose and approached the receptionist's desk. The woman simply pointed with her pen to the door leading to the room wherein Garson had been so embarrassed two days before.

Inside, Diane encountered another nurse, who seemed slightly more human than the receptionist.

She was told to remove all her clothing and given a carton in which to store her things. The nurse handed her a medical gown and told her to lie on the room's one empty gurney. Both the gown and the sheeting bore numerous bloodstains that repeated washings had not entirely removed.

The nurse went into another room. "The Garson girl is waiting, Dr. Schmitt," she announced. "She's the one who isn't pregnant. Do you want to just go through the motions?"

Schmitt thought for a moment and stubbed out a cigarette as he sat down at the desk in his office. "Hell, no. She's paid her hundred dollars, hasn't she? Let's give her a bit of a show. Something for her money. We'll use the saline solution." He sat back and rested his feet on the desk.

The nurse registered surprise momentarily but quickly recovered her professional mien. "Yes, Doctor."

She returned to Diane with a tray on which was a lather mug, a brush and a straight razor.

"I'm going to have to prep you," she said.

Quickly, she lathered and began to shave Diane's pubic hair.

"Do you have to do this?" Diane pleaded.

"Yes. Don't worry. Everything will be all right."

"Father Brown would have solved it by now," said Sister Clotilde.

The three other nuns chuckled at her insistence.

The Sisters, all assigned to Sacred Heart Seminary, were engaging in their "recreation"—mending the clean laundry before returning it to the seminarians.

Sister Clotilde, in her eighties, had been a teenager when the lengendary Father Brown was created in 1911 by G. K. Chesterton. She had grown up with Father Brown mysteries during her early career in the convent. Later, she had occasionally read other mystery heroes such as Nero Wolfe and especially Philip Marlowe. She considered Raymond Chandler's writing to be nearly as careful as Chesterton's. She never touched Mickey Spillane.

When a murder affected the Catholic community in any way, as The Red Hat Murders surely had, Sister Clotilde entered into the investigation from her armchair position.

"Now, Sister," Sister Dulcilia chided, "you know it's too early in the book for Father Brown to come up with one of his elaborate solutions."

Sister Dulcilia, sixty-five, had been searching assiduously for a button to replace one missing from a brown shirt. Not finding a suitable button, she began sewing shut the buttonhole.

"Not at all. Not at all," said Sister Clotilde. "The case is closed."

"Closed?" Sister Mary George seemed surprised. "How in the world would you know a thing like that?"

Sister Mary George, having first inserted a darning egg, was darning a black sock. At sixty-three, she still could dance the Charleston, if anyone asked. People who knew, regularly did ask.

"Why, my dear," said Sister Clotilde, "because the gentleman who killed those three poor souls did so on Saturday, Monday, and Wednesday. Every other day, you see." She looked up from the laundry tag she was repairing. Her companions appeared to be paying attention. "Well, you see, too much time has passed since the last killing. If he were going to have killed anyone else, he would have done so last Friday, and so on."

"Have you told the police all this?" Sister Paulita asked seriously.

Sister Paulita was patching a T-shirt that was a study in patches. It was beginning to resemble Joseph's coat of many colors. From time to time, Sister Paulita looked in the laundry basket, adjusted her glasses and studied an article of clothing.

Sister Clotilde laughed softly. "Oh, the police don't need any help from a little old lady."

"Do you think there is any chance that the killer could be a Catholic boy?" asked Sister Dulcilia. Having failed to find yet another appropriate button, she was stitching up yet another buttonhole.

"Oh," exclaimed Sister Clotilde, "I'd be very surprised if he were not a Catholic!"

"Why is that?" asked Sister Mary George.

"Did any of you read that article on the murders in Sunday's *News*?" She checked her companions. None seemed to have read it. "Well, it explained how carefully the red hat and these statues have been selected to match, in significance, the alleged occupations of the victims. I'm sure only a Catholic would establish that M.O."

"Oh, dear," sighed Sister Dulcilia.

Sister Paulita peered again into the laundry basket. She seemed puzzled. She reached into the basket and extracted a spanking clean athletic supporter. She studied the laundry number. "Who has laundry number 302?" she asked.

Sister Clotilde consulted her list. "Vito Lombardo."

Sister Paulita sighed, took the athletic supporter to the board and ironed it. Before placing it in the laundry bag marked 302, she pinned a note to the supporter.

The note read, "This pair of undershorts is beyond repair."

For the third time in two days, Colleen Farrell was spilling forth the gruesome details of her and Charlie Papkin's make-believe marriages. Details replete with abuse, infidelity, and chemical dependency.

Farrell and Papkin sat in the Reverend Mr. Ramon Toussaint's office at St. Cecilia's rectory.

Toussaint listened silently to Farrell's tale of woe. He took no notes. He barely moved. Papkin became aware of the deep penetration of his eyes. It was almost as if he could see into one's soul.

Farrell finished her story. There were a few moments of silence.

"I am sorry. I am unable to help you," said Toussaint, as he rose and opened his office door. "And I am unable to think of anyone who could help you."

Before they knew what had happened, Farrell and Papkin found themselves standing outside the rectory. It was as if they had been struck by a black tornado.

Papkin agitatedly jiggled the change in his pocket. "Well," he said, "that was fast."

Farrell shook her head. "Charlie," she said, "we had to find someone who was willing to say, 'The hell with Church law,' and marry us. I really thought Toussaint would be the one."

"Disappointed?"

"Crushed."

"You know what, Coll? I think we've been the victims of reverse discrimination."

"Thank you very much," said Joe Cox as he hung up the phone.

Cox inhaled deeply, held his breath for a few seconds, then exhaled. He glanced over at Nelson Kane, who was editing copy. Kane's blue pencil flashed over the page. Cox moved to Kane's desk and seated himself in the chair beside it. The chair was known by those in the city room as "the hot seat." And rightly so.

Cox waited until Kane's pencil slowed and the editor looked up.

"I don't think you're going to like this, Nellie, but this story shows every possibility of becoming another of those 'on-the-other-hand' features."

Kane looked at Cox uncomprehendingly. His lack of comprehension was a silent demand for clarification.

"The Community and Economic Development Department story," Cox said. "There aren't any good guys or bad guys, just lots of halftones."

Kane seemed disappointed. One thing that always contributed to a gloomy atmosphere in the city room was a disappointed Nelson Kane. Staff writers tried sedulously to preclude this state of affairs.

"This Willoughby guy who heads the C&EDD seems like a good man and competent. He's no token black, by any standard. But he's the obvious target when projects don't get off the ground or lie uncompleted for a long time.

"The problem is the red tape—all the bases that have to be touched. And the red tape is the result of well-founded precautions. The city didn't want to create a monster. So, when it created the position of head of the C&EDD it surrounded that position with red tape so the city wouldn't get ripped off.

"I don't think Willoughby is the sort to rip off the city,

but how do you know you're going to find a Willoughby before you find him?"

Throughout the explanation, Kane had listened impassively.

"Dammit, Cox," he said, matter-of-factly, "there's never a time when there's not a bad guy. There are poor people who should have better housing and don't; there are poor neighborhoods that should have parks and don't. If the *system* is the reason everything is happening the day after tomorrow, then the *system* is the bad guy. Write it that way."

Kane returned to his editing. The matter of how to approach the C&EDD story had been concluded.

Cox rose, but instead of returning to his desk, he crossed over to Dennis McNaught's desk.

"How's it goin', Denny?"

A startled McNaught looked up. "Oh, pretty good, Joe." He had rolled paper into his typewriter God knows how long before. As regularly happens with professional writers, he had been staring at the paper waiting for inspiration but lost in a permissive fugue.

"How's the Red Hat case coming?"

"'Bout the same as it was when you asked me this time yesterday, Joe. I think the cops are trying to mop up the investigation. And I get the impression they don't have many leads. They may even have a timetable for closing it for good."

"Looks like they figure it's all over?"

"Yeah. I can't say I blame them. Why spend years trying to find a guy when if you caught him the mayor would probably be pressured to give him the keys to the city?"

They laughed. Cox started back to his desk.

Now this, he thought, was a story wherein there were good guys and bad guys, albeit in somewhat reversed roles. Unless it were true there had been some paid assassin who'd wasted three of Detroit's top hoods, there had to be someone who, thinking he had the best of reasons, had rid the city of its worst filth.

The nice thing about working on a murder story, he thought, was that the heart of the story was solid. Somebody's life ended early. And somebody else ended it. Having bodies, even heads, around was much better than the study of a beleaguered bureaucrat hopelessly enmeshed in sticky red tape.

Those in a position to know claim there are 400,000 manuscripts submitted to publishers in the United States each year. Of these, some 40,000 become published books.

Donna Halliday of the *Free Press* sometimes musingly considered the possibility that all 40,000 were sent to her and were, indeed, on one of her two desks. The book editor's present contemplation of stacks of books was interrupted by a ringing phone.

Answering it, she then rolled her chair a couple of feet north to get sight of film critic and Anonymous Gourmet Larry Delaney.

"Larry," Halliday said, covering the mouthpiece, "this is the manager of the Summit. He wants to know when you're going to publish your critique of his restaurant."

Delaney had been studying the Pontchartrain Wine Cellars' menu, trying to recall every aspect of the meal he and his companions had enjoyed there. It took some moments for the question to register.

"Sometime after I eat there."

She relayed that information.

"He says you ate there just last week."

"Tell him he's out of his—wait a minute . . ." Delaney recalled the mysterious call from Mario's. "Ask him what I look like."

Halliday returned to the phone.

"He says you were disguised as a priest. You're tall, bald, a bit overweight, and you wear glasses."

Delaney ran his hand through his full head of hair with

its Mondale forelock, looked with unspectacled eyes at his trim waist, and mentally acknowledged he was tall.

"Who was I with?"

"You were with two other men also dressed as priests."

"Did the manager extend me and my party any particular courtesies?"

"He had your table changed to one with a better view. He wants to know why you don't remember any of this."

Delaney smiled and shook his head. Some tall, bald, paunchy myopic priest was engaged in a little pious fraud. There wasn't anything he could do about it. Besides, he *was* planning to visit the Summit.

"Tell him there'll be a review soon."

Halliday returned to the contemplation of books.

It did not occur to her to wonder why calls for the Anonymous Gourmet came to her desk. If it had, and if she had investigated, she would have learned that the switchboard crew had concluded that she was the Anonymous Gourmet.

"The trouble is, Miss," explained the uniformed officer from the Wayne County Sheriff's Department, "the damn thing—excuse me, Miss—the thing is twenty-seven miles long."

The thing to which the lawman referred was the Middle Rouge Parkway. Most people called it Hines Park because Edward Hines Drive curled through the park, following the course of the Middle Rouge River.

The tree-lined parkway could be breathtakingly beautiful. Lately, one's breath was taken by fumes from motorcycles, the sickening sweetness of smoldering dope, and the smell of beer. After some particularly active evenings, it was difficult to see the grass for empty beer cans and other debris.

Officer George Elliott was trying to explain to Pat Lennon why conditions here were so out of control that even residents whose property bordered on the parkway traveled many miles away from home to picnic elsewhere.

Lennon had difficulty concentrating on what Elliott was saying. Carloads of young people raced by, horns blowing, and shouting obscenities. Periodically, a phalanx of motorcycles roared by, their riders resembling zombies on their way to creating a master race.

The *News'* crack photographer, Don Carlson, was busily snapping shots, mostly of the parade of American youth. Some of them would point proudly to their pictures in the *News*. Some of their parents who hardly ever saw their children would wince at seeing them in the paper.

"Trouble is, Miss," Elliott said, "this park is like a long thin balloon. You squeeze one trouble spot down and it bulges out somewhere else along the line. This is like one long free-swinging singles club."

"You mean there's nothing you can do about it?" Lennon peripherally noticed a late-model Lincoln move swiftly by. Bare buttocks protruded from a rear window. Somebody was mooning.

The little dears, Lennon thought; they're not deprived, they're depraved.

"Miss," answered Elliott, "it would take a small army to control an area this size."

"Don't the citizens in this area complain?"

"Constantly."

"What do you do about it?"

"Just as I've indicated, Miss. We go in and squeeze off the area being complained about and trouble springs up in three other areas."

"Isn't there any plan for improving the situation?"

"Just one, Miss. We're going to start making arrests. Giving out tickets has no effect. They pay their fines, if they show up in court at all, and forget about it. We'll just see if spending some time locked up reaches them."

Just then, from an open convertible, a full can of beer arched in their direction. It smashed into the camera Carlson was using, pushing it into his face. The photographer reeled backward, nose bleeding profusely.

It was a fluke, but whoever threw the can had to be responsible for the damage and injury.

"Now that," said Elliott, "is too much!"

He slid behind the wheel of his patrol car, hit the flasher and siren and gave chase.

Diane Garson did not go from the clinic to her job at the A&P.

She had spent an hour in the recovery area of Services, Inc. After the first half-hour, she had been regularly urged by the receptionist to get up and leave. After an hour, she had been ordered to leave. In more pain than she'd ever experienced, she drove directly, if unsteadily, home.

She spent the afternoon and evening in bed, alternately shivering and perspiring as she thrashed about.

It was evening. Her mother and father were sitting on either side of her bed. She was conscious, but confused and on the verge of delirium.

"Please, baby, won't you tell us what happened?" her father asked, repeating a question he had asked many times this evening. "What is it did this to you?"

"No, no, it's a disgrace," she mumbled, "I can't do that!"

"Fred," said her mother, "she's getting worse. I think we ought to call an ambulance."

Fred Garson hesitated. It wasn't so much the expense of a private ambulance as it was he didn't want her out of the house and their care if he could help it.

"No, Louise," said Garson, "let's just wait another few minutes and see if she doesn't start to pull out of this."

"What will you do to me if I don't do it?" asked Diane of no one. Her head flopped back and forth on the sweat-soaked pillow.

"Tell us what happened, baby," said Fred Garson. "What is it did this to you?"

Suddenly, Diane's small body stiffened. She seemed to lapse into unconsciousness.

"Fred," said Mrs. Garson tensely, "I think she's going into shock. I'm calling the ambulance."

"O.K., Louise. But call the private service. We don't want her taken to some second-rate hospital."

"I was really hard up for a job," said Linda Ryder, "but I don't know about this one."

Ryder, a registered nurse, had been employed recently by Services, Inc. A tall, attractive redhead, she was standing in the reception room drinking coffee prior to opening the clinic this Thursday morning.

"You'll get over it," assured Patricia Teague.

Teague, of medium height, in her mid-fifties, with graying hair, had been registered nurse-receptionist at Services, Inc. for the past five years. Long ago she had "gotten over it."

"It's funny," said Ryder, "when I graduated, an RN could get a job almost anywhere. I never thought then that I'd be unemployed for eight months."

Teague smiled. "The market isn't what it used to be," she commented.

"But," a troubled expression clouded Ryder's face, "I don't know about this place. I mean, I don't have any qualms about abortion. If a woman wants one she ought to be able to get one. But this place! That Dr. Schmitt is so sloppy. It's a wonder he doesn't kill somebody!"

"We haven't lost one yet. Not that we know of, at any rate," Teague added.

"Then there was that poor kid yesterday. You know, the one in the morning. She wasn't even pregnant. Why did we accept her anyway?"

"That's the way we eat. We earn money. That's what we're here for, dearie. Don't forget that: money."

"Well, can you explain why we used the saline solution? That's not normally used till midterm. Why would Dr. Schmitt use it when there wasn't even a pregnancy?"

"One thing you ought to keep in mind about Schmitt." Teague looked up from the records she was sorting. "Besides being sloppy, he has a strong sadistic streak. Dr. Schmitt does not like women. He's the opposite of the physician who tries not to cause pain.

"Oh, I know he puts on this high-and mighty I'm-only-here-to-help-you-my-dear attitude, but don't you believe it. He figures if they're stupid enough to get themselves pregnant, he'll make sure they learn their lesson."

A song from "Man of La Mancha" leapt to Ryder's mind. "He's only thinking of them," she murmured.

Teague, unfamiliar with either the song or the implication, missed the irony. "No, he's only thinking of money."

Then, noting her co-worker's distressed expression, she snapped, "And so are we or we wouldn't be here!"

Ryder took a final sip of coffee and vowed that at the first opportunity she'd seek employment elsewhere. There had been no mention of money in the pledge she'd taken when they'd capped her on graduation.

"What have we got here, Doc?" asked Lieutenant Tom Bourque.

"We've got a mess that started bad and got worse," said Dr. John O'Donavan.

Bourque, head of Homicide Squad One, had been called earlier by Koznicki, who had informed him of the suspicious death at Holy Cross Hospital.

Bourque was standing with the head of Holy Cross' Pathology Department in the hospital's basement.

"The identity is Diane Garson," said O'Donavan, "eighteen years of age."

Bourque busily took notes as O'Donavan related details of the case.

"The cause of death is septicemia—blood poisoning. It may have little to do with your investigation, but you might like to know this little girl suffered a lot before she died," O'Donavan added.

Bourque shook his head in sympathy. Beyond a general humanitarian interest, the victim's suffering was of no value to an investigation, and thus, of no value to Bourque.

"At this point," O'Donavan continued, "we are quite certain the infection that caused the septicemia began in the pelvic region. The endometrium, the lining of the womb, has been freshly shed. We found unusual amounts of saline solution in the tissues of the uterus, which, in some areas, has been damaged by the solution."

Bourque looked up, tapping his pen against his note pad. "An abortion, Doc?"

"Looks like an abortion," O'Donavan confirmed, "that was only a small level above the back alley kind."

Bourque's expression invited amplification.

"Either," O'Donavan continued, "the lining of the vagina was not sterilized, or the object inserted, probably a pump, was contaminated, or both. In any case, the infection began in that area. There are definite signs the abortion was performed in a clinic but probably in a badly run clinic."

"Looks like homicide," Bourque opined.

"There's one more thing you ought to know," said O'Donavan. "It may not bear directly on the investigation, but it may help to know what kind of person you're looking for."

Bourque waited.

"The Garson girl either wasn't pregnant at all or she was in the very earliest stage."

"Yes?" Bourque knew there was more.

"A saline injection is used for abortion only in the middle stages of pregnancy. There was no need whatever to use it on the Garson girl in her early state."

"Which means?"

"Which means you're looking for someone—with at least some medical training very probably—who missed his vocation when he was born too late to run a Nazi death camp."

"We don't know the age of this butcher, Doc," said an impressed Bourque, "maybe he's one of those Nazis who got away. But if he is," Bourque paused for effect, "he won't get away this time."

"The thing that really pisses me off, Leroi, is that you lied to me!"

Georgia Thomas, young, black, slightly overweight, sat on the passenger's side of Leroi Jackson's rusted old Ford. Jackson, lean, black and sullen, slumped against the door, his left hand toying with the steering wheel, his right holding a cigarette.

There being no verbal response, Georgia continued.

"Sure, sure, big man. You were gonna go out and get yousse'f fixed. An' that was gonna take care-a us. Well, then, big man, 'spose you 'splain to me if you is fixed, then how come I is pregnant!" She almost spat out the final word.

Jackson shifted uneasily in his seat. Taking a final drag on his cigarette he dropped it over his shoulder to the curb, where the car was parked in front of Services, Inc.

Jackson's continued silence encouraged Georgia to resume her harangue.

"An' like I say, man, the worsest thing is you lied to me. Man, I know ever'thin' 'bout you." After a slight pause, she added explosively, "exceptin' for the fack you never got no operation!"

Jackson lit another cigarette.

"Baby," he said, at length, "I had to lie to you."

"What you mean you *had* to?" she snapped.

"Well, you said you were tired of always bein' the one to take the percautions. You said the pill gave you a headache." He grew more aggressive. "Then you wouldn' use the coil. An' then you claim the foam waren't no good. Shit, woman, you wouldn' do *nothin'*."

"That's when you stepped in, big man. 'I'm gonna git myse'f fixed,' you said. You're so *fixed*, I'm gittin' an abortion!"

"Well, I'm payin' for it. Don't ferget that!"

"You're payin' for it! Big deal! Who's *gittin'* it?"

"But you're not gettin' it in some burnt-out buildin' from some smartass who's quick with a hanger."

"No, one step up. Good ol' Doc Schmitt."

Georgia Thomas had played her trump. Jackson lapsed into silence.

Georgia consulted her watch.

"Well, it's time. You better be waitin' here when I get outta there, you turkey, or I'll tell all your other chicks that you ain't fixed."

Jackson winced. That last shot was unfair, he thought. He was faithful to Georgia Thomas, in his fashion.

Detective Larry Rogers resembled an oversize Sidney Poitier. He and his partner, Detective Donna Osborn, both of Homicide Squad One, had the Garsons' permission to search their home for leads to their daughter's abortionist and murderer.

Osborn, of medium height and build, was going through Diane Garson's belongings in her bedroom. Rogers was talking with the Garsons in their living room.

"So neither of you knew that Diane had been to an abortionist?" asked Rogers.

Mr. Garson shook his head. Rogers noted that during their conversation, he scarcely ever raised his head.

"No," he said, "she never mentioned it."

"You see," said Mrs. Garson quietly, "we are Catholics and abortion is very much against our religion. I am surprised that Diane seemed to have gotten in the family way. But I'm not surprised she didn't tell us she was thinking of getting an abortion. I'm sure she knew we would have tried to talk her out of it."

"She must have been very frightened," Mr. Garson said softly.

"If she *was* pregnant," said Rogers, "do either of you have any idea who the father might have been?"

Mr. Garson shook his head, still without looking up.

"She dated a few boys," said Mrs. Garson, "none of

them seriously . . . we thought . . . until this . . ." Her voice trailed off.

Damn, thought Rogers. We'll probably not get any of them to admit they had intercourse with the girl. Too bad. One of them may have driven her to the abortionist.

"Mrs. Garson," said Rogers, "could you give me the names of her boyfriends, and their addresses? And also her girlfriends; she might have confided in one of them. We're trying to check every possible lead. And so far, there are very few."

"Certainly." As Mrs. Garson rose to comply with the detective's request, Sergeant Osborn entered the room. She held a small rectangular leather-bound object.

"Mr. Garson, Mrs. Garson," she said, "I've found Diane's checkbook. It shows she recently withdrew a hundred and fifty dollars, which left only twenty in her account. Her savings account is empty. Do either of you know of anything she might have spent that amount on within the last few days?"

Garson shook his head.

"No," Mrs. Garson answered. "I know of nothing she bought recently. Why?"

"Because," Osborn responded, "one hundred and fifty dollars is a ballpark figure for an abortion in the early stage of pregnancy."

Damn, thought Rogers again, that means she didn't pay by check. So we've got no record and no name. There's got to be a break in this case. There must be; he felt it in his bones, but where was it?

Leroi Jackson waited a full four hours for Georgia Thomas to emerge from Services, Inc. Now he was sorry he had.

She had come out barely able to walk.

Jackson's first reaction to any stressful situation was to panic. And this emotion did not desert him now.

Georgia had not spoken a word to him. She sat on the passenger's side of the front seat, curled into a semifetal position. Occasionally, a low moan escaped her. Jackson noticed blood on her calves.

His initial instinct was to run from his own car. His second was to drive to a remote field and dump her. His third was to drive her to her home.

Suddenly, it occurred to him that, for once, this was not his fault. Or at least not by *his* lights.

He looked up and saw, as a visiting angel of mercy, the white-on-blue sign indicating the presence of Detroit Memorial Hospital. He knew Detroit General was nearby. He started his car and homed in on the hospital a few blocks away.

While the now unconscious girl was wheeled into the emergency room, Jackson stayed on the scene and gave the admitting clerk all the details of where Georgia Thomas had been and what had been done to her.

He was quite proud of himself.

Rarely had he remained at the scene of any crime. But then rarely had he been innocent of the crime in question.

The Highland Park A&P was seldom crowded on Saturday mornings.

Sergeants Osborn and Rogers had informed the store's manager of their investigation. Osborn was questioning the market's department heads. The interrogation was being conducted in the large meat packing room. It was cold. The manager had suggested that room not because it was the largest or most suitable, but because of the temperature. He wanted to hurry things along.

Rogers roamed the aisles talking to employees as he encountered them. He was getting the clear impression that several of the girls knew more than they were willing to say. The old don't-get-involved syndrome. The kind of attitude that let Kitty Genovese die in New York City these many years ago.

Out of the corner of his eye, he caught sight of a small form standing just behind him to his left. It was a checkout clerk he had already questioned. He turned as he consulted his note pad, searching for her name.

Oh, yes, Sylvia Trotter. "What can I do for you, Ms. Trotter?"

"Well, I been thinkin'," the small attractive black girl began, hesitantly, "it just ain't right."

"What just ain't right?"

"What happened to Diane."

"You mean her death?"

"The whole thing. I mean, Diane, she was a good girl. Not like some of the trash that works here. I can't even believe Diane went and got pregnant. And all the rest of that stuff, well, it just ain't fair."

"We all agree with you, Ms. Trotter. It just ain't fair. But what are we going to do about it?"

"Well, I been thinkin'. That old man been gettin' away with this too long."

"What old man?" Rogers scarcely dared to breathe. This was the break; he sensed it.

"Old Doc Schmitt."

"Old Doc Schmitt at Services, Inc.?" Schmitt was infamous. But so far no one had been able to prove he did anything illegal.

"Yeah, old Doc Schmitt and his Tinkertoy abortions."

"What did he do?"

"He's the one Diane went to. She told me she was goin'. I tried to talk her out of it, but I couldn't. She didn't have much money and she was scared. But it just ain't right, 'specially with a girl like Diane. Somebody outa put a stop to old Doc Schmitt before he kills us all."

"Honey," said Rogers, "I think you just did."

If he'd been able to get off his feet, he would have kicked his heels.

The atmosphere was particularly dank in the autopsy room of Detroit General Hospital. Two people stood in the room, in the hospital basement, where the naked dead body of Georgia Thomas lay on an aluminum tray.

"What have we got here, Doc?" asked Lieutenant Bourque.

"It's very simple and very sad," said Dr. Jane Browne, the head pathologist. The small trim black woman looked as if she would be more at home behind a stove than delving into dead bodies. But she was very good at what she did. There were those who said she would one day succeed Wilhelm Moellmann, the White Tornado.

"Her name was Georgia Thomas," the doctor began. "She was twenty years old, she was unmarried, and she was pregnant."

The lieutenant thought there was a lot of that going around.

"Yesterday, she had an abortion. The doctor—and I use that title recklessly—while he was performing a dilation and curettage, perforated her uterus with his curette. Peritonitis set in. The peritonitis was untreated and septicemia occurred, probably from an improperly sterilized curette. The complications of both the peritonitis and the blood poisoning killed the poor girl."

"Do we have any witnesses?" Bourque asked.

"Yes, a young man named Jackson brought her in. They have his address at the desk."

Bourque began to think the presence of a witness was too good to be true.

"Do we know the abortionist involved?" asked Bourque.

"Dr. Robert Schmitt," she said, with a certain grim satisfaction.

This *is* too good to be true, Bourque thought. I've been trying to get that old S.O.B. for years.

A nurse appeared in the doorway. "Telephone call for you, Lieutenant."

"Bourque," he identified.

"Rogers," was the reply.

"Yeah, Larry, what've you got?"

"This is our lucky day. I found a girl at the A&P where the Garson girl worked. She can tie Garson's abortion to none other than our old friend Doc Schmitt."

Bourque whistled.

"Double lucky day, Larry. I just got done talking with Doc Browne at General. Old Doc Schmitt killed another girl yesterday. And we have a material witness."

"Zowie! Why don't we go over to Doc Schmitt's office and take a look at his records."

"I'll get a court order and meet you there," said Bourque.

"It's time to round up the bad guys," said Rogers gleefully.

It was times like this it was unmitigated fun being a detective.

Even on Saturday afternoons, Carl's Chop House hosted a goodly number of diners.

At promptly 12:30 P.M., Dr. Robert Schmitt left his Cadillac with the parking attendant at Carl's entry.

Services, Inc. was open only till noon on Saturdays. Schmitt generally lunched at Carl's on Saturdays and Sundays.

It was a rather chill day. Schmitt left his coat and hat at the check stand and was greeted rather coolly by the maitre d'.

Near the entrance to the dining room was a tank of live lobsters. Schmitt selected the one he wished boiled for his lunch.

He was seated at a table that would be served by a recently hired waitress. It was sometimes difficult finding a waitress who would serve him. His reputation forcefully preceded him.

Schmitt was a rich man. A millionaire many times over, some thought. And as such he was generally shown deference, at least publicly.

But what he did and how he did it were quite well known. He had no social life. He liked to think he had friends, but, if asked, he would not have been able to name even one. His wife was dead. She had not been his friend.

He did not care. He wanted money and he had it. He wanted luxuries and he had them.

Schmitt had lived in Germany from his birth in 1908 until after World War II. This was common knowledge. He had not been assigned to any of the notorious Nazi death camps, although he had been in the Medical Corps. This was common knowledge. He had counseled the medical officers in the death camps on methods of experimentation on human victims and methods of inhuman extermination. This was known by very few. And they were not talking.

Schmitt nodded curtly to the smiling new waitress.

"Would you like a cocktail before your meal?" she asked, as she handed him a menu.

"No," he snapped, "coffee. I don't need a menu," he spat out as he flung it across the table, "I always have lobster!"

The waitress gingerly picked up the menu and retreated. Other diners looked over during the brief scene, then looked away in sympathetic embarrassment for the waitress.

Oblivious to fellow diners, Schmitt sat back and let his mind wander. His thoughts, as they often did, turned to his military career. He regretted not a moment of it. He had been paid well. And he had kept most of what he'd earned. Early on, he had learned the value of the Swiss and their banks.

"Ouch!" he cried.

A black busboy, pouring Schmitt's coffee, had spilled a little in the saucer. In his attempt to sop it up and already nervously fearful of the diner, he had jabbed Schmitt's hand.

Schmitt glanced at his hand but could see no blood.

"Stupid fool!" he shouted.

Again, nearby diners looked up.

But the busboy had disappeared from view.

The trouble with Hitler, Schmitt thought, was that he had selected the wrong race to eliminate. Schmitt had no doubt the Führer eventually would have gotten around to the Negro race, but he should have put them ahead of the Jews.

Schmitt was very comfortable with being a member in good standing of the Master Race.

With his disposition, only Schmitt could enjoy his lunch.

The nurses at Services, Inc. were tidying the interior of the locked clinic when they were, as they put it, "invaded" by a pride of police.

Several members of Homicide Squad One proceeded through the various rooms of the clinic. Some took photos of the rooms, furnishings, equipment, and gowns. Others carefully gathered and sealed in cartons the instruments and implements used in the abortions.

Lieutenant Bourque and Sergeants Rogers and Osborn were in the reception area with nurses Teague and Ryder.

"You don't remember either a girl named Diane Garson or a Georgia Thomas?" asked Bourque.

"No, neither," Teague answered quickly.

"How about you, Miss?" Bourque addressed an obviously unnerved Ryder.

"No," she said uncertainly. "Why do you want to know?"

"They're dead," Bourque said flatly.

"As a result of the treatment they received at this clinic," Rogers added.

Ryder gasped.

Teague blanched but retained her noncommittal expression.

Osborn had been busy for several minutes checking the records in the desk. The records did not reach very far into even recent history. But they did cover the past few days.

Teague scarcely took her eyes from Osborn as the detective riffled index card after card.

"I hope you understand that our investigation could end in either or both of you being charged with being accessories to homicide, manslaughter, conspiracy, and/or with-holding evidence."

Ryder appeared on the verge of tears. Teague, un-changed, kept her eyes riveted on Donna Osborn.

"They're both here," said Osborn, a note of triumph in her voice. Her index finger marked the spot where she had found the record of Diane Garson's visits, and the file was open to Georgia Thomas' more recent visits.

"Great!" said Bourque and Rogers simultaneously.

"I should have destroyed them," muttered Teague.

"I was going to tell you!" Ryder seemed near a break-down. "I was going to tell you, honest!"

"Shut up, Ryder!" Teague warned.

"Those poor kids," Ryder babbled, ignoring her, "it shouldn't have happened to them. It was all Dr. Schmitt's fault. In all my years of nursing, I've never seen anyone so unprofessional and callous."

The police had a bird and she was singing.

"Miss Ryder," said Bourque soothingly, "why don't you go into the next room with Officer Osborn. She'll be glad to take your statement."

"Larry," he turned to Rogers, "take this lovely lady," he indicated Teague, "read her her rights, and book her on everything that comes to your mind."

The good guys are winning, thought Rogers.

"The best part," Bourque continued, "I must admit I've reserved for myself. I'm going to Grosse Pointe Farms and tell dear old Doc Schmitt the good news!"

Sometimes it was a sheer joy to be a cop.

Following an impulse more than anything else, Dr. Rob-ert Schmitt returned to his office rather than going home after lunch at Carl's.

Laboriously, he worked his short stocky body from be-hind the wheel. He saw nothing unusual about the clinic's exterior. The police and clinic personnel were gone and nothing outside the clinic had been disturbed. He was un-aware that anything out of the ordinary had occurred.

At the door, he paused after inserting his key in the lock. A frown crossed his porcine face. Removing his Homburg, he ran a hand over his bald pate. He was perspiring. Something was wrong, he sensed it.

All looked in order in the reception room. He quickly moved to the rear of the clinic. All his equipment, all his instruments—gone. A robbery? Should he call the police? If it were a robbery, why just his equipment and instruments? Why not the rest of the furnishings? The typewriters?

Another thought, a far worse possibility, occurred to him. He returned to the reception room and jerked open the desk drawer. Gone. All the records gone. This was no robbery. This was a police action. He fell back into the chair, limp.

He was undecided whether to leave town hurriedly or go to the police and face whatever charge they might bring against him.

As his head began to clear and he was putting his thoughts in order, he became aware of a strong foreign odor. It pierced the normal strong disinfectant smell. He could not clearly identify the odor, but it seemed to emanate from one of the back rooms.

Curiosity engaged, Schmitt started again cautiously toward the rear of the clinic.

As he passed from the reception area, he was able to identify the odor. It was of burning human flesh and hair. But why here? In his clinic? In the middle of Detroit? He was confused. Badly confused.

As he progressed further to the rear, the smell of burning flesh increased till it was nearly unbearable. He pressed his handkerchief over his mouth and nose but the maneuver did little good.

He reached the large rear office but oddly it was as if someone had installed a glass door that covered the entire entrance to the room. And the glass was clouded as if by steam.

He rubbed a corner free of mist with his handkerchief.

He peered in. He saw two men wearing striped uniforms. As if in slow motion, they were picking up naked dead bodies of men, women, and children and tossing them into a gigantic furnace. With the approach of each body, the flames leapt from the furnace to greet the corporeal fuel.

As the stench grew to almost suffocating proportions, shrieks of terror assailed Schmitt's ears.

He rubbed more mist from the glass. He saw men, women, and children compressed by their sheer number. Gas was being pumped down at them from the ceiling. Instinctively, they knew immediately it was poisonous. They screamed and tore at each other.

There was a clap of ear-shattering thunder.

Schmitt spun about. He was standing in a black room. He sensed it was huge. A hissing sound echoed all around him. With the gas chamber and crematorium behind him and this room in front, he had no escape.

Slowly, a string of fluorescent lights brightened the central portion of the room to reveal a high, almost judicial bench. Seated behind it was a group of people, all women. Schmitt recognized most of them. Diane Garson was there, along with Georgia Thomas, and so many more women he had butchered. There was even a small baby who had emerged alive during one of Schmitt's sloppier abortions. Schmitt had smothered the little girl. He recognized her due to the blotchy burns covering her body. The result of saline injection.

One by one, each woman extended her right arm, hand fisted, thumb turned downward. As the last woman gave her sign, all of them disappeared. There was another clap of thunder. Schmitt again spun about.

Now no glass separated him from the condemned. They had stopped screaming. The gas had ceased. They were laughing at him maniacally.

Those in the front ranks grabbed Schmitt and pulled him into their midst. Bodies pressed upon him so tightly he could scarcely breathe. Hands tore at his clothes and at his flesh. All he could see were grinning, laughing mouths. Mad hysteria was all about him.

The crowd moved Schmitt ever closer to the furnace. Now he was directly in front of it, and forced to look inside it. It was filled with gold. His gold.

The gold began to melt. It sizzled. Bubbles appeared. Steam rose. It became molten. It began to boil.

Two men raised Schmitt's struggling body over their heads. They hurled him, writhing, into the furnace. He extended his arms before him in a futile gesture of self-protection. His face contorted in terror. He shrieked one resounding "NOoooo—"

Unlike the days of yore, seminarians' attendance at weekday Mass was spotty at best. But they invariably rose to the challenge of the Sunday liturgy.

Not only did all resident seminarians attend the Sunday Mass, there were also visitors. Friends and relatives of the seminarians or faculty as well as some of the homeowners or apartment dwellers in this benighted area of Detroit.

The music, carefully rehearsed, usually included everything from a bit of Gregorian Chant to the polyphony of Palestrina to traditional to folk. The seminary choir religiously avoided all the execrable music that had been composed before but mostly after Vatican II.

While this Sunday's visitors were being shown to their places in the huge Gothic chapel, faculty and students were aligning themselves in the dark corridors outside the chapel. Seminarians were garbed in cassocks and surplices, a very rare occurrence. The clergy faculty were vesting in Mass robes in the large sacristy.

"Did you hear what McNiff, out at St. Mary Magdalen in Melvindale, said the other day?" asked Father Osborn. He eased the long white alb over his shoulders and let it hang down to his ankles.

"No, what?" asked Father Burk eagerly.

Father Patrick McNiff was such a colorful character that

the news of what he did and said was always grist for clerical gossip.

"Well," said Osborn, "McNiff's associate pastor, young Harry Doyle, comes up to him the other day. It is obvious that Doyle is very upset."

"Yes?" Burk's complete attention was given to Osborn as Burk automatically adjusted and tied his cincture.

"So," said Osborn, carefully placing the stole over his shoulders and securing its position with the cincture's loose ends, "young Doyle has just received another notary job from the Tribunal. It seems he has received many previous directives from the Tribunal to take testimony from various parishioners on marriage cases. He feels as if he is being used by the Tribunal—"

"Who doesn't?" Burk interrupted.

"In any case," Osborn continued, "Doyle is very angry. So he comes up to McNiff and says, 'Father, what can they do to me downtown if I refuse to take this testimony? I mean, what can they do to me if I simply refuse to do this?'"

Burk, who had stopped vesting entirely, waited expectantly.

"Well," said Osborn, "McNiff told him, 'Father, they can't do anything to you. You're already here!'"

They laughed.

"It reminds me," said Osborn, bringing himself under control, "of another incident Doyle told me about. A while back, Doyle received a document from the Tribunal and was ordered to place the document in the parish's secret archives."

Somewhat against his will, Burk was busy working the heavy chasuble, the outer vestment, down over his head. He didn't want to miss a word of a McNiff story.

"So," Osborn continued, "Doyle came to McNiff and asked in all sincerity just where these secret archives were. Well, McNiff draws young Doyle close to him and whispers in a conspiratorial tone, 'Father, they are so secret even I don't know where they are!'"

They laughed again.

The students had finished assembling in the corridor. It was 10 A.M. The procession was scheduled to begin. But it would wait until all the clergy faculty was vested and ready.

Four buddies had managed to group themselves together.

"Gentlemen," announced Vito Lombardo, "I propose an atrocity!"

"Dandy," agreed Dick Kiefer, "we've been too long without one."

"What is the nature of your atrocity?" Kevin Dunne demanded.

"You all know Leo Ramrod," said Lombardo.

They all knew Leo Ramrod. They leaned toward each other till their heads were nearly touching. It reminded each of them of an episode from the old "Mission Impossible" series.

"Leo Ramrod is the sacristan," Lombardo needlessly reminded his colleagues. "Thus, Leo will be busy until late this evening, what with cleaning up from this morning's liturgy and preparing for tomorrow's."

His three lieutenants nodded their continued understanding.

"I propose the following atrocity, gentlemen," said their leader. "We will place Leo's bed on top of the plasterboard stalls in the dormitory. Not only will Leo not be able to get his bed down by himself, he is too short to even reach the bed!"

Stifled guffaws from the three soldiers.

"One thing," insisted Joe Smolenski, "we are all in this together."

It was a valid point. It would be somewhat more difficult to fix cruel and unusual punishment upon inevitable apprehension on four than on one poor soul.

"Absolutely," agreed Lombardo.

The four piled their hands one on top the other.

The procession began.

"Have a happy liturgy, Joe," Lombardo stage-whispered to Smolenski. Both snickered.

The immense pipe organ, supported by three brass instruments, boomed out "A Mighty Fortress is Our God." The seminarians and faculty boomed right back. Both visitors and participants felt a thrill. It was a sound to set one's blood moving.

A straight-back chair had been placed in the sanctuary near the congregation.

As soon as he noticed it, Lombardo breathed a fervent, "Oh, God!"

As each noted the chair, the exclamation was repeated by nearly all the seminarians. For the chair signified that old Monsignor Klenner would be the main celebrant and, worse, that he would deliver the sermon.

Klenner's knowledge of Latin, Greek, German, and Sanskrit, among other languages, was internationally famous. Now in his eighties, he was physically not very strong. However, the opportunity to be seated while he preached added thirty minutes to his delivery.

Klenner never wanted to know the sermon topic before vesting for Mass. That lack of foreknowledge assured his homily a sense of freshness—and seemingly interminable length.

As the time for the homily arrived, Klenner seated himself. His audience tried to make themselves as comfortable as possible. Some prayed for the merciful gift of sleep.

"Ze topic uf today's homily," Klenner began, words clouded by his heavy German accent, "iss ze Ainchels. Now," he launched himself, "ze vord 'Ainchel' comes from ze Greek *'angelos-angelou-haw!'*" he said, adding the gender identification.

Lombardo counted the pillars and wondered about their foundation.

Smolenski mentally replayed yesterday's Tigers game.

Kiefer tried to estimate how long it would take the authorities to solve the Ramrod caper.

Dunne managed to capture an impure thought and entertain it.

Twenty-five minutes passed.

There was a rustling. Could Klenner be finishing?

"Und now," Klenner intoned, "ve come to ze *bad* Ainchels!"

The heat generated by all these bodies, the closeness of the air, the boredom created by the speaker all reached Sister Clotilde. Unassumingly, she slid off her pew and landed in a heap on the floor.

As regularly happens when someone simply faints in church, overreaction springs from as many sources as possible.

Lombardo hurdled three consecutive pews to reach the fainted woman. Her nun colleagues shrank back. Gradually, almost everyone in the chapel was gathered around the area where Clotilde's body lay. No one was able to remember, later, whether Monsignor Klenner had continued his sermon on the angels to its projected conclusion.

Paul Burk eventually took charge.

"Back! Get back!" he commanded. "Give her air!"

Burk knelt and cradled Clotilde's head in his lap, and fanned her face with a handy hymn card.

Air, indeed, was what Clotilde needed to return to consciousness. Little by little, her eyelids fluttered and then opened tentatively.

"Someone get some water," Burk ordered.

Slowly, as her focus grew more clear, Sister Clotilde became aware that she was looking at a head. One that wore a mask of horror. The lips seemed to be shouting a silent "NO!" And the head had no body.

Sister Clotilde screamed and returned to unconsciousness.

Chills ran up and down everyone's spine.

And that was without their even having yet seen the head.

Six

ST. JOSEPH'S

"What can I say after I say I'm sorry?" asked Lieutenant Ned Harris.

"There's no need to apologize," Inspector Koznicki reassured him.

The two were quite literally huddled in Koznicki's small office.

"Besides," Koznicki added, "the fact that this is another in the series of Red Hat Murders has not yet been established."

"No, I know that," said Harris. "But my squad is on the scene at the seminary. Especially after having been fooled before, they were very careful with all the details before sending the head on to the Medical Examiner. They're sure it's the Red Hat murderer."

"But you say the head was found on the *floor* of the chapel?" Koznicki asked.

"That's right."

"Well, doesn't that deviate from our killer's M.O.?"

"No, no, Walt. You see, the head of this statue had been carefully removed and Schmitt's head placed on its shoulders. Sometime before its discovery, probably due to the heat, the head must've softened slightly and rolled off the statue and fell to the floor where it was found. The head seemed drained of blood and there was no sign of embalming."

"We're still going to have to wait for Moellmann," Koznicki observed.

"Yeah, I know."

"You want me to go down and get the verdict?"

"Oh, no, Walt. If Moellmann was interested enough in this to come downtown on a Sunday, the least I can do is go over and get his findings in person."

Harris shoved his chair back to the wall. There still was not room for him to rise.

"You know," Koznicki said, "this is going to upset Lieutenant Bourque."

"Bourque? What's this got to do with Bourque?"

"Squad One was just about to collar Schmitt for two counts of homicide."

"No kidding!" Harris looked surprised. "I knew Schmitt was giving abortion a bad name even among those who favor it. But I didn't know we were ready for a collar. Did it look good?"

"Excellent case. Witnesses, records, evidence. A nice strong case. Bourque himself went out to Schmitt's home in the Farms to make the arrest. Waited till early evening, then put out an all-points."

"By that time, our Red Hat killer probably had him."

"Probably. We'll see if Moellmann can give us a time."

"Oh, yes, Moellmann," Harris remembered. "I think I'll just run over to his office and take my medicine."

"You do that." Koznicki smiled, pulled in his stomach, pushed his chair back against the wall, and pulled the desk toward himself.

Only thus did Harris have room to rise and leave.

"What can I say after I say I'm sorry?" Joe Cox asked Nelson Kane.

"There's no need to apologize," Kane reassured him.

"After all," Kane continued, "I agreed with your guess that The Red Hat Murders was a series that was finished."

"Yeah, but it was my idea," said a disconsolate Cox.

The two were talking with each other by phone. Cox had

heard a WJR news bulletin that another suspected Red Hat Murder had been discovered during a liturgical service at Sacred Heart Seminary.

First Cox had apologized to Pat Lennon and acknowledged that her theory that there would be more murders had been correct. Then he called Kane, who hadn't heard the news.

Lennon, at times descending to charades, kept urging Cox to get off the phone and leave it open. She wanted to get to the seminary and get on this breaking story. But she was sure her assistant news editor would call and make it all official.

"Are they *sure* it was another Red Hat Murder?" Kane asked.

"I don't know, Nellie. All I know is what I've heard on the radio so far."

"Now," Kane cautioned, "don't get sucked in on another red herring. Remember the Fitzgerald murder!"

"I know, Nellie, I know. I have Fitzgerald's name pinned to my desk like an idiot card."

Lennon was standing in front of Cox, waving her arms semaphorically.

"Nellie," Cox's voice was rapidly taking on an urgent tone, "don't you think I should be getting over to the seminary? I'll bet the *News* has heard about this by now. And besides, you'll be wanting to call some more of your crack staff to get on this one."

"Are you trying to tell me my business?" It was the good old aggressive tone filled with hostility.

"Did Moses advise God on how many plagues it would take to free His people for the Promised Land?"

"O.K., Cox, get on it!"

"Right, Nellie," said a relieved Cox.

"And Cox—"

"Nellie?"

"Get a little luck."

"I thought you were going to tell me to break a leg."

"No," said Kane dryly, "I'll do that to you if you don't get a little luck."

Lennon had been correct. No sooner was Cox out the door than the phone rang.

As she lifted the receiver, she noted it was hot. Either the pressure of Joe's ear, she thought, or the blistering heat of Kane's words.

"What can I say after I say I'm sorry?" asked assistant news editor Bob Ankenazy.

"There's no need to apologize," Lennon reassured him.

"Well," said Ankenazy, "I was the one who pulled you off The Red Hat Murders and put you on another assignment. I was the one who thought that series had been canceled. You were the one who insisted the option would be picked up again."

Lennon was growing to like Bob Ankenazy. Almost to the point of being fond of him. He had an engaging ability to laugh at himself, as well as a lively wit. If it weren't for Joe Cox . . .

"That's not important now, Bob," she said. "We don't even know for sure whether this might not be another Fitzgerald imitation."

"Well, I just wanted you to know, Pat," he said, "that if there's any flak about this in the city room, I insist on taking it and handling it."

"It's good of you to tell me this, Bob."

"Not at all, Pat. I also wanted to tell you your series on Hines Parkway is superior. But I'm going to put somebody else on it. From here on until the end, The Red Hat Murders is your baby. And I'll back you every step of the way."

"It's really super great of you to say so, Bob," she said warmly. "Now, let me get over to the seminary where I will, as they say in show biz, break a leg."

"Don't," he said, "they're too pretty."

She couldn't tell from his tone whether he was serious or kidding.

"Thanks," she said.

Where, she wondered, was all this leading?

"Lewtenant," Marge drawled, lilting the final syllable as if it were a question, "do yew thank it wood be at all poss'ble for yew to fahnd yore hayuds on weekdays instead of week*inds*? Ah wood shorely 'preciate it."

"We can surely try, Marge." Harris grinned. He could not think of anyone who did not 'preciate Marge. Not only was she dependably efficient and strikingly attractive, her Texas accent simply wouldn't quit. To the point that there were times when the northern ear could not comprehend what Marge was trying to communicate. But she never tired of repetition till she'd gotten the message across.

"But," Harris continued, "it's not so much that we are finding these heads on the Sabbath as it is this killer is leaving them around town on weekends."

"Ah weeyul except theyat explanaition for the tahm bean. But ah weeyul remahnd yew theyat the Lord mint the Sabbath for rest, and ah intind to git mahn!"

"Gotcha." Harris made an imaginary pistol out of his right hand, aimed at Marge and fired his thumb.

Down the hallway, Dr. Wilhelm Moellmann trudged from his second-floor laboratory. His hands were clutched behind him, his head bowed.

Harris, saying nothing, positioned himself in Moellmann's path, much as a basketball player on defense would get position on a charging offensive player in hopes of drawing a foul.

Moellmann stopped just short of bumping into Harris. The doctor stood inches away, staring at the watch chain on Harris' vest.

"Do I know you?" Moellmann asked, looking up.

Harris sighed. "Harris, Lieutenant, Squad Six, Homicide Division, Detroit Police Department."

"Oh, yes. Oh, yes. I wonder why it is I never can remember you."

"Because," Harris explained, "you're getting old now,

approaching senility, and it's hard for you to remember names."

"That must be it," said Moellmann without really listening to Harris. Wordlessly, the doctor led the way into his inner office.

"Now what is it you want?" Moellmann asked.

Harris could never be sure when the doctor was being droll, when absentminded, or when merely irritating.

"The head," said Harris.

"The head," Moellmann echoed.

Harris sighed again. "The head of Dr. Robert Schmitt."

"Oh, yes." It was as if Moellmann were recalling a distant memory. "I was meaning to ask you about that."

"Ask me?" said Harris, "Ask me about what?"

"Why you brought me the head of a distinguished German physician of this community?"

"Distinguished—!" Harris was almost speechless. "Why, that guy ran an abortion mill."

"Abortion is legal," Moellmann reminded.

"Abortion is legal," Harris agreed, "but your friend Schmitt was about to be arraigned on two counts of homicide. And the case against him was very strong."

"Ah, that explains it better." Moellmann seemed inwardly satisfied.

"Well," Harris prodded.

"Well, what?"

"Is it another Red Hat Murder?"

"Oh yes. Oh yes, indeed. Same M.O. Same drained head. Incision in the same place in the neck area. Same remarkable strength in the removal. And same saw. Oh yes. Oh yes, indeed."

"Well, thank you, Doctor. That's what I came for. Could you establish a time of death?"

"Sometime between 11 A.M. and 3 P.M. yesterday."

"Thank you once again, Doctor." Harris turned to leave.

"I would like to mention one thing more about this series of murders," said Moellmann.

It was rare that the Medical Examiner volunteered information. The offer took Harris by surprise. He turned back to give Moellmann full attention.

"It occurred to me after the Fitzgerald incident," Moellmann said. "One of the ways we determined that Fitzgerald's death did not fit the pattern established in the Red Hat series is that the head was embalmed."

"I remember."

"Well, it occurred to me at this time that the reason Fitzgerald's head was embalmed was to enable it to appear to have a look of great terror."

"Yes."

"This—this visage of ultimate fright—appears to be achieved by the real Red Hat murderer naturally. He doesn't need the artificial aid of embalming. It appears his victims are scared out of their wits by the time they die."

"And the conclusion?" asked a very interested Harris.

"If my conclusions prove correct, you are looking for a young, extremely powerful, meticulously planning, dedicated, very spooky fellow."

The pickup truck was freshly painted red and apparently in excellent condition. So good was its condition, it seemed out of place in this neighborhood. Stenciled on the doors and back paneling on either side of the truck were the words, "McCluskey Roofing and Repair."

The truck slowed to a stop in front of a well-kept house on Pulaski Street near Joseph Campau in Hamtramck, a city entirely within the boundaries of Detroit. Once known for its near one hundred percent Polish population, Hamtramck had become increasingly black.

The home on Pulaski Street belonged to Mr. and Mrs. Stanislaus Krawczak. The Krawczaks had lived there forty years, nearly all their married life. Krawczak was retired from the Dodge Main plant and the couple lived on a meager fixed income.

As the familiar old neighborhoods changed, most of the Krawczaks' friends had moved, many to the nearby suburb of Warren. A number of Polish parishes, with enormous church buildings, closed. The storefront ministry was the wave of the present, both for Baptists and Catholics.

The Krawczaks, after attending Mass this Sunday morning, had come home to a modest breakfast. Now they were seated on their front porch. Stan Krawczak planned a quiet afternoon listening to the familiar voice of Ernie Harwell broadcasting the Tigers game on sturdy WJR. Margaret Krawczak was knitting. She planned to start the stew shortly.

The Krawczaks had always taken meticulous care of their house and lawn, as did most of their neighbors, black and white.

They were surprised that a repair truck had stopped in front of their house and even more surprised when the driver and his companion, after a careful study of some papers resembling blueprints, approached their home.

"Well, now," said the middle-aged, slightly paunchy blond man who wore coveralls and a facsimile of a Tigers baseball cap, "you two young folks would be Mr. and Mrs. Krawczak, wouldn't you? And isn't this a spankin' nice day?"

The Krawczaks exchanged glances, wondering how this stranger could possibly know their names.

"Name's McCluskey, Tod McCluskey," the man continued. "This here's me assistant, Mulrooney," he said, indicating the shriveled, venal-looking man standing on the front lawn. "And that," gesturing toward the vehicle, "would be me truck."

The Krawczaks remained bewildered.

"Now you'll be wonderin' what it is brought us here," said McCluskey. "We—Mr. Mulrooney and meself— would be contractors for the county. Which, of course, as you both well know, includes the city of Hamtramck, where we find ourselves this very moment."

"But what—" Krawczak began.

"But what," picked up the garrulous McCluskey, "would we be doin' at yer fine house this day, ye're askin' yerself. Well, ya see, Stan—I can call ya Stan, now, can't I, Stan?"

McCluskey peered up at Krawczak from beneath the visor of the Tigers cap. "Ya see, Stan, county records show it's very likely that yer roof may have some trouble, what with the age of the house and all."

"But we—" Krawczak attempted to enter the one-sided conversation.

"I know, Stan, I know. Good people like yerselves try to keep up yer property like God-fearin' folk. Not like yer niggers."

"But we like—" Krawczak tried to protest his affinity with his neighbors.

"But face it, Stan," McCluskey plowed on, "how often is it a man yer age is able to get up on his roof and really carefully study its condition?"

"Well, I—"

"Not often, God help us. And whose fault would that be?"

"I—"

"Certainly not yers, Stan. But the county is after wantin' homes like yers to stay in its right good shape. Keep the neighborhood on its toes, as it were."

"Well—"

"So if there's no objection on anyone's part, I'll just ask Mr. Mulrooney here," McCluskey motioned his sidekick into action, "to climb up and give a look at yer roof."

Mulrooney wrestled a ladder against the side of the Krawczak house and clambered toward the roof.

Mrs. Krawczak had dropped several stitches during this monologistic exchange. As Mulrooney crawled about the roof, Krawczak rose from his rocker, came to the railing and looked up, craning his neck in an attempt to locate the elusive Mulrooney.

"Now look here—" said Krawczak.

"I know, I know how ya feel, Stan," McCluskey assured him. "Here we are, perfect strangers, disturbin' yer Sabbath, as it were. But I can promise ya this: if there's any work to be done to yer roof ye'll bless the day McCluskey Roofing and Repair came into yer life. That ya will."

Mulrooney descended. He and McCluskey caucused near the truck. There was much head-wagging and mumbled argument. Finally, the huddle broke and McCluskey returned to the apprehensive couple.

"Well, Stan, old friend, I've good news and I've bad news. The bad news is that ye'll need major work done to yer roof to bring it up to county code."

The Krawczaks instinctively drew close to each other. They felt as if a tidal wave were about to engulf them.

"The good news is that McCluskey Roofing and Repair is here to help. Well I know what it's like to be on a fixed income. Isn't me own mother suffering the same financial burden."

"Well," McCluskey continued, after honoring the mention of his mother with a respectful pause, "Mr. Mulrooney and I agree we can take care of yer roof, bring it up to code, and remove all yer worries for just $5,000."

With this, a beatific smile appeared on McCluskey's face.

"Here, then." He presented the Krawczaks with an order form that needed only a signature to become an official contract. "Ya just sign this, Stan, and let McCluskey take on yer worries."

Obviously overwhelmed, Krawczak hesitated. He looked at his wife, who now stood close to him clutching his arm. She nodded. Signing seemed their only choice. He scribbled his name on the bottom line.

"That's all the money we have, Stan," said Mrs. Krawczak as the red truck disappeared around the corner.

"I know, Margaret, I know."

"That's all the money they've got, you know," Mulrooney observed as the firm of McCluskey Roofing and Repair rode forward to new conquests.

"I know, I know," McCluskey acknowledged, dropping the brogue. Posing as an appropriate official, McCluskey always checked in advance data such as bank reserves and realty holdings.

"What made you try for the whole thing?" Mulrooney was barely able to suppress laughter as he rubbed his hands in glee. It was not every day they got $5,000 for hammering a few shingles back in place and daubing a bit of tar around.

"I don't know, Johnny. It was a spur-of-the-moment decision. They just looked scared enough to fall for it." McCluskey glanced at his partner and winked broadly. "Just lucky, I guess," he observed.

"Ah, yes," Mulrooney did an impression of the late Barry Fitzgerald, "the luck o' the Irish!"

The two roared with laughter.

In its more than half a century, there had never been more bedlam within the Gothic vaults of Sacred Heart Seminary's chapel than the present pandemonium.

Students, still garbed in cassock and surplice, and clergy faculty members, still wearing their Mass vestments, mingled with police, television and radio news staffers, and newspaper reporters.

"This side chapel, where the head was found," Detective Fred Ross was gathering facts as usual, "was it currently or recently in use?"

"No," Father Burk answered. "These altars off to the side were used years ago for private Masses. But they haven't been used for anything for years."

"They seem to be well kept up," Ross persisted.

"The nuns," said Burk, "they and the janitorial service keep the chapel pretty clean. They even change the linen on these altars, though we no longer use them. I guess they just don't like to see things go to seed. You know how women are."

Ross looked up from his note-taking. "Possibly even better than you do, Father," he said.

Burk thought of Father Andrew Greeley's forgettable treatise on "Sexual Intimacy." "Yes, Sergeant, you're probably right. Only not all of us realize it."

Ross was not sure he understood all of Burk's implications but decided the matter was not worth pursuing.

Brilliant television lights were on in front of the shrine where the head had been found. A blond, chunky, well-groomed man stood before the camera, holding a microphone.

"We have with us," he announced, "the person who first saw the severed head of Dr. Robert Schmitt. I've been told that, oddly enough, Sister Clotilde had been of the opinion that the series of killings known as The Red Hat Murders was over. How ironic, then, that she should be the one to find the latest Red Hat Murder."

"Sister Clotilde," the camera pulled back to pick up Clotilde, obviously shaken and ashen-faced, "what were the first thoughts that passed through your mind when you saw the severed head of Dr. Schmitt?"

Sister Clotilde's eyes slowly rolled back in her head as she gradually crumpled to the floor and out of the picture.

The camera came in tight to a head-and-shoulders shot of the TV reporter.

"This," he said, a look of panic crossing his face, "is Dwayne X. Riley, Channel Four—oh, hell, guys, scrap it. Somebody take care of the nun."

"Had you ever seen Dr. Schmitt before, Father?" asked Joe Cox. "I mean had he ever attended services here at the seminary?"

"No," said Monsignor Al Martin, in his characteristically thoughtful manner. "I am here for almost everything the seminary does or sponsors. Certainly, I am here for all liturgical events. To the best of my knowledge, I have never seen the doctor before today. And, given the present circumstances, I wish I had never seen him at all."

"Thanks, Father." So distracted was Cox that he had failed to catch the monsignor's proper title. Damn, he thought, another blind alley.

Pat Lennon had found a pay phone near the seminary residence wing labeled "St. Thomas Hall."

She had been put on hold and was waiting for Father

Leo Clark. She had declined the suggestion of St. John's switchboard operator that Clark return her call. She preferred holding the line to preclude anyone else's reaching him first.

"Miss Lennon?" The voice was becoming familiar to her. "Father Clark. What can I do for you?"

"They've found another Red Hat victim, Father."

"Where?"

"In the chapel at Sacred Heart Seminary."

"Oh my God, no! Who was it?"

"A Dr. Schmitt. I doubt you knew him. A very bad abortionist. Another one who deserved to die." She heard herself say the last few words and, on reflection, couldn't believe the words had been hers. She who all her adult life had been in ethical opposition to capital punishment. She vowed she would return to reexamine this apparent gut reaction later.

"I take it the head was found in conjunction with some saint's statue," Clark surmised.

"Yes, Father. St. Bridget."

"St. Bridget." He paused. "Irish. But I can't tell you too much more off the top of my head. This will only take a moment. Do you want me to call you back?"

"No, no, Father!" Her tone was simultaneously imperative and pleading. "I'll hold the line."

"All right."

She could almost hear him chuckle at her peculiar vehemence.

"I have it," he said after a few moments' research. St. Bridget of Kildare. Do you want the details of her life?"

"No, I don't think so, Father. Just tell me: is she patroness of something or other?"

"Let's see. She died in 625 A.D. She is usually depicted holding a light, lamp, or candle."

"That's what the now headless statue in the chapel is like: it's a woman holding a lighted candle."

"Let's see now: Bridget is the patroness of cattle, dairymaids, fugitives, Irish nuns—wouldn't you just know it—and midwives and newborn babies."

Lennon tensed. "What were those last two, Father?"

"Midwives and newborn babies. Of course," he exclaimed, "that's it, isn't it? He was an abortionist, so his head would be found on a saint who was patroness of midwives and newborns!"

"That's it," Lennon affirmed. "How do you like playing detective, Father?"

"It's as good as chess ever was. Father Brown, one side: watch my smoke!"

The front doorbell rang. That in itself was an event at this rectory.

Old St. Joseph's parish, just off Gratiot, not far from downtown Detroit, was a shadow of its former self. Once it had been a German national parish. Which meant it had no territorial boundaries. Any and all Germans of Detroit could be members if they wished. And most did.

St. Joe's had gone through both urban decay and renewal. All the original old houses were gone. In their place were new high-rises, townhouses, and condominiums.

With all these new and fairly affluent people around, St. Joe's could have been a much more active parish. But Father Donald Curley, the pastor, preferred a passive apostolate. Rather than going about ringing doorbells and bringing in new sheaves, he opted for waiting for the sheaves to find him and St. Joe's.

Casting his vote in favor of this passive apostolate was Father Edmund Sklarski, retired and living at St. Joe's. Sklarski had been professor of speech at Sacred Heart Seminary and, briefly, pastor of St. Norbert's in Inkster.

When asked by the speech professor at St. John's Major Seminary whether they had ever had a course in speech, not one of Sklarski's erstwhile students admitted to ever having had such a course. The denial stood as a monument to his nonteaching ability.

Actually, the doorbell rang several times. Father Curley,

tall, paunchy, bald and myopic, was also very hard of hearing. So it was only gradually that he became aware of the active doorbell. And when he did, he scarcely believed his own poor hearing.

Curley, wearing brown trousers and a sport shirt, since he was headed for a few holes at the St. John's Seminary links, made his way to the door.

"Good afternoon," said the well-dressed gentleman at the door. "I wonder if I could see a priest."

Curley said nothing. It wasn't registering. *He* was a priest. He had forgotten that in his mufti, a stranger would not recognize him as such.

"I'm attending a convention here," the man, uncomfortable at having to give particulars, explained. "I'm staying at the Plaza. I won't take more than a few minutes of Father's time. I just want to go to confession."

The picture became clear to Curley.

"Certainly, sir," he said, "I'll get a priest for you. Only one thing," he added, building a scenario for no reason except the hell of it, "the priest is very hard of hearing. You'll have to speak up."

"Oh, that's quite all right," said the man. "I'm just grateful I caught Father in."

Curley left him standing in the hallway.

He went upstairs to Sklarski's suite and leaned into the sitting room. "There's a guy downstairs who wants to see you, Ed. Only one thing: he's very hard of hearing. You'll have to speak up if he's going to hear you. But that should be no trick for an old speech prof."

"No, no, none at all." Ordinarily, Sklarski would have reacted negatively at having his Sunday afternoon rest interrupted. But the challenge of projecting enough so that the deaf might hear was too tempting to grouse about the bother of it all.

"Peoples, moneys, panorama," Sklarski commented meaninglessly as he descended the stairs.

Grinning, Curley gathered his golf clubs and quietly went out the kitchen door.

"How do you do, Father," the man shouted. "I am attending a convention in town and I would like to go to confession."

"I'm Father Sklarski," Sklarski shouted. "Let's go in this parlor and you can make your confession."

Both his visitor and Sklarski marveled at the tendency of those who were hard of hearing to shout as if everyone were similarly afflicted.

There were no passers-by outside St. Joe's rectory this Sunday afternoon. If there had been, they would have discovered that a conventioneer had committed adultery with the chairwoman of his subcommittee. And that he had received a penance of ten Our Fathers and ten Hail Marys.

Whereas the scene inside Sacred Heart Seminary's chapel was bedlam, the interior of Services, Inc. was pastoral by comparison.

This was the second time in two days the Detroit Police had visited Services, Inc. Both visits were by the Homicide Division; first Squad one, now Squad Six. It was, in part, due to the thoroughness of Squad One's search that Squad Six's investigation was going so smoothly. Squad One had gathered all available evidence, and there was no sign that any additional evidence had sprung up since the previous day's search.

Most of the local news people had come and gone.

Once Joe Cox learned there had been a warrant out for the arrest of Schmitt, he quickly called Lieutenant Bourque and got some priceless quotes on the charges against Schmitt, as well as a sketchy account of the evidence.

Cox made this the lead to his story. What, Cox reminded himself, do lurid pathological maniacs do? They sell newspapers.

Pat Lennon did not file her story as quickly. She had missed Bourque, since the Lieutenant, immediately after talking with Cox, had headed out for some sailboating on the Detroit River.

Lennon was able to contact Detective Donna Osborn of

Squad One. From her, Lennon got much of the same information as Cox had from Bourque, though not all the explicit details.

Lennon stayed on the trail a while longer. She was able to turn up and contact one of Schmitt's old German cronies. She learned of Schmitt's wartime activities and—the old man was willing to talk now that Schmitt was dead—his tenuous but definite connection with the Nazi death camps.

An even better backgrounding! What do mass murderers do? They sell even more newspapers.

Lennon was now making a final tour of Services, Inc. in the company of Detective Colleen Farrell.

Having been briefed by Osborn and now Farrell, Lennon still experienced an involuntary shudder as she walked through the offices of Services, Inc. and thought of the brutality that Schmitt had perpetrated here.

The rooms had been stripped. Instruments, tools, records, and file cabinets had been taken as evidence. Only a few furnishings remained.

One object, a statuette, on a windowsill near a potted fern, attracted Lennon's attention.

It appeared to be a man in the armor of the old Roman Empire. One of his feet was crushing a bird, from whose beak issued, in the fashion of comic strips, a balloon-enclosed word: *Cras*. The soldier's right hand held a sword, with which he was pointing to a cross, which bore the inscription, *Hodie!*

Lennon began to laugh. The combination of the deadly serious business of this day along with this ludicrous statuette tickled her funny bone.

"May I pick this up?" Lennon asked Farrell.

"Yes, it's been dusted. Go ahead."

Lennon lifted the statuette. It was lightweight plaster of paris. The sort of thing that could be bought inexpensively, once you found a shop that sold it.

She turned the statuette upside down. On the bottom was etched the letters, "Exped."

Lennon, even with her extensive Catholic background, could not make heads or tails out of the statuette.

She asked to see Linda Ryder, one of the nurses at Services, Inc., who had cooperated with the police and was now in the clinic for questioning.

"Linda," Lennon asked the still-frightened girl, "do you recognize this?" She offered Linda the statuette.

"Yes." Linda responded without taking the object in her hands.

"Where did it come from? What's it doing here?"

"It came in yesterday morning's mail. It was odd, but then Dr. Schmitt used to get some odd things in the mail. I was going to ask him about it, but he was unusually gruff and rushed yesterday..."

Linda Ryder broke down in tears. Even Schmitt, she thought, had not deserved the death that had been described to her.

Lennon waited a few moments.

"Linda," she again addressed the nurse as the tearful girl regained her composure, "can you tell me how it was delivered?"

"It came in a plain brown wrapper. I put it on the shelf there. I meant to ask Dr. Schmitt about it on Monday morning..."

She broke down again as she realized there would be no Monday morning for Dr. Schmitt.

Lennon took the statuette over to where *News* photographer Don Carlson was happily snapping shots of the clinic's various rooms.

"Don," Lennon presented him with the statuette, "would you take shots of this from every angle, including the bottom of the base?"

"Sure." Carlson took the statuette and began laughing. "Is this somebody's idea of a joke?"

"Maybe," Lennon conceded. "Then again, it may prove to be the missing link."

"The what?"

"Never mind. After you're done with that, I'd appreciate

it if you'd come back to the paper with me. I'd like to go through our library."

"Looking for a particular photo?"

"Yeah. I seem to remember it. But first I've got to find it."

Lennon was positive she had seen a statuette similar to or identical with this one. She was nearly certain she had seen it in connection with The Red Hat Murders. But she had paid no attention to it before.

There must be a reason for all this.

Beulah Blackstone, elderly, black, and widowed, shuffled toward the front door of her modest old home on Doremus Street in the shadow of the Chrysler Assembly Plant.

Why, she wondered, can't people stay home on Sundays. No peace. No peace even for an old lady who lives alone.

As she neared her front door, she looked past the formidable figure in the doorway to the shiny red truck parked outside. She didn't like the look of it. Not at all.

"Good afternoon to ya, Miz Blackstone," the blond man in coveralls and Tigers cap greeted her.

A little too familiar and friendly for her taste.

"Miz Blackstone, me name would be McCluskey, Tod McCluskey of McCluskey Roofing and Repair Company, as me nice shiny new truck out there by the curb will attest."

McCluskey could barely see through the closed and locked screen door. Two white eyes peered out at him suspiciously.

"Ah, Miz Blackstone, would ya be after wantin' ta come out here on the porch? We surely mean ya no harm. No harm at all."

There was no movement from inside the house. If anything, the peering eyes grew more suspicious.

"We've been empowered by the county to make sure the roofs in this neighborhood come up to code, Miz Blackstone." McCluskey decided to go directly to a power play with this reluctant customer. "So, then, if ya have no objection, Miz Blackstone, I'll just ask me assistant down by the truck, Mr. Mulrooney, a fine man, to take a quick look at yer roof. Ya don't want fer yer fine home to descend to the level of the white trash in the neighborhood."

Mulrooney was on the roof. There still had been no sound from the old lady whose sad eyes continued to stare at McCluskey from behind the locked screen door.

" 'Tis really a fine, fine day out, Miz Blackstone. Ya really ought ta come out and enjoy it!"

Still no movement.

"Ah, well . . ."

Mulrooney was down from the roof. He and McCluskey converged at the truck. There was much mumbled argumentation and debate. In the end, McCluskey returned to the door.

"Well, now, Miz Blackstone, as ya must have suspected, a roof as old as is the one of this very house has been up there so long it's in desperate need of repair. And I remind ya, Miz Blackstone, we're not talkin' of a matter of choice. Yer house just must meet the demands of the code. However, ya can bless this day, Miz Blackstone, that it was McCluskey Roofing and Repair and none other that called upon ya.

"We'll be able to take care of yer precious roof, Miz Blackstone." McCluskey shifted to his left foot and took a breath. Even McCluskey had to breathe from time to time. "And it's not gonna cost ya an arm and a leg. So what's it gonna cost, ya ask? I tell ya, it's gonna cost ya no more than just fifteen dollars a month at just eighteen percent compounded interest. And ye've got years to pay. No pressure. No pressure at all, Miz Blackstone."

Still no sound from inside.

"Now I'll just have ta have ya sign this requisition order, Miz Blackstone. I'll tell ya what I'll do, since ya seem to be a bit reluctant ta open yer door. And I don't blame ya fer a minute what with all that's goin' on in the streets this day. I'm just gonna leave this form on yer front porch along with my pen. What I'd like ya to do is, I'll leave the porch and ya just sign the form and, please Miz Blackstone, ye'll keep the pen like a nice lady, won't ya?"

McCluskey left the form attached to a clipboard on the floor on the porch near the door.

Mrs. Blackstone sighed. She was being ripped off again. She knew it. She did not even understand how much this would cost her over the long run. They always made it sound like such a little bit. It always became an awful lot.

But, she thought, McCluskey made it clear she had no choice; after all he *was* from the county.

She opened the screen door a crack and pulled inside the packet McCluskey had placed there. After a moment, the door reopened and the packet was replaced.

McCluskey retrieved the packet.

"Ah well, then, ya didn't have ta return the pen, Miz Blackstone."

Even the eyes were gone from behind the screen.

Poor bitch, McCluskey thought as he returned to his shiny red truck, you should have taken the pen. It's the only thing you're going to get out of this deal.

"How'd we do?" asked Mulrooney as they drove away.

"Sometimes, Johnny boy, you have to take it in dribs and drabs. Rest assured, we got all we could. And even if we don't get it all during her lifetime, we'll have a legitimate claim on her estate when she dies. Some estate!" He chortled. "We might even end up owning that old house."

"I found it!" exulted a triumphant Don Carlson.

Pat Lennon's heart skipped a beat. All the pieces were falling into place.

It had always been thus. Even many years back when Detroit had had a third major daily, the *Detroit Times*, a Hearst publication. When there was a breaking story, the *Free Press* would send one or two reporters to cover it. The *Times* would send three to five. The *News* would send up to fifteen staffers. The *News'* pictorial library reflected this blanket coverage. It was two to three times the size of the *Free Press*' library.

Lennon and Carlson had spread the contents of all the folders on The Red Hat Murders across the immense photo desk. For the past hour, they had been going over the pictures with magnifying glasses.

To this point, Lennon had found Strauss' statuette, on a shelf otherwise filled with uppers and downers in the drug kingpin's headquarters, and Carlson had just located Harding's replica atop a bureau in the pimp's plush pad. The statuette was partially hidden by a framed photo of Harding in full pimp regalia.

"O.K.," said Lennon, after confirming Carlson's find by means of her magnifying glass, "on to Rough Rudy Ruggiero and we'll have a full house!"

They were ebullient. They felt like research scientists on the verge of a major breakthrough.

As the minutes ticked by, discouragement set in. Try as they might, they could not discover another "Exped." statuette anywhere in the photos of Ruggiero's base of operations. They even exchanged stacks of photos to scan them all again with a fresh perspective.

It was no use. There was no "Exped." anywhere, at least not in the photos of the various places of business or pleasure belonging to Rough Rudy.

"Damn!" Lennon said in frustration. "Why isn't it there? It's got to be there. It ties the murders together. You're sure this is the complete file on Ruggiero?"

"I'm sure, Pat. Don't feel bad. You're not the first reporter ever to see a pet theory go down the drain."

Lennon sat, drumming her fingers on the desk top. The photos near her hands did an erratic dance responding to the rhythm of her tapping.

Suddenly, "The house!" she almost shrieked.

"The what?" Carlson seemed jolted by her excitement.

"The house!" she repeated. "Ruggiero's home. I remember now. The police report: Ruggiero's home resembled a cockamamie church or chapel. There were statues and votive lights all over the place."

"So?"

"So, that's where 'Exped.' is. That's where he's got to be!"

"Pat, don't get your hopes up too much."

"Don, he's got to be among all those statues. Nothing makes sense unless he's there!"

Lennon picked up the phone and called Homicide Squad Six. This was her lucky day: she reached Lieutenant Harris.

She explained all she and Carlson had accomplished. She described what she anticipated could be found among the statues, reliquaries, and holy pictures in Ruggiero's chapel-like home.

In Harris she found a sympathetic ear and responsive action.

She hung up and headed for police headquarters.

The fifth hole at St. John's Seminary golf course was a very easy par five. The elevated tee led to a marshy valley, then to a gentle upgraded slope; a dogleg to the right led to the green, which was open in the front and rear, with sand traps on either side. It was relatively easy to reach the green in two.

The four clergymen golfers were almost alone on the course this Sunday afternoon. They stood on the elevation preparing to tee off.

"Remember when the barn burned down?" Father Joe Sheehan looked at the vacant area between the tee and Sheldon Road.

"Why that must be nearly thirty years ago," said Father Fred Dolson.

"Yeah," Sheehan acknowledged, "but I think of it every time I tee off here."

"Uh-huh," Father Don Curley agreed. "Fathers Hubbard and Latham played right through it. Said afterwards, it was a bit warm but they'd got off decent shots."

"And Father O'Brien up in his room," Sheehan was beginning to break up over the memory, "kept calling the switchboard to report the burning barn. And Harry kept telling him they were burning leaves. And he said, 'Oh, O.K.,' even though he could see the damn barn burning."

They all laughed as they remembered the barn filled with valuable farm implements and fertilizer going up in smoke while a number of Sulpician Fathers watched it go with no more than academic interest.

"Simply one more indication," said Curley, "of why it takes seven Sulpicians to confer one sacrament!"

Curley teed up, took a couple of practice swings, and sent the ball whistling down the fairway. The slight fade played the dogleg perfectly. Whatever else one was tempted to say about Curley, he did golf well.

"Nice shot," said Father Ted Neighbors, Curley's partner.

"Didn't any of you guys hear anything about another Red Hat Murder?" asked Sheehan.

"How many times do we have to tell you we didn't?" snapped a short-fused Curley.

Neighbors' drive sliced badly. The ball disappeared in a forest that resembled the jungles of equatorial Africa.

"Damn!" Neighbors swore, "Can't you guys think of anything to talk about besides the damn Red Hat Murders?"

Curley guffawed. "That's right . . . and how is St. Frances Cabrini?"

"I understand she hasn't performed any miracles lately," said Sheehan. "Terrible headache."

All laughed, save Neighbors.

Sheehan's drive barely made the top of the hill on the other side of the valley. Not much distance, but he would have a clear shot to the green.

"Well," said Sheehan, "on the way here I thought I heard a radio news bulletin about another murder."

"There aren't supposed to be any more Red Hat Murders," Curley observed.

"That depends on which paper you read," said Sheehan. "The *Free Press* says the series is over. The *News* says there's more to come."

Dolson's drive split the middle of the fairway. With no fade, he would have a long way to the green.

"Personally," said Dolson, "I think it's a good way to handle criminals. There's too much mollycoddling nowadays. The only ones who have any rights are the criminals. You don't see cops reading their rights to victims, do you?"

The foursome began their descent from the knoll.

"Fred," said Sheehan, "I think in a former life you were in charge of the Spanish Inquisition."

Rather than begin a futile search, Neighbors dropped another ball at the base of the marshy valley. If successful, this would be a tricky shot. He would have to bring the ball up sharply and either slice it to conform to the hole's dogleg or arch it over a tall tree. Neighbors' confreres stationed themselves behind the ball to help track its course.

Neighbors selected a three-wood.

"Don't you think you ought to go with a low iron?" Curley asked.

"Silence!" Neighbors suggested.

Neighbors took a mighty swing. Turf, mud, and goop flew in every direction. His confreres peered through the debris trying to trace the flight of the ball. None was able to find it.

Finally, Curley looked at the spot where the ball had lain. A small white object was barely visible. Neighbors had hit the ball on its top and buried it.

Curley began to laugh. He pointed at the white dot. "You took the head right off 'er, Ted!"

The blood slowly drained from Neighbors' face as his three companions fell to the ground clutching their sides in hysterical laughter.

It was uncertain whether the match could continue.

"They found it." Harris hung up the phone. He was solemn. He always was when he sensed he was nearing the end of a difficult investigation.

"Where was it?" Pat Lennon had difficulty controlling her excitement. Her theory was proving itself.

"In among all the other statues and bric-a-brac," said Harris. "Bernhard found it after a brief search ... funny how easy it is when you know what you're looking for."

"How was it delivered?" asked Inspector Koznicki.

The three were seated by themselves in Squad Six's squad room.

"By mail. The day before Ruggiero's murder," said Harris. "Mrs. Ruggiero thought it was from some missionary—she supports so many. She just put it up among the other statues and thought no more about it."

"Well," said Koznicki, "that completes the circle. Each of our victims received this particular statuette shortly before his death. Now, what does it mean?"

"Miss Lennon," Koznicki addressed the reporter, "you've led us this far with, I must say, some brilliant observations. Do you know anymore about this statuette? Is it a saint? If so, which saint?"

Lennon was somewhat surprised. "You mean," she said, "you'd allow me to continue along with you on this case?"

"Certainly." Koznicki's huge hands made an open, welcoming gesture. "At least to some extent. As far as Lieutenant Harris and I are concerned, neither of us cares who solves or helps solve a case, only that the case be solved.

"I propose we collaborate now. If and when we are ready to make an arrest, you'll be the first to know. Meanwhile, we'll let you know what is on or off the record and we will trust you to cooperate."

Lennon was elated.

"Then let me try my primary source." She picked up the phone. "May I?" she asked.

Harris pushed the button that would give her an outside line.

"Father Clark? This is Pat Lennon again."

"Good heavens, a few days ago I'd never heard of you.

Now I receive a couple of calls a day from you."

"I've got another saint for you."

"Gracious! You mean there's been another murder?"

"No, no, Father. This may be a clue that will help us find the murderer."

Lennon started to describe the statuette. Before she could complete her description, Clark began to chuckle.

"Oh, yes," he said, "no doubt about it. It's old St. Expeditus."

"Expeditus?" That was a new one on Lennon.

"Yes. I'm afraid, Miss Lennon, that Expeditus is a myth. Like Philomena, Christopher, and good old St. George and his fire-breathing dragon. Expeditus is a figment of someone's fertile imagination."

"Can you tell me anything about him?" Lennon's frustration level was getting a workout.

"No, sorry, not really. I pay very little attention to mythical saints. But feel free to call me when you have a real one."

Lennon turned to the two officers.

"At least," she said, "we have a name for our friend here." She picked up the figure and studied it. "St. Expeditus."

"Saint who?" asked Harris.

"Expeditus," said Koznicki. "I've never heard of him."

"Let me check with my backup source." Lennon dialed again.

"Father Koesler? Pat Lennon. I've got one for you that Father Clark couldn't solve."

"If it baffled Leo, I wouldn't hold out much hope for me."

Lennon explained about the statuette and the circumstances under which it had been found. As she continued, she was struck by the difference between the way Clark and Koesler reacted to St. Expeditus. While Clark had laughed at the mythical holy man, Koesler was deadly serious.

"You say Inspector Koznicki and Lieutenant Harris are with you?"

"Yes."

"I think I can help you with St. Expeditus, but my explanation may strain your credulity somewhat. Would it be possible for the three of you to drop by the rectory here?"

Lennon checked with her companions.

"We'll be there in about twenty minutes, Father."

"Very good. That will give me time to do some research."

The Lions were playing the Vikings. Football from Metropolitan Stadium in Bloomington, Minnesota.

Joe Cox had the game on TV. Only sporadically did he pay attention to it. Even Bud Grant, the Vikings' stoic coach, did little to establish philosophical tranquility in Cox's life.

He missed Pat Lennon.

And he didn't know what could be keeping her. He had filed his story on the latest Red Hat Murder hours ago. And it was a damn good story, if he did say so himself.

If his story was that good and he had finished it so long ago, his roommate should long since have returned to their apartment. He could not imagine her finding that much more to the story than he had.

Minnesota scored. A pass from Lee to Foreman. Pat would have squealed. She always did at a touchdown. Especially a Minnesota touchdown. Pat preferred Minnesota even to the hometown crew.

TV viewers would now be treated to stop-action instant replays from every conceivable angle. Cox used to try to bet with Pat on the replay action. Only if she had been distracted during the live action would she consider wagering on what she didn't realize was a replay. She was always furious when she realized what had happened.

Cox smiled at the memory.

At times like this, Cox wondered whether it mightn't be a good idea to join the paper chase and propose marriage to

Pat. He had no reason to believe she would accept. But it might give a sense of permanence to their lives which, when there was no Pat Lennon present, he missed.

He decided to make a large salad. It would both distract him and keep in the refrigerator till Pat returned.

The Lions fumbled. A Minnesota lineman picked up the loose ball and, accompanied by what appeared to be a herd of elephants, ran it in for a touchdown.

Pat would have squealed.

Damn! Damn! Damn!

He'd grown accustomed to her squeal.

"You may wonder," Father Robert Koesler opened his explanation, "why I think I know more about something than Father Leo Clark does."

He addressed this remark to Pat Lennon, to whom he had given Clark's name as an expert in just about everything hagiographical.

The two were seated on a couch in the living room of St. Anselm's rectory. Seated opposite them on an identical couch were Inspector Koznicki and Lieutenant Harris.

Koznicki, having previously experienced Koesler's attempts at instant coffee, had declined the priest's offer. Lennon and Harris had tasted the coffee served them. Their nearly filled cups rested on the end table. Koesler was the only one Koznicki knew who could ruin instant coffee.

"The reason I have taken a special interest in St. Expeditus will have to wait a few minutes," said Koesler. "First, let me give you a few interesting facts about this saint who probably never existed."

"Excuse me," Harris pushed his coffee cup still further away, "but how could someone who never existed be a saint?"

Koesler smiled. It was a source of never-ending surprise to him how much one took for granted if one were born and raised Catholic.

"In the early Christian centuries, Lieutenant," Koesler leaned forward, "some pious stories and myths became enshrined and retold so regularly they gradually became accepted as fact."

"Father Clark mentioned St. Christopher as an example," said Lennon.

"Ah, yes," said Koznicki, "the saint who adorns so many dashboards."

"A good example," said Koesler. "Legend has it that this man carried a small boy across a dangerous stream. The boy was Christ. And the man was dubbed Christopher—or 'Christ-bearer.'"

"Then what's he doing in all those cars?" Harris demanded.

"A good example of a myth being taken for a reality," Koesler answered.

"But now we come to St. Expeditus." Koesler selected a book from among several stacked before him on the coffee table.

"Expeditus," Koesler paraphrased from the martyrology he held, "was one of six soldiers put to death for their Christian faith. He allegedly died with Caius, Aristonique, Rufus, and Galatas, all of whom were companions of St. Hermogene."

"I hate to tell you, Father," said Lennon, "but this is not very interesting."

"It gets better." Koesler continued from the martyrology. "Supposedly, they were put to death in Melitene, in what was known as Armenia. Not only is their exact date of death unknown, so is the period in which they lived. With all of that, they do have a feast day, April 19th.

"Now, in about the seventeenth century," Koesler selected another book from his stack, "a packing case containing human bones from the catacombs was sent from Rome to some nuns in Paris. On the case was inscribed the word '*spedite*.' Did that mean the case held the mortal remains of St. Expeditus—or that the case was to be delivered with speed and dispatch?"

His guests smiled.

"See," said Koesler, "I told you it would get better."

"But what, if anything," Harris interjected, "does this have to do with The Red Hat Murders?"

"Give him time, Ned." Koznicki knew how his priest friend needed to build a logical explanation leaning heavily on Aristotelian logic.

Koesler nodded unspoken gratitude to Koznicki. "Along about the eighteenth century, Expeditus became a firm fixture in the religious piety of both Sicily and Germany. He became the patron saint of—what else—dispatch. He was the saint to be invoked against procrastination."

"The statuettes that were found at each of The Red Hat Murders?" Lennon asked.

"Exactly," said Koesler, "it's the traditional depiction of Expeditus. Leo Clark is one of the few who would recognize it. You have a man in a uniform of ancient Roman times. The raven is a creature which, to the Latins, was an emblem of interminable delay. The word coming from the raven's mouth is *cras*, Latin for 'tomorrow.' All this is intolerable to Expeditus, of course. So he crushes the raven beneath his heel. And points with his sword to the cross on which we find the word *hodie*, Latin for 'today.'"

Koesler looked quite pleased with himself. As if he had just successfully completed teaching a very practical course to attentive students.

"That's very interesting, Father," said Koznicki, "but it is still not clear to me why anyone would send this statuette to someone who was about to become a murder victim."

Before Koesler could answer, Harris uttered a muted exclamation. "Oh, my God," he said, very deliberately. "I think I know."

The others turned their attention to the Lieutenant, who, in turn, looked very intently at Koesler.

"You think it's voodoo, don't you?" Harris asked.

"Yes," said Koesler.

"Voodoo!" Lennon and Koznicki exclaimed simultaneously.

Koznicki ran with the ball. "Really, Ned," he said, "we are living in the middle of Detroit in the middle of the twentieth century! You can't expect anyone to take voodoo seriously!"

"Walt, I don't care whether you take voodoo seriously," said Harris. "All I want you to know is that the practice of voodoo is far from dead in beautiful downtown Detroit."

"He's right, Inspector," said Koesler. "And now we are getting close, in the circuitous path my ratiocination takes, to the reason for my interest in St. Expeditus."

For the first time in this conversation, Pat Lennon flipped open her note pad and began scribbling her version of shorthand.

"You see," Koesler recommenced, "during all those years I was with the *Detroit Catholic*, I built up strong bonds with Detroit's black community. That was due partly to the physical location of the newspaper in the heart of Detroit and also to some controversial positions I took.

"In any case, it was through some of my connections in the black community that I was informed of a few of the voodoo cults that are very active in Detroit."

"I can't believe I didn't know this was going on." Koznicki experienced a rare moment of surprise concerning his city. Ordinarily, he made it his business to know everything that was going on in Detroit.

"They don't advertise, Walt," said Harris.

"Have you attended any of these voodoo rites?" Koznicki asked Harris.

"No," Harris answered, "but I'm well aware they're going on."

"How about you, Father," Koznicki persisted, "have you ever attended?"

"No," Koesler answered. "To be perfectly frank, I find the notion of voodoo worship somewhat frightening. But the knowledge that rites were being conducted in Detroit —and in most other major cities of the country—started me on some research.

"Voodoo," Koesler self-consciously again cast himself in the role of a teacher, "began in Africa many centuries ago. As the natives were taken to other countries, usually as slaves, they took with them their voodoo faith and practices."

"Do you have any idea, Father," Lennon asked, "which countries are most affected by voodoo?"

Koesler consulted yet another volume from his stack. "Well, according to this account, it's most prevalent among the native populations of Africa, Haiti, and the West Indies, as well as some South American peoples. Also, forms of it are indigenous to Australia, New Zealand, and the aboriginal populations of various Pacific islands."

Lennon jotted all this down.

"What is truly amazing as one studies this," Koesler continued, "is the incredible adaptability of these people. Most of the native Africans under slavery were virtually forced to become members of one or another of the Christian denominations. Most were forced to become Catholic."

An apologetic blush tinted the priest's cheeks.

"Yet," he went on, "they were able to blend voodooism with Christianity in ways the early missionaries could not have imagined. And that is particularly so when it comes to the saints. You see, the spirits in voodooism are called *loa*. And, while not all *loa* are saints, all the saints are *loa*."

"And that," Harris presumed, "explains your familiarity with good old St. Expeditus."

"Why, yes, it does." It was Koesler's turn to be surprised. "As it so happens, Expeditus is one of the predominant saints in the voodoo *loa*. St. Expeditus is invoked particularly when an evil curse, perhaps even death, is to be delivered. Expeditus, as we have already seen, does not suffer delay. And when an enemy is to be dispatched, it is essential the curse be delivered with dispatch."

Koesler was pleased with his pun. The others seemed unmoved by it.

"There's one more thing I think you ought to know." Koesler selected a book with a brightly colored dust jacket. "This book, *The Mind/Body Effect*, by Herbert Benson, M.D., makes, among other things, a strong case for the physical effects, including death, that voodoo can have on people.

"I want to read you one short passage wherein Dr. Benson cites what happened to an Australian who had been marked for death by an aboriginal rite of pointing a bone at him. *'The man who discovers that he is being boned by an enemy,'*" Koesler read, *"'is, indeed a pitiable sight. He stands aghast, with his eyes staring at the treacherous pointer, and with his hands lifted as though to ward off the lethal medium, which he imagines is pouring into his body. His cheeks blanch and his eyes become glassy, and the expression of his face becomes horribly distorted . . . He attempts to shriek but usually the sound chokes in his throat. His body begins to tremble and the muscles twist involuntarily. He sways backward and falls to the ground, and after a short time appears to be in a swoon; but soon after he writhes as if in mortal agony, and covering his face with his hands, begins to moan . . . His death is only a matter of a comparatively short time.'"*

Koesler's listeners were silent. The description of an apparently voodoo-caused death had reached them.

"I was particularly impressed," Koesler said, "with this description of blanched cheeks, glassy eyes, distorted face, and a mouth that seems to be trying to shriek. This pretty well describes the condition of the heads you've been finding, doesn't it? I mean, all I know is what I read in the papers." He inclined his head toward Lennon.

"Yes, that could well describe the heads," Koznicki said thoughtfully. "But, with the possible exception of Stud Harding, it is probable that none of the victims even saw their statuette before they died. And, in the case of Dr. Schmitt, it is certain he did not see the statuette. The nurse was going to show it to him tomorrow."

Everyone seemed to find the word "tomorrow" jarring. So many things had happened since the discovery of Schmitt's head that it was difficult to keep in mind it had happened only a few hours earlier.

"And, in addition to that," Lennon observed, "don't the

233

victims of things like voodoo curses have to believe in their efficacy before a curse can actually work?"

"That's my understanding," said Harris. "It's the power of suggestion that does it. Not some kind of primitive power in voodoo."

"I must confess," Koesler admitted, "that is the point Dr. Benson makes in this book. But I have told you all this for a specific purpose. The only connection I can see between the presentation of a statue of St. Expeditus and each of the Red Hat victims lies in voodoo.

"The victims each appear to have died under strange, possibly even ritualistic, circumstances. So much so that when the red herring—who was it, Fitzgerald—was slipped into the picture, only embalming could come close to duplicating what the real killer is capable of accomplishing by some awful natural means. I just read you an eyewitness description of a real voodoo death. It would seem to match the death masks of the Red Hat victims.

"The only argument against these deaths being the result of a voodoo curse is the belief that a voodoo curse can't happen. As rational people in the middle of Detroit in the middle of the twentieth century," Koesler nodded toward Koznicki, whose phrase he had borrowed for the rebuttal, "we know there can be no special magic in voodoo. If it works at all, it must work through the power of suggestion.

"Don't mistake me. It's not a bad argument. I would probably make it myself if I were not playing devil's advocate for the moment.

"But if I were you, conducting an investigation or doing some investigative reporting, I wouldn't totally discount the possibility that voodoo may possess some sort of magic force of which we are simply unaware. These, after all, are the days of psychokinesis and extrasensory perception. I just don't think we yet know the extent of—whatever you care to call it—psychic or spiritual power. After all, as we in the Church keep reminding people, faith can move mountains."

A long silence followed. It reminded Koesler of the silence liturgically recommended after the homily of the Mass. He was never sure his homilies were worth silent consideration. Evidently, what he had just said was being seriously considered.

"End of sermon," Koesler said at length.

His guests stirred and began preparing to leave.

"May I get you more coffee?" Koesler offered.

"Oh, no! No!" Harris protested.

"Oh, please no!" Lennon pleaded.

Koznicki merely smiled.

"As per our deal," Lennon said to both officers, "is what went on here this afternoon on or off the record?"

Harris and Koznicki exchanged glances.

"It's on the record," said Harris. "If there's somebody or some group out there messing about with voodoo in these murders, it won't hurt to let them know we're thinking about them."

"It might help an intended victim to know about it," said Lennon.

"Or be the cause of his death, if the power-of-suggestion theory is correct," added Koesler.

"Come on, Father," said Harris, "you can't have it both ways. You just made a convincing argument in favor of the unknown power of voodoo."

"I also explained," said the priest, "that I was acting as devil's advocate."

Harris shook his head.

"Ned," said Koznicki, "you said you've never been to a voodoo ritual. But could you get into one? I'd like to see it."

"You do like to live dangerously, don't you, Walt? O.K., if you're game, so am I. Let me make a call, and you and I should have ringside seats tonight."

"You sure there'll be something going on on a Sunday night?"

"Weekends are the best bet."

The meeting was breaking up. Pat Lennon was headed back to the *News* to write the best exclusive she'd ever had. The officers were making their arrangements for an evening of voodoo.

"How about you, Father? Are you game?" asked Harris.

Koesler felt ambivalent. He did not want to be dragged into a murder mystery. He had quite enough to do without adding a measure of amateur detecting. But there was no denying he was into it, and he did find the mystery exciting.

He also knew that until this case was solved, priesting, plans for homilies, and so forth, would be distractions from what would be his principle preoccupation, The Red Hat Murders.

"Now, remember, not a word out of any of you that I'm the *Free Press*' Anonymous Gourmet!"

Fathers Joe Sheehan and Fred Dolson greeted Father Don Curley's admonition with blank stares. Father Ted Neighbors, who had been through this routine before, smiled indulgently.

The profession, made while the maitre d' was passing the line of people waiting for tables, led to the clerical foursome's premature seating. Murmured complaints came from hoi polloi as the four were ceremoniously plucked from the line and seated ahead of some ten who were left waiting. Comments heard by an uncomfortable Joe Sheehan as he was whisked along, included, "It's time for another French Revolution, Ed." And, "I don't care, Helen, I believe in the separation of Church and State!" Followed by, "You mean the separation of Church from Privilege, you idiot!"

"What do you mean," asked Sheehan after they were seated, "by saying you're the Anonymous Gourmet? You have trouble keeping your golf score!"

"Be gentle with him, men," said Neighbors, "at least we're not standing in line anymore."

"That's right," Sheehan heatedly rejoined, "and we've antagonized a lot of people who are angry—not with the *Free Press*—but with the Catholic Church."

"Take it easy, Joe," said Dolson. "They'll get over it."

Just to be on the safe side, Dolson kept alert for signs of any possible attack. He didn't have any of his guns with him now. But the fingers of his right hand gripped the handle of the knife beside his plate.

If Joe Muer's, on the corner of Vernor and Gratiot, was not the finest seafood restaurant in Detroit, it generally enjoyed that reputation. It almost always boasted a line of people waiting to be seated.

"Now," Curley cautioned, "don't be too eager to order drinks or the meal. These places are all different. Some give the good old Anonymous Gourmet more than others."

The waiter attended their table promptly. Curley told him they would study the menu before ordering.

Yet another foursome, two couples, entered Joe Muer's and took their place at the end of the long line. Larry Delaney checked his watch. His review of the restaurant would include a report on how much time was spent waiting to be seated.

The waiter returned to the priests' table. There was no offer of complimentary drinks. Curley nodded and he and the others ordered libations.

Muer's had changed over the years. It had expanded and Delaney did not particularly care for the present decor. He so commented to his attractive date, who agreed.

"Oh, come on, Sheehan," said Curley, gently stirring his extra-dry martini, "come off your high horse. The people in line will forget about this. Rank, after all, has its privileges."

The line was moving, but imperceptibly. Delaney checked his watch. He frowned. This was a long holding pattern. But he'd wait his turn. Any kind of privileged treatment at this point might end in assassination at the hands of justly aggrieved queuers.

The waiter visited the priests' table. Joe Sheehan wanted to order dinner. He was outvoted three to one. Each had another drink.

The Delaney party was almost to the head of the line.

Delaney conferred with his date and their guests. The four-some determined in general what each would order. Delaney would taste everything served, but he would take the opinions of his fellow diners into consideration in his total critique of the meal.

"I hope somewhere in the annals of golf," Curley was saying, "there can be enshrined your second shot on five, Ted. There's got to be an award for burying a ball on the fairway."

All laughed save Neighbors, whose face reddened in anger. Curley's tone was a bit loud. He was conscious of being slightly tipsy. But he knew all would be well as soon as the food was served.

The Delaney party was next in line to be seated. Delaney casually looked over the patrons who were already seated and at various courses of dinner. His eye was caught by four priests at a fairly prestigious table. He was particularly taken by the priest who seemed to be doing the most talking. Bald, paunchy, looked as if he might be tall. Wearing thick glasses, he had a habit of cupping his ear when others spoke, as if he were hard of hearing.

"Can you imagine a Ted-Neighbors-conducted funeral?" asked a gasping Curley. "They get to the cemetery and Teddy beats the corpse into the ground with his three-wood!" Curley convulsed with laughter. Smoke was about to escape from Neighbors' ears.

"Excuse me." Delaney caught the maitre d's attention. "Could you tell me if you have the *Free Press*' Anonymous Gourmet here tonight?"

The maitre d' clearly was surprised. "Why, yes; yes, we do. But you'd never guess who it is!"

"Let me try. Is it that bald, paunchy, myopic gentleman over there disguised as a priest?"

"Why yes! However did you know?"

"Just lucky, I guess."

On his way to being seated, Delaney detoured to the priests' table. He leaned over Curley's shoulder.

"I just wanted to tell you," said Delaney, loudly enough

to be heard by Curley's table companions, "how much I enjoy your column in the *Free Press*."

"Hunh?"

"We usually plan our dining-out based on your reviews."

"Wha—"

"I've always wanted to ask your opinion of *kleiner Liptauer* as an hors d'oeuvre."

"I'm—"

"Generally, we serve *celeri-rave rémoulade* for salad. Do you think that complements *kleiner Liptauer*?"

"Uh—"

"And would that combination logically lead to *paupiettes* as the piece de resistance?"

"Uh—"

"Finally, do you think it appropriate to conclude with *croquembouche*?"

"Hunh?"

"Well, thank you very much."

Curley was destroyed, at least temporarily. His three companions had all but fallen off their chairs in laughter.

Delaney had memorized Curley's physiognomy. He would check the *Free Press* photo library the next day and discover the identity of this clerical fraud.

Ned Harris was having second thoughts. He was beginning to be sorry he had pressed Father Koesler into joining Koznicki and himself at tonight's ritual.

In addition to urging Koesler to accompany them, and assuring him of safety, Harris had suggested the priest dress in mufti. For the occasion, Koesler had donned black shoes, black trousers, a black jacket, a white shirt and a black tie.

Harris felt less than comfortable in the company of the only two white people in the room. One was as large as any two men there. The other resembled a mortician in mourning.

Though the night air was decidedly chill, due entirely to body heat it was very warm and close. Nearly fifty people were in a room that measured roughly twenty by thirty feet.

Most of the onlookers were pressed against the walls. A circle of chairs near the center of the room was occupied by men and women attired in simple but obviously ceremonial robes.

Adding to the closeness was the incense burning near the open door. A light breeze wafted the fragrant smoke throughout the room.

Somewhere out of sight someone was drumming on what they later discovered was a conch. The hollow-sounding rhythm had a mesmerizing effect.

The seated men and women began to sway to the rhythm. Some had closed their eyes as their lips formed silent words. How like, thought Koesler, the altered state of consciousness that sometimes accompanies contemplative prayer. Strange how such disparate cultures produced such similar prayer structures.

In a small wire cage in the center of the room was a live chicken. The cage was surrounded by foot-high statues of saints. Koesler recognized the Virgin Mary, St. Joseph with his flowered staff, St. Patrick crushing a snake. Several other statues each undoubtedly represented a specific saint but could easily have represented any saint. And there in the middle of them all was good old St. Expeditus.

When Koesler caught sight of Expeditus, he nudged Koznicki. However, the two officers had noted the statue shortly after entering the room.

Suddenly, a thundering sound was heard. Four large men entered in solemn procession. They bore heavy drums which they were pounding in almost savage rhythm.

The quartet was followed by a frail-looking woman of uncertain age, who swayed and dipped to the drumbeats. When she reached the center of the room, she turned to the chicken and began shrieking at it. To the three outsiders, her words seemed unintelligible, but, in any case, they were drowned out by the drums.

"She's telling our troubles to the chicken," Harris' contact whispered to the three.

"I wouldn't lay too heavy odds on that chicken's future," Harris commented in a whisper.

"Who is she?" Koesler asked.

"That," explained the contact, "is a *Mambo*—a voodoo priestess."

The drums stopped as suddenly as they had begun.

An odd antiphonal chant began between the *Mambo* and a deep-voiced male assistant.

"*Tousa Tousa rè lè Tou Salonggo Tou*," the *Mambo* chanted, "*sa Tou sa rè lè Tou Salonggo Tousa Tousa rè lè Tou Salonggo.*"

"That," explained the contact, "is a song of worship to a voodoo god."

"*Misereatur nostri omnipotens Deus,*" chanted the assistant, "*et dimissis peccatis nostris perducat nos ad vitam aeternam.*"

"You don't have to tell me what that is." Koesler smiled as he recognized the familiar Latin of the old Tridentine Mass.

"*Filé na filé fem Dambala Wèdo,*" chanted the *Mambo*. "*Filé na filé Dambala Wèdo ca conclèv oh! lèv oh!*"

"*Indulgentiam, absolutionem et remissionem peccatorum nostrorum tribuat nobis omnipotens et misericors Dominus,*" the assistant replied.

The exchange continued for about twenty minutes. Koesler found the blend of cultures fascinating. He was particularly in awe at how easily the ancient voodoo faith had absorbed the Catholic intrusion.

No sooner had the dialogue between the *Mambo* and her assistant ceased than the drums began again with their intoxicating rhythm.

The people who had been seated rose and began to dance within the circle formed by the chairs. Their arms flailed in all directions. Occasionally, as one would pass by the statue of a favored saint, he or she would bend over backward until his or her head was nearly touching the floor.

Many of the contortions seemed physically impossible.

As the drums continued their thunder, the *Mambo* danced in ever-narrowing concentric circles around the caged chicken, which appeared to be in a twitchy stupor.

Suddenly, with a movement almost too rapid for the eye to follow, the *Mambo* jerked the chicken out of its cage. Her head snapped. Koesler, horrified, thought she had bitten the chicken's tongue out. But he couldn't be sure, as everything was happening too fast.

There was no doubt, however, about what she did next. With a shriek, she wrung the chicken's head from its body. It all happened so quickly that, Koesler was sure, the chicken could not have felt anything.

Still dancing, the other participants moved ever closer to the *Mambo*. Stretching out their hands, they wet them in the blood spurting from the chicken's neck.

The *Mambo* moved outside the circle of dancers, the chicken's body held between her two hands. Snapping the chicken like an aspergillum, she sprinkled its blood at the audience.

Oddly, Koesler didn't mind. He was too spellbound. Oddly, too, with a target the size of Koznicki, the blood missed the Inspector entirely. Harris looked down in sartorial horror at the spot of red on his blue tie.

Not long afterward, the ceremony wound down to a finish. The *Mambo* left the room visibly shaken and spent. Some of the dancers had to be carried out.

The three visitors sat in Koznicki's car parked on West Euclid near Rosa Parks Boulevard. With them was Harris' contact, who was introduced as Andy Beeks.

"Is it like this all the time?" asked Koesler.

"Pretty much," said Beeks.

"Isn't it ever any different?" Harris persisted. "Don't they have a ceremony where they put a curse on someone?"

"Oh, yeah." Beeks brightened. "I see what you're gettin' at. Yeah. Tonight was a regular Sunday night ceremony. Like goin' to church on Sunday, or," acknowledging Koesler's presence, "goin' to Mass."

"But when do they place the curse?" Harris prodded.

"That's a secret ceremony. Strangers like you could never get in to see somethin' like that. Most of 'em here tonight couldn't even get in for that!"

"Have you ever been to one?" asked Harris.

"No." Beeks looked frightened. "But I've heard tell of 'em. They pray to Gede, who lives in cemeteries behind a cross. And to Baron Samedi who also lives in cemeteries. Then they send a *Wanga*—that's an evil charm. Then they bury St. 'spedite's statue upside down in the cemetery. Then, if it all works, Baron Samedi sends a dead person to enter the victim's body and kill him."

Koesler shuddered. He felt as if his flesh were creeping.

Koznicki and Harris exchanged glances.

"Andy," asked Harris, "how many voodoo groups would you say there are in Detroit?"

Beeks shrugged. "I got no idea . . . must be at least a dozen, maybe two dozen."

"Is there any way," Harris asked, "that we can learn about one of these groups that has been casting a series of death spells?"

A broad grin grew on Beeks' face. "You lookin' for the Red Hat murderer, aintcha?"

"Yeah," Harris admitted.

"No, I got no idea," said a very solemn Beeks. "Unless you can find all the *Mambos* and *Houngans*—that's the male voodoo priests. And I don't think you're gonna find 'em. And if you found 'em, I don't think they would tell you what day it was."

Koznicki had driven Beeks, then Koesler, home. He was now driving Harris back to headquarters so Harris could retrieve his car. It was very late Sunday night, actually early Monday morning.

"Has it occurred to you, Ned?"

"What?"

"That it was one week ago yesterday that the Red Hat murderer struck for the first time. And one week ago today that we found Rudy Ruggiero's head in Cardinal Mooney's hat."

"Yeah. So what?"

"Just this: if our murderer *has* started another series, he will kill again tomorrow and we will find the head on Tuesday."

The two rode in silence for several minutes.

"Squad Six is going to be very busy tomorrow," Harris broke the silence, "looking up and interviewing *Houngans* and *Mambos*."

"You want some help?"

"All I can get!"

"You got it."

They had never expected to find a genuine *Houngan* working on the Ford assembly line. On the other hand, before this Monday morning, Detectives Patrick and Lynch had never heard of *Houngans* or *Mambos*. Now they were about to interrogate one. A policeman's lot may not be happy at all times, but it is frequently educational.

It was almost as difficult to get Ahmed Baka, the alleged *Houngan*, off the lines as it would have been to get an interview with Henry Ford II. Only when the officers identified themselves as members of the homicide division did Baka's foreman initiate the procedure that would get Baka off the line.

Patrick and Lynch were shown to a waiting room while a sub was dispatched to relieve Baka.

"I've never quite gotten over the effect that word 'homicide' has on people," Lynch mused.

"Yes, indeed," Patrick agreed. "It's really weird how people will confess to almost anything else when you talk to them about murder."

"That's true even when they're not even involved in a murder." Lynch sat on the black Naughahyde couch and stretched his lanky frame.

"It's just awesome thinking of ending a human life." Patrick continued pacing in the small room.

"Unless it becomes your business."

"What do you make of this guy Baka?"

"Don't know." Lynch toyed with an ashtray. "I've never met a *Houngan* before." He smiled. "At least not that I know of."

"He's gone back to an African name. So his consciousness has been raised. We may have a tough time getting anything from him."

"Let's see what kind of magic the word 'homicide' will work," said Lynch laconically.

A short, powerfully built, very black man entered the room. His clothing was grease-smudged.

The detectives identified themselves. Baka said nothing. His eyes moved from one officer to the other as they displayed their credentials.

"Mr. Baka," Patrick opened, "we have been informed that you are a *Houngan*. Is that correct?"

"Is that a crime?" Baka was unsmiling.

Patrick guessed from his accent that Baka had come from another country. Possibly somewhere in South America.

"Not unless that occupation leads you to the commission of a crime," Lynch replied.

Baka neither responded to nor seemed affected by Lynch's statement.

"You did not answer our question, Mr. Baka," Lynch pursued. "Are you a *Houngan*?"

"And you have not answered mine," returned Baka. "Am I being charged with a crime?"

"No, Mr. Baka," said Patrick. "We are not at the point of charging anyone with a crime. We need a little information that may help us clear up a series of murders."

"I know nothing of murder," said Baka.

"Mr. Baka," said Patrick, "have you conducted any voodoo ceremonies for the purpose of putting a curse on someone to the point of wishing him dead?"

"Is it a crime to wish someone dead?" Throughout the interrogation, Baka had not changed his noncommittal expression.

"No, Mr. Baka," said Patrick, "it's not a crime to wish someone dead. But the wishing might lead someone, maybe someone in your congregation, to go out and actually perform the deed."

"I know nothing of a death conjure," said Baka.

"Mr. Baka," Lynch rose from the couch, "we have not used the term 'death conjure.' Why would you use such a precise term if you know nothing about it?"

Baka said nothing.

Lynch whispered to his partner.

"Mr. Baka," said Lynch, "we'd like you to come with us to headquarters and answer some more questions."

"And if I refuse?"

"You may refuse, Mr. Baka," said Lynch, "but if you do, we'll have to put you under surveillance."

Baka thought a moment. He took a deep breath. "I will go with you," he said.

Baka's interrogation at headquarters was intense. It elicited only one vaguely relevant fact. When not otherwise gainfully employed, Baka had been a part-time caretaker at Dutch Strauss's headquarters.

But, as Baka would and did remark, was it a crime to work for Strauss?

It was not a crime. But it was a lead that was pursued to its dead-end conclusion.

The smoke from the burning incense curled up and around the walls, filling the room with its sweet odor.

Six black candles burned before a makeshift altar. On the altar was a miniature coffin about one foot long, lined in black.

"Coté ma prend Coté ma prend Médi," the Mambo chanted, "oh! Aanago Coté ma prend Coté ma prend Médi oh! Ana go Cotéma go."

"Credo in Deum," sang her assistant as he gently swung the censer, out of which came puffs of incense, *"Patrem omnipotentem. Creatorem coeli et terrae."*

"Bonjour papa Legba, bonjour Baron Samedi," chanted the *Mambo,* *"bonjour ti moun moin yoma pé man dé ou con man non yéma pé man dé, bonjour papa Legba, bonjour Baron Samedi."*

"Credo in Spiritum Sanctum, sanctam Ecclesiam catholicam, Sanctorum communionem, remissionem peccatorum, carnis resurrectionem, et vitam aeternam," sang the assistant.

The *Mambo* picked up a crudely made rag doll. With a sharp knife she cut a slit in the doll's midsection. Her assistant handed her a slip of paper on which was printed the name "McCluskey." She tucked the paper in the doll's belly. She then placed the doll in the open coffin.

"Héla grand père éternal sin joé Heé-la grand père," the *Mambo* sang, *"éternal sin jozé do co agué."*

"Gloria Patri, et Filio, et Spiritui Sancto," her assistant responded, *"Sicut erat in principio, et nunc, et semper et in saecula saeculorum."*

She took an agitated chicken from its wire cage and pressed it to her breast. Then, still holding the chicken close, she quickly wrung its head from its body. Blood spurted over the *Mambo* and across the floor. She sprinkled the blood on the floor to the north, south, east, and west. She then placed the body of the still quivering fowl in the coffin next to the doll.

Her assistant handed her a statuette. It was a man in ancient armor, one hand holding a sword pointing at a cross, his foot on the neck of a bird. This she also placed in the coffin, then closed the lid.

Together, in honor of St. Expeditus, the *Mambo* and her assistant prayed.

"Pater noster qui es in coelis, sanctificetur nomen tuum. Adveniat regnum tuum, fiat voluntas tua, sicut in coelo et in terra. Panem nostrum quotidianum da nobis hodie. Et dimitte nobis debita nostra, sicut et nos dimittimus debitor-

ibus nostris. Et ne nos inducas in tentationem: sed libera nos a malo."

The *Mambo* sat back, exhausted.

Her assistant removed the statuette from the coffin. It was covered with the chicken's blood, as was the doll.

At a postmidnight hour, he took the blood-drenched statuette to a nearby Catholic cemetery, where he carefully buried it head downward in the consecrated ground.

"I didn't think a *Mambo* would be working as a domestic," said Colleen Farrell as she rang the doorbell of a fashionable mansion in Grosse Pointe Farms.

"Oh, come off it, Colleen," said her partner, Pat Karnego, "until today you didn't even know there was such a thing as a *Mambo*!"

A discomfited expression passed across Farrell's face. "Well, you're right, of course. It's just that being a *Mambo* sounds so important, I just wouldn't expect such a person to work as a maid."

"Buck up, Colleen. You are about to meet what you are fond of saying the Catholic Church needs, a female priest."

"And she's about to meet what few people believe in, two female members of a homicide squad."

The door opened. A small, matronly, well-groomed black woman stood before them.

The detectives identified themselves. Mrs. Evalla Johnson's eyes widened. Told it was she they had come to see, her eyes grew even wider.

"Please, Missy," said Mrs. Johnson, "if you don't mind, could we talk out here. I don't want to disturb the Missus." She gestured vaguely into the interior of the mansion.

She got her coat and rejoined the two officers at the portico. It was a sunny but brisk September day. The officers invited her into their car.

"That's right, Missy, I am a *Mambo*. Or at least I used to be. Don't do it no more at all. It's the work of a young woman, I always believed. Why, I'm a grandmother now." She smiled at the thought of her grandchildren.

"I see," said Karnego. "But would you know of anyone, a practicing *Mambo* or *Houngan*, as it were," the terms were foreign to her and she was unsure of their usage, "who would be conducting voodoo rituals to curse or cast fatal spells on people?"

"Oh, no, Missy. I don't keep up with that sort of thing no more. Even when I was a *Mambo*, there wasn't hardly anybody doing the killing hurts. Why, I got enough trouble now just gettin' to Mass on Sundays."

A few questions later, Mrs. Johnson stepped from the car and made her way back to the mansion.

She entered the house, a derisive smile on her face.

It just so happened she did know of a *Mambo* who was using the death conjure lately. And very effectively.

The firm of McCluskey Roofing and Repair was housed in a crowded storefront on Detroit's west side.

There was no reason the firm should be better housed. It did a lot of business and very little work. Tod McCluskey owned the business. There was but one employee, John Mulrooney. Neither knew much about carpentry or repair. McCluskey was able to frighten or coerce most helpless victims into believing they had no alternative but to use his firm if they needed repairs—or even if they didn't. Mulrooney was able to climb up on the roof to pronounce it in terminal condition.

Scarcely did they ever get complaints from their victim-customers. McCluskey carefully selected his targets from those who seem to be fate's favorite butts.

As it was near lunchtime, McCluskey had sent Mulrooney out for a couple of fast-food orders.

McCluskey was going through his mail. He was running late. Yesterday had been such an outstanding Sunday for business that he and Mulrooney had celebrated a bit too fervently last night, resulting in their oversleeping this morning.

Like most businesses, his was afflicted with an enormous amount of junk mail. A few bills. Nothing personal.

A small package. McCluskey ripped off the plain brown wrapper. It was the plain brown wrapper that fanned his hopes the package would contain something pornographic. His hopes were dashed when a peculiar statuette emerged. Something that looked like a Roman soldier. He appeared to be standing on some kind of bird and pointing with a sword to a cross. Words were coming out of the bird's mouth, and there was also a word on the cross. McCluskey understood none of them.

Probably more junk from some Catholic outfit, he thought. People with Irish—and Polish and Italian—names were forever getting unsolicited things like religious cards, rosaries, holy pictures, and statues in the mail. The dunning letter would follow. Of all people, McCluskey knew a con when he saw one. He did with the statuette what he always did with religious junk mail. He dropped it in the wastebasket.

His copy of the *Detroit News* would not be delivered for several hours. It would contain a very interesting story, on just such a statuette, bylined by Pat Lennon.

As McCluskey deposited the statue in the wastebasket, there was a knock on his office door.

"Yes?" McCluskey responded.

A tall, middle-aged black man entered. He appeared to be husky, particularly for his age. He held his hat in hand subserviently. He even seemed to shuffle a bit.

Whatever this might be, McCluskey knew he had nothing to fear from this man. "Is there somethin' I kin help ya with, then?"

"I don't mean to interrupt you, sir," the man said apologetically.

"No, no, not at all, at all. What is it I kin do fer ya?"

"It's my roof." The man spoke in a deep rich bass.

"Yer roof! Glory be ta God! The mountain comes ta Mohammed!"

"I beg your pardon, sir?"

"Nothing. A phrase, nothin' but a phrase."

"I believe my roof is in bad need of repair. I saw your sign. You do make roof repairs, don't you?"

"Is the Pope a Catholic?"

"I beg your pardon?"

"Oh, just an expression. Just an expression. Think nothin' of it."

"Now," McCluskey said deceitfully, "we wouldn't want to give ya any kind of a estimate without we examine yer roof. Else we might overcharge ya. What we could do is just come over ta yer house and give a peek ta yer roof. Then we kin give ya a daycent quotation of a price."

"We would really be appreciative of that, sir."

"Not at all, not at all. We are at the service of our customers. Now, sur, if ya wouldn't mind just leavin' yer name and address with me, we'll be right over this very fine day."

"Oh, sir, tomorrow will be fine."

"Tomorrow it is, then. Here, if ye'll just write yer name, address, and phone number on this card here."

The man reached across the desk to use McCluskey's pen.

"Ouch!"

"Oh, my dear sir," said the man, "I am so sorry. How clumsy of me!"

"Not at all, not at all," said McCluskey, rubbing his right hand. "Ya must have a sharp edge on yer ring there."

McCluskey squeezed the back of his hand. A small drop of blood appeared. He put his hand to his mouth and sucked the blood, hoping the prick would clot quickly.

"I am so sorry, sir," repeated his ostensibly embarrassed customer, "I seem to have hurt your hand."

"Think nuthin' of it. We in the carpenter's trade learn to live with far worse wounds than this."

"Well, that is very kind of you, sir. Very thoughtful, indeed."

The man wrote his name, address, and phone number on the sheet McCluskey had proffered. Alvin Thomas. His address was only a few blocks from McCluskey's office.

"Ah, practically in the neighborhood, aren't ya?"

"Yes, sir," said Thomas with a respectful bow.

"Well, we'll be after seein' ya tomorrow, Mr. Thomas. And," McCluskey added with a wink, "we'll see ya git a special price in a right neighborly way."

"Oh," said the man, bowing his way out of the office, "thank you very much, sir. I am deeply obliged."

Damn nigger, thought McCluskey as his new customer departed. He'll get a special price all right. About a third more than the already outrageous price he would have been charged anyway. All as a reward for having cut him with that damn ring.

McCluskey squeezed the back of his hand again. Again a spot of blood appeared. Damn cut wasn't healing. He sucked the blood again.

Where in hell was Mulrooney? How long does it take to get fast food? Why is it called fast food if that idiot Mulrooney can't get it fast?

He was tired of sucking blood. He wanted a 'burger.

He was beginning to get into a foul mood.

Pat Lennon hung up the receiver. She had just talked with Lieutenant Harris. His replies to her questions had filled her in on the previous night's voodoo ritual and the interrogations now being conducted by several of the homicide squads in addition to Squad Six.

Harris' cooperation was almost total. He held back only the special knowledge shared by the Medical Examiner and the police on the method of severing that so far clearly identified four decapitations as the work of the Red Hat murderer.

When Lennon looked up from her notes, Bob Ankenazy was standing at her desk. He was smiling indulgently.

"Great work, Pat," he said, "great story. I don't know how you put it all together, but you've got the *Free Press* playing catch-up and that's the way we like it."

"Thanks, Bob," she replied, returning his smile. "It's nice of you to take the time and trouble to tell me."

"Do you feel ambivalent about it?"

"About what?"

"About beating your old rag, the Friendly Freep."

Lennon thought a moment. "Yeah, I guess I do. I had a lot of good days there and left some good friends behind." Her jaw jutted. "But anytime I start feeling sorry for the Freep, I just think of Karl Lowell and I could kick up my heels."

"Lowell is that bad?"

Lennon nodded.

"I've heard tales about the bastard, but I've found it hard to believe them."

"Believe!"

"It's almost as if the S.O.B. were out to destroy the *Free Press*."

"You're sure he isn't in the secret employ of the *News*?"

They laughed.

"Anyhow, keep it up," Ankenazy said. He gave her hand a pat. "We want to keep this winning combo intact."

She watched as he returned to the far west side of the huge office.

He wasn't making a play for her. That was different. Bob Ankenazy was a happily married man with two kids. And he was not making a play for Pat Lennon. It was perfectly possible, even in this day and age, for a man and a woman to work together on a professional level, have a platonic relationship without a demand or even a hint of hanky-panky.

She would have to inform Joe Cox of this phenomenon. She was sure he would never believe it.

Tod McCluskey couldn't believe it was the 'burgers. It must be all the booze he'd consumed last night. Even so, it was difficult to pin the blame just on the booze.

He had to admit he had never felt worse in his life. No, he amended that: he had never felt as bad in his life.

He was nauseated. But that was the least of his problems. He was filled with a pathological fear. He could not identify the cause of this fear. He was perspiring as he never had before. Yet he knew it was a bright, brisk day. And the doors were open, letting in the air.

He rose from behind his desk and began to walk toward the small toilet. He felt he was about to be very sick. When he reached the area where the toilet was, it wasn't there. He looked back across the office. The toilet had been moved to the other side of the room. That was crazy. Or was he going crazy?

"Mulrooney! Jack boy! Will ya come in here!"

"What is it, Mac? What's the matter? You sounded all excited!" said Mulrooney.

But it wasn't Mulrooney. It was that trouble-making priest who used to hound McCluskey's dad and who had warned McCluskey that if he didn't shape up, he would end his life in eternal hellfire. What was *he* doing here?

"Father O'Brien," McCluskey exclaimed, "what the hell are you doing here? Have you come to hound me then as you did my father? I tell you I'll have none of it!"

"What are you talkin' about, Mac? It's me, Mulrooney. Jack Mulrooney!"

"I told ye before, Tod, that ye'd come to an evil end and, indeed ye have. I've come to take ye before the Judge and I can promise ye it won't go good with ye."

"The hell you say. I'm still a young man. I'll not be goin' to the other world. Not at this age, I'll tell you. You're a lyin' mick, just as you always were. And I don't believe you now anymore'n I ever did just 'cause you wear your collar turned 'round!"

"What is this talk, Mac? What's wrong with you, man?"

"Ye won't be goin', eh, Tod? Then watch careful at what happens now!"

"You can't scare me, you bloated devil!"

"I'm not tryin' to scare you, Mac! What's got into you?" The priest was gone.

Slowly through the doorway came a procession of people. At first, McCluskey thought they were strangers. Then he began to recognize most of them. They were former customers. People he had swindled and conned and bilked. It was a most solemn procession. Each of them carried a piece of lumber. Heavy lumber that might be found in the walls or roofs of houses.

"What are you people doin' here?" McCluskey screamed. "You've got no business here. We're done with our business. You were treated fair and square. Now get out of here!"

"What people, Mac? Get hold of yourself, man!"

They did not retreat as McCluskey had commanded. They continued their slow, measured march, forming a wide circle around McCluskey.

He became aware of a powerful odor invading the room. It resembled burning sulphur. McCluskey recalled the stories the Sisters used to tell and the pictures in the catechism books of hell, the eternal fire that would not consume and would not be quenched. He began to shiver, even as he continued to perspire.

"Now I'm givin' you fair warning," McCluskey shouted, "get out of here while the gettin's good. Or I'll have the police on you."

"You're out of your head, Mac," cried Mulrooney. "You're the very one who called me in here!"

Miraculously, the wood left their arms and formed itself into a coffin at McCluskey's feet.

He stared at it transfixed.

The floor next to the coffin gave way, revealing a burial pit.

The crowd grabbed at McCluskey. Their hands were on him everywhere. They lifted his struggling body off the floor, dropped him rudely into the coffin and forced the lid closed.

"What do you think you're doing?" McCluskey screamed as the perspiration coursed down his body. "You can't do this to me! It isn't my time! This isn't human!"

"What's not human, Mac? Come out of it, man! You're having a dream! A bad daydream!"

Slowly the crowd lowered the coffin into the pit. They

began kicking dirt into the pit and over the coffin. The boards did not completely seal the coffin's lid, and dirt trickled through.

"You can't do this!" McCluskey pleaded. "It's not human! Whatever I've done to you, it wasn't this bad!"

"Wake up, Mac!" Mulrooney began slapping McCluskey's face. His action seemed to have no effect. "Wake up, Mac! Now you're scarin' me!"

McCluskey tried to ward off the dirt trickling into the coffin. He could not. Now the dirt covered the coffin's lid. There was very little air.

McCluskey clawed at the wood, leaving bloody tracks where the wood splintered into his fingertips.

"No, no, I can't breathe! Don't do this!"

Mulrooney watched in horror as McCluskey fell to the office floor, grasping at his throat. Mulrooney quickly bent over him and loosened his collar.

"There now, Mac! Maybe you can breathe easier now!"

"No! No! NOoooo!"

"Mac, get that horrible look off your face! Mac, I can't stand to look at you. Mac—Jesus, Mary and Joseph, I think he's dead!"

Mulrooney was just able to phone for an ambulance before he got very, very sick.

"I don't like it, Joe," said Nelson Kane, "we're playing catch-up and that's not my kind of ballgame."

"I know, Nellie," said Cox, "but I can't get ahead of Pat on this story. About a week ago, in this very room, I told you I thought she had a special feel for this story. All she's doing is proving me right."

"Cox," the two were returning zigzag-fashion from the water cooler to Kane's desk, "the best way to lose a game is to admit you can't win."

It was one of those simple truths Kane had a way of expressing, usually couched in a sports metaphor, that had a way of clearing the air.

Cox stopped abruptly at Kane's desk. The water in his

Styrofoam container sloshed and nearly spilled.

"You know, Nellie, you're right. It's simplistic, but I guess I conceded The Red Hat Murders story to Pat from almost the beginning. It didn't make that much difference then. But now, she's working for the enemy."

"Exactly!"

"Thanks, Nellie," Cox said, slapping himself lightly on the cheek, "I needed that!"

"Now, why don't you get your ass over to headquarters and see if you can make friends with Lieutenant Harris."

"Better than that, I'll see if I can get back in with my old friend, Inspector Koznicki.

"But," Cox added before leaving, "I've got to hand it to Pat for coming up with that voodoo angle."

Kane dismissed him with a wave of the hand. "Why don't you go see if there aren't some more surprises around?"

"He was D.O.A.?"

"Yes, Doctor."

A small group stood near a gurney on which lay the dead body of Tod McCluskey. They were in the pathology section of Detroit General Hospital.

Dr. Jane Browne, head pathologist, and her assistant, Dr. Fred Smith, stood on either side of the body. At the foot stood a badly frightened John Mulrooney, hat in hand. The body was unclothed. There did not seem to be a visible wound on it.

"Mr. Mulrooney," asked Browne, who had requested the presence of McCluskey's associate, "you say Mr. McCluskey was acting strangely?"

"Oh, yes, indeed he was!" Mulrooney had an instinctive fear of the dead and was extremely uncomfortable among these vaults and in the immediate presence of his recently deceased employer.

"Tell us what happened," said Browne.

"Well, we had just had our lunch—'burgers which I had purchased from a Big Boy franchise, if you please—"

257

"Did you both eat the same food?" Browne asked.

"Oh, yes, indeed. A Big Boy, fries, and coffee. We had an order apiece."

"Go on."

"Well, it was sometime after lunch, maybe a half hour, when Mac—Mr. McCluskey—calls for me."

"How did he sound?"

"Anxious, kind of scared, like he was suddenly struck sick."

"Then?"

"So I come in, and the strangest thing, he never recognized me presence in the room at all. I kept talkin' to him. I'd say, 'Mac! Mac! Get hold of yerself, man!' But he kept talkin' to them."

"Who?"

"I dunno. People only he seen. One was a priest. I think his name was Father O'Brien er O'Riley er somethin'. Then there was a whole flocka people. I think he thought they were old customers. They were threatenin' to do somethin' horrible to him, and then I think he thought they done it."

"What do you think he thought they did to him?"

"I don't like to say it."

"It may help us learn how he died."

"It sounds stupid and spooky all at the same time."

"What?"

"I think . . . I think he believed he was bein' buried alive!" The words spilled out in a hushed, almost reverential tone.

The three gazed at McCluskey's body in silence. Somewhere a faucet dripped.

"That would explain the death mask, do you think, Fred?" Browne addressed her assistant.

"Yes, I guess it would," Smith replied.

"You know, Doctor," Smith continued, "something's been knocking on the fringe of my consciousness from the first moment I saw this body."

"What's that?"

"The resemblance of McCluskey's death mask to the ones of those other murder victims."

"The Red Hat Murders," Brown supplied.

"Exactly."

"It's the same thought I had, Fred. It's almost a carbon copy of those others. I'm glad you agree. And since you agree..." Browne extracted a note pad from one of her oversize pockets and began writing on it "...I am shipping this body over to the Wayne County Medical Examiner."

"Doctor," said Smith, smiling, "I think you are going to make Willie Moellmann's day. Or," checking his watch, "his tomorrow."

"My dear friends, I'd like to talk to you this evening on the evils of steady dating."

He must be out of his mind, thought Father Donald Curley, as he stood in the vestibule of old St. Joseph's church. This is just a Novena Mass honoring St. Joseph; the average age of this congregation must be in the sixties, and the man wants to talk to them about steady dating!

"I know you're thinking, 'What does this have to do with me?'" preached Father Edmund Sklarski in his best Boanergian tones. "But I tell you, my friends, the devil is no respecter of persons or ages. He roams about the world seeking the ruin of souls!"

The congregation, small in number and generally elderly, dozed serenely, followed their own streams of consciousness or contemplated the myriad statues and pictures that were nearly everywhere in the church. Some few were actually listening to Sklarski. Somehow he was always able to introduce the subject of S-E-X into his sermons. It was occasionally entertaining to anticipate how he would work it in.

"Many of us, my dear friends, deplore the emphasis now given to sports, especially on the high school level. Why, sports have become more important than the traditional three Rs!"

Sports, another of Sklarski's recurring themes. But how,

his few listeners wondered, would he bridge his way to the Other Topic.

"However, there are, we must admit, my dear friends, some obvious if fringe benefits accruing from this early emphasis on sports. Some of our racial minorities are enabled to continue on to a higher education as a result of athletic scholarships. An education that could be achieved in no other way. And then, too, my dear friends, an early interest in sports prevents the premature and unhealthy pursuit of girls!"

Ah!

As he circled outside the church and entered the sacristy from the rear, Curley formed a plan. As pastor, he had recently decreed that no sermon was to last longer than fifteen minutes. A blow aimed directly at Sklarski, who, when he launched on a homily, gave every indication of never intending to see shore again.

Sklarski would never be able to wrap up so pregnant a topic as steady dating in the prescribed fifteen minutes. From the sacristy, Curley planned his attack. Strangely, he was reminded of Scarpia plotting the coercive seduction of Tosca from within the church.

"I call your attention, my dear friends, to the picture over here," Sklarski gestured expansively toward the right side of the nave, "depicting the conversion of St. Paul."

How would he get from the conversion of St. Paul to S-E-X?

"There's Paul, on his way to Damascus. He's going there to find Christians and persecute them. But God knocks him off his wild horse. Wild horse! What might be *your* wild horse? Women? Sex?"

Ah!

Fifteen minutes. Curley flipped the switch turning off the public address system.

The effect was dramatic. Sklarski's volume level dropped to near inaudibility.

"So!" Sklarski boomed, "you pull the plug on Sklarski? Sklarski simply raises his volume!"

And on he thundered, afloat on his uncharted seas of sexual entrapment.

Meanwhile, back in the sacristy, Curley slumped into a chair, defeated. He wondered if having Sklarski's warm body around to help out was really worth it.

No matter that she had worked there for years, it still required several minutes to get used to the strong smell of the various powerful chemicals.

Emma Lewin was going on her fifth year as night custodial worker at the Wayne County Morgue.

It no longer bothered her that the long narrow metal trays she was cleaning had been and would be used to hold a parade of cadavers that would be sliced, carved, and dissected by teams of pathologists. She no longer even adverted to the bodies stacked in their private shelves all about her.

Emma was whistling "Some Enchanted Evening," steadily changing musical keys as she progressed. This was one of the reasons she preferred working alone. She loved to whistle but could not carry a tune. None of her companions in the basement of the building would complain about her misshapen melodies.

As she scrubbed a tray at the far end of the room, something white at the doorway caught her eye. She looked up from her work. It was a black man in a white uniform. He wasn't in the doorway. He was in the hall. He was not in the light, so she couldn't see his face clearly.

He waved at her and smiled. "Laundry," he explained, as he continued down the hall, dragging a large laundry bag.

She thought little more of the incident—although it was odd: in her years of nightly work, there had not been a laundry pickup or delivery that she could remember.

But if she had learned one thing from working here it was that this whole place was odd. Odd sounds, odd odors, odd sights, and some fairly odd people.

After a brief interval—she was uncertain of the precise

length of time—the white-clothed figure passed the door again.

"'Night," he said as he left. He pulled the laundry bag after him.

Emma selected "Somewhere Over the Rainbow" to mangle.

Pat Lennon and Joe Cox sat at opposite ends of the long wooden bench to one side of the entry to the Medical Examiner's office.

Lennon was there at the invitation of Lieutenant Harris, Cox at the invitation of Inspector Koznicki. Neither Lennon nor Cox cared for the competition of the other in this professional capacity. But there was nothing either could do about it.

Koznicki and Harris paced together in front of the office door and along the open second floor corridor. They seemed nervous. An emotion neither often felt. It might be more accurate to say they were eager. Eager for the news Dr. Moellmann would soon bring.

"The thing that puzzles me most, Walt," said Harris, "is identification. If the guy's head is still attached to his body, how can he be identified as a Red Hat victim?"

"I think we'd better leave that in the capable hands of the good doctor," Koznicki answered. "I've seen him pull rabbits out of some hats in my time. He's good."

"God, Walt, it makes me tingle to think we finally have a body. If it's really a Red Hat victim, we ought to get a cause of death and be able to come up with a charge that'll stick."

"Yes, friend, it does seem we may see light at the end of the tunnel."

"What time is it?" Lennon asked.

Cox looked at his watch. "About ten after eight." He looked at her and, for the first time that morning, smiled. "What are you worried about? You work for an afternoon paper now."

Lennon returned the smile. It was difficult for the lovers

262

to remain cool to each other, even when professionally separated.

"What did they say that guy—McCluskey—did for a living?" she asked.

"Uhmm," Cox consulted his notes, "McCluskey Roofing and Repair."

"Sort of a carpenter?"

"Yeah, I suppose. Why?"

"Oh, nothing. Just want to stay on top of things."

"Speaking of which," Cox slid closer to her on the bench, "would you consider a return to the apartment after this conference? We *are* in the neighborhood, you know."

Lennon shook her head. "Joe, if only you were afflicted with impotency, you would probably win an annual Pulitzer."

"Meaning I am not concentrating enough on my job?"

"Meaning let's find out what comes out of this conference before we make any dates."

Marge, Moellmann's secretary, timed her emergence in the corridor to coincide with the moment Koznicki and Harris passed in front of the office door.

"Would y'all care fer sum coffee?"

As it turned out, all four would. Cox black, Lennon with cream, Koznicki with sugar, and Harris with cream and sugar.

"Then y'all kin come in an' get it!" said Marge, with a gesture indicating her head was swimming.

"Whah don't y'all mike yorse'ves comfortable?" Marge said as the four helped themselves to coffee and a variety of ingredients. "It my be a period 'fore the doctor returns." She sighed. "At least he was happy 'bout havin' a whole *in*tahr body to work with!"

It was with a great deal of anticipation that virtually the entire team of Wayne County's pathologists gathered in the basement of the morgue to begin the autopsy of Tod McCluskey. Their curiosity had been piqued by the preliminary report sent with the body by Dr. Jane Browne of Detroit General.

Dr. Paul Werner, with a theatrical flourish, pulled open the shelf and, with a dramatic flourish, threw back the covering sheet.

There was a collective gasp.

"Gott in Himmel! Scheisse!" swore Dr. Wilhelm Moellmann.

"I don't believe it!" said Werner.

The mortal remains of Tod McCluskey had no head.

"Wir hätten mindestens einen Kopf in der Hand halten können!" With his back to the wall, Moellmann tended to revert to his native tongue, as he wondered why his department couldn't hang onto the heads entrusted to it.

"Did any of you remove this head?" Werner asked.

Of course none had.

"Ich scheisse auf diese Idioten!" was Moellmann's assessment of his staff.

Werner looked helplessly at his Chief. "Sir, I don't know how this could have happened!"

"So sitzen wir wieder in der Scheisse!" was Moellmann's assessment of their present situation.

"Well, find out!" he suggested to Werner.

Dr. Werner and several colleagues obediently peeled away from the group to try to track down the how, why and wherefore of Tod McCluskey's missing head.

After a moment to appraise the situation from several other angles, a smile began to play about Moellmann's lips. He reassembled the remainder of his staff, moved what was left of McCluskey to the table and began cutting furiously.

Moellmann slowly ascended the stairs en route to his office.

As soon as he came into view, Lennon and Cox were off the bench and pumping him with questions.

"What's the verdict, Doc?"

"Is it another Red Hat case, Doc?"

"Did you determine the cause of death, Doc?"

"Later," answered Moellmann, motioning for the two police officers to follow him into his office.

"Hätten wir nicht einen einzigen Kopf in der Hand behalten können?" said Moellmann to no one as he passed through the outer office.

"What was that?" asked Cox.

"He said," explained Marge, "'Couldn't we even hold on to a single hay-ud?'"

"Oh." And then, as the possible import penetrated, "Oh?"

"Roughly," Marge added. Among the many talents for which Marge had been hired, not the least was her ability to understand Moellmann whether he spoke in English, Low German, medicalese, or high dudgeon.

Moellmann, Koznicki, and Harris entered the doctor's office. Moellmann shut the door behind them and indicated they should be seated. The doctor, however, began pacing behind his desk.

"Verdammtes Pech!" Moellmann said. Then he added, "Actually, not such bad luck after all."

"Could you explain?" Koznicki asked.

"Overnight, someone decapitated McCluskey."

"Decap—you're kidding!" said Harris.

"Would I?" Moellmann asked. "A cleaning lady who works alone at nights saw him, a tall black man. She did not see him well enough to identify him, only that he was tall, black, and had a deep voice. He posed as a laundry man."

"We'll have to interrogate her," said Harris.

"You'll have her name," said Moellmann. "But there's more." He looked thoughtful. "With his head on, I don't think it could have been other than highly speculative for us to have identified McCluskey as another Red Hat victim. With his head off, there is no doubt." Moellmann appeared very pleased. "The same flawed saw. He removed the head in four or five strokes, even as awkward as that must have been with the body in the drawer."

Moellmann ceased pacing and stood facing the two officers. His excitement increased the scope of his gestures.

"This," he said, "is where the good news gets better. This is the first time in this series of murders that we have a body. Our preliminary autopsy indicates a foreign substance in the body."

Harris and Koznicki leaned forward.

"I can't be sure, but I think it could possibly be snake venom."

"You can't be sure!" Harris almost exploded.

"You think I am God?" Moellmann returned the volley.

It was the first indication Harris had that the doctor might not think of himself in divine terms.

"Easy," Koznicki cautioned Harris. He turned to Moellmann. "What do you plan to do?"

Moellmann paused long enough to permit his neck muscles to relax. "I have called in a toxicologist. He will be here by noon. We'll have all your answers then."

It was a dismissal. ——

"We'll have to check your lab for prints and interrogate that woman," Koznicki reminded.

"Of course."

The officers left.

Outside the examiner's office, the two were bombarded by Cox and Lennon.

They briefed the reporters on what they had learned from Moellmann, omitting the specific clinical details of the beheading that enabled them to identify the killing as another in the Red Hat series.

"This guy, McCluskey," asked Cox, "what kind of guy was he? I mean, why would he be selected by the Red Hat murderer?"

"If I were you, I'd check the General Assignment Unit," said Harris.

Cox was off.

"Oh, my God!" Harris exclaimed. "It just dawned on me. I guess I didn't think of it because I wasn't expecting McCluskey to be decapitated."

"What?" asked Koznicki.

"McCluskey's head," said Harris. "It's probably in some Catholic church right now!"

"My God!" said Koznicki, "you're right! But which one?"

Lennon, who had been taking in the exchange, asked, in a tone of mounting excitement, "This McCluskey, wouldn't he be classified as kind of a repairman, a kind of carpenter?"

The officers agreed he would.

"Then I think I know where the head is. Just give me a minute to call my photographer."

Sergeant Terri Scanlon was searching her records.

She was one of only four Detroit police officers who made up the General Assignment Unit.

"Tod McCluskey," said Scanlon, "the name is definitely familiar, but I can't quite place it."

"Don't get me wrong, Terri," said Joe Cox, "I'm not trying to put your unit down, but if your unit would be working on a guy like McCluskey, he wouldn't be one of Detroit's major criminals, would he?"

Scanlon smiled as she continued to finger through the files. "No, Joe, we don't work on the Al Capones. And you're wondering what he'd be doing in our files if he's a target of the Red Hat murderer."

"How did you know that?"

"Joe, Homicide is just down the hall, same floor."

"Oh."

"Hmmm," she said, "yes, we do have a file on McCluskey. Not a very large one, though."

"What was he into?"

"Fraud, mostly. Nothing big league and nothing you could even make an arrest on. The tenth precinct handled most of the calls. McCluskey operated outside the tenth's jurisdiction, in a variety of precincts, just often enough for our unit to be called in occasionally."

"What was his game?"

"He was a con man. Very minor league, but very nasty. He would convince people, mostly old people—"

"Picking on the lame and the halt, eh?" Cox interrupted.

"Yes, that's about it. He would convince them they needed roof repair, usually. And usually, the victims were too old or crippled to get up there and check it out. Generally, they would end up paying nearly all they had in savings or they would pay outrageous interest rates for pretty nearly the rest of their lives—until the grave freed them. And even then, the bastard would put in a claim for the balance from their pitiful estates.

"But this is the kind of con," she continued, "that's almost impossible to prosecute. Not all his customers would complain by any means. Most of the people he picked on were used to being victimized as a way of life. And he always made sure he had a valid contract. So there were no grounds for prosecution."

"You're telling me that McCluskey was just another slightly dishonest businessman?"

"That's right."

"He merely took advantage of his customers?"

"That's about it."

Cox whistled softly. "Good grief. But that's the All-American way of doing business. They might not all be as bad as McCluskey, but can you think of a major business that doesn't take advantage of its customers?"

"No, I guess not," she said, after a moment's thought.

"Terri, you know what this means? Almost everyone who deals with clients in this area is a possible candidate for the Red Hat murderer's hit list!"

It was Terri Scanlon's turn to be impressed.

Cox had his story. It could practically write itself.

Half a dozen cars arrived at old St. Joseph's almost simultaneously. One belonged to Pat Lennon, another to *News* photographer Don Carlson; the rest were police vehicles.

Several uniformed officers discovered, by trying every door, that the church was securely locked.

"If the damn head is in there," said Harris in a tone of near frustration, "how in hell does he get in and out of these churches so easily?"

Officers were ringing the front, side, and rear doorbells of the rectory.

A bewildered and disheveled Father Donald Curley appeared at the front door. His bewilderment increased when he saw the assembled cars. Their number would be representative at a Sunday Mass.

"Father," said Detective Patrick, "—you are a Father, aren't you?"

"Yes." Several smart-alec replies to that question passed through Curley's fertile brain, but, in present circumstances, he discarded them all.

"Father," Patrick pressed on, "your church is locked."

"That's right. The first Mass isn't scheduled until ten minutes after noon."

"Well, Father, we'd like it opened now, if you don't mind."

"Now?"

"Right now!"

"What the hell is going on down there?" Father Sklarski bellowed from a front window of the second floor. "Can't a poor priest get a little rest even in retirement?" Sklarski was wearing an old-fashioned nightshirt and nightcap.

Everyone but Curley all but broke up.

"It's O.K., Ed," Curley called up to his confrere. "Go back to bed. I'll handle it." He turned to Patrick. "Just let me get the keys."

Curley unlocked the church's front door and the flood quickly passed through the portals.

"Where is your statue of St. Joseph, Father?" asked Lennon.

"Up front, on the left."

Lennon grabbed Carlson's arm and made a beeline for the shrine dedicated to this church's patron.

There, resting securely on the shoulders of the statue of St. Joseph, was the head of Tod McCluskey, its horrified and horrifying death mask intact.

Lennon involuntarily winced, then shuddered.

Outside of the police photographers, Carlson was the only one to get a shot of the head on its resting place. Many photographers and cameramen from the *Free Press*, wire services, and television stations would visit this scene later. Only the *News* would have the grisliest of all photos.

"How did you know?" Harris asked.

"McCluskey! When you told me he would be considered a carpenter, it had to be St. Joseph. That's the way he made his living. I didn't go through parochial school and a Catholic college for nothing. I didn't even need Fathers Clark or Koesler for this one."

"You saved us a lot of time. And time is of the essence now," said Harris.

"We got our story and our pictures," said Lennon.

"So we start again, even." Harris enjoyed Lennon for no more complicated reason than that she was a beautiful woman.

"By the way," low-keyed Lennon, "what is it made McCluskey a victim of the Red Hat murderer? I've never even heard of him before."

"Neither have we," said Harris. "He has no record in Homicide. I'm afraid I'll have to refer you to our General Assignment Unit."

"Is this déjà vu? Somewhere, someplace I've heard that before."

"It's the same answer to the same question I gave your pal Cox half an hour ago."

Lennon experienced a momentary pang and then remembered she worked for the *News* now. Poor Joe. He got that story first but he wouldn't be able to get it published until the one-ball, which wouldn't reach the presses until 8:15 that evening. With any luck, Lennon's story would hit the streets that afternoon. She almost felt sorry for Cox as she departed for her interview with Sergeant Terri Scanlon

—who would have the answers to Lennon's questions fresh at her fingertips.

Father Donald Curley suffered in solitary woe. He could foresee the sensational treatment his parish would receive from the news media. He could anticipate the negative reaction to all this sensationalism from his staid parishioners. He could not bear to think of the abuse that would be heaped upon him by all those he had verbally abused in the past—and their number was legion. He tried to block out entirely what he would suffer from Father Ted Neighbors, who, unlike all the king's men, had already started to put his St. Frances Cabrini together again.

Seven

ST. JOHN'S SEMINARY

Eleanor Breitman drove her five-year-old Mercury Comet into Dessalen's Garage, one of the largest and busiest auto repair shops on Detroit's west side. She got out of her car and looked nervously about. She ran her hands restlessly over her purse.

Elmer Dessalen himself came over to greet her. He tried to attend all customers who appeared to know nothing about what was wrong with their cars and would be easy targets for a small game of fraud. This lady appeared ideal.

"Good morning," he said, "something wrong with the old Comet?"

He startled her. She hadn't seen the small black man approach.

"Why, yes," she said, "can you help me?"

"If I can't, nobody can. I own this place. Name's Elmer Dessalen. What seems to be the problem?"

He had an odd accent. She couldn't place it. Spanish or Portuguese, something like that.

"Well, for the last several days, I've had an off-and-on problem starting my car."

"Oh?"

"Yes. Sometimes when I turn the ignition on, all I get is a click. Nothing turns over."

"Well, let's see."

Dessalen opened the hood and peered around the interior, poking this and pressing that. Straightening up, he continued to look meditatively at the engine.

"You'll have to leave it overnight. We'll have to work on it all day. Sounds like your ignition system is shot or just about worn out. We may have to replace the whole system."

"Oh, my! How much would that cost?"

"I don't want to give you a firm price before we know all we're dealing with. But I'd say somewhere between fifty and a hundred dollars."

"Oh, my!"

She was clearly in a dilemma. Her eyes darted back and forth.

"It could die on you any minute," he added.

"Do you have any courtesy cars?"

"No, ma'am, they're all out. But the Grand River bus runs right past the front door."

"Oh, very well."

Dessalen got all the necessary information. Mrs. Breitman joined the line of commuters, mostly black, awaiting the arrival of the overdue Grand River bus.

Dessalen gave the keys to the Comet to one of his mechanics.

"Whatcha got there, Chief?" asked Ben Jones.

"Bad starter, Jonesie," said Dessalen. "Unless I miss my guess, if you look above the right front wheel, you'll find a connection in the ignition system that's rusted out. Sand it down and that mother will start like a fine horse."

"Want me to rustproof it?"

Waving his cloth cap, Dessalen whacked Jones on the side of the head. "Dummy! Don't you ever want to see that lady again? Planned obsolescence, that's the name of the auto game."

They laughed uproariously.

Jones pulled the Comet into a stall. In fifteen minutes he would have the car repaired. The actual cost to Dessalen's Garage: perhaps a mill for wear on a piece of sandpaper.

* * *

Nelson Kane sat at his desk studying the copy editor's suggested headline for Joe Cox's latest piece on The Red Hat Murders. It read, "Red Hat Murderer Threatens American Way of Business." It was marked to be set in two lines, three columns wide. Kane did not object to the headline size; he merely wondered whether it overstated the facts.

Cox stood waiting to gain Kane's attention. Kane was in an odd mood and Cox didn't know why. He wasn't sure he wanted to know why.

At last Kane looked up. "Well?"

"I can't figure it, Nellie. I don't know where Pat went after the briefing at Moellmann's office, but she was bound to touch base with Scanlon at the General Assignment Unit. And she's got time on her side. She'll be able to get her story in this afternoon. I beat her but she'll likely beat me. It ain't fair."

"So you don't know where Lennon went after the briefing?" Kane pushed his chair back from the desk with deliberation. Cox was getting more certain by the minute that he would not want to know the reason for Kane's odd mood. He was equally certain he was going to know.

"Well, let me fill you in: she took the cops and a *News* photographer over to old St. Joseph's church, where they found McCluskey's head!"

Cox's mouth dropped open and hung open.

"They tell me," Kane continued, "that the *News* photographer got a shot of McCluskey's head on the statue. If what I hear is correct, it's the only media still of any of the victims where the Red Hat killer left them."

Cox closed his mouth. It was getting dry.

"I sent McNaught over," Kane added, "to cover that scene."

Cox blinked several times as if he were not sure this was real.

Kane looked at him with a mixture of pity and disappointment. "Didn't you say earlier that Moellmann was going to state his findings on the McCluskey autopsy around noon? Cox, if I were you, I'd get the hell over to the M.E.'s office. If you can't beat Lennon, you'd damn well better not fall far behind."

Cox raised his hand as if to say something.

"Damn good story, Joe," Kane patted the fifteen-page double-spaced text. "Let's see if Lennon can write one that good." He looked again at the headline. "If I saw this headline," he asked himself aloud, "would I buy this paper?" After a moment's thought, "Damn right!" he answered, and yelled for a copyboy.

Father Robert Koesler took a toothpick from his shirt pocket and inserted it in his mouth where he would worry it to death.

He was seated in the Toussaint living room, telling his hosts of his experience two nights before.

". . . and after it was all over," he concluded, "I must've gone on hearing those drums for hours. Until I finally fell asleep."

"It is an exciting experience, isn't it?" Emerenciana enthused.

"That sort of brings up what I wanted to ask you." Koesler looked from Toussaint to his wife. "Has either of you ever attended a voodoo ceremony?"

Emerenciana smiled engagingly. "Of course we have, Bob. We used to go often in the old country. And we've been to a few in this country."

"I knew, though only from reading about it," said Koesler, "that there is a heavy blending of Catholicism in the voodoo rites. But I was surprised to actually hear the old Latin liturgy, especially in that context."

"You see, Bob," said Toussaint, "when the slaves were brought from Africa, the British looked on them merely as property. The French, however, considered the slaves to be people. Albeit with no rights." He smiled. "So the French had their slaves baptized.

"Baptism meant little to the slaves already bewildered by confinement in a foreign land. So they simply continued with their native religion. For example, voodoo has many *loa* who vaguely correspond to our Catholic saints. So the slaves simply blended the *loa* with the Catholic muster of saints.

"Dambala, for instance, is none other than your old friend St. Patrick." Toussaint smiled as he said this. He knew that although his friend bore a German surname, his mother's people had come from Ireland.

Koesler smiled back. "Fascinating," he said, as he deposited a mangled toothpick in the ashtray. "And even more fascinating is the theory that the Red Hat murderer is a practitioner of voodoo."

"Yes," said Emerenciana, "we read about it in the papers."

"This gentleman I told you about," said Koesler, "gave us a sort of play-by-play account of the ceremony, and talked to us afterward. He told of ceremonies in which a curse is placed on someone. Is there any way you know of that I could get into one of those ceremonies? If I could get into one, I'm sure I could get into others. I might even stumble across the Red Hat murderer."

"And if you did, Bob," Emerenciana asked, "do you think you'd stumble away alive?"

"Yes, I do," Koesler stated firmly. "I'm convinced that whoever the Red Hat murderer is, he's making a powerful statement on sin. And while I'm no saint, I don't believe I quite rank with the sinners he's disposing of. I don't think he would kill any of us under any circumstances."

"And what would you do with him even if you did come across him—turn him in or give him a medal?" Toussaint went on before Koesler could reply. "Besides, there is not a chance of your getting in for one of those death conjures. Nor any chance of our getting in, for that matter. Such ceremonies are by invitation only. Otherwise you could end up being the object of the death conjure."

"I guess that makes sense," Koesler reluctantly agreed. He stood and prepared to leave. "I've got to get out to St. John's. I've got a luncheon date with Father Clark, then we're going to play a round of golf."

"Give our best to Leo," said Emerenciana.

As he reached the door, Koesler sniffed the air. There seemed to be a trace of incense.

"Fumigating again, Ramon?"

"Why not?" answered Toussaint with a shrug. "Cockroaches been on earth lots longer than humans. They get angry when we take land from them and build on it."

Koesler began his journey to the seminary laden with that feeling of guilt that core city people could lay on suburbanites any time they wanted.

Tom McCoy drove his three-year-old Chevrolet into Dessalen's Garage. That is, he almost drove it in. As he turned into the service drive from Grand River, his car stalled. He started it, gunned the engine, and brought it to a rocking stop in front of the entrance. He got out of the car and circled it, kicking each tire soundly.

It was Elmer Dessalen's opinion that anyone who treated his car in such fashion did not understand automobiles and probably would have no idea what was wrong with it. Thus, the owner personally attended this customer.

"Problems?" Dessalen asked needlessly.

"Damn car!" McCoy fumed. "Every time I turn a corner the damn things stalls."

"That's a problem!"

"I've stopped in at I don't know how many gas stations —nothing!"

"How long's it been doin' this?"

"Last few days."

Dessalen opened the hood and began to explore. His finger inside the carburetor picked up a gritty substance. He rubbed it between his fingers. Sand.

"Looks pretty bad," Dessalen shook his head sadly. "I'd say it was your fuel pump. Probably needs to be replaced."

"How long will it take you to do it?"

That, thought Dessalen, was good. Time was more important to this car-owner than money.

"Get it done for you this afternoon. Have it ready on your way home from work."

"Great! I'll leave it with you and take a cab downtown."

Dessalen wrote out the work order.

"Now, Mr. McCoy," Dessalen called as McCoy was about to leave, "if we find any more problems, I'll phone you to see if you want 'em fixed."

"Fine! Great!"

Ben Jones watched the departure.

"Whatcha got there?" asked Jones.

"Jonesie," said Dessalen, "I think if you take this gas tank off, you'll find a ton of sand. After you dump the sand, give the nice man a new fuel pump. And if you see anything else that looks replaceable, let me know."

"Why," said Jones, "we could build the man a brand new car."

"Not too much now, Jonesie. Moderation," Dessalen cautioned.

They laughed.

Dessalen counted heavily on Barnum's having been right when he observed that there was a sucker born every minute.

The buildings were the same as he remembered them a quarter of a century earlier, but everything else had changed.

As a student at St. John's Seminary, Robert Koesler had been one of a full house. In his day, St. John's had housed from 200 to 250 students. The faculty was composed entirely of Sulpicians, diocesan priests whose sole task was the training of seminarians. The school rules were considered to be the will of God. The training tended to produce macho but disciplined and obedient, if slightly adolescent, men.

Now the Roman Catholic province of Michigan felt fortunate to have fifty to seventy-five seminarians. The faculty comprised everyone from priests, nuns, and Protestant ministers to the laity. There were no rules in the strict sense. There were a few "suggestions," such as silence, for the sake of the small community, after 10 P.M. A suggestion that was never observed.

St. John's was a huge complex of buildings searching for a purpose.

Three deacons had joined Fathers Koesler and Clark at lunch. Another departure. In Koesler's day, students had dined at their tables and faculty at theirs.

A duplication of this group would be rare. All five were men. Koesler was old enough to be a father to the three deacons. Clark was old enough to be their grandfather.

"What I'd like to know," Deacon Ed Landregan asked, "is what did priests used to do before there were all these meetings?"

"Yeah," Deacon Mike Shanahan agreed, "it's end-to-end meetings out there. Staff meetings with the pastor, parish council meetings, council committee meetings, vicariate meetings, archdiocesan meetings—"

"And that," Deacon Dave Ballas interjected, "does not count the experts who are brought in for speeches in the parish, the region, the vicariate, the diocese—"

"And the beat goes on," Landregan concluded.

Koesler chuckled. "You're right, of course. But before the meetings, and before your time, there were convert classes. Twenty years ago and earlier, everybody wanted to be a Catholic."

"That's right," Clark added, "just about the time you were ordained, Bob, the whole conversion business peaked."

"Yes," said Koesler, "I started with as many as four or five prospective converts each evening, and several during the day. Then there were the marriage problems, family troubles, financial woes. It could and did fill the day and night."

"And now?" asked Shanahan.

"Now there aren't all that many prospective converts, and most people take their troubles to professionals," said Koesler.

"And so," said Clark, "to fill the time, we meet."

Koesler refilled his soup bowl. "Can any of you join Father Clark and me for nine holes after lunch?"

"No, thanks," said Ballas, "we've all got to get back to our parishes."

"Kind of brisk for golf, isn't it?" asked Shanahan.

"Got to keep Leo supple," said Koesler, "or he'll roll into a little ball and be blown away."

"Careful, Bob," said Clark, "or I'll resurrect Cardinal Mooney's old electric golf cart and ride the legs off you."

"Ah, the golf cart," Koesler recalled, "Mooney's was the only one ever used here. Is that thing still around?"

"It must be," said Clark. "Unless they buried it with him in the crypt chapel."

When no one laughed, Ballas asked, "You mean Cardinal Mooney is buried here?"

It was the turn of the other four to be surprised.

"You mean," said Koesler, "you've been here almost four years and you didn't know Cardinal Mooney is buried in the crypt chapel?"

"I've never been back there," Ballas said defensively.

"There's no reason for the students to be there anymore, Bob." Clark's tone bore a touch of regret.

"Well, David," said Landregan, "you are not going to win any Explorer Scout merit badges with that kind of isolationism. Right after lunch we'll go visit the Cardinal's grave. You'll like it. It's spooky!"

Clark was right, Koesler thought. The crypt chapel was a memory of the past. In his day as a seminarian, five priest faculty members had offered daily Mass simultaneously, each at his own altar in the crypt. They were called the "whisper Masses," because the Latin was whispered and the bells barely sounded so as not to distract the others.

Today, no one but the most staunch conservative would say Mass privately. Community was the central thought in the liturgy.

Mooney had been buried in the crypt at a time when the

chapels there were the hub of early morning activity each day.

Well, Koesler thought, the best-laid Cardinals often go unvisited.

"You probably never even knew this, Leo," he said, "but one day your sacristan, Dick Kulaski, taped the clapper to the side of the little bell. Two or three of us stood in the shadows to watch Ted Neighbors, who was serving your Mass, try to ring the bell. It was all we could do to keep from revealing our presence and disgracing ourselves when Ted first tipped the bell and finally waved it like a flag."

"I vaguely remember a Mass without a bell. I had no idea why it had been so quiet." Clark laughed.

"Poor Ted and his fractured Cabrini."

"Waste no pity," said Koesler. "Teddy fell in and came up smelling rosy. The sculptor agreed to repair, or if that proves impossible, entirely redo the statue, gratis."

"Two Cabrinis for the price of one," said Clark.

"Yes," said Koesler, "I believe Teddy has managed to impress even his parish council."

The five rose. Each said a private after-luncheon prayer.

"What would you say, Bob, if I offered you a nip of wine before we attack the course?" asked Clark.

"I'd drink to that."

Moellmann called Koznicki and Harris into his office. He wanted to speak privately with them before the news conference.

"The foreign substance in McCluskey's body proved, as I thought, to be snake venom."

Koznicki looked interested; Harris, plainly pleased.

"Dr. Moody, an expert in the field, has identified it as the venom of the king cobra."

"But how—" Harris began.

"We're not positive how the venom was introduced into the body," Moellmann interrupted. "It's probable it was injected into the back of the right hand. There was an extremely small puncture there."

"It looks like we've got a homicide!" Harris was very pleased.

"But that's not all." Moellmann gestured at Harris, who apparently was ready to leave.

"That a small amount of cobra venom was present in McCluskey's body is one fact," Moellmann stated. "The other fact is that the venom was not the cause of death."

"Not the cause of—"

"No," said Moellmann. "McCluskey died of heart failure. Those are the two facts we have. From them, it is possible to make some suppositions, draw some conclusions."

"But the death mask, Doctor," Koznicki asked, "the probable cause?"

"Fright, most likely," said Moellmann.

"If my memory does not betray me, is it not possible for venom to cause a victim to hallucinate?"

"Yes, that's true," said Moellmann.

"Is it possible," Koznicki pressed, "that the venom caused hallucinations so terrifying that the victim, in this case Mr. McCluskey, would be frightened to death? And that you would then conclude, quite correctly, that he died of heart failure? And the venom thus was the contributing factor, or the initial or primary cause of the heart failure?"

"Yes," Moellmann acknowledged, "not only is all that possible, your theory matches mine exactly, Inspector. But it remains a theory. I do not believe a strong case could be made in a court of law."

Both Koznicki and Harris were dejected.

"However," said Moellmann, "find me another one. Find me another body of a Red Hat victim containing venom and I believe your case will be quite strong indeed. Either, in this as-of-now hypothetical case, the venom will cause death—in which case you have your homicide plain and simple—or the coincidence of two identical deaths will tend to confirm the venom-hallucination-heart failure sequence."

"Damn!" said Harris. "We uncover bodies almost every

damn day. Not one has been another Red Hat victim."

"I say this, gentlemen," said Moellmann, "only to encourage you. All is by no means lost. Find me another body. Find me another body." He was almost like a child asking for candy.

"I think I'll call your Father Koesler," said Harris.

"Why?" Koznicki asked.

"We haven't got a body and we need a prayer."

With the exception of the specific clinical details of the actual decapitations, Pat Lennon knew as much about The Red Hat Murders as the Detroit police. And so did the readers of the *News*.

The delay in Moellmann's news conference had made it impossible for her to make the late-afternoon edition. But she had interviewed Sergeant Terri Scanlon and learned the wide dimensions of this case.

Her page-one story was headlined, "Red Hat Victims: Hard and Soft Core Crooks." It ran with the gruesome photo of McCluskey's head atop St. Joseph's statue.

She had just finished closing her copy on the Moellmann news conference. The story was now locked in the CRT directory for editing.

"I just wanted you to know, Pat," said Bob Ankenazy, joining her at the water cooler, "that everybody here has been talking about your coverage of The Red Hat Murders. It's been terrific. In the finest tradition of the *News*. You got it first and you got it right."

"Thanks, Bob," said Lennon. "I'm sorry I didn't get the Moellmann angle in for the four-ball."

"Not your fault. Moellmann's delays slowed things up."

"I know. I guess it just burns me that Joe will beat me on that one."

"I wouldn't let that worry me. You've stayed so far ahead of Cox he'll never catch up."

Lennon finished the water and threw the paper cup in the wastebasket. "I've had the creepiest feeling ever since the Moellmann conference this afternoon."

"Why's that?"

"Just imagine," Lennon shivered, "what it would be like to be scared to death, literally."

"Very probably," said Ankenazy, "there will be more than a few local businessmen pulling a few fast ones who just might be literally scared *of* death when they read your story."

"Of course, Mrs. Grimes. I'll be glad to handle the case for you."

Charles Lebaron, attorney-at-law, was seated behind his large desk in his office in the CNB Building. Across from him, seated in a wheelchair, was a lovely young woman— no, what had been a lovely young woman. Now, her body was twisted, her skin scarred, her eyes pained far beyond her years.

Mrs. Grimes, her husband, and their two small children had been passengers in a commercial jet that some months before had crashed, killing most of its passengers and crew and severely injuring most of the survivors, many of whom would be maimed for life.

Mrs. Grimes and her young daughter were in the latter category; her husband and son had been in the former.

Even with all the money in the world, life would not be easy for either Mrs. Grimes or her daughter, both of whom faced years of operations, plastic surgery, and physiotherapy, not to mention psychotherapy to combat the recurring nightmares and survival-guilt syndrome.

It was a cut-and-dried case. A first-year law student could prove liability. The groundwork had been laid by several of the big national law firms who specialized in airline liability cases. The airline had already paid off several of the heirs and survivors; juries were certain to award huge amounts to the remaining victims. And if the airline attorneys were smart—and they were—they would try for an out-of-court settlement. One look at the photos of Mrs. Grimes and her daughter as they had been and as they were now, and there was no doubt a jury would make a record-setting award.

Lebaron mentally licked his chops. Either way, his share would be magnificent. For a few hours of dictation and paperwork, a few phone calls, some postage, possibly a court appearance or two, he would be on easy street. He made a note to be sure to thank the Galandt Funeral Home, who had buried her husband and son, for recommending his services to Mrs. Grimes.

"What? Oh, my fee. Well, Mrs. Grimes, a case like yours involves a lot of work—yes, a lot of work. I'll have to shelve some other matters. There'll be a lot of documents to file. But I'll charge only the normal amount. In liability matters, as you know, the attorney gets one-third of all settlement monies—plus expenses, of course—and you will get two-thirds."

Lebaron's gaze dropped to the picture of Tod McCluskey on the front page of the afternoon *News*. He tapped his finger against the desk's polished surface.

"On the other hand, Mrs. Grimes, you have your daughter to think of. And you've been through so much. And no amount could ever repay for the loss of your husband and your son. I'll tell you what: I'll cut my fee to a straight one-fifth—and I'll absorb the expenses."

Mrs. Grimes wept.

"My estimate for moving your furniture and belongings to Dallas, Mrs. Tiefer," said Duane Kelleher, "is $2,500."

"It's going up, isn't it?"

"Yes, ma'am. Moving and everything."

"I mean, it only cost us $1,500 to move here from Kalamazoo last year."

"Well, you probably accumulated more things, it's a lot longer distance, and gas is out of sight. And, of course, no one can promise you a lower price than we can, because all moving companies must operate under the same tariff, according to ICC regulations."

"All right. The important thing is, when can we expect

delivery? My husband has to report for class Monday. He's going to teach at the University of Dallas."

"Well, let's see: We can pack you tomorrow, that's Wednesday, and pick you up on Thursday. If there aren't any other loads to pick up, we should have your stuff there on Monday all right."

"Oh, that's fine. That will be just perfect. I'll just phone and tell my husband the good news while you're filling out your order sheet."

Mrs. Tiefer left the room. Kelleher could hear her talking on the phone in the kitchen. He glanced around the room. The photo of Tod McCluskey stared up at him from the newspaper on the table. Drawn by the horror of the picture, Duane Kelleher picked up the paper, and scanned Pat Lennon's accompanying article.

He laid the paper down slowly. He thought of the critical gas situation. He thought of the additional pickups he was pretty sure the driver would have to make. He thought of the company's crowded warehouse. And most of all, he thought of the company computer in Indianapolis—the computer that could withhold trucks and hang up people's furniture for weeks.

Mrs. Tiefer reentered the room.

"Uh, Mrs. Tiefer," Kelleher said, "I should tell you there is the possibility of a delay on a move like this, a long delay."

"What do you mean?"

"I mean as much as a month."

"A month!"

"Or even longer. It's possible. It would be possible with any moving company at this time of year. I just think it's important for you to know that. I'd keep it in mind when you pack your car. You might want to take along some extra things, like more of your husband's shirts, for his new job. And some sheets, towels, and cooking utensils you'll need until your household goods can be delivered."

"Oh, and Mrs. Tiefer, I'd suggest some extra damage

insurance. Our people aren't always as careful as they should be—and things do get broken."

"Well, thanks, I guess, for telling me. I don't know how we would have managed if you hadn't."

"Thirty-five thousand dollars is the very finest we have."

Wilson Menard, owner of Menard Funeral Homes, didn't expect his callers to actually choose a $35,000 funeral. But Louise Seymour *had* asked about the best.

Both Louise and her sister gasped.

"Louise, don't be an idiot!" said Rose.

"But," Louise's hands and eyelashes fluttered, "you know Loretta never had the best in life."

"All the more reason she'll be satisfied with less than the best in death," said Rose.

"Don't say death!"

"Why not?"

"It sounds so final."

"It is."

Wilson Menard tugged at his vest and cuffs. He knew from years of experience the exact maximum funeral fee he could expect from a couple of spinsters on behalf of their sister.

"Miss Seymour," he addressed either or both sisters, "the most popular funeral we have is priced at $2,400. It is not lavish, but it is most respectable. And that price includes everything from transporting the deceased here to the actual burial."

"Well, that sounds more reasonable," said Rose.

"Do you really think it's enough for Loretta?" asked Louise.

Menard's eye caught the afternoon edition of the *News*, which he had carefully folded so that sickening picture would not be visible. But he remembered it.

"Actually, ladies," he broke into their conversation, "almost the identical service is available to you for $1,600. I recommend it."

"Would you excuse us for a moment?" Rose Seymour

had grown suspicious. She drew her sister aside for a caucus.

While they were gone, Menard picked up the *News* and once more scanned the story of Tod McCluskey's death, the series of murders, and the wide variety of future possible victims.

The two sisters returned.

"Your sister was quite elderly?" he asked.

They nodded.

"There are not many survivors, are there?"

They shook their heads.

"Then I would like you to consider cremation. Four hundred and fifty dollars for a simple sturdy coffin, five dollars for a permission certificate, and a hundred and twenty dollars for the cremation."

The sisters looked at each other in wonderment.

"Father Koesler?"

"Yes?"

"Lieutenant Harris."

"I thought I recognized your voice."

"I know it's a little late, but do you have a few minutes?"

"Yes, of course."

"I wonder if you could provide me with a little more information about your friend Ramon Toussaint."

"Why, is something wrong?"

"Oh, no, Father. Just an effort to understand everything I can about all aspects of the case we're investigating."

"What can I help you with?"

"Those Ministers of Service Toussaint created; how do they fit into things Catholic? Are they unique?"

Koesler chuckled. "Yes, I guess they are, Lieutenant. I've never thought about it quite that way. But as far as I know, there's nothing like them in the world."

"And why was it Toussaint got this group started?"

"Well, there was a program begun about ten or twelve years ago to reestablish a permanent diaconate—men who would not become priests but would remain deacons."

"Why wouldn't they become priests?"

"They could be married and still be deacons."

"Oh. O.K., go on."

"They can perform some of the rites that formerly only priests could. They can baptize, distribute communion; they can anoint, they can witness weddings, they can preach. Things like that.

"Well, anyway, Ramon predicted the black Catholic community simply wouldn't buy this program, especially since it required two years of rather intense study. And he was right. It became a white man's program. The black Catholic community would be once again without any black Catholic leaders.

"So Ramon began, all on his own, the Ministers of Service. He, along with several sympathetic inner-city priests, teaches them, and turns them out in a matter of two or three months."

"And are they the equivalent of deacons?"

"Yes and no. They can't witness weddings. They would not be recognized by either civil or Church law. But by and large, at least from time to time, they do pretty much everything else a deacon does.

"The Church in Detroit—that would be Archbishop Mark Boyle—sort of lets them be. The problem of attracting black Catholic leadership for black Catholics is so desperate, the thinking seems to be, 'Don't rock the boat.'"

"And does it work?"

"Better than anything anyone else has developed."

"And Toussaint?"

Koesler chuckled again. "The Archbishop ordained him a deacon without making him go through the entire deaconate training. Sort of a reward for helping to solve an enormous problem."

"Then you would say that Toussaint was not the type to wait around interminably for the solution to a problem?"

Koesler thought a moment. "Yes, I think I would agree

with that statement. And add that I find the quality admira-
ble."

"Good! Thanks for your time, Father."

"That's all?"

"Pray for us."

An odd way, Koesler thought, for a police officer to
conclude a phone conversation.

He poured a nightcap and sipped it slowly, thinking of
his years of friendship with the Toussaints and all Ramon
had done for the blacks of Detroit's Catholic Church.

That night, Koesler had an odd dream. He dreamed of
Ramon Toussaint garbed in the ancient uniform of Imperial
Rome. He was walking on the heads of white deacons who
were shouting, *"Cras!"* And he was brandishing a sword
and marching toward a group of black Ministers of Service, who were chanting, *"Hodie!"*

Larry Ranger was not a prayerful man. But he prayed his
four-year-old Lincoln Continental would make it to a garage or service station. He felt a special sense of gratitude
then, when he saw the large sign, "Dessalen's Garage." He
pulled into the service area.

A small black man approached Ranger. Dessalen tried to
personally determine the etiology on luxury cars. It was his
philosophy that anyone who could afford gas for those
guzzlers could afford a whopping repair bill.

"Troubles?" asked Dessalen, chomping on a fresh cigar.

"Damn car didn't start this morning," said Ranger. "I'm
just lucky my neighbor had jumper cables."

"That's trouble," Dessalen affirmed. "Nothin' worse
than when the damn car won't start."

Dessalen opened the hood and began poking about
among the wires and engine parts. Finally, he emerged,
wiping his hands on a rag.

"It doesn't look good," he said.

Ranger was more concerned with the time he was losing
than the possible cost. He continued shifting his weight
from one foot to the other.

"Looks like your starter is shot and I don't like the look of that battery. Have to test it, though."

"Listen," said Ranger, "do what you have to to make the damn thing run. I'll have my secretary call later today and find out when it'll be ready."

Dessalen got the necessary information and completed the service slip. Ranger flagged a cab and headed for downtown Detroit.

"Big mother," Ben Jones commented.

"This one's gonna pay for a couple of vacations," said Dessalen. "Inside there you'll find a loose cable. Tighten it so the damn car will start. Then replace the starter, battery, and just about anything else that doesn't look new."

"Man must be made of money."

"Not when we get done with him."

Blood was splattered nearly everywhere. The dead chicken, whose blood it was, lay on the floor. A heavy cloud of incense hung high against the ceiling. The ceremony was nearly over.

"*Adia ban moin zui poto tou félé,*" the *Mambo* sang, "*Adia ban moin zui poto tou félé.*"

"*Placeat tibi, sancta Trinitas, obsequium servitutis meae,*" her assistant chanted, "*et praesta, ut sacrificium, quod oculis tuae majestatis indignus obtuli, tibi sit acceptabile.*"

"*Adia bon moin zui zui ya ma qué félé. Adia ban moin zui poté tout félé.*"

"*Mihique et omnibus, pro quibus illud obtuli, sit, te miserante, propitiabile.*"

The assistant bowed low and left the room. He carried a statuette of St. Expeditus. He would bury the statue head downward in a Catholic cemetery.

"Lady, you don't understand. We don't make house calls."

"But, sir, I'm old and crippled and can't get out of the house. I can't even lift the television set. And it's supposed to be portable." Her tremulous voice broke with a combination of worry and desperation.

"I can't help that, lady. You gotta bring your set in. If I have to come and get it, I'll have to sock you with a big service charge."

Mark Owens, proprietor of Owens TV and Radio Repair, was losing his patience and time trying to convey to this old lady the idea that her TV set had preceded her to the grave.

"No, sir, please, I don't want you to take my TV. Please sir, couldn't you come and fix it here? It's not so bad. The picture just keeps flipping. I think it must be the vertical hold button. Please sir, I'm going to miss all my programs." It was as if she were pleading for the life of a loved one. In reality, her TV set was her only companion. It was very ill.

"Look, ma'am, I really don't have time..." In boredom, he had been drumming on the desk with his fingers. Well, not directly on the desk. He'd been drumming on his copy of the morning *Free Press*. He looked at the story he'd read earlier about the Red Hat murderer and about the type of person who could be his next victim.

"...uh, wait a minute, ma'am. Did you say it was just your vertical hold? Listen, give me your address. I think I can fix that for you at your apartment."

"Right here? You won't have to take it away?"

"That's right, ma'am."

"Oh, God bless you!"

"I hope so."

In the Detroit area, used cars find their way to Livernois Avenue the way elephants find a burial ground.

In the Paulsen Used Cars lot, some extraordinary activity was going on.

Arnold Paulsen, owner of the lot, armed with wet sponge and grease pencil, moved from auto to auto slashing prices.

Earlier in the morning, he had consigned three of his vehicles to the junk heap.

In the wastebasket of Paulsen's office was a rolled-up copy of yesterday's *News*.

A decree had gone forth to the meat department that henceforth there was to be no more wrapping of fresh ground meat around stale hamburger.

Stanley Pace, manager of the supermarket at Cass and Seldon, and author of the decree, sat at his desk with the morning *Free Press*. For the third time, he was reading Joe Cox's latest account of developments in The Red Hat Murders. Pace slowly shook his head.

Fred Roper tucked a copy of the morning *Free Press* in his saddlebag and mounted his impressive Harley Davidson. He was about to kick the monstrous motorcycle into life and spend a few moments revving it with ear-splitting bravado. He followed this routine at least once a day.

Roper paused and looked at the nearby convalescent home. For the first time he thought of the patients whose tranquility he was about to shatter.

He walked the motorcycle out of the driveway and into the street. He started it and drove away without a single varroom.

Leo Richmond, corporation executive, sat near the window of his suite in St. Paul's Commodore Hotel, where he was staying while attending a business conference.

He had just read the early edition of the *Pioneer Press*. As had nearly all the nation's newspapers, this one carried a wire service account of the latest developments in The Red Hat Murders.

Richmond looked out the window contemplatively. In his mind's eye, he could see the tons of taconite tailings his company was accused of dumping into Lake Superior's Silver Bay daily while the farce dragged on in the courts.

For the first time, he felt ashamed—and nervous about the charges.

"I've got to hand it to the guy," said Harris. "He sure started at the top."

"Absolutely," Koznicki agreed. "I wonder how he ever got through to them."

Koznicki had not only every available Detroit police officer on the Red Hat case, he also had the full cooperation of the Wayne County Sheriff's Department, and was now himself actively involved in the investigation.

He and Harris, in Harris' car, were en route to a meeting of local black clergymen, mostly Baptists, who might give the officers a lead toward that elusive voodoo ceremony for which they were searching.

"I've got a hunch," said Harris, "we'll have to find him in order to learn how he got to people like Ruggiero, Harding, and Strauss."

"Sensational!" Koznicki commented. "I must admit I couldn't duplicate his feat at least as far as a Ruggiero and Strauss. Not only was his ability to kill and decapitate them amazing, but his timing was exquisite."

Harris shook his head. "So a guy who can touch the untouchables is now working on comparative small fry."

"Yes. He probably did not know that we were about to collar Dr. Schmitt. So he probably thought he was eliminating an evil man who operated above the law. That certainly was true with McCluskey. One of those small-time crooks who operates within the law. And if he uses the same M.O., he'll kill again today."

"But who?" Harris asked. "The world is filled with business people who are at least morally dishonest with their customers, their clients. I can't help it, Walt, for some reason I feel very vulnerable."

"It is a feeling, I assure you, that is shared by many, many people in our city this day," said Koznicki, as they passed Dessalen's Garage.

* * *

It was late in the afternoon. Father Koesler sat at the desk in his small office at St. Anselm's.

All through the day, he had been monitoring the hourly news bulletins on WJR radio. No news yet of another Red Hat victim.

Koesler had been almost dragged into this case. But now he could not avoid his involvement. From the time he had offered Mass this morning, he had pondered virtually nothing but The Red Hat Murders.

The series of killings was a statement, of that he was convinced. A statement on sin. Sin as the using and misusing of people.

Ordinary citizens, parishioners, tend to think of people like the king of vice, the top pimp, the head of the drug empire as criminals, rather than as sinners. But if they are truly criminals they are truly sinners. The worst of sinners. Guilty of the most heinous abuse of the innocent.

But then people like the abortionist and the repairman— not *all* abortionists or *all* repairmen by any means, but the two selected as victims by the Red Hat killer—were guilty of the very same crime, the same sin, only on a smaller scale. They too used and abused people.

Obviously, it was the avenger's purpose to demonstrate the similarity of the crimes, the similarity of the sin.

After that, the series of murders seemed filled with symbolism.

Three killings in a week. The Trinity. The days between the death and resurrection. The days spent by Jonah in the whale. A popular Biblical, mystical, and religious number. If he killed today, it would again be three in a week. Three at the top, then three very ordinary sinners.

Completion?

The possibility engrossed Koesler. The statement would be complete. Three outrageous sinners. Three sinners closer to our everyday lives. All suffering the same fate. Capital punishment, using the pun to go with both "hat" and "head."

Would it be possible, if his theory were correct, to anticipate the identity of today's victim? No, no; utterly impossible. The killer had practically the entire city to choose from.

What chance was there of intercepting him?"

The place he would leave the head! Was there any way of guessing where he would leave the head? Especially without knowing the victim's identity, or perhaps better, the victim's occupation. The pimp found with a model of purity and chastity. The drug king with an angel who represented angel dust. An abortionist with the patron of midwives. The repairman with St. Joseph the Carpenter.

And the next victim? Which occupation was the vehicle for his sin? Where would his head be found?

At long last, a possibility occurred to Koesler. He tried to discard it, but it continued to resurface. And then it simply wouldn't go away.

Well, he thought, why not? At worst, he could lose a night's sleep. And that was little enough price to satisfy his curiosity.

Elmer Dessalen closed his garage. He ascended the stairs to his office, whose windows overlooked the stalls still filled with cars to be worked on first thing in the morning.

Dessalen's routine required going through the day's mail, counting the day's receipts, and cleaning up. Then a late dinner, followed by a little fun.

The junk mail he disposed of unopened. There were a couple of trade journals he'd take with him to browse through over dinner.

Finally, there was a package wrapped in plain brown paper. He tore away the paper. Immediately, his hands began to tremble. Awkwardly, as if he feared doing an irreverence to the statuette, he placed it on his desk. He could not take his eyes from it as he backed into a corner of the office.

As he retreated, the figure of St. Expeditus grew suddenly larger and larger until the saint was larger than life-size. He towered over the cringing Dessalen.

The eyes of Expeditus burned into his. Dessalen could see in the saint's eyes a parade of every ordinary bewildered vulnerable driver he had defrauded. Instinctively, Dessalen knew that Expeditus had come as the avenger.

Expeditus advanced. Dessalen compressed himself into his corner. No sound was uttered.

In two majestic arcs, the sword of Expeditus severed Dessalen's arms at the shoulders. Strangely, he felt no pain. He looked from side to side and saw blood gushing from both wounds.

Expeditus pointed with his sword to the garage repair area. It had disappeared. In its place was a huge vat of oil. Bubbling, boiling oil that sent up a pungent odor.

The office walls had disappeared. Expeditus prodded Dessalen toward the floor's edge. At last, with the sharp point of his sword, the saint tipped Dessalen over the edge.

Down, down, down, into the oil-filled vat.

The pain was searing. Dessalen surfaced covered with the sizzling petroleum. In agony, he fought to keep his head above the surface. He had no arms to help him stay afloat. He gasped for air; his lungs were seared by the foul fumes. The heavy oil dragged him down, down, down. To nothingness.

A tall black man entered through a door at the rear of the large building. He wore coveralls, a leather jacket, and a felt hat, all of which had seen much better days. He looked around the empty garage.

He climbed the stairs. As he entered the office he seemed startled by the figure lying on the floor. He approached it, and with head cocked to one side, studied it. After a few minutes, he shook his head. He smiled. He removed a ring from his right hand and carefully put it in a small case he took from his pocket.

He went down the stairs and out to an old Plymouth parked behind the garage. Putting plastic coverings over his shoes, he returned to the office carrying an immense canvas bag. He removed a small case from the bag, opened it and removed a venerable handsaw. Squatting by the dead body, in a few strokes of the saw he removed the head. Blood covered the floor. He replaced the saw in its case and put the case and the head in the plastic-lined bag.

Making certain he had left no fingerprints, he exited the building.

He placed the bag in the trunk of his car, removed the plastic coverings from his shoes and disposed of them in the trashcan behind the garage.

Resolutely he drove out Grand River. It was very dark and quite chill.

Meanwhile, on Stoepel Avenue, a plainclothesman arrived to take up surveillance outside the home of Lieutenant Harris' chief suspect in The Red Hat Murders.

Father Koesler had seldom felt so foolish.

He wanted to view his vigil at St. John's Seminary in the dramatic setting of those stereotyped prolonged police stakeouts. But all he could honestly liken it to was the "Peanuts" cartoon strip wherein Linus annually spends all Halloween vainly waiting for the appearance of The Great Pumpkin.

In the darkness, he was all but invisible on the second-floor porch over the seminary's front entrance. He had been standing there for slightly more than four hours.

It was an excellent vantage. He could see for miles. He could see every road that approached the entrance to the seminary grounds. There was very little traffic on these roads during evenings. Outside of a few farms, most buildings in the area were institutions like the seminary and its distant neighbor, the Detroit House of Correction.

Not even a book to read, he thought—even if there were

light. This place had been spooky even when he had occupied it as a student a quarter of a century before. Then, nearly overflowing with students and faculty, it had had the smell of newness. But even then, it had been filled with dark places that seemed impossible to illuminate sufficiently.

By now, the building had developed its own sounds—creaks, squeaks, whispers and moans. In addition, there was almost no one around. The few students living at the seminary were either in bed or gulping down the last few beers. In either case, they were in the rear of the building, which now seemed miles away.

Koesler's eyes wandered restlessly over the roads. If he had been a profane man, he would have cursed the theory that had brought him there. Instead, he shrugged the feeling away. He was tempted to leave. But, like the rationalization for the prolonged U.S. presence in Vietnam, he felt he had invested too much time to leave without knowing his hands were doomed to remain empty.

At that moment, he saw a car turn into the seminary drive. As it turned in, the car's lights were turned off.

It could have been many things, not the least a student returning late. But Koesler determined to follow this through. It was the only out-of-the-ordinary occurrence thus far.

Instead of continuing the path of the circular drive, which would have brought it directly beneath Koesler, the car took the alternate drive leading to the seminary's north side.

As it passed out of Koesler's view to the side, the priest turned and ran down the stairs to the main floor. There he slowed, deciding to walk swiftly with arms outstretched, rather than running. Doors might be closed, and there was no moonlight, so all was thoroughly dark.

The door to the north cloisters was ajar. It had been closed and locked when he'd checked it before his vigil. A car was parked outside. He could not discern the license number, but it appeared to be an old Plymouth. And that was vaguely familiar.

As he turned the corner into the transverse cloisters, Koesler thought he saw someone disappear into the entrance that led to both the main church and the crypt chapel. The figure had been carrying something—a bag, or a pouch, or a sack.

The only illumination came from a few lights still on in the residence halls across the courtyard. Not enough to see clearly.

Koesler hurried along the cloister but hesitated as he reached the entrance to the chapels. It was pitch-black. He fumbled for the light switch, found it, flipped it. Nothing.

Damn!

Cautiously, he felt his way along the wall. Suddenly, he touched something. He didn't want to touch it again. He forced himself. It was cold, it was slimy and, whatever it was, it was dead. With a shudder, he pulled away from the object. In doing so, he backed into something unyielding. It was not a wall.

Koesler spun about. His eyes were becoming adjusted to the dark. He was able to perceive a human form easily as tall as himself. But who was it? Was he about to strike? Koesler raised both arms in a protective stance.

But there was something. A body odor. Not unpleasant, but distinctive. In an intuitive flash, it all came together.

"Ramon!" Koesler exclaimed in a voice barely above a whisper.

The figure turned and darted down the staircase toward the crypt chapel.

Koesler, several steps behind, ran in pursuit. I'm too old to be playing cops and robbers was his only thought.

At the basement level, Koesler swung through the door to the crypt chapel and turned toward where he remembered the light switch to be.

With that, he crashed into an ancient, ornate, and rigid kneeling bench. Koesler went up and over it in the same fashion as a running back who suffers a roll block at the knees. Except that professional athletes are better prepared for such bone-jarring collisions.

The back of Koesler's head made first contact with the concrete floor. He thought this a great indignity. Then he lost consciousness.

Everything was very fuzzy. With this head, he thought, I should be enjoying a hangover.

As things began to come into visual focus, he tried to remember what day it was. Thursday. Yes, definitely Thursday. But if it's Thursday, what am I doing on the floor?

This was going to be a day for one thing at a time.

First, rise.

That may have been a mistake, he thought. In an upright position, his head throbbed still harder.

Even though the students seldom pass through the crypt chapel, you'd think someone would occasionally dust the place. His black suit was covered with dirt.

Crypt chapel!

It all came back to him. He stopped brushing his suit and tentatively peered around the corner into the central area of the crypt chapel.

It was there all right. In the center of the large plaque covering Cardinal Edward Mooney's final resting place was a human head. It had been a black man. Koesler did not recognize him. Outside of the picture that had appeared in the *News*, the priest had not seen the remains of any of the previous Red Hat victims. He would never forget the look of utter horror on the man's face.

The police. The police must be notified.

But not by me, he thought. Not right now. The police would want to know how I found the head, what I was doing here. I'm not quite ready to tell them everything I know or suspect. Not, at least, till my head clears.

He would take the elevator to the third floor and use one of the guest rooms to clean and freshen up.

And then deal with the head.

He looked back at it and shuddered again.

Several luxury autos driven by several very agitated people had arrived at Dessalen's Garage. Just the sort of vehicles and persons Elmer Dessalen so enjoyed taking for all he could. Still, he had not made an appearance.

Ben Jones' curiosity became worry. He asked, but none of the mechanics had seen Dessalen.

Seizing the senior mechanic's prerogative, Jones climbed the stairs to his employer's office.

"Christ!" Jones could clearly be heard by those in the vicinity of the office. A couple of mechanics mounted the stairs to join him.

First to catch Jones' eye was the floor nearly covered with blood. Then the body. Though Jones had never before seen a headless body, he knew instantly it was that of Dessalen.

One of the other mechanics called the police. He had to; Jones was too sick to do so.

It was time for Lauds. As with all else, attendance was not compulsory. So, very few St. John's seminarians attended. Delaying the commencement of Lauds was the fact that none of the lights worked in the huge main floor chapel.

"Listen, Dave," said Deacon Ed Landregan, "since I was kind enough to take you on a tour of the crypt chapel the other day, you know where the fuse box is. Why don't you go downstairs and reset it?"

Deacon Dave Ballas could think of no reason why he should not be the one to set things right, except that since Landregan had thought of it, Landregan might be the more logical choice. But Ballas didn't care to argue the point. It was too nice a day. One of those September days that makes a Michigan autumn something to brag about.

Ballas descended the stairs very carefully. With no trouble, he found the fuse box and reset the switch.

Since his first visit had been just two days ago, he decided another quick look was in order. He wanted to see again that interesting plaque on Cardinal Mooney's grave.

Landregan began to wonder what had happened to Ballas. He had been gone several minutes longer than necessary. Had he gotten lost? Hurt himself? Fallen downstairs? Landregan began to worry. He felt responsible. He tested the light switch in the chapel. The lights worked. He went in search of his friend.

He found Ballas and he found the head. Ballas had not returned because he had become sick. Very sick. Fortunately, Landregan did not follow his example. On this occasion, he did not pass out. After caring for Ballas, he coolly called the police.

Showered and shaved, his suit sponged off, but still with a splitting headache, Father Koesler descended from his third-floor aerie to discover the head had been found and the police notified.

This was the first happy discovery he had made this lovely day.

While making this discovery, his presence in the seminary was noted by many of the faculty and students. His presence at that early hour and on this day would be considered by all to be noteworthy. Koesler guessed that someone would be bound to mention this. But there was something he had to accomplish before he spoke to the police.

He used the pay phone outside the central office.

"'Ciane, this is Bob Koesler. May I please speak with Ramon?"

"Of course. Just a moment."

"Bob," Toussaint's mellifluous voice came over the wire, "how are you?"

"O.K., I guess. Tired. And I've got a headache that won't quit."

"I am sorry to hear that. I checked you over carefully

before I left and saw that you were unconscious but not badly hurt."

So there was to be no dissembling. All the better.

"Ramon, I must see you."

"Of course, Bob. What do you say to meeting at Sacred Heart Seminary? It's a very nice day. We can walk around the grounds while we talk."

"That sounds good, Ramon. I'll get a bite to eat first. Maybe it'll help the headache. An hour?"

"I'll see you then, Bob."

Some toast and coffee with three aspirins couldn't hurt. With any luck, he'd be gone before the police investigation became too intense.

As Harris hung up the phone, he thought that seldom had he detected such naked excitement in Koznicki's voice. He hurried toward the Inspector's office.

When he entered the office, Harris remained standing. It was too much trouble struggling into a chair in that small room for any but the most solemn occasions.

"Ned," Koznicki opened, eyes dancing, "about half an hour ago, the Plymouth Police called. A severed head was found at St. John's Seminary."

"Whose?" Harris readily contracted the excitement.

"They have not made identification. But more on that later."

"Did they give permission for us to join in the investigation?"

"Of course. And since Plymouth is in Wayne County, there was no problem in their getting the head to Moellmann.

"But that's only half the story. Just a few minutes ago, I got a call that a headless body was found at Dessalen's Garage on Grand River. The body has been tentatively identified as that of Elmer Dessalen, owner of the garage. That's been shipped to Moellmann too. Do you think we could get lucky enough to have this head and body belong to each other?"

"I feel it in my bones," said Harris. "Are you as eager to get over to Moellmann's as I am?"

"I'm too old to race you, but let's go!"

"By the way," Harris asked as the two strode swiftly down the corridor, "what statue was wearing the head?"

"Odd," Koznicki responded as he pressed the elevator call button, "there was no statue."

"No statue?"

"No, the head was found on old Cardinal Mooney's tomb."

Harris was silent during the ride to the main floor.

"That doesn't seem to make any sense," he said as they reached the street.

"I don't find any pattern in it either. I think I'll put in a call to Father Koesler and ask him to stop by. This may be a matter for our theological experts."

"Not every police department has them."

"Damn right!"

They were too ebullient to bother driving. They walked briskly to the Wayne County Morgue.

Around and around they walked, following the brick path circling the spacious grounds at the rear of Sacred Heart Seminary. Each in black, with clerical collar. Approximately the same height. The dark man noticeably older and more powerfully built than the white man.

Koesler had offered his theory on the motive for the killings.

"That was it, wasn't it—a statement on the nature of sin?"

"Exactly correct, Bob." As always, Toussaint's pronunciation of "Bob" rhymed with "daub." "And it was particularly brilliant of you to properly deduce the conclusion."

"Well, I thought that depended on two elements. One, that the killer—you—that you were making your statement in two series of threes. First, the more notorious sinners, followed by more inconspicuous sinners.

"And second was the use of 'cardinal' as a pun. 'Cardinal' in its etymonic sense of being the hinge on which all else swings. That, along with the further pun that Pat McNiff came up with on the use of the red hat and the heads, a pun on the Latin *'caput,'* meaning 'head.' So it was capital punishment.

"And St. Expeditus would not wait until tomorrow to enforce capital punishment. He would insist on its being today."

Was the gleam in Toussaint's eyes amusement or admiration? Or both? "You're right, of course. But tell me, Bob, how did you know to wait for me at St. John's?"

"I didn't, really, or I wouldn't have been alone. It was just a hunch."

Koesler was silent for a minute, his mind a kaleidoscope of images. "But everything seemed to have a sort of symmetry. And so it seemed to me that the third victim of the second week would be the final element of the killer's—your—statement.

"And while each of the four heads was found with an appropriate statue, the first head was found with one of the only two relics we have of the late Cardinal Mooney—his red hat. The only other relic we have is his mortal remains.

"Add to that my notion that the killer—" Koesler shook his head wryly, "—*you*—intended the word 'cardinal' to be used in its strictest sense, as a hinge on which the entire enterprise swung, and . . ." he stopped walking and looked earnestly at Toussaint, who had also stopped and was regarding him gravely, "well, it just all led me to believe you would finish where you had begun."

"Excellent, Bob, excellent!"

As they resumed pacing, Koesler tried to stop feeling like a student who was being given extremely good grades.

Abruptly, he again stopped pacing. Again his companion was forced to stop also.

"Ramon! What in hell was that I touched hanging from the wall of the cloister, just before I bumped into you? It felt cold and slimy and dead! It wasn't the head, was it?" At the memory of the head, Koesler felt revulsion at the possibility of having touched it.

A smile played at the corner of Toussaint's mouth. "It was a cold and slimy and dead chicken, Bob."

"Chicken!"

"Yes. It is used in the death conjure. It is hung while the rite is completed."

If he had to to touch something slimy while not knowing what it was, Koesler thought, he'd prefer a chicken to a cadaver.

But there was something missing in this picture. Toussaint had not just come over on the boat. He was cultured —easily one of the most cultured, civilized, self-disciplined people Koesler knew. Even though Toussaint, by his own admission, was the Red Hat murderer, Koesler still could not make all the pieces fall in place, especially the magical pieces. It was as if the James Bond character were to rely on prayer rather than technology.

"But why voodoo? Where did that come from?"

"Emerenciana. She is a *Mambo*."

"A voodoo priestess? 'Ciane!"

"One of the best!"

"I find that hard to believe."

"Oh, no, Bob; she really is one of the best."

"No, not that. That she's a *Mambo*."

"Well, believe me, she is."

Koesler had little success envisioning the elegant and stately Emerenciana as a voodoo priestess. The priest had pictured 'Ciane as a most cultured woman, certainly above the practice of voodoo. But as he continued this consideration, he wondered why he would place voodoo "below" anything. To the Africans and at least some of their descendants, it was as meaningful a religion as Christianity was to Western civilization.

As he thought of voodoo, another impression emerged. An odor.

"The incense!" Koesler exclaimed. "It wasn't because of fumigating. It was part of a voodoo ritual. You conducted them in your own house."

Toussaint nodded.

Koesler had the irrelevant notion that if Madison Avenue ever got hold of this, eventually they would advertise a "new and improved home voodoo kit." He dismissed the distraction as an additional question occurred to him. Had Toussaint had a belt-and-suspenders approach to his mission?

"But if you had voodoo ceremonies, where did the snake venom come in? I read they found a trace of venom in that fellow—what's his name, McCluskey."

Toussaint lowered his head, shook it slowly and smiled. "'Ciane and I decided together to make this statement. After that I could not let her take full responsibility for the killings because of her death conjure. She does not know, but I was going to tell her later, if it seemed appropriate.

"It is something like the execution by firing squad. One marksman is given a blank instead of a live bullet. No one knows who has the blank. So theoretically none of them knows whether he killed the condemned. In this instance, neither 'Ciane nor I would know by whose hand the condemned was executed."

"But you can't believe in the power of voodoo." Koesler looked sharply at Toussaint. "The very fact you used venom indicates you don't."

"You misunderstand, Bob. I've explained why I injected the venom. Besides, you may very shortly learn that voodoo *is* effective."

Koesler wondered what possibly could convince him that voodoo had any practical effect. He was reminded of a young man he had counseled years before. The youth had been reluctant to tell him of what he thought was the bliss and beauty to be found in drugs for fear that, even though it might be against his religion, he, Koesler, might sample them!

Just as there was no possibility Koesler would drop into the drug culture, so he saw no way he could believe in voodoo.

"Bob," Toussaint continued, "there are so many things we know little of. I think all those men died of fear. But I am not certain what caused that fear. Perhaps the death conjure. Perhaps the venom. Perhaps an hallucination brought on by one of the two, or both. Or perhaps guilt helped them toward a vision of their life in eternity."

"That's right," said Koesler thoughtfully. "In all these studies of people who have returned from a death experience, thanatologists say that in addition to those who have a heavenly experience, there are many who experience some kind of hell. Most of the time, it literally scares the hell out of them."

"And those are merely the ones who admit their terrifying experiences," agreed Toussaint. "Not everyone is willing to admit he is so evil he nearly went to hell."

"Amazing!" Koesler automatically inserted a toothpick between his teeth.

As they continued their peregrination, several fire trucks sped by, sirens wailing. Koesler pressed both hands against his temples.

"Oh," Toussaint said solicitously, "your head! I am so sorry about that, Bob. I was only trying to lose you. I did not intend you to meet so violently with that priedieu."

"It was my own stupid fault." Koesler grimaced. "By the way, Ramon, you wouldn't happen to have any aspirin on you, would you?"

"Sorry, Bob."

Koesler had no intention of interrupting their dialogue. But he did wish an aspirin vendor would pass their way.

Which led to another consideration.

"Just to satisfy my curiosity, Ramon, where does one find snake venom in Detroit?"

"For your pharmacological information," Ramon smiled, "cobra venom when dried and properly handled retains its potency almost indefinitely. A *Mambo* in Africa sent it to me. There is a network of voodoo practitioners so vast you might not believe it! I relied on the members here to get me work uniforms, to tell me of habits and routines, to show me hidden switches, to duplicate keys—especially to the churches. Why, a *Houngan* was the caretaker at Dutch Strauss' headquarters!"

"You're telling me that because of this voodoo network, you could have access to almost anywhere and anyone in Detroit?"

"In the world. The whites did a fairly thorough job of introducing Africans and their descendants to all the rest of habitated earth."

It was mind-boggling. If Toussaint was not exaggerating, this voodoo network could be more far-reaching and powerful than any group on earth, including the Mafia, Interpol, and General Motors.

But there was still the individual to consider. At one time, Toussaint, as well as Koesler, had been under some suspicion.

"What about your alibi?" Koesler asked. "Didn't you have to provide the police, as I did, with an alibi for the times of the killings?"

"I lied."

"And the corroboration?"

"A lie."

"But, at best, that makes the end justify the means."

"You should not be surprised, Bob, that someone who executes six sinners who deserve to die will lie because it suits his purpose.

"Besides, the traditional objection to the end's justifying the means represents the theology of the Haves. The end must be able to justify the means for the Have-Nots or they will have nothing forever."

It was like first principles, axioms or givens. Koesler had never doubted, never even questioned, theological statements such as the end's not justifying the means. He began to wonder if his personal theology and conscience had been formed with a blindness toward an alien but legitimate culture.

It was too broad a concept for the moment. He would have to think this through at a later time.

"But are your means justified when they involve a

friend?" asked Koesler wryly, as he pondered his mangled toothpick. "If you *are* the one, you must have left those masticated toothpicks in Strauss' apartment. Why did you do a thing like that to me?"

Toussaint's chuckle was throaty. "First, I made certain you had a firm alibi or I would not have done it on that occasion. But I was eager for the police to begin suspecting the clergy. I wanted them to get to me so I could give them my alibi and have them forget about me.

"But apparently, it did not work as well as I had hoped. Later, they sent two officers to see if I had no regard for bad Church law and would perform a canonically invalid marriage. I ushered them out of the rectory so fast their heads must have been spinning."

"Are you sure they were police officers?"

"Bob, I studied all of Homicide, especially Squad Six. I know the names and faces of all of them. We did not attempt our statement on the nature of sin without preparation."

The priest thought for a moment of the preparation that had gone into The Red Hat Murders. It was the antithesis of spontaneity. The amount of study, planning, and plotting had to be exceptional. Determining when these victims, some of them extraordinarily protected, would be dependably vulnerable demanded split-second timing.

Which brought still another question to mind.

"Why weren't you able to retrieve the body of that McCluskey character? And while we're at it, what did you do with the other bodies?"

Toussaint looked slightly perplexed. "I am not sure about McCluskey. He died earlier than he should have. But then he was the only one who noticed the pinprick on the back of his hand and sucked on it. That might have spread the venom throughout his system sooner, thus advancing the hallucination. I just don't know.

"As for the other bodies, Bob, all over the city things are burned and, as you have seen, I have friends all over the city."

Koesler discarded the mangled toothpick.

"That pinprick you just mentioned: is that how you injected the venom?"

Toussaint removed a small box from his pocket, and opened it to reveal an innocuous-looking ring. "The stone is hollow; the needle is concealed by the stone. When I press the ring against flesh, the contents are ejected through the needle. Don't touch it, Bob. It still contains venom."

Koesler recoiled. "But how did you get close enough to—"

"Oh, Bob, in this country, if a black man is wearing an appropriate work uniform, whether it be coveralls or a busboy's jacket, nobody notices him, pays any attention, or even knows he's around. He is not only faceless; he might as well be invisible—a nonperson."

There are few things worse, Koesler thought, than being so far removed from consciousness as not to be noticed. Until this conversation, he had thought he empathized with the plight of minorities in this country. Now, he would agree, there was no way of really tasting prejudice without being black-, brown-, red- or yellow-skinned—or female.

"Bob, I don't think you know what it is to see someone trapped in a life of prostitution, enslaved by drugs, torn apart by an uncaring abortionist, or becoming a victim in the countless ways people have of taking advantage of others. You don't know what it's like to see all this and know that the law will never right these wrongs, will never protect the helpless!"

Koesler felt as if Toussaint had read his mind. And yet, he thought, there was something overly simplistic in Toussaint's contention.

"I think you may be overstating the case, Ramon. The laws of this country and their enforcement are not all that bad. More often than not, criminals are arrested and punished."

"Arrested yes; punished sometimes. But not always and almost never promptly!"

"St. Expeditus!"

"St. Expeditus," Toussaint echoed. "Not tomorrow. Punishment *today*. Frustrations build from watching evil flourish. Some are impelled to make a statement, as were 'Ciane and I.

"But now, Bob, it is over. Our work in Detroit is done. Our statement has been made. I have accepted a position in a parish in the Mexican area of San Francisco."

"Isn't that a bit premature?"

"How is that?"

"There is the matter of six murders, executions, whatever you want to call them, in Detroit. From a conversation I had with him the other night, I think Lieutenant Harris is suspicious of you. And now I have to wrestle with my conscience on whether to tell the police all I know."

Toussaint smiled broadly. "I did not freely give you all these details so you could become the prosecution's star witness, Bob. I think you will find they have no case at all."

"There may be no case, Ramon, but there remain six dead men. Even now, I find it difficult to believe you are responsible for that. But there they are.

"Now Ramon, as you very well know, we can make all you've told me a matter for confession. Do you want to make this a confession?"

"For confession, Bob, you must have sin."

"Yes."

"In this, I am guilty of no sin!"

I suppose, thought Koesler, that the principle holds true in or out of the sacrament: *credendum est poenitenti tam pro se quam contra se loquenti*—a penitent, or sinner, must be believed whether speaking for or against himself.

Shortly thereafter they parted.

Koesler phoned his rectory and discovered a concerned Mary O'Connor. Good grief, in all the excitement, he'd forgotten this morning's Mass! Some fifteen bewildered daily communicants had trudged home sans sacrament, not knowing that at that hour their unconscious pastor was sharing a room with Cardinal Mooney's bones and Elmer Dessalen's head.

In addition, Inspector Koznicki had phoned. Would Koesler please meet him at Police Headquarters as soon as possible.

The priest began to wonder if his friend were as safe as he thought he was.

Dr. Moellmann was deadly serious. He could be when there was need. This was his second time through the explanation of his autopsy of the late Elmer Dessalen. Midway through his initial explanation he had sensed that both Koznicki and Harris appeared a bit dazed. And he wanted to be sure they understood.

"There is no doubt," said Moellmann, "that Dessalen's head was removed by the same hand that severed the other five heads in what is popularly known as The Red Hat Murders.

"There is also no doubt that the cause of death was heart failure, as it was in the case of McCluskey, whose body is the only other one in this series of deaths we have. However, unlike McCluskey, there is no suspicious foreign substance in the body.

"You may recall I told you at the time of McCluskey's autopsy that were you to find one more body that fit into this series and in which there was a substance that was fatal and/or hallucinatory—ideally, venom—that you would have a good chance at building a case of homicide.

"However, with the scant scientific evidence available to us, I think we must conclude that instead of six homicides, we more probably have six deaths of natural causes—heart failure."

"That's just silly, Doc," said Harris. "They were homicides, six homicides!"

"I'd say your chances of proving that with the evidence we have run from poor to nil," commented Moellmann.

"What if voodoo works?" Harris mumbled.

"What?" asked a startled Koznicki.

"What if voodoo works?" Harris' tone was argumentative.

"Ned," said Koznicki, "I remind you: this is the twentieth century!"

"He has a point, Inspector. There *are* deaths that have been attributed to voodoo. But in all the documented cases, the victim must believe totally in the power of voodoo to kill him.

"If I understand correctly, the Lieutenant is wondering whether Dessalen and any or all of the others believed in voodoo."

"Right." Harris affirmed Moellmann's assessment.

"Even if they did, I wouldn't want to bring voodoo into a court of law," said Koznicki, "unless I wanted to launch a career as a stand-up comedian."

"It's the Inspector's point," Moellmann judged. "Even if you identified the person who has been removing the heads, I'm sure you couldn't charge him with murder. The evidence simply isn't here."

"I think I know who it is," Harris said flatly. Today's events had taken all the zest out of his intense search for the killer.

"You do?" asked Koznicki. "Who?"

"I think it's that deacon, Toussaint. It's not much more than a gut feeling. I have no solid proof. But I think if I stayed on it long enough I'd nail him—for something. I've put him under surveillance. But now," Harris shrugged, "what's the use if we can't bring him up on homicide?"

There was a lengthy silence.

"Say," said Harris, finally, "isn't it some sort of crime to decapitate even a dead person?"

"I think you're right," said Koznicki, searching his memory, "uhmm . . . mutilating a dead body, I believe."

"Desecration of a human body," Moellmann corrected. "I knew a pathologist who was charged with and acquitted of the crime. It is a felony, but I have no idea what sort of sentence goes with it."

"Couldn't we get him on that?" Harris clearly wanted to

get someone for something. He had worked tirelessly on the special challenges this case had presented.

"I doubt it, Ned," said Koznicki. "Most of the citizenry want the mayor to give him a medal. It would have been hard enough to prosecute him for homicide. But what the hell, why don't you check with the prosecutor?"

"Damn it, I will!"

Harris returned to headquarters. First Moellmann, then Koznicki faced the press, neither happily.

Father Robert Koesler pondered many things as he drove the relatively short distance to police headquarters. He experienced a brief period of mental torture almost every time he found himself knowing some fraught fact nobody else knew, or found himself in possession of portentous knowledge to which he alone was privy.

Only two people knew all the secrets of The Red Hat Murders.

The tendency among priests, generally, when entrusted with a secret, is to evaluate the nature of the secret. Is it a secret protected by the seal of confession, a professional secret, or the sort of confidence shared between friends?

There was no doubt that Toussaint had not gone to confession to Koesler. So the secrets that Koesler now knew from Toussaint himself were not protected by the seal.

But what, the priest wondered, if Toussaint had made his detailed narration of murder a confession?

There was no automatic excommunication or other ecclesiastical penalty attached to murder, unless one killed a cleric. In the Red Hat killings, Toussaint would have had to agree to take care of any consequent problems. If there were any needy widows or orphans resulting, for instance, Toussaint would have had to be determined to do his best to take financial and to some extent emotional responsibility for them. Then, Koesler would have absolved him.

After which he would then have issued Toussaint some sort of prayerful penance to perform, possibly to go on a private retreat to reevaluate whether the end does justify the means. But, especially since no innocent party was being charged with the murders, Koesler would not need to require Toussaint to move from the internal to the external forum and confess also to the police.

If it had been a confession, Koesler's present dilemma would have been solved. Under no circumstances would he be able to reveal any of what Toussaint had told him. The details would have been protected by the inviolable seal of confession.

But it was no use. It was impossible for Koesler to perceive his friend as a murderer. For the moment, Koesler preferred to look upon it as an as-yet undefined form of justifiable homicide.

Which was neither accurate nor real, but it was the best Koesler could come up with for the moment. Learning a close friend could murder coldly took some getting used to.

However, all this was academic.

As a result of following his own theories, Koesler had deduced that Cardinal Mooney's grave would be the final scene for the placement of the last severed head. That surely would not be protected by the seal no matter what might or might not have been confessed. It was knowledge Koesler possessed completely exclusively of the confessional in any event.

He had thought he recognized Toussaint in the darkness of the seminary cloisters. Yet, he could not have sworn that it had indeed been Toussaint. Only that it had seemed to be.

Beyond these two details, which would carry little weight in a court of law, all the rest of the specific details Toussaint had just given him would have been inviolably protected by the seal if Toussaint had placed his tale within the context of the sacrament.

Two things were crystal-clear: Toussaint did not believe that what he had done was sinful. His conscience was clear. And he was supremely confident that the police would not press charges.

Koesler knew that according to Catholic doctrine, one's

conscience, unless hopelessly pathological, was the supreme personal arbiter. He could only hope Toussaint was accurate in his assessment of the police reaction.

Much would depend on conditions as Koesler found them when he reached police headquarters.

He decided to pray, without being quite certain what he was praying for.

Lieutenant Harris had spent the past three-quarters of an hour on the phone with the Wayne County Prosecutor.

Painstakingly, he had explained the history and present status of the investigation, and Dr. Moellmann's evaluation, as well as his own wish to continue the case with the possibility of prosecuting on the charge of desecration of a human body.

It had been a lengthy monologue and Harris completed it breathlessly.

There was a pause. Harris sensed it was an irate pause.

"Do you mean to suggest, Lieutenant, that we should seriously prosecute the Red Hat murderer for the crime of severing a head from a dead body?" the prosecutor asked in his most intimidating tone.

"Yes," Harris responded, intimidated.

"My God, man, that would be like prosecuting Robin Hood for establishing a multiple dwelling in a wooded area!"

Harris massaged his ear.

"Dammit," he said to no one, "he didn't have to slam it!"

"You've done a magnificent job of showing the connection between Mooney's tomb and Dessalen's head, Pat." Bob Ankenazy perched informally on the edge of Pat Lennon's desk.

"Thanks, Bob."

"Do you think the cops really believe this is the end? That there won't be any more Red Hat Murders?"

"It makes sense." Lennon rested her chin in the palm of her hand and looked thoughtfully out the window. "Two series of three murders, in two separate weeks, the executions on identical days of the week, first the prominent criminals, then the more common variety."

"Incidentally," she looked up at Ankenazy, "Dessalen was a real sleeper in the criminal category until we got some quick reaction from some of his mechanics who were pretty scared and some of his customers who were pretty angry."

"How about you, Pat; do you think it's over? After all you were just about as close to this case as anyone."

Lennon smiled. "Yeah, I think I do. Especially since it all began with the Cardinal's red hat and seems to have ended at the Cardinal's grave. The moment I learned this morning where they had found Dessalen's head, I just had the overwhelming feeling that this was the period. The end."

After a moment, she added, "For now."

"For now?"

"Yes, for now. Whoever that avenging angel is out there, he's still out there. And it's certain that bureaucracies and businesses will continue to grind up their subjects. What's to stop him from starting again? As a matter of fact," she laughed infectiously, "I've noticed myself treating my interviewees and sources more courteously."

"To be perfectly frank," Ankenazy admitted, "so have I."

They laughed.

"Well," Ankenazy stood, "I just stopped by to compliment you on a job well done. I can't remember anyone with as good a debut as you've had with the *News*."

"Thanks, Bob."

She watched him walk away. A genuinely nice man who'd gone to bat for her from the start, with no strings attached. A guy who could work closely with a pretty woman without making even the hint of a pass.

Oh, yes. She was definitely going to have to tell Joe Cox about Bob Ankenazy.

"It's not just me, Walt," said Harris. "These dead-end unsolved cases are bad for the morale of the squad. They've worked damn hard on this investigation and they're going to feel rotten if I have to give them the official word that it's over."

Harris and Koznicki were once more squeezed into the latter's office.

"And it's you, too," reminded Koznicki. "You still want to get somebody for something."

"Damn right!"

"I don't blame you, Ned. I've been in your position, Lord, I don't know how many times. We've got to face the fact that not all murders are solved. And not all the ones that are solved are brought to trial. Especially when you have a series this cleverly and carefully planned . . ." Koznicki allowed the sentence to drift off.

"There's somebody out there," Harris was quietly but obviously chagrined, "smiling smugly because he beat the police."

"And you think it's Toussaint."

"I do."

"Have you any proof?"

"No!"

"Take a realistic look at the odds, Ned. We have a medical examiner, acknowledged expert in his field, who tells us we have no medical evidence to sustain a homicide charge. And a prosecutor who does not want to go to court with a desecration charge. In a game like this, I think all we need is two strikes like these to be out."

"Maybe we could locate another body. Or maybe the news media would put on enough pressure to force a trial."

"Maybe," Koznicki allowed. "But while we are pursuing your maybes, we will expend thousands of man hours, hundreds of thousands of dollars—while homicides that could be solved rest on the back burner. Meanwhile, we will have one of our best specially trained squads out looking for a body that may not even exist anymore.

"Or we'll wait for the media to push for the prosecution of an unidentified somebody the public would like to congratulate."

Koznicki fell silent. He hoped he had convinced the tenacious Harris of the futility of continuing this investigation.

"As far as we know," he said, "we have only one person who even recalls seeing him—the night attendant at the morgue—and she can't even describe him."

"It's as Moellmann says, we all look alike."

"Ned, you're bitter. And I don't blame you. Why don't you take the rest of the day off?"

Harris bit his lip and stared at the ceiling. Finally, he brought his gaze back to Koznicki.

"No, Walt, that won't be necessary. I'm O.K. Guess I just had to talk it out."

He squeezed out of the office.

The Inspector was certain Harris would shortly be himself again. Not only was he one of Koznicki's closest friends, he was one of his best officers. And Koznicki empathized with him on both counts.

"Personally," said Joe Cox, "I'll be glad if the cops are right and The Red Hat Murders are history. This story has handcuffed me from the beginning."

"Don't be so hard on yourself, Joe," said Nelson Kane. "You didn't do all that badly. The stuff you wrote was good. I guess we'll all just agree that the kudos for this story belongs to Pat Lennon. But this is not the last story we'll ever cover."

The two sat on either side of Kane's desk.

"Besides," Kane continued, "this story isn't over yet."

"What do you mean?" Cox was surprised. He'd already turned in his article stating the police believed this series of murders was over, finished, completed—while warning it could begin again.

"We're getting reports from all over town on how incredibly nice people are being."

"Oh? We always get Good Samaritan stuff."

"Not like these!" Kane began to rifle through the notes on his desk. "Here's one where an insurance agent declined to sell an old couple a policy. He proved to them they were already overinsured.

"Here's another one about a restaurant owner on Jefferson. He was taking a percentage of his waitresses' tips. Now he's not only going to let them keep all their tips, but he's raised their wages.

"Here's one where a kid was yelling obscenities at an old lady. A gang of his own buddies ran him off.

"And here's one about the owner of that factory that's been polluting the Rouge. He's volunteered to pay for a cleanup of that whole stretch of the river.

"I could go on and on. But you get the idea."

"Wow!" Cox was impressed.

"In all my years in this business," said Kane, "I've never seen anything to equal this rash of 'good news' stories."

"Maybe not for the best of reasons," said Cox. "But, as the Bible says," he smiled condescendingly, "'The beginning of wisdom is the fear of the Lord.'"

"Proverbs, Chapter Nine, Verse Ten."

Cox's mouth hung open.

"Every once in a while I can surprise you, can't I, kid?"

He was surprised by the question.

Father Koesler had expected to be queried about his knowledge of The Red Hat Murders or at least about his presence at St. John's Seminary that morning.

Instead, Inspector Koznicki has asked his opinion of the motive for the placement of Elmer Dessalen's head on Edward Mooney's tomb.

Koesler cautiously explained what he now knew to be a fact, not a theory, about the heads, the hat, and the tomb.

Koznicki then explained the latest developments in the case, and informed him that the police, reluctantly, were terminating the investigation.

Koesler was amazed. Toussaint had been correct.

As Koznicki continued his explanation, in great detail, Koesler's mind was restless. What was he to do with all the information Toussaint had given him? Was he obliged to reveal it to the police?

What good would it do to even indict Toussaint? The series of executions was finished. Bringing Toussaint to trial would not bring back any of the dead men.

More compellingly, he strongly doubted Toussaint would have so completely bared his soul if Koesler had not been a priest. Toussaint had spoken not just to a friend, but to a friend who not inconsequentially *was* a priest. This placed the knowledge solidly in the professional secret category, he concluded.

Professional secrets could not be revealed unless the public good demanded it or unless, without the revelation, someone would greatly suffer. For example, if an innocent person were facing trial in Toussaint's stead.

Koesler honestly could find no legitimate reason to violate this professional confidence. His resolution became firm at about the same time Koznicki finished his explanation.

". . . and so, Father," Koznicki concluded, "it seems this case is closed, at least for the present."

"For the present?"

"One never knows. A body might be found without its head . . ."

Koesler was privately positive that particular eventuality would not occur.

"By the way, Father," Koznicki said, deliberately changing the subject, "Wanda and I were thinking of attending Mass at St. Anselm's this Sunday. What time are you offering Mass?"

"What? Oh, ten and twelve."

"Why don't we plan on attending the noon Mass and then perhaps you would join us for lunch."

"Yes, of course. That will be fine."

Lieutenant Harris stepped out of the squad room just as Koesler was passing by on his way out of the building.

"Father."

"Lieutenant."

"Your prayers didn't help all that much after all."

"Pardon?"

"The case didn't get solved; it got closed."

"Oh . . . oh, yes, that's right."

"By the way, how's your friend, Deacon Toussaint?"

"Oh, he's fine. As a matter of fact, he's accepted an assignment in San Francisco. He and his wife will be leaving soon."

"I guess that's best for everyone. I'll be interested in how he makes out in San Francisco. You might tell him that."

Koesler wondered what he meant by that. But he wasn't going to ask. He'd just gotten that can of worms closed.

Eight

DÉJÀ VUDOO

"There it is again, dear." Emerenciana Toussaint fussed as she pointed to a paragraph in Sunday's *News*.

She and her husband were seated on one of the oversize wooden benches in the mammoth vaulted old Michigan Central Depot. They were waiting for the Amtrak train that would take them on the first leg of their journey to California.

"There's *what* again, 'Ciane?" Toussaint responded, leaning near to read the section at which she was pointing.

"It says here that Mr. McCluskey's body bore a trace of snake venom. What does that mean?" she asked.

"I don't know." Toussaint removed his hat and scratched his head. "Maybe the doctor made a mistake. Maybe the newspaper made a mistake. Or maybe it was the death conjure. You know there is no telling what side effects that can have."

"That's true. But it's very strange."

Toussaint wore a dark suit but not his clerical collar. Looking like a priest while traveling with a woman without the simple justification of being Episcopalian might mean answering questions all the way to the coast.

Emerenciana was dressed in her Sunday finest. She looked smashing.

Toussaint excused himself and walked to the drinking fountain at the far wall. As he did so, he looked about.

This must have been really impressive back in the days

when rail travel was popular, he thought. Now, with its extraordinary size and dearth of customers, it was almost the personification of a white elephant.

As he sipped the water, out of the corner of his eye he noticed black shoes and black trousers. He followed the black motif upward to the smiling face of Father Koesler.

"Going somewhere?" asked Koesler.

"Not your way, unfortunately," said Toussaint. "I did not expect you to be here," he added.

Koesler became serious. "I wasn't sure I would come."

The knowledge that two of his dearest friends were capable of murder had shaken Koesler to the core. He could look at Toussaint's dark impenetrable eyes and see a mass murderer. He could blink, look again, and see one of the most dedicated, selfless, gentle men he had ever known.

Koesler had tried to view what his friends had done through their eyes.

Justice immediately satisfied.

Old Testament-style retribution.

Crime and punishment joined.

A form of justifiable homicide.

But he had been unable to carry it off.

Middle-class morality?

Whatever. He did know that such action, carried to its extreme, would find people all over the world doing away with their auto mechanics, butchers, candlestick makers. A solution, he supposed, to the population explosion, but untenable as a means of righting wrongs.

Besides, there was that Old Testament precept that God desires not the death of a sinner but that he be converted and live.

Several times, Koesler had been on the verge of calling his friend Koznicki and unburdening himself of his secret knowledge.

Only the awareness that with the evidence available to them, the police, even if they knew the culprit's identity, still would not have a court case, convinced Koesler that nothing but further evil could come from his revelations.

That, plus his awareness that this barbarous revenge was concluded and that the Toussaints were headed for a new and peaceful ministry in San Francisco, had made him resolve to keep his knowledge to himself.

And, characteristically, once he determined to maintain silence on the matter, Koesler had put it out of his mind.

Today he had but one purpose: to bid farewell to two dear friends. It was his considered opinion that, in his shoes, Jesus would have done the same.

The two men shook hands warmly, then walked toward the bench where Emerenciana sat absorbed in her newspaper.

"Do not mention anything to 'Ciane," warned Toussaint. "She does not know I told you."

"Of course."

"Look who is here," Toussaint called to his wife.

"Bob!" she exclaimed, welcoming him.

Koesler sat next to her. They kissed lightly.

"I would have come sooner, but I went to lunch with the Koznickis."

"We got here only a little while ago ourselves," said Emerenciana. "We stopped at the kiosk downtown. See Ramon bought a Sunday *News* and a *San Francisco Chronicle*. I'm reading of my two homes, the one we are leaving and the one we are headed for."

She seemed very pleased.

"We're going to miss you," Koesler said to both.

"And we will miss you and all our Detroit friends," Toussaint said sincerely, "But we can write, and it is not so big a country. We can visit. It is a good mission, Bob. A very poor Mexican parish. We will be needed and wanted."

"And you will give of yourselves selflessly, as you always do," said Koesler.

The three sat in silence, holding hands.

The trackman appeared at the central door to announce the train departure.

The thirty to forty passengers gathered their luggage and packages and started down the ramp.

"Goodbys are difficult at trainside," said Toussaint, "let's say them now." He extended his hand to Koesler. "Friends?"

Koesler embraced him. "Always!"

Emerenciana embraced Koesler.

All three embraced. Tears flowed.

Toussaint gathered their few bags. He and his wife walked swiftly down the ramp. They climbed a flight of steps and disappeared from Koesler's view.

The tall black couple walked along the platform, located their coach, climbed aboard, and settled into their seats.

Emerenciana paged rapidly through the *Chronicle*, her smile broadening until she was beaming.

"Would you just look at these prices in San Francisco, Ramon!"

He leaned over her arm to scan the list.

"Look at the price for candles. And they have large black ones, too! And see this for live chickens! And," she turned several pages, "look at the incense!"

"Very reasonable, dear." Toussaint smiled broadly and settled back into his seat. "Very reasonable indeed."

ABOUT THE AUTHOR

William X. Kienzle, author of the widely acclaimed *The Rosary Murders*, was ordained into the priesthood in 1954 and spent twenty years as a parish priest. For over twelve of those years, he was editor-in-chief of the *Michigan Catholic*. After leaving the priesthood, he became editor of *MPLS Magazine* in Minneapolis. Until recently, Kienzle was Director of the Center for Contemplative Studies at the University of Dallas. In addition to writing, Kienzle spends his time playing piano and organ, listening to classical music, and participating in various sports activities. He and his wife live in Detroit, the setting for both of his novels.

While readers puzzle through the compelling mystery of *Death Wears a Red Hat*, William Kienzle is already well into the writing of his third Father Koesler mystery.